SOHO BLACK
SOHO BLACK
SOHO BLACK
SOHO BLACK
SOHO BLACK
SOHO BLACK

SOHO BLACK

CHRISTOPHER FOWLER

WARNER BOOKS

A *Warner* Book

First published in Great Britain by Warner Books 1998

Copyright © Christopher Fowler 1998

The moral right of the author has been asserted.

A CIP catalogue record for this book
is available from the British Library.

ISBN 0 7515 2559 6

Typeset by Solidus (Bristol) Limited
Printed and bound in Great Britain by
Clays Ltd, St Ives plc

Warner Books
A Division of
Little, Brown and Company (UK)
Brettenham House
Lancaster Place
London WC2E 7EN

For Richard Woolf

Acknowledgements

This novel was inspired by three things: life inside Soho's 'School Of Cool' The Creative Partnership; a notorious Cannes party; and the endurance-test lifestyle of lunatic producer Damon Bryant, who should know better and thankfully doesn't.

Love and respect to top pal Jim Sturgeon, group hug to Mike, Sarah, Jo, Graham, Di, David, Seb, Alan, Jez, Bruce, Jeff, Damien, Mia, Joey, Loren, Bal, Maggie, Poppy, Amber, Pam, Sally and Gary.

Special thanks to Jude and Sadie, Ewan, Jonny Lee, Sean, Tom, Brad, Viv and anyone else from Natural Nylon with whom I spent a 'Double Games' period in Soho.

This novel is brought to you by my effervescent agent Serafina Clarke, editor Andrew Wille, Nann du Sautoy, Jennifer Luithlen and Lora Fountain, designer Martin Butterworth, photographer Jay Eff, models Polly, Danny, Troy and crew.

Kath, Bill, Steve, Sue, Clare, Charlotte, I couldn't do it without you. Tales of death are about life, and this is a celebration of the happier state, dedicated to all Soho-ites who spend their days, nights and wages in the service of celluloid.

Prologue

My life is now a major motion picture.

I am waiting for the lights to dim and the curtains to open. These minutes spent in anticipation are delicious agony. I know that the screen never appears until seconds after projection of the film has begun. During my childhood years I imagined that the curtains were translucent, and revealed the glowing picture through the material. Finally I realised that the images were projected in a beam above my head, and superimposed upon the parting cloth.

This time when the curtains open, they reveal something very familiar. The screen takes us flying. A helicopter shot, looking down at an aquamarine mosaic racing past. The English Channel gives way to white cliffs, then gently sloping hills. A waterlogged patchwork of dark green fields. The sepia scars of factory sites. The ugly sheet-steel roofs of shopping malls and retail outlets. The curving tangerine closes and crescents of suburbia. Finally, the great grey conurbation of the city.

The music swells with pride. London from above. Grown taller and broader with each post-war generation, sprawling and ugly in the West, strapped with wide arterial roads, striated with railway lines in the North and South, attenuated with mirrored concrete in the East.

As we lose height, following the line of the river, we recognise individual features. Tower Bridge. Waterloo Bridge. The Houses of Parliament. The Albert Hall. The Tate Gallery. The structures that stand out most clearly are built in strong white stone, reminders of the city's Palladian heritage, an Italian affectation now despised by the architects who are peppering the city with tents of glass and steel cable. We are above Whitehall, Green Park, the hub of Piccadilly, and a low, squarish area of old houses. Soho. Architecturally unremarkable, its dull sienna buildings barely register from the air. But it is within the confines of this little district that my story takes place.

I shift in my seat, rigid with anticipation. Everyone I know is in the audience, and they are all here to see my movie. Once we enter this territory, there will be no escape for the next one hundred and seven minutes. And I warn you, my imagination runs away from everything rational and orderly. This is my script, I told them, I'm the director and I'll shoot it any damned way I please. As the camera swoops across the approaching matrix of grey streets, the film's title appears.

You have to see the whole picture. If you need to go to the toilet, you should have gone earlier. This drama must be played out to the end of its final reel; just one week in a long hot summer a year before the end of the century, but a week that changed many lives and even ended some, including mine. For, like *Sunset Boulevard*, this is a tale narrated by a corpse.

The credits fade. The film begins.

Monday

One day more is one day less
That is to say that every day is more
and every day is less

That's why
there is no addition that doesn't subtract
there is no subtraction that doesn't add

There remains
clear like an adventure
the day.

'Clear Accounting', Juan Octavio Prenz

One Eighty Runs Out of Extra Strong Mints

'**She's wearing** a wire but the police can't hear what she's saying because the neon all around her is interfering with it.'

'What do you mean?'

'The neon. From the strip-club signs. It's interfering with the wire she's wearing. Messing up the reception.'

'What the fuck are you talking about? Neon is just gas in a tube. It can't affect radio waves.'

'Well, it does, all right? The sound goes all crackly. So she ends up in this porno booth with the bloke and he tells her not to look around, right, but she can't stop herself and sees he's turned into a werewolf, and the experience traumatises her so badly she has to go to a woodland retreat where she can get therapy. But it turns out that everyone at the retreat is already a werewolf.'

'So?'

'So? Isn't that kind of a stupid coincidence? She could have gone to a thousand different therapy centres to recover but she picked the one that just happens to be full of werewolves?' One Eighty pulled a sour face and shifted in his seat. He tugged his shirt cuffs below the sleeves of his jacket and narrowed his emerald eyes. 'Doesn't that strike you as unrealistic?'

Waldorf wound down the window and flicked out his cigarette butt. 'Man, the whole concept of werewolves strikes me as unrealistic. Not to mention stupid. They always show you the hair-growing stuff, but never let you see what happens when they turn human again. I mean, does the hair go back in? Does it just fall off? And what happens to the nails? I once saw this film, *The Two Faces of Dr Jekyll*, right, and each time the geezer turned back from Mr Hyde his goatee reappeared.'

'Goatees are satanic. All devils in old movies have goatees. I tried growing one once. It was all right until I tried to trim it. I took too much off one side, tried to even it up by taking a bit off the other side, then had to take a bit more off the first side.'

'What happened?'

'By the time I did that, it was gone.' One Eighty shook a manicured hand at the Soho crowds passing before the tinted windscreen of the van. 'You wanna see men turn into real monsters, just watch this crowd getting fucked up on a Friday evening.'

'I like it. The concentration of light.' Waldorf smiled. 'Where there's light there's life. Death is just black.'

'What the fuck are you on about?'

'This place. Everyone living on top of each other. It's so crowded. Like *Soylent Green*. Ever see that movie?'

'It was a book first. *Make Room, Make Room*.'

'What?'

'That's what the book was called.'

'Oh yeah, you read, don't you.' He made it sound like *you molest children*.

'At least they're not eating each other yet.' One Eighty sighed and unwrapped another Extra Strong mint. His partner's chain-smoking reminded him how badly he wanted a cigarette. 'See, the trouble with movies,' he paused to rattle the sweet to one side of his mouth, 'is that nobody ever thinks things through. It's like chick-in-peril flicks. They get attacked by maniacs with machetes, but nobody ever comes around from the flat next door to complain about the noise. I'm sorry, but you *cannot* run up and down a hallway scream-ing your fucking head off without some old bitch com-plaining about the noise, not in town. Christ, you can't even turn your stereo above Four without someone calling the noise police.'

Waldorf patted his smartly waxed hair back in place. He had glossy black curls. Chicks loved glossy black curls. One Eighty had a billiard-table crew-cut and a broad stubble-blue chin that made him look like Superman's stunt-double. He worked out too much, with the consequence that most of his clothes fitted him badly. As usual he had stuffed himself into an expensive black suit and shirt, but the collar was cutting into his neck and the sleeves were too short. Both men were physically imposing, and the van was the only vehicle that offered them decent leg room. They spent a lot of time in the van.

'How much longer before we can go in?'

One Eighty checked his watch. 'Ten minutes. It's like in my screenplay . . .'

Waldorf groaned and sank in his seat. 'Man, don't tell me about your fucking screenplay again.'

'At film school they tell you to avoid unbelievable

situations. They obviously never saw Tom Cruise fly through the fucking Channel Tunnel in *Mission: Impossible*. I've watched millions of popular films and I still don't get it.'

Waldorf sighed. 'What don't you get?'

'Suspension of disbelief. If films were realistic, James Bond would have a briefing session with his osteopath, not fucking M. It's like horror films. Endless punch-ups between good and evil, or a bloke with a knife creeping round to the kitchen door from the outside. Fucking rubbish.'

'That's a cultural difference, man. American kitchens aren't in the same place as ours.'

One Eighty ignored him. 'And another thing. There's always a McGuffin.'

Waldorf gave him a blank look. 'A what?'

'A McGuffin. You know what that is, right?'

'Sure. Like a round egg on a piece of ham, in a bun.'

'That's a McMuffin, you mook. A McGuffin is a thing the plot revolves around, like a briefcase full of money or a computer disk with secrets on it, or the Maltese Falcon, or a priceless amulet. It's valueless except as a jump-start to the plot. Real life doesn't have a McGuffin. See, we secretly want movies to remain unbelievable. What we can't handle is any portrayal of real ugliness. Films adopt a tough posture because it's cool. It's like musicians. They talk radical in their lyrics and live in expensive suburban houses like elderly stockbrokers. Posture is acceptable; reality is not. Children get murdered. Life traps you. Love is disappointing. Can we face up to it? No, the truth has to be glossed over for public consumption.' He looked over at Waldorf, who was feigning catatonia, and crunched the mint. It sounded like he was breaking his teeth.

'You can't write what you feel,' mumbled Waldorf.

'Why not?'

'Because it's boring. No one would pay to hear your opinions.'

'They would if I had them read out by a naked bird with big tits and a chainsaw. Oscar Wilde said give a man a mask and he'll tell you the truth. Not that it did him any fucking good. Oi, kid, what are you looking at?' He turned to Waldorf. 'What is this mook kid looking at?'

A boy was crossing Meard Street, walking in front of the van. As he passed he cupped the light from his eyes, trying to see in through the tinted windscreen. One Eighty stuck his head out of the side window and yelled.

'Here, why don't you take a fucking Polaroid, it'll last longer.'

Waldorf opened one eye and peered out. 'Relax, he's just a kid. What a stupid haircut. If he really wanted to see you, he just got a good look.'

One Eighty fidgeted in his seat and turned around, peering into the rear of the van. 'You think we can re-use that bag in the back?'

'You were supposed to clean it out.'

'I told you, I couldn't do it. My flatmate never leaves the lounge. She sits there all night eating junk food and vomiting into a bowl.'

Waldorf's train of thought was checked. 'What – how does she get the food if she never goes out?'

'She pays the deaf kid next door to do Mickey D runs. I couldn't bring the bag through the flat Monday night because there was about a quart of blood in the bottom of it, and we've got cream carpets. I drained out as much as I could but it needs to be scrubbed in a sink. Remember what happened when we tried to get rid of the bags? A bright idea that was, dragging a fucking body through reception in a pink candle-wick bedspread.'

'So you left it stinking up the van. Christ.' Waldorf lit a fresh Camel. 'What's wrong with her, anyway?'

'Who?'

'This flatmate.'

'Bulimia.'

'I figured out that part. What I meant is why.'

'Fuck knows. Low self-esteem. Extremely well deserved in my opinion. She works from home. Minicab controller. Spends all day shouting into a microphone. I've got to find a new place to live. Somewhere in Soho.'

'You couldn't afford it.'

'Other people do. Glory does.'

Waldorf shifted uncomfortably at the invocation of her name. 'Yeah, but she has to, doesn't she?' He thought it best to change the subject. 'You think this Tyler bloke will come through with the money?'

'I guess. Another sweaty executive scared of his own shadow. If he doesn't, he's a dead man and he's going straight in the bag. Fuck, I'm out of mints.'

'Do you have to keep eating them?'

'As long as I'm stuck in here with you smoking, yeah. What you got?'

Waldorf dug in his pocket. He had two fruit pastilles left, one blackcurrant, one lime. Reluctantly, he handed over the lime. 'If we manage to get through this week,' he said, 'you'll be able to buy all the mints you want.'

CHAPTER TWO

Lunch With Pachyderms

Elephants are really good swimmers, apparently. You'd never think it to look at the bulk of them, but I knew for a fact that it was true. My potential new client, an arrogant young twerp in crocheted novelty headgear and a purple nylon high-button collar that looked as if it was choking him, told me he'd purchased a script about a demonic rogue elephant that killed people, and described their abilities over lunch that Monday.

Part of my job at the film company consisted of listening to the bizarre ideas of total strangers, and in the course of this pursuit I accumulated reams of useless information. From the aggregate of the previous week's script meetings I could recall that:

The city of Winchester is wrongly considered to be King Arthur's 'Camelot' because it has a round table in its castle hall – *The Legend of Lancelot*

Your IQ is the ratio of your mental age to your actual age expressed as a percentage, so if a ten-year-old has a mental age of nine, his IQ is ninety – *The Boy With the Big Brain*

If a whale is caught near the British coast it becomes the property of the crown – *Thar She Blows*

The Caterpillar Club was started by a parachute company in World War Two who awarded a gold caterpillar pin to any RAF airman forced to bail out in action – *Caterpillar Troop*

King Midas had his golden touch removed by a river that, for ever after, rolled over gold sands – *Touched By the Sun*

'Gloria mundi, Sic transit' does not mean 'Gloria was sick on the bus last Monday' but 'So passes away the glory of the world', intoned during the coronation of a pope over the flickering, dying light of a burning reed. It is a classic statement on the transitory nature of human vanities – *The Pope John Paul Story*

None of these films has a hope in hell of ever being made. I remember virtually nothing about the men and women who outlined their plots. All I could recall was that most of them wore black suits and smelled of Calvin Klein scent, many were arrogant, argumentative and idealistic, and a few actually listened to what I had to tell them. Most had clever visual ideas but very little else. Their image of the film industry was clichéd, naive, ridiculous. They thought audiences were dying to see their stories, and they weren't prepared to listen to me telling them otherwise.

That was the problem. Ask around Soho and anyone would tell you; my name meant absolutely nothing in the business. Richard Tyler, ring a bell? Thirty-two-year-old film exec with years of experience but no films to his credit, undergoing a mid-life crisis a decade too soon? No? I knew what the problem was. I lacked confidence. I was convinced my clients saw right through me; they recognised this tall, indecisive liberal who clearly had trouble choosing his own clothes, and marked me as a careful, nervous man whose only outward signs of stress were his fingernails, which admittedly I gnawed during the many tense moments that lacerated my working days. These were boom years for British film. There were fortunes to be made. But not, it appeared by me.

I didn't know where I was going wrong. I worked in the industry and followed the fashion. This year's fashion was to develop projects about damaged people, rites-of-passage stories involving misunderstood misfits, psychopaths, losers. Other current UK trends included scripts set in the seventies featuring sub-Tarantino gangster capers, teenagers trying to escape stifling family life, unlikeable women who become friends during road trips, and Irish comedies about rascally drunks pulling off minor scams. Our company never referred to them as 'films' any more. Beresford Elliot, known as Berry, explained that a 'film' was a project during its development, and a product during its distribution. During its conception, when it was just the first draft of a script, or an optioned book, or perhaps a single sheet of typewritten paper, it consisted of nothing more than an idea, a protean thought that might somehow be parlayed, after two or three years' hard work, into a blueprint for a motion picture. Only at this early hopeful point, when enthusiasm was infectious and optimism still unquenchable, might it be referred to as a film.

Much later, when the director has miscast the project, bowdlerised the script, blown the budget and left the editor hopelessly trying to salvage the cut, it becomes a product, to be shelved and dusted down under another title for sell-through release to video bargain bins everywhere. During production, interest runs high. As soon as it's finished, the word is on the street; it's a hit or it's a dog, and the interest compounds or evaporates. There's nothing you can do to alter the word of mouth, and if you're caught trying to, you're really in trouble. Understandably, the film-maker will never say that his film stinks. If it actually makes it into cinemas and the box office is lousy, why then, the campaign was wrong, it opened against too much competition, it failed to find its audience, it was too sophisticated to become a popular success. Nobody ever says it was a total bone-burier.

I suppose I should never have attended the lunch. Thinking about it superstitiously, that meal marked the start of the nightmare. It was a *lunch* lunch, clients going yatter yatter from the moment I walked towards them with my hand outstretched and a smile so wide it fitted around my head like a lampshade, yatter yatter all the way to the Dean Street restaurant dressed up with Big Bad Art and emaciated wait-persons (why are there no fat waiters any more? What has happened to them all?) languidly drifting between tables exuding simply-can't-be-arsed-to-serve-you attitude despite the probability that the bill for four would come to around two hundred and eighty pounds without service, and I longed to be somewhere else, somewhere impossible like Jupiter or Elsinore. Instead, I had to sit there hopelessly attempting to spear hazelnuts with my fork (some kind of rocket salad – the nuts came as a surprise because I had not studied the menu properly. I could never concentrate on the food when I was listening to clients) while the couple opposite pitched their film concept.

That was when they informed me that elephants could

swim. The entire climax of the script hinged on this fact being correct; the hero thinks he is safe from the demon elephant because he is marooned on a river bank, but the elephant swims through the pounding current to attack him. The film was to be billed as Action-Adventure even though it was Horror. Nobody ever said 'horror movie' any more; too audience-limiting. Unless it was something produced by the guys who made the *Scream* films; those were horror hits, and therefore exempt from the ruling. The bottom line was that everyone was chasing the next crowd-pleaser, even so-called 'art film' makers. When it came to niche-marketing, there wasn't much difference between *Anaconda* and *Anna Karenina*.

They were looking to shoot in India because their company had tax-breaks over there. I explained that although over seven hundred local films were made in Indian studios each year, reaching an average national audience of 12.5 million admissions every day, the producers' flexible-rate loan system had attracted all kinds of shady underworld characters, and shooting there was problematic. Forget the delays that would be caused by union problems, unavailability of equipment, impossibility of rushes, weird weather, medical crises and the sheer red tape of Indian bureaucracy – their backers were going to save money by shooting on location, so to them the idea was justified.

When the main course arrived, it turned out I had ordered ostrich instead of cod. It was delivered on a brilliant white plate the size of a manhole cover, the food constructed in a tower consisting of two brownish fillets balanced on leeks, then something squidgy and crimson that could have been red cabbage or a patch of stomach lining, then a layer of tiny hard flatulence-inducing beans and finally a dry-looking potato cake. Soho was going through a phase at that time when everything you ordered came balanced in a miniature skyscraper, with a glistening puddle of sauce surrounding the food like a moat. If there were enough of you it was possible to construct a diminutive city, with little roads between the buildings made from spears of asparagus and shreds of carrot.

There were four of us: me and Berry representing Film Creation Incorporated, Marcie Beech and Red Banner representing Shattered Glass Productions. Marcie and Red looked to be about nineteen, but exuded the confidence of fifty-five-year-old investment bankers. Middle-class English children were currently sporting the kind of names found in bad American TV shows. Presumably their parents thought it would give them a head start in the media world. Red and Marcie's company, like many production companies, had yet to produce anything significant. They had made some money from a quiz show format they'd sold to a number of European cable stations, and were now, in their opinion, ready to make a film. I don't know if Red had personally been involved in the development of the elephant script but he said he had, and that was all that counted. What they needed from FCI was a commitment to develop the project, help in raising money, finding co-producers, creating sales agreements, setting up production, then providing publicity and marketing services after the film was complete. The Soho film industry was in a state of flux. New service combinations were being tested, and FCI now offered itself as a total production package. So far, it hadn't made much of a splash.

What Berry and I wanted in return was a hefty service fee, and a percentage cut of the projected territory sales if Shattered Glass got the script rewritten to everyone's satisfaction and pulled in the rest of the funding with FCI's help.

Red and Marcie completed each other's sentences, so excited were they about their project. Red had a suspiciously runny nose. Berry did most of the talking on Film Creation's side of the table. He was mainly concerned with the acrostics of film finance. I could see the arithmetic vaulting about behind his beady eyes as he lowered his fork and removed the sweating plank of parmesan that had been balanced on his salad like a discarded sheet of yellow hardboard tossed on to a rubbish dump.

'Let me see if I understand this,' I said. 'The elephant goes after him because it recognises him . . .'

'. . . As the guy who desecrated the temple, yeah. It's like invoking a curse.'

'. . . He's an avenging elephant, sent from the gods to destroy infidels,' completed Marcie.

'How do we know this elephant is demonic? I mean, are there any outward signs that it's supernatural in origin?'

'There could be –'

'– Could be. Its eyes could glow.'

'What I mean is, it can't fly or anything like that.'

'Well, when we first see it, it's coming down out of the sky in a trail of flame, like the monster in *Curse of the Demon*.'

'Ah. You didn't mention –'

'Well, we figured, CG effects.'

'Computer graphics.'

'But doesn't that undercut the climax?' I felt impelled to ask. 'I mean, if we've already seen the elephant flying across the sky like some kind of satanic Dumbo, won't the swimming thing come as a let-down?'

A horrible silence descended on the table.

'No, Richard,' Marcie began, 'because we can . . .'

'. . . Spice up the swimming sequence with even bigger effects,' Red finished uncertainly.

'And there's another point I think I'd better raise.' I faltered. Everyone looked at me, daring me to throw more cold water on the project. 'I've heard there's a film with a similar premise that may be going into production at Universal . . .' The Universal script had yet to be given the green light, but it was a big production with a good budget and an 'A' list cast.

Red and Marcie groaned in unison.

Everyone was attending the lunch for a different reason. I was there to articulate the company's involvement and enthuse about the proposed script. Berry was handling the financial connections and attempting to elicit a fat fee. Marcie was there to extract advice and contacts, and establish the package. She had casting proposals, pencilled commitment dates, director choices, studio finance details, everything investors needed to know before parting with their money. Red was there to pitch the script, show enthusiasm and convince everyone of his ability to deliver the rewrite. But what we talked about mostly – what we laughed and joked with each other about – was other movies, the real ones seen by millions all over the world, the big American ones like *Titanic* and *Godzilla*. We complained about the blandness of scripts (carefully avoiding the fact that most British films were just as bad), the unreliability of current box-office receipts, the impossibility of finding enough screens, the agony of dealing with the London Film Commission, the Hollywood distribution stranglehold, Shattered Glass's recent doomed film about London street gangs which collapsed one week before the start of principal photography, and demonic rogue elephants, the Florence-Chadwick-capabilities-of.

These topics, with the pachydermal exception, were what everyone in the restaurant was talking about because, this being Soho, the restaurant had a dedicated clientele, and in this particular eaterie the diners were all involved in film. The professional groups occupying the area were more territorial than Sharks and Jets. Advertising executives ate in the French joint next door, music people ate in the Mexican opposite, video people ate in the Chinese place around the corner and TV people ate modern British cuisine down the road, each group grimly locked within its compound. Film people considered TV people to be vulgar purveyors of rubbish, and TV people considered film people to be childish egotistical dreamers. Both groups considered video people to be opportunistic louts. Publishing people were regarded as bewildered Dickensian throwbacks. The advertising industry was populated by right-wing carrion producing imitative, self-congratulatory style-dross, the music industry was run by drug-addled, menopausal youth-draining vampires, cable people were human slurry lower on the evolutionary scale than blowflies, movie-gossip journos were skin-crawling illiterate half-wits who missed the blindingly obvious, and the cruellest joke was that we all desperately needed each other in order to survive.

It was generally accepted that the media-world pecking order ran roughly like this: films and music, publishing, television, video, advertising, cable, and finally, showbiz journalism, or in zoological terms, lions, tigers, wolves, jackals, vultures and hyenas, the difference being that, unlike the natural world, in Soho the vultures were as much in control as the lions and had a lot more ready cash. The only non-residents in the social groups were journalists, who, to their horror, had been shifted out of Fleet Street to the hinterlands of Canary Wharf, from where it was virtually impossible to keep tabs on the city's ever-refining zeitgeist.

For the first hour of lunch we discussed everything but the topic we were there to debate, i.e. who was going to pick up all the bills on this project, starting with lunch. In the second hour we discussed specifics with a certain amount of guarded honesty. By dessert we were assigning responsibility and arranging the next lunch, and Berry was looking at me as if I had said the wrong thing again. I could not remember the last time I ate a meal that didn't come with a hidden subtext.

Later, I sat in my office thumbing through documentation on the India project (now titled *Quincy's Rogue*), resting my head against the green leather padding of the armchair as my panicked mind began to lose its focus.

The ostrich had not settled. Visual recall of the creature proved more lurid than that of the humble cod, and conspired to prevent digestion. A daydream-fragment involving backstroking elephants followed, drawn forth from the linking of pachyderms and ostriches, last seen waltzing together in Walt Disney's *Fantasia*. The segment was presented inside my brain in a Technicolor Panavision 2.35:1 screen ratio, although I think the original was 1:85. Films fill my dreams. I close my eyes and super-saturated images race across a panoramic horizon at twenty-five frames a second. When I open them again, everything becomes monochrome and unreal.

CHAPTER THREE

The Celluloid Slipstream

Every single event of my life has suggested, at some point, a film reference. Everything I do and say reminds me of a movie – and not just the famous ones, or even the good ones. The smile of a waitress will recall the voluptuous, ill-fated twenty-three-year-old Susan Denberg in *Frankenstein Created Woman*. The frown of a traffic warden will bring to mind Bryan Pringle's overbearing *maitre d'* in *Brazil*. I walk in Regent's Park and the rain-beaten trees return me to the final reel of *Withnail & I*. I go to the coast and the desolate promenade takes me back to Tony Hancock and a little boy dashing through the downpour in *The Punch and Judy Man*. I try not to be a bore about it. These days I keep my conversational movie references to a minimum, for fear of seeing that familiar I've-just-been-shot look appear in the eyes of my companions. But I think them all the time. They are woven into my reality. Everything reminds me of a scene.

But this was why Berry kept me around. I have an encyclopaedic knowledge of the motion picture. Berry could barely remember the title of each picture he discussed. In that sense our working relationship was symbiotic, but deep down I had always known I was being carried. The real difference between us, I supposed, was that I still saw films as something mystical and Berry saw them as cash-cows, products to be sold, like washing machines or cars. Artistic integrity was not a profitable quality.

I love American movies, but they don't mean as much to me as English ones. The culture doesn't connect. There's no happy smile of recognition in Californian high school court-ship rituals, no identification with the squeaky clean con-sumerism of American teens. I'm embarrassed to admit it, but *Carry On Cleo* is more memorable to me than *Casablanca*. 'Infamy, infamy, they've all got it infamy' sticks in my mind more than 'Here's looking at you, kid'. The appeal of *Gone With The Wind* – or *Forrest Gump* for that matter – remains lost and beyond my reach.

Films have the power to haunt my sleep. Not just the celluloid stories themselves, but the whole process from pro-duction to projection. I loved the peculiar smell of a working sound stage, the vast background cycloramas pinned down like marquees, the ceilings filled with dangling chains and wooden rafts, the bored technicians and extras passing time with the tabloids behind dazzling *trompe l'oeil* sets. How could the crew casually ignore such magic in the making, when just a few feet from where they sat lines were intoned that the world would turn into familiar catchphrases? I loved the old cinemas, the big art deco fleapits that smelled of damp plaster and disinfectant, evocative, beautiful buildings that all but vanished with the arrival of plasticky popcorn-stinking multiplexes.

My mind was forced back to reality; I knew I could not

afford to let it wander, not today. Looking around the cramped office at the half-read scripts lining the walls, I prepared to defend myself. I felt bilious with fear. It was pretty much my normal state, but today was uniquely nerve-shredding. I decided to see if throwing cold water over my face would help. In the bathroom, it was hard to believe that the sweating, frightened man staring back at me was only thirty-two years old. The grey-eyed creature in the mirror, while not entirely unattractive, had worry-lines and a bald patch that was gradually appearing like a winter sun through thinning clouds.

My contract, you see, was about to be terminated with extreme prejudice.

Berry had given me plenty of warning. I worked on commission, but it wasn't generating enough money to live on. Everything I had was tied up in this venture. I had honestly believed that my move to FCI would work out, but I had been proven wrong. I had spent my savings, remortgaged my home. There was nothing left that I could sell, no other way that I could raise finance. My tenure at Film Creation Incorporated had been an unmitigated disaster. Two weeks ago I had been forced to sell my car, half of which technically belonged to Miranda. But she was no longer at home to remind me of that particular humiliation. Like a cat scenting an approaching storm, she had left with a pair of suitcases, magnanimously – or foolishly – leaving behind the car keys.

She said she no longer had faith in me. Explained that the situation had been developing for months. Assured me she was not running off with anyone else, simply needed time to be alone and think the relationship through. Our son had been taken by friends (not real friends but 'Friends of the Clinic') to the Sussex coast for a fortnight. Gregory was five, in poor health, and severely autistic.

Nobody seemed to know enough about autism. The doctors thought it was something that had occurred in his genetic make-up, but I felt otherwise; it had been a long and difficult pregnancy, and I was sure something had happened to Miranda during that night. A tube, a vein, a clot; oxygen might have briefly failed to reach the child's brain. I had accused the hospital of making an administrative error; they had pointed out that autism was just one of those unfortunate occurrences. Gregory could not walk, eat or defecate without assistance. He could not speak, and although his hearing was sound, failed to comprehend human speech. He could not be left alone at night for fear that he might turn face-down and choke. He could, however, experience certain emotions in varying measures. He knew joy and sorrow, pleasure, anger, even jealousy. His cognitive ability, as with many autistic children, could be extraordinary. His mind vividly read parts of the picture, but would not put them together to form an overall view. Although the doctors had suggested that he would be best looked after in a private care facility specialising in his condition, I had insisted on having the boy at home. For a while I had felt sure he was making progress. Then I began to have doubts.

About a year ago, Miranda had shocked me by suggesting that the time had come for Gregory to be sent away. The rift in our relationship grew from that point. I still loved her very much, but my faith had been shaken. Miranda would not be able to conceive again. Gregory was our only chance for a child. How could she even consider giving him up? We started spending our time with him separately, because Miranda criticised everything I tried to do for him. She had decided that I was wasting my time, and it annoyed her. Why, she asked, could I not see that our son would have a better quality of life being looked after by experts?

I began to feel like a boat dropping its lines and drifting away from the safety of a familiar shore. Miranda and I stopped sleeping together. We stopped being a family. Six months ago Gregory managed to remove the cover from the special duvet that lay on his cot, and became wrapped in it. The material knotted around his neck and nearly strangled him to death. The day after that happened I finally relented, and signed the papers that would allow my son to be placed in a care facility twenty miles from our house. The boy's summer holiday was part of the 'breaking in' period designed to settle him comfortably with his new carers. By this time, Miranda had moved out. It was hard not to feel that I had lost my son, my wife, my job, my home, and my sanity. In short, the whole thing was a fucking mess.

If my life really was a movie, it was a box office disaster.

CHAPTER FOUR

Berry Suggests Joining a Circus

Julie Saito, FCI's incredibly efficient production manager, passed my office door. 'Berry called in on his mobile to tell you he'll be another ten minutes,' she warned.

'Where is he?'

'Stuck at Tottenham Court Road tube. There's some kind of drama going on there. Apparently the place is swarming with police and they've closed off the stairways with that yellow "crime scene" tape. The officers won't let any of the passengers out until they've cleared the station.' If ever there was a problem of a criminal nature in the underground system, it always occurred at Tottenham Court Road tube. I sat back and nervously awaited Berry's arrival.

Finally I heard him approaching along the corridor. It was the moment I had been dreading. I couldn't afford to have this happen.

'I don't want to talk to you here, old sport,' said Berry. 'Let's go over to the club.' That boded ill. The only reason Berry could have for not wanting to talk with me in the office was because he knew that there would be no displays of temper in a public place. We left our gloomy third-floor offices situated above a trendy pastel-hued gay bar in Rupert Street and headed across to Old Compton Street.

The Soho Villa was the film industry's latest designated watering hole, the place where everyone went to get away from the area's endless vulgar hustle in order to conduct a more exclusive, orderly hustle of their own. At the Villa, accessible only via a swipecard, mobile phones were banned to ensure that its patrons talked to each other instead of calling people on the other side of the world. Executives who were determined to speak to the West Coast did so from the roof terrace. This veneer of civilisation extended throughout the club, from the handwritten menus that always contained at least one esoteric culinary term, to the neat stacks of doom-riddled industry newspapers, the coke-friendly marble toilet tops, and the chatty walkabouts of the manager who dispensed creepy bonhomie over the vodkas and cappuccinos. The members were comfortably assured of their privileged status as they conducted press interviews and held court, guest speakers at a liars' convention. The air of good-natured hyperbole was such that one half-expected to see Pinocchio and Baron Munchausen swapping industry horror stories. It was an ideal location in which to hire someone, but not to fire them.

'You always were too damned polite, Richard,' Berry complained, wedging his girth behind a tiny brushed-steel table and tapping out a Marlboro. 'You could have told them the real truth.'

'Which is?'

'That their film has zero chance of getting decent pre-sales with the wanker director they've chosen.'

'You never know,' I ventured, 'Mackay might come through.'

'Yeah, right, and Hugh Grant might make a successful comeback. Listen, Mackay's made three rock promos, two unscreened experimental shorts and a thirty-minute documentary about a Scottish housing estate. He'd shit himself shooting on location with a crew of a hundred and fifty. Once a film crew scents directorial weakness it becomes impossible to control.'

Berry was that unusual commodity, a producer who had actually made films. None of them were any good, but all had made their money back. The trick was selling them to America, a feat akin to trading refrigerators to Eskimos. This final monumental task was the only one that had managed to defeat him, although he had twice come close to achieving his goal. He was the kind of guy the West Coast liked, a no-nonsense facts and figures man who wore white short-sleeved shirts and bright cheap ties. His hands were large and dry, his shoulders broad, his attitude positive to the point of insensitivity. The square chin, paunch and neat greying hair added to his image as the kind of man who would have made a decent living selling station wagons in the Eisenhower era.

'It's depressing how you always look for the best in people, you know that? Mackay's a total arsehole, and he'll screw up on Day One. The backers will get scared, take outside advice and start checking the rushes, then they'll panic and pull the production cash, but at least we could have got our cut up front if you hadn't opened your big mouth about the Universal project.'

'I couldn't pretend I didn't know, Berry. They'd have found out sooner or later. A little honesty –'

'. . . is great if you're a doctor or a nun, and you're neither. It may have escaped your attention, Richard, but you haven't closed a decent deal since you've been with the company.'

S o h o   B l a c k

'That's not fair –'

'I'm not counting the piddly stuff you brought in from your pal's agency.' He waved away the protest as he relit his cigarette. He had as much trouble keeping them alight as other people had with cigars. I guess he was a really wet smoker. 'I'm talking about the real money. There are too many production companies in town these days. Too many know-all brats graduating from too many fucking media courses. Every kid in town has a script in his back pocket. Are any of them good? Maybe one in a hundred. You wanna make that good film? No. Because you'll raise the stakes. Provide a new benchmark. Critics will bitch: why aren't all films like this? One good movie kills a dozen bad ones. Great ones really fuck up the system, and nobody wants that. We need multiplex fodder. We need to keep expectations low. Christ, we live in a world where people happily watch *Coronation Street*, it shouldn't be that difficult.' He threw his soaked cigarette aside. 'Have you read any Dickens recently? Dickens wrote for the people, ordinary people loved his books. In the last five years it's become impossible for any Londoner to read *Bleak House* from cover to cover. No one has the attention span any more. No one can remember the plot, the names of the characters, no one can spare the time. We've dumbed it all down, the language, the beauty, the sheer thrill of invention. We've turned it from a craft into a science, the science of making money, and it works better this way. You think you might be instrumental in fostering art? You think what you do for a living is important? Not any more. No one would give a shit if all the artists vanished tomorrow. If there's another world war they'll be in the front line because they're cannon fodder, sport.'

He gripped the edge of the table and shifted nearer, bringing me within range of his pungent, sweet aftershave.

'Do you understand the business world at all? Have you got the concept of buying and selling locked clearly in your head? Forget film. Think of those people we had lunch with today as the manufacturers of a new product. They come to us and say, "We're going to build something and we want you to help us." It doesn't matter that the product won't give consumer satisfaction, it's not important if its fucking legs drop off after a couple of weeks, the initial sales will recover the cost of manufacture and turn a profit. Our job is not to point out that the product won't be wonderful, but to assist in its creation and aim it at the people who are prepared to buy the fucking thing.'

'You don't have to talk to me as though I were a child,' I protested.

'Well, you have to admit that you think like one. Jesus, before your move into the glittering world of showbiz you were selling discontinued lines of sportswear. What were you doing before that? Cold calls for a double-glazing company, wasn't it? Tell me something I don't understand.' He jabbed a fresh cigarette, making little smoke rings. 'What put it into your head to enter the film industry? It's tough enough for a self-confident man to make it in an environment so filled with neuroses and insecurity, but for someone like you . . . don't get me wrong, you're a lovely unreconstructed liberal, Richard, a true people's friend, but you should be running a garden centre, flogging knackered begonias to OAPs, something where you only have to tell the customers little lies. How the hell did you end up here?'

'I'm not entirely sure,' I admitted. 'Maybe I thought I could help to make something good. I guess you took a chance with me.'

Berry narrowed his eyes through exhaled smoke. 'I should have known better.' He leaned forward confidentially. 'I have to let you go, old sport. Believe me, I'm doing us both a favour. You've got to get out of the business. Soho is the opposite of Wall Street. All the rules are up-ended here. The only people who can make sense of them are those who are sure of their direction. You need to get far away. Then we can all relax.'

I wanted to discuss the matter reasonably but could feel my chest tightening, my breath growing shallow with indignation.

'Let's just say you didn't fulfil your early promise. I made a mistake. You're not cut out for this kind of life. You give money to tramps, for Christ's sake!'

'They're not tramps, Berry, they're homeless . . .'

'Richard, listen to me. You're never going to be a producer. Look at you, you've lost so much weight your shirts don't fit. Fear is a cancer that eats you up, pal. You're not the kind of person who thrives on it. But I am. I can wine 'em, sign 'em, sixty-nine 'em, get to bed at five in the morning and still be in their lawyer's office by nine. That life's not for you. Remember what I said when you joined? You have to be an ironman. Thick skin. Steel heart. I'm not pretending it's easy. I've been going to the gym for fifteen years; hell, you only get ten for armed robbery. The lining of my nose has worn so thin you can look up my nostrils and see my brain. Look at your agency mate, the one who died, Pete Harris –'

'Paul Ferris . . .'

'Yeah, him. He was a nice guy, put together some good deals, but finally he couldn't hack it. He was a lightweight.'

'Christ, Berry. He was a decent man.'

'And what does that mean? That his wife never shouted at him for coming home late? That he spent quality time with his kids? They found him hanging from a light fitting in a fucking restaurant toilet, Richard.'

'Ruth said he'd been depressed for a while.'

'Listen, I know you're disappointed but you can't say this has come as a surprise. There's no immediate rush, but I need you to clear your desk by the end of the week.'

'Berry, it's going to take me time to find another job,' I pleaded. 'I need an office. What if I –'

'I'll have someone new starting next Monday. I've got to move while the company's reputation is still intact. Our sales agent had nothing to sell at Cannes this year. Buyers forget fast. Luckily, this is a more forgiving industry than most. People are prepared to put their faith in you for trying to make a film at all, and producers stand a better chance of survival than actors or directors. We'll be back in big deal territory without anyone realising we've been away. And you, you'll be a free man. Trust me, Richard, you don't want to be shackled to this shit. When it comes to packaging movies, there are only two states of being. You're either a winner or you're a cunt.'

I winced at his choice of words, and in doing so confirmed Berry's opinion of me.

'You went to the doctor again last week, didn't you? What did he say?'

'He told me not to get overwrought. Gave me some pills.'

'Well, it's time to take his advice. You mustn't let it knock your confidence. You know, there are things about you I'll really miss. I don't know who will go through the trades every morning. Or all those unsolicited scripts. You're the only one of us who bothered to read anything.'

'I don't know what I'm going to do, Berry. I have a mortgage, outgoings . . .'

Berry looked around the packed club and blew a thin jet of smoke into the air. His goodwill was evaporating. 'I know you owe money, and it's got nothing to do with your mortgage. You shouldn't have lived with a woman who had such expensive tastes, then you wouldn't have so many debts. And you want to lay off the coke for a while. It can be an expensive habit.'

That was rich, considering it was Berry who sold it to me. 'You don't understand what I'm going through –'

'I understand enough to know that a couple of guys will come around and break your legs in an alleyway if you don't give them something on account before Saturday. You make very loud phone calls, Richard.'

'I wouldn't ask you to lend me money, Berry –'

'Then don't. Sell your furniture, run away, go travelling, live in a caravan, join the circus, then film the story of your life and prove I made a mistake by selling it to a dozen overseas territories including the US.' He smiled. 'And above all, lighten up. Let's have another drink.'

CHAPTER FIVE

The Butterfly Boy

Obviously, it was a dead body.

What it was doing trussed up and standing on its head in the cleaner's cubicle at Tottenham Court Road station was another matter. Arthur Bryant took a slow walk around it, prodding, peering and wincing. Periodically he released a sharp little sound reminiscent of a small animal in pain. He was considering the side effects of sudden death. Everyone else was outside the cubicle, pacing about in boredom, waiting for him to finish.

The floor surrounding the corpse was slippery with blood. Each step Bryant took gave the forensic team palpitations; the elderly detective had a grudging regard for their work, but could never keep his hands to himself. Even now he was poking about beneath one of the benches, plastering his fingerprints everywhere.

'Look, Bryant, couldn't you keep your mitts in your pockets until we've had a chance to finish up in there?' asked the team leader, leaning around the door.

'I'll be through in a minute, Willis. Ah.' Bryant rose from the floor with something in his hand.

'I hope you're not thinking of removing anything before

we've had a chance to photograph the room.'

'Bugger off for a mo, there's a chap.' Bryant shoved the door shut and looked back at the body. A skinny young man in his early twenties, about six feet tall, wearing faded jeans, a Miami Dolphins sweatshirt and a black leather jacket. His waistband had a size 30 tab. He had to weigh something like twelve and a half stone. What would it physically take to turn him upside down, and why would someone bother? It was macabre, disrespectful, and made no sense at all.

Bryant liked that in a murder.

A grey metal bench was fixed along one wall. Something at the back of it caught the detective's narrowed eye. He hiked his sleeve and thrust an arm into the gap. A grey box was wedged there at an angle, as if the boy had suddenly released it from his right hand. Bryant bent down and worked it free. Straightening his legs, he examined it, then carefully unclipped the polythene lid.

Two dozen fiery red butterflies flew out, batting into the walls and filling the tiled cubicle with colour. The elderly detective turned about, the box still open in his hand, and watched in astonishment as the butterflies whirled and danced around him like sparks from a bonfire. Tiny crimson drops were flicking from them, spattering the white walls.

'How extraordinary,' he muttered, carefully stepping over a bundle of broom handles and emerging from the booth. He closed the door tightly behind him.

'You're telling me,' grumbled Willis. 'Killing somebody and turning them upside down like that, it's undignified.'

'I meant the butterflies,' he said, guiding one along his forefinger. 'Have you ever seen anything so beautiful?' He tucked his scarf into the top of his overcoat and took another peep inside the booth, shaking the insect from his hand. The lepidoptera were sinking down to feed from the blood on the floor.

'Probably belonged to some collector. You get all kinds of stuff turning up in Lost Property. I'm surprised they're still alive.'

Bryant halted and touched Willis's arm. 'Why do you assume the boy was killed first, then turned upside down?'

'You mean he wasn't?'

'Look at his face.' Bryant rapped a knuckle on the wired glass and pointed with his thumb. 'His body's been emptied of blood, but his head is purple.'

Willis gave him a blank look.

'Well, it wouldn't have happened if he'd been killed the right way up, would it? He was hung upside down and his throat was pierced. He was left to drain, like an animal. I'd say he's been here over twenty-four hours.'

Willis gave him a funny look. 'Aren't you hot in that?'

Bryant pulled his scarf a little tighter. 'No. Why?'

The boy also had two large calibre bullets in his body, in the thigh and the upper abdomen. At first they had both assumed this to be the cause of death. Bryant knew what Willis was thinking now; if the victim was hung before dying he must have put up a fight, which increased their chance of finding decent prints.

'You won't find much,' he said gloomily. 'Looks like someone tied his hands and feet together, then hung him from the ceiling.' He pointed to the alloy bars that criss-crossed the upper section of the room. 'There are burns on his wrists and ankles. Too broad and shiny to be rope. Most likely nylon cords of some kind. I imagine the assailant removed the restraints after his victim stopped moving, and took them away with him. The premeditated actions of, well, not necessarily a professional but someone who'd done it before, I'd say.'

'You would, would you?' The forensic expert looked thoroughly annoyed. He stepped back from the booth and peered down the rail line. 'At least there won't be anyone wandering through here,' he said, looking for something positive to say. 'No dirty great feet trampling around the murder site. The area's beyond public limits.'

'Which makes you wonder what he was doing in it. Has anyone been up to East Finchley?' Bryant scanned the silent group.

'No,' said one of the officers, 'why?'

'That's where the boy boarded the train.'

Bryant handed Willis the bloodstained ticket that had fallen to the floor, and strolled off along the platform to rain blows on the chocolate machine.

'I'm going to Brighton, so just say you couldn't find me.' John May rezipped his holdall and hoisted it on to his desk. It weighed a ton. It would weigh more coming back, given his sister's penchant for experimental chutney. 'Tell him I'm on leave. Tell him I've died. No, better not say that, he'll be inclined to believe you.'

Sergeant Janice Longbright, newly transferred to the division from the West End, slipped her hand over the mouthpiece and looked over imploringly. 'He knows you're here, John,' she whispered. 'He says it's important.'

May stared back at the telephone and hovered, undecided. If he took the call he would have to be firm and say no, absolutely not. He hadn't had a holiday in –

He snatched up the receiver.

'Look, Arthur, I haven't had a holiday in –'

'Your whole life's a holiday,' shouted Bryant. He was standing at a phonepoint in Upper Street, Islington with a finger in his ear, trying to blot out the sound of road drills. He had signed out a mobile phone the previous day, but had already managed to leave it on a number 53 bus. 'You love what you do for a living. How many people can honestly say that?'

An articulated lorry passed and blotted out his partner's reply, which was just as well.

'Besides, you'll like this case,' he bellowed. 'There's something about it that's odder than the taste of your sister's chutney.'

'Not a good enough reason for staying,' said May. 'You have all the resources you need without requiring my presence.'

'You don't expect me to believe that you'd rather be trudging through a sheepfield with Gwendoline's satanic children than tracking down a bizarre murderer in London, do you?'

May lowered his holdall. 'How bizarre?'

'We found a bloody alien toeprint in the cubicle. And I mean a toeprint; the killer wasn't wearing any shoes or socks. And that's not all.' He told May about the lepidoptera. 'The boy's prints were the only ones on the lid of the box, so don't tell me the butterflies belonged to an absent-minded collector. I really need your help on this, John.'

May looked back at the packed holdall and thought about the fortnight ahead. Overcooked roasts. Soggy vegetables. Rain on the cliffs. Visits from ancient relatives. The smell of wet anoraks.

'Well,' he said, replacing the bag on the floor, 'if you really need me, I suppose we all have to make sacrifices.'

Mornington Crescent

'The young man's name was Malcolm Cotton. Australian, twenty-three, originally from Melbourne, had taken a year off to travel through Europe, arrived in London nine weeks ago.'

Arthur Bryant was peering over the top of the fax machine in the North London Serious Crimes Division. The police unit had been developed to handle London's long-standing unsolved cases, and was housed in a maze of rooms above Mornington Crescent tube station. He had been installed here with his partner John May for eleven months – since transferring from his former Bow Street headquarters – and had still not worked out how to operate the unit's most basic technological devices.

'The paper will come out by itself, Arthur, there's no need to pull it.' May had long since given up trying to drag his partner into the twentieth century. Bryant was intractably marooned in the past; but that was part of the reason why their partnership had survived the decades. Although John May was in his early sixties, he was still taller, fitter and three years younger than Bryant. Immaculately attired, he had a keen eye for the female form, sported a fashionable haircut and kept himself conversant with the latest scientific and sociological advances. He drove a restored twenty-year-old Mercedes and could occasionally beat his nephew on the latest Nintendo unit. Nevertheless, his approachable, friendly demeanour hid an unhealthy fascination with all things strange, and this was where his interests bisected Bryant's.

Arthur Bryant reminded his staff of an ancient London monument, being an essential part of the landscape that was badly in need of repair. He was irascible, stubborn, perversely old-fashioned and astoundingly rude to almost everyone. Hunched up like a hibernating tortoise, lost within the shapeless coils of his scarf and his amoeba-like overcoat whatever the season, bald, grumpy and myopic, he frightened the juniors and got in the way of everyone else. It was odd, then, that he balanced his partner in almost every respect. His knowledge of arcane trivia, forgotten law and irrelevant detail proved valuable only when coupled with May's practical knowledge. In their work together, Bryant could see the way ahead and May knew how to get there.

The system, such as it was, worked, and proved useful in investigating the city's more extraordinary crimes. Lately, the Mornington Crescent division had developed a reputation for being able to clear up outstanding files. After the pair's success with the so-called 'Leicester Square Vampire' and their well-publicised involvement in the 'Darkest Day' murders, the detectives were now being sent all kinds of odd leftover dossiers. Often these were forwarded by TV companies hoping to film some kind of Holmesian resolution, but that never happened. The usual outcome made lousy television. Old cases were cold cases.

Even though they were still answerable to the Met, the detectives had no problem handling esoteric demands. Due to their unusual connections with London's less savoury fringe elements, they were often the only officials who could help out. They were the final line of attack, and the last resort. John May was friendly with computer anarchists; Arthur Bryant knew psychic healers and clairvoyants. They often eschewed traditional procedures in favour of more controversial methods. They consorted with known criminals. They collected advice from unreliable sources. Inevitably, this led to a certain amount of acrimony between their division and the regular Met officers who were bitter about being weighed down with the endless assaults, burglaries, drink and drug offences that Bryant and May's division never had to handle. Strictly speaking, an offence committed in Soho's north-easterly corner was beyond their jurisdiction, but as the officer on duty there was a part-timer (during the rest of the week he worked as an interior designer for Anouschka Hempel) they felt within their rights to step in and initiate an investigation.

'Thing is, the boy's father is a bigwig in Australian politics, and he's kicking up a hell of a fuss about the death. Who can blame him?' Bryant finished reading the fax. 'The son's clean in this country at least, not so much as a parking ticket, so one could assume he just happened to be in the wrong place at the wrong time.'

'You mean he witnessed a drug transaction in the cleaner's cubicle, something like that?' May snorted in disbelief, and moved to the great curved window that looked out across the heat-blurred road. 'They must have been pretty angry drug dealers to hang him upside down and drain his blood.'

'Drug-related violence is endemic to the area, John. You can never tell what terrible things junkies get up to.'

May pointed a finger at his partner. 'We don't say

"junkies" anymore, Arthur, we say "chemical-dependants".
You smoke dope, don't you?'

'If you're referring to the marijuana plant I keep in my
conservatory, I'll thank you to remember that it's medicinal,'
said Bryant huffily. 'For my arthritis.'

'You haven't got arthritis.'

'Not any more, I haven't.'

'There's something else,' said May. 'The bullets removed
from the body are of a calibre no one has produced for years.
Why would anyone carry such an old gun? It's a bit of an
obvious calling card.'

'You might as well ask where the boy obtained his
butterflies.'

'I'm working on that,' said May. 'Did you get a chance to
examine the box they flew out of?'

'No, Willis spirited the thing away before I could get my
hands on it.'

'Wise man. It had a polythene base and lid, aluminium
mesh and a tiny lightbulb.'

'A breeding box?'

'I imagine so. Janice went through the Yellow Pages. She
looked under butterfly breeders and drew a blank. The zoo
weren't missing any. I suggested taxidermists. The only one we
could find near here was Get Stuffed in the Essex Road, so we
arranged an appointment with them. Fancy coming along?'

There was a heat-shimmer on the tarmac as they drew to a
stop in the Essex Road. The area had changed little in a
century, and narrow shop-fronts still poked out from yellow
brick terraces. In an area known for its fake Victoriana the
little corner shop had a genuine Dickensian quality; in its
window predatory hawks and gimlet-eyed owls loomed over

cowering field-mice. A cobra gripped a moth-eaten mongoose in its coils. Prissy little bluebirds perched sanctimoniously beneath glass domes. A huge grey deep-sea fish with a face like a Donald McGill mother-in-law glared down from the rear wall of the store. None of these creatures looked too pleased about being preserved for posterity.

'North London only has one registered breeder of butterflies,' said the manageress, Miss Evadne Petty, running her finger down the page of an enormous catalogue. 'We occasionally get stock from him. I have a feeling he's in Finchley.'

'And you stuff them, do you?' asked May. 'What do you use, tweezers?'

'Good heavens, no, we don't stuff them, they're wired and used for decoration on some of our tableaux.'

'Finchley,' mused Bryant. 'That's where Cotton boarded the train on Saturday night.'

On the counter in front of the manageress lay an envelope containing one of the butterflies Bryant had removed from the floor of the waiting-room. 'It's a monarch,' she told him, 'very pretty but not particularly rare. Many butterflies drop specks of blood as they break from their cocoons, but this one seems to be smothered in it.'

'If you could just let us have the address of the breeder,' prompted May. Miss Petty returned to her catalogue and copied out the details.

'I'll be happy to help you anytime,' she smiled, handing John May a slip of paper. Bryant snatched it from him.

'Thank you,' he said. 'I've a cat that could do with stuffing. I'll threaten him with a visit to your establishment if he doesn't behave.'

'I don't know why women always do that when they talk

to you,' said Bryant disgustedly as they walked back to the car.

'Why they do what?'

'You know very well. The thing with the eyes. Going all girly.'

'They can sense my charisma,' said May, unlocking the passenger door.

'They can smell your aftershave. What do you keep it in, a fire extinguisher? Can't I drive for once?'

'No, you cannot. Not after last time. Forcing that ice-cream van off the road. Get in.'

Bryant's ancient blue Mini belched and chuntered north through an opalescent summer haze of exhaust fumes, on its way to East Finchley.

CHAPTER SEVEN

The Midas Touch

If anyone could see her now, they would wonder how on earth she had come to be in this ludicrous predicament. They would laugh in disbelief. Certainly they would not take her seriously. Who in their right mind would? Such things didn't happen in the city, certainly not in the centre of Soho on a hot Monday in August, with so many people passing by her window.

She sat in the middle of the chaotic lounge amid shards of glass and pieces of broken china. Folding her legs beneath her, she began to lay out the pieces of her scrapbook. There was nothing else to do.

As she worked with the tape and scissors, droplets of sweat fell from her nose and forehead on to the pages, staining them like tears. Gluing in the photographs, the ticket stubs, a drawing of a tiger, the cover from a book of matches, her thoughts were drawn back to those first days at the beginning of July when she had met Midas, and the events that led to the grotesque situation in which she now found herself trapped.

Everyone knew about the Midas touch. Those M's were among the few pieces of mythology anyone still remembered:

the Medusa, the Minotaur and Midas – the man with the golden touch. She should have been warned by his name.

Hers was Judy Merrigan, another M and no myth, just an ordinary Mrs. She was twenty-nine years old when she moved from Arizona to England to be with her husband for the four inglorious years their marriage lasted. She and William met in Phoenix, Arizona, where he taught military history at the university. He took her out to dinner and asked if he could take her home, although it turned out that he meant all the way home from Phoenix to Sussex, quite a culture shock.

It was her first trip to Europe, but she didn't see any of the things Americans were supposed to see. Even Texan boys got to visit Paris when they graduated, but Judy found herself marooned in a silent English suburb with funny little front gardens and round red mailboxes and bay-windows, looking after a man who needed a mother more than a wife.

She had given up a successful career as a graphic artist to do this. There was no way she could keep her clients from her new overseas base, and starting afresh was impossible without contacts. Besides, William did not approve of her working. They separated because he wanted more children, and Judy wasn't crazy about the ones he already had.

She had no intention of returning to Phoenix and subjecting herself to her father's barbed remarks about the failure rate of modern marriages; she decided to stay on in England so long as she could move to London. Her divorce papers came through and suddenly she was on her own in a city she hardly knew. Most people would have been thrilled at the prospect of independence, but Judy was petrified. William had spent four years bullying the confidence out of her. As she walked down an impossibly crowded Regent

Street, she realised just how much she had distanced herself from the world outside.

When her mother died, she left Judy some property investments, one of which turned out to be a small apartment owned by her deceased sister in London. As not much was forthcoming from the divorce settlement, Judy used the bequest to fulfil her dream. She took over the property, reclaiming it from the rental market, and she spent every penny of her savings fixing it up.

It was not the kind of place William or her father would ever have approved of – that was part of the appeal – an inner-city flat, cosmopolitan and chic and central to everything. It was the top floor of a renovated two-hundred-year-old building with polished hardwood floors and three small but light rooms, opposite the old Rank Organisation offices in the heart of Soho's original film district, Wardour Street, above Shaftesbury Avenue and below Fitzrovia (she loved those names), where the sidewalk cafes and corner pubs and late-night stores and market stalls steeped with displays of vegetables made it the closest you could get in Central London to a New York neighbourhood.

It was the first time Judy had a place she could truly call her own. She decided to use part of the lounge as a studio and resume her interrupted career. She got herself a deal with an illustration agency in Lexington Street, made a few contacts, but the industry had changed while she'd been away – computers had replaced illustration work with photo-composites. Spirits undampened, she enrolled in computer design courses for Photoshop and Adobe. At the start of that hot thundery summer she leaned out of her window watching the world pass below, convinced that somebody somewhere would still need watercolours, gouaches and pencil sketches, and that she would produce them from her beautiful penthouse eyrie.

There were others in the building: an invisible woman in the apartment below, and an old Greek couple in the first floor flat above the dry cleaners. The smell of cleaning fluid permeated the building, but it was clean and pleasant, a reminder of childhood. There was one more apartment opposite hers, separated by a small dark landing. The brass sign on the door read 'Midas Blake', but Judy never caught sight of the tenant. Maria, the Greek lady, told her he was strange.

'What kind of strange?' she asked.

'Very quiet,' Maria explained, 'keeps his door closed. Comes and goes late at night. Doesn't have a job, but always has money.' That didn't sound so bad.

'A nice man, though?' asked Judy.

'Oh yes,' said Maria, smiling with her big white false teeth, 'very nice.'

And then one night there he was, rattling his key at the lock as she arrived, looking over his shoulder at her. Judy did not introduce herself. The neighbours nodded awkwardly and turned their backs to each other. He closed his door and she closed hers. She didn't see him again for an age. Never heard his latch click, or any sound from his apartment. For a big man he seemed to be very light on his feet.

Then one hot Monday morning at the start of July, she had her bag snatched on the tube platform by a fourteen-year-old, a child strong and fast enough to break her shoulder strap and hightail out of the station. The policeman to whom she complained at Tottenham Court Road took details indifferently, another statistic to be tallied.

Judy cancelled her credit cards, bought a new wallet, then

realised that she was missing her spare keys. When she got home, Maria's husband Ari stopped her on the gloomy landing, where he was repairing a junction box. He was a tiny man, as soft and grey as a waterlogged potato, very gentle, always giving advice, not all of it good. He told her that she should change her locks, just in case.

'More expense,' Judy complained. She was up to her spending limit for the month, with a week still to go, so the lock stayed as it was.

The good thing about London was the lack of summer brownouts. The bad thing was, she had no idea how to fix an English fuse. On the Thursday of that week she came home late to find the stairway in total darkness. She managed to grope her way up to the second floor, then heard someone on the landing above, and there was something about the sound that told her it wasn't right. She felt her heart beating faster and set down her shopping bag, listening. There was an angry shout, a scuffle of boots, the sound of someone being punched or slapped, and suddenly that someone was coming towards her at great speed, stamp stamp stamp, crashing past her and downwards, out of the door at the bottom of the stairwell.

'Are you all right?' asked a deep male voice, cultured, out of breath.

She replied, 'Yes, I'm fine,' and in the flare of a match she found herself being introduced to Mr Midas Blake.

He had long dirty-blond hair that touched his shoulders, a stubbled chin scarred at the jawline, pale light-sensitive eyes. Quite beautiful, but big and crazy-looking, six foot three, maybe more. His presence seemed to fill the staircase. He was larger than life.

'You sure you're all right?'

'Yes,' she said again, puzzled now.

'Your shopping got knocked over.'

'Did it?' She could not see – too dark. How could he tell?

'I'll fix the lights. I'll bring up your purchases.'

And that was it. He showed Judy to her apartment and waited with another match while she dug around for her key. As soon as she was through the door he pulled it shut behind her. A few moments later she saw the hall lights go on and found her shopping stacked neatly on the doormat. Of her neighbour, there was no sign. She nearly crossed the landing and rang his bell, but decided to let it go. In cities like London it was hard to figure out where the boundaries of privacy began.

And now it is the first Monday in August, just one month after meeting him, and look at me, she thought, sifting through the photographs in front of her. Someone shrieked in the street outside. What sounded like a scream of terror turned into a fit of hysterical laughter. She listened, and once more her situation presented itself with terrifying clarity.

I shall be dead by the end of the week if not before, she reminded herself, dead and unloved in the heart of Soho, and I do not want to die like this, like an abandoned animal, not here, not now. With infinite care she aligned the snapshot to the corner of the page and taped it neatly into place.

CHAPTER EIGHT

Power and Glory

It was a sweltering Monday night in London's most crowded square mile.

Soho was buzzing with executives, editors, artists, producers, personal assistants, waiters, performers, players, media stars, models, chefs, dancers, designers, fashion victims, semi-celebrities, wheeler-dealers, suburbanites, homeless teens, crooks, losers, chancers, junkies, thieves, drunks, whores, rent-boys and tourists, most of them awash with alcohol, food and chemical stimulants in various combinations. Driven by the power of their own opinions, they shifted between the restaurants, bars, clubs and offices, noisily acknowledging one another, waving, backslapping, backstabbing, air-kissing and arse-kissing themselves into a steamy stupor of self-gratification.

It seemed as if everyone was having a good time except Lucas Fox.

What was the point of having a birthday if you had no one to share it with? On Friday he would be twenty-one, and he knew he would be lucky to get so much as a card from his mother and father, who were divorced and living in Ontario and Majorca, respectively. His sister had opted for married death on a housing estate just two miles from where she went to school, and clearly had her own problems. Few other people knew he was alive.

The drawings beneath his arm began to slide out again. He rested the too-new black nylon portfolio on his knee and realigned the pages. On the next corner, a bedraggled mariachi band freelanced its way through a samba routine to the indifferent response of their al fresco audience. The diners seated outside the Italian restaurant gave a round of half-hearted applause as the musicians launched into another old Gypsy Kings song, as if hoping that a collective show of strength would drive them away. On a night like this even the pavement appeared to be sweating. Lucas could feel the heat trickling between his shoulderblades as he set off along Dean Street.

He had failed to cultivate many friendships since leaving film school. He found it difficult to be a part of his new world. He had taken a summer job at a production company trading under the pretentious title of Film Creation Incorporated, and worked there as a runner. Although menial, these positions were highly prized because running – delivering film cans and tapes, mostly in the Soho area – covered every aspect of the media industry, and provided a first-hand look at job opportunities. Most positions were filled within hours of becoming available. Some were taken by the sons and daughters of people who already worked in the field. Others went to students from St Martin's, the style-conscious art college in Charing Cross Road. Because the job paid badly, country kids never got a look-in unless they could find somewhere to stay in town and get their parents to foot the bill.

Everyone seemed urbane and knowing, the skinny girls

who accentuated their thinness by shaving their heads, the chubby stripe-shirted businessmen slipping into the Groucho Club, the club-geared bar-boys sipping morning-after coffee in Old Compton Street, the well-fed restaurant owners, the black-clad film executives, the dressed-for-lust PAs in tight suit-skirts and high heels, everyone seemed to know exactly where they were going. Lucas came from Leicester and had known nothing of London before he stepped from the coach at Victoria to attend classes.

Since graduating from film school without distinction, he had felt there were times when the city's legendary unfriendliness seemed to be personally directed at him. He had gone drinking with a few of the other runners, but they were different, tougher and more ambitious. Many of them were the offspring of film industry professionals. Some had no need to work at all, and kept the job purely as a chance to socialise and network. Sadly, he wasn't one of those.

He wished he could find a way to talk to the girl with magenta hair who always smiled at him across the street. She was a receptionist in the production company opposite his building, and stood on the front step every morning at the same time, smoking a guilty cigarette. He surreptitiously watched her through the window, trying to imagine what she was like undressed.

He knew several things about her; she ate at the Pollo Bar in Old Compton Street, but never sat with any of her friends, never joined the little cliques that were created and divided by each passing local fashion. He did not know her name, and whenever he saw her out of office hours, she entirely failed to notice him. In the bars she ran with an older crowd, hip looking men and women in their mid-to-late twenties. He wondered if she had found a way of making money by taking an evening job in Soho. Many of the studios and post-production houses worked through the night. It would certainly explain her choice of companions. Odd, the way she ate with students, worked alone and drank with executives, like she was several different people.

His only chance of finding her alone was at the Pollo. He checked his wallet for cash and decided that it was as good a place as any to start looking. Tonight, he felt, was his lucky night.

Which was when the van very nearly ran him over. It was a black vehicle with a red light on the roof and red Water Board lettering that read 'Leak Detection Service' on the side. It pulled up so sharply in front of him that he thought at first it had hit something in the road. But then a side door slid back with a bang and a man jumped out, throwing him a furious look before slamming the door shut and disappearing into the entrance of the nearest building. The driver remained behind, staring sullenly through the darkened windscreen at him. Like his companion, he wore wraparound shades, a smart black suit and a matching black round-collared shirt. He gave Lucas a look of such uncoded malevolence that the boy's natural reaction was to quickly turn away. When he looked back, the driver mouthed an obscenity at him.

It wasn't until he had walked several yards from the vehicle that he remembered seeing it the day before, parked outside the reception bay where the girl with magenta hair worked. The more he thought about it, the odder the encounter seemed. It was impossible to walk across Soho without being brushed by cars and motorcycles. Every type of motorised vehicle imaginable – including, recently, some jerk in a beige Chieftain tank – could be seen negotiating the chaotic streets. But why, he wondered, would a Water Board van be painted black and driven by such elegantly attired men?

By the time he reached the Pollo, he had forgotten all about the encounter. A lurid sunset filled the sky with soft striations that slowly parted like crimson ink dissolving in water. The warm glow in the air made even the drug addicts look healthy. London brick shone with the effulgence of Italian terracotta. Midges danced before his eyes. On some distant stereo system, Marianne Faithfull was singing 'The Ballad of Lucy Jordan'. As Lucas walked, the evening imperceptibly slowed. Above Soho's low buildings, the sky gently deepened to diamond blue.

The restaurant was packed with students, its windows steamed over, but the girl with magenta hair was nowhere to be seen. He wasn't downhearted; it was later than the time she usually liked to eat. She had probably gone to a pub. The one she favoured was far from the rest of the college crowd, the Sun and Thirteen Cantons near the end of Beak Street, where the roads began sloping down towards Piccadilly Circus. Cursing his decision to bring the portfolio with him, he straightened the drawings and set off once more.

She was not there, but the Water Board van was. Parked in the shadows of an alleyway opposite the pub, its driver and passenger seated side by side like a pair of Action Man dolls. It was almost dark now, but they were still wearing their shades. As Lucas passed the bonnet of the van, the driver removed his glasses and narrowed his eyes, speaking to his companion without turning to face him. The van's crimson emergency sign shone in the darkness between the buildings. They certainly weren't Water Board officials, he decided. Besides, if the van was real it would have an area-specific logo emblazoned on its side. Soho was covered by Thames

Water, and the company logo had a distinctive design. Perhaps they were following him . . .

Unnerved, Lucas entered the pub and ordered a half of cider. He seated himself on a bench at the window, where he could keep an eye on the van. After fifteen minutes had passed, a statuesque woman appeared beside the vehicle. She wore dark glasses and black high heels. Her tight black dress, a feminine redesign of their own clothes, was cut low across her breasts and barely covered her buttocks. At first he looked without seeing. There were a thousand women just like her in the neighbourhood. It took him a while to recognise Glory in the black wig; her usual blonde colouring always seemed a part of her personality. She was a stripper, working at the old burlesque house on Dean Street; at least, that's what everyone said she was. He saw her in a different street almost every evening, presumably on her way to various stripping gigs in the neighbourhood. She always wore extraordinary clothes, and one night had passed him wearing an immense black-spangled outfit with diaphanous wings fitted at her shoulders. When he looked back she had faded into the low evening light like some species of deadly spectral butterfly.

Now she revealed her identity in the way she moved, absently placing her hands on her shoulders, inclining her head as if listening for some faint, special sound beneath the traffic noise. The slow-burn smile was final proof. There was something insubstantial about her, as if any minute now a gust of warm evening air might lift her from the street and send her drifting away across the rooftops.

Lucas rose from the bench, his first thought to wait until she had finished talking, then cross the road to get a closer look. She displayed an unconscious sensuality he had not seen in any other girl. Glory looked braver and more experienced than any man, impossible and even dangerous to know.

Fascinated and slightly unnerved, he watched while she spoke with the driver of the van. As their conversation intensified, her companion replied in a growing state of agitation. Several times she tried to reassure him by laying her hand on his arm. Each time he pulled away. Finally he began speaking so loudly that Lucas could almost hear their conversation. Glory just smiled and walked away.

Everyone knew of her, but no one seemed to know her. In the office he'd overheard Beresford Elliot describe her as one of Soho's 'trouble-blondes', women who always left fights in their wake.

Darkness deepened in the street, until all that could be seen of the van in the alleyway was its ruby roof light. Lucas was sure that the two men were still inside because the pub's windows were wide open, and from here he would have heard the van doors slide back. He drained his glass, feeling more depressed than ever. He had no one to celebrate his approaching birthday with, nothing to do except get drunk alone – and not enough money to even do that properly.

He wished he had finished college and applied for a place in a production design studio, where he could produce work that would gain him recognition in the film world. He wanted to be like the people he saw through the windows of smart restaurants. Nobody in his family had ever been like that. At lunchtime today he had watched his bosses accompanying a pair of cool, power-suited executives from an expensive Dean Street restaurant, discussing movie production as if it were the most natural kind of conversation they held every day of the year. As they passed by, he had heard

Berry Elliot say 'Sure, you can shoot it there, but the cost of trained elephants will fuck the budget. You'd be far better off completely creating them with computer graphics.' He had wanted to follow them from the restaurant back to the office, listening to their conversation and offering his opinion on their design problems, but he had videotapes to deliver.

That was the trouble with growing up outside London. Until he moved here, the only famous person he had ever seen in his life was somebody from *Coronation Street* who had come to open a local fête. Not that he was bothered about meeting famous people. He just wanted to be near the centre of things, to be where the decisions were made, so that he could see how it was done and become a part of it. In ordinary jobs like insurance and banking it was something you waited years to do. The young were not allowed responsibility. But here it was different; in Soho the traditional rules did not apply. A person could become successful overnight and fail just as quickly. Here the system actually favoured the young. You only had to look at the club flyers left in stacks on the window ledges of every café and bar to see the sheer wealth of design talent the area offered. He wanted to be inside their world, to be one of the sombre-suited men and women who wielded the real power in Soho.

He checked his Swatch and saw that it was almost ten o'clock. He was sure that the girl with magenta hair wasn't coming, and in a strange way he no longer wanted to see her now that he had seen Glory. She was on a higher plane. She showed everyone else in their true light; made them slaves to their earthbound immaturity.

The bar had become crowded with groups of half-cut Regent Street shop assistants noisily celebrating birthdays and dismissals. The sound of sliding metal skewed his attention back to the van. The driver and his passenger climbed out and walked around the vehicle, opening the rear doors wide.

Lucas tried to watch without drawing attention to himself, and the more he studied them, the more he was intrigued. The driver took something from the back and stepped inside a doorway further along the alley. After a moment, he reappeared and beckoned to his companion. They were gone for just over five minutes. When they returned, they were carrying a black nylon sack between them, a bag tall enough to hold a man. They held it upright, supporting the top by gripping a pair of steel tabs, moving as if there was something bulky inside. They carefully laid it on the floor of the van, first checking to make sure that no one was watching. The rear doors slammed shut. The side doors slid forward. The engine chugged into life, and they were gone.

Tuesday

Sidney James: 'Why do you always have to make a mystery out of everything? Every second we're getting older. Do you realise that as I'm talking this very minute all your working parts are slowing down, wearing out, slowly falling to bits, grinding themselves to a standstill until one day – *phhht!*'
Bill Kerr: 'I didn't realise we were falling to bits.'
Tony Hancock: 'See what you've done, you've set him off now. He'll be holding his breath and looking in the mirror all day, waiting for something to drop off. You're all right, Bill, you're going like a bomb, you're ticking away like a mad thing. You've got four or five years left in you yet.'

Galton and Simpson

Beyond Normal Laws

The sun had shifted above the trees of the square. Beneath branches shivering in the silvered morning air, iridescent caterpillars of light wriggled in the damp emerald shadows. An elderly Chinese man performed leisurely stretches on the grass. Motorcycle couriers, their movements constricted by their riding suits, strode slowly across the concrete paths like leather astronauts. Lycra-legged cyclists muttered into their transmitters. A sprinkler hissed, its tone flattening as the shimmering spray fell on stone. Two young women tore buttery chunks of croissant from paper bags, chewing and staring at the wet lawn. A gardener unravelled a yellow hose-pipe. A peaceful start to the day.

I sat on my usual corner bench, balancing my café latte on the green slats, removing the plastic wrapping from a semi-frozen sandwich. The sunlight sifted gently through the upper branches of the great plane tree above my head. I shielded my eyes and watched the falcon launch itself towards the ground. Its wings made the sound of someone shaking out an umbrella. It swooped low and came to rest on the handler's glove. A group of German tourists gave the bird a round of polite applause, and the secretaries retreated back into private conversation as the falconer wandered away.

What I loved most about Soho Square was its sense of distanced camaraderie. Here there was an amused tolerance for the unusual. You were allowed to walk on the grass, smell the flowers, don national dress and start speaking in tongues for all anyone cared. In these closing moments of the twentieth century, the square still had two churches, a bank, a coffee house, small businesses, a charity house, several large office buildings and, until 1997, a hospital for women. In earlier times, at the end of the eighteenth century, when Oxford Street was still Tiborn Road, there were no trees, just a few immaculately trimmed ornamental bushes, a formal gravel path and a statue where the keeper's absurd fairytale cottage now stood. The residents had been diplomats and parliamentarians. Nobody lived around the square any more. Its population was migratory, appearing at nine each morning and vanishing promptly at six. It was my favourite place to sit, the one spot from which I could gain a vantage point on the day.

Every building here had a history. The drab block in the north-east corner behind me had once been the home of the first earl of Fauconberg, then Wright's Hotel and Coffee House, a musical-instrument maker's, the Crosse and Blackwell soup bottling plant, a cinema and finally a dance club. I loved learning about the area's chequered past. Here in the course of a single day occurred more strange stories than Hollywood could muster in a year. But nobody was bothered with the people of Soho Square. Instead they made movies about aliens, drug lords, funny dimwits, teenagers in love or trouble or both. Those were the stories that made people rich.

My dream was to see a return to great film-making in Britain. In the sixties and early seventies every possible kind of movie had been produced; intelligent, incisive epics like *The Charge of the Light Brigade*, *Zulu* and *Lawrence of Arabia*, romances like *Dr Zhivago* and *The Go-Between*, comedies like *The Italian Job* and *Alfie*, dramas like *Get Carter* and *If...*, the Hammer horror films, experimental features like *Blow Up* and *Performance*. What had we managed to produce in the last few years? Grim little slices of life from the BBC and Channel Four, the odd silly comedy aimed at America. Where were the epic modern dramas, the great stories of history? Why weren't they being presented on the screen? I knew I was not personally capable of writing or directing one, but I might be able to produce it, even if it proved to be unprofitable.

'The things you love doing don't make money,' my father had once told me. 'Nobody enjoys their work. It wouldn't be work if they did, would it?'

That was why I decided to do something I loved. But since entering the world of my dreams, life had stopped making sense. The square made sense. It centred me, calmed me. I saw the same familar faces here, whatever the weather. Within five minutes' walking distance was a land of madness, where nothing and nobody behaved according to the laws of rationality, where deals turned on incomprehensible rules and money was made by lunatics, where people discussed supernatural elephants and I had to take them seriously, and if they told me they were encoring the scene with a hippopotamus performing star-jumps, I was expected to give the idea serious consideration.

I had begun to feel that the rules of common sense governing the lives of normal people had stopped applying to me. I was losing any concept of real life. I had idealised the good things in my world, and demonised the bad. My vision of this tiny park as an earthly paradise, for example, was quite wrong. I watched a bedraggled pigeon with a red stump for a leg wobble over to the bench, searching beneath it for filthy crumbs. You saw oil-covered seagulls dragged from the sea in better condition. The outer edges of the bushes around me were stunted by the exhausts of trucks. The leaves had thick dust on them, and something else beneath it, something sticky and unnatural that wouldn't come off your fingers.

The city crippled people, animals, birds, plants. Everybody knew that. Maybe Berry was right, it was time to get out. To do that, though, I needed to generate money. I had accumulated credit-card debts that were now being turned over to collection agencies. Miranda had set up a casting partnership with my help, and I had allowed her access to a joint account. I had not reckoned on the exercise costing so much. She had promised to pay me back, but had no head for finance. The debt deepened daily.

I needed a gameplan. Successful men always had gameplans. Hell, I needed a job. What was I going to do after today? How far down the ladder would I have to fall this time? How would I survive if Miranda never came back? I remembered how insanely beautiful, how completely carefree she had been when I first met her. There is nothing more terrible than the pain of loving someone who no longer loves you.

I needed to find some practical answers, but all I could think about was the sun in the trees, the breeze that ruffled the hairs on the back of my neck. I was alone and in trouble, with no way out and no idea at all of how to save myself. And this morning, instead of concentrating on my predicament, I was thinking about a funeral.

But that was when I saw her.

She drifted across my line of vision in a torn robe that

gleamed with a dull copper sheen at her shoulders and turned to midnight blue at her feet, as if in thermal reaction to the cool grass. Her glazed blonde hair was so fine that the breeze lifted it about her immobile face. Long, tapered legs switched back and forth in a swirl of damaged fabric, her ceramic-pale arms lifting slightly away from her body as if testing the air for flight.

She turned, scanning the background, her sight touching me and sliding on, disinterested. The tattered gauze robe lent her an injured vulnerability, as if she had spent the hours before dawn fighting off an attacker. I was startled, entranced by this spectral woman who belonged to no time, but who moved with such confidence and purpose that it seemed as though the square – and perhaps the whole of Soho – was property belonging solely to her.

It was the first time I saw Glory. I did not understand then, of course. All I know is that I came to associate her with everything beautiful. Everything dreadful. Everything dead.

The Funeral Network

It **was** too hot for a funeral. The cemetery's flora looked shop-soiled and exhausted in the day's migraine-inducing sunlight. Bouquets hung limply on the roofs of the cortège as it wound its way around the chapel's gravelled crescent, the limousine tyres raising low clouds of dust. I alighted from the first car and held open the door for the others. Beyond the high hedges I could hear the dull roar of summer traffic heading north. Even this place of final rest was not safe from the intrusion of the modern world.

The girl in the last car was called Tiffany, and the great black hat topping her slender body appropriately lent her the appearance of a lamp. Tiffany had latched onto our group and was watching the other mourners with unconcealed curiosity. Grief was the only excuse for a lack of respect, and she did not appear to be grieving.

'I didn't actually know the deceased,' she admitted as she gripped my arm, 'but my boss thought it would be a good idea to attend if I wanted to get my face seen. He said there would be a lot of industry people here, and I'm trying to get a job as a production assistant. I used to be a location manager but it's not really sexy, is it, phoning councils about parking

arrangements all day long. Who are you? Are you important?'

'My name is Richard Tyler,' I said, 'and no, I'm not.'

She raised the brim of the black saucer and rebuttered her
lips with a fierce, whorish crimson. 'It was really short notice
too, but I guess that's the beauty of working in Soho. You
always have the right wardrobe.' She indicated her tight crêpe
dress. 'Soho Black.'

'I thought brown was the new black,' said a petite woman
walking behind us who may have been joking.

'They say that every season, but everyone still wears black,
don't they? Don't you?'

As Tiffany slammed her compact shut, I noticed a slim
envelope of coke wedged behind the face-puff. I hoped she
wasn't considering doing drugs during the actual funeral.
That kind of behaviour was unacceptable prior to the wake.
Mind you, I had cut myself a short line before I set off, just to
cope with the ordeal.

'So much black,' sighed Barbara Hanning, a sexy, acidic
producer who developed scripts for Miramax. She always
reminded me of the French actress Fanny Ardant. High cheek-
bones, glossy auburn hair, a wide luxurious mouth, unnerv-
ingly direct eyes which at this moment were studying the
networking executives gathered in front of the cars. 'When did
the colour of death get to be so chic? Look at this crowd. My
meetings look like funerals and my funerals look like meetings.
It's getting so I can't tell which is which any more. I have to ask:
are we brunching together or did somebody die?'

'Do you know which one is Beresford Elliot?' asked
Tiffany. 'Apparently he's really important.'

'He's standing over there, talking to the red-haired lady,' I
replied, pointing.

Tiffany tipped on to her toes and squinted through the crowd. 'What's he like?'

'Berry?' Barbara thought for a moment. 'A viking with Tourette's Syndrome.'

The image proved too complex for Tiffany to conjure. After a moment's concentration she pulled focus back to her make-up. She sprayed something pungent and floral into her cleavage, then tilted her hat over her eyes and puckered her face. 'How's my lipstick?'

Barbara considered the pouting crimson diamond beneath Tiffany's nose. 'You could suck cock for days without smudging it, darling.'

'That's pretty much the effect I was going for. Wish me luck.'

They watched as she staggered away to the calibration of heels on gravel.

'Tiffany should go far,' said Barbara, tapping sharp nails on the roof of the car. 'Berry's never been able to resist the obvious ones. I do adore men who can't stop themselves from falling for the oldest female tricks. Of course, Berry would go down on a howler monkey if it was wearing french knickers, but that's the charm of him. I must say, though, he's not looking himself today.'

I realised the truth at that moment; Barbara didn't know that Berry and Miranda had once had an affair. I'd assumed it was common knowledge among our set. I considered telling her, but decided against it. Miranda and I had been well on the road to separation when it happened. Their relationship had only lasted a few weeks; what good would come of raking over the past? I suppose I should have hated Berry, but I didn't. I knew how irresistible Miranda could be. That's what we wishy-washy liberals do, we find excuses to forgive.

The Church of England service was brief and bland. Tiffany's mobile phone went off during the Lord's Prayer, and she actually took the call. After passing two truncated hymns and a prayer through throats strangled with embarrassment, the congregation filed out and the coffin slipped behind a pair of shortened purple curtains, the kind that hung in caravan windows. Ruth, Paul Ferris's widow, seemed blind to her surroundings, and had to be steered about by her parents. She hugged me so hard that I felt her nails digging into my back, but as she let go she pushed me away, and I knew she was releasing the thought of any continued friendship between us.

As I watched the mourners networking, I kept thinking that Miranda should have been here. Why wasn't she here? She had cared a great deal about Paul, sharing my concern over his excessive behaviour, frustrated by the way he shrugged off our worries. Did she even know that he had died? I had not spoken to her in over a week. I tried to think but my migrained head would not clear. A passing stranger grasped my hand and offered me his condolences. The funeral party dissolved itself into a sombre kaleidoscope until I could no longer recall why I was there, or whose funeral I was attending. All I knew was that I had lost someone very close to me, and my life would not be the same again.

The cars were discreetly leaving the urban necropolis. Fresh wreaths were stacked beside stale bouquets, city dust settling equally on all. A strange vision appeared to me unprompted; Glory walking slowly and steadily between the marble rows in her sparkling death-moth gown, stopping to stare at each inscription in turn, searching out the plots that rightfully belonged to her.

The wake was held in a sweltering Italian restaurant that proved unable to cope with group catering. No eulogies were delivered, and I got the impression that people wished they had not come. I sat in a sunny corner of the patio with a wine bottle at my feet and thought of my old friend. Paul had been my mentor, the only person I had ever looked up to. Once, before he was married, he and I chartered a boat and spent a weekend together on the Thames. The trip had proved to be disastrous. The riverside residents were pathologically unfriendly to Londoners, the weather was awful, the locks a dull chore, but Paul loved the lunacy of it and had spent the whole time doubled in paroxysms of mirth. It was the last time I remembered him laughing. Nine long years before his death.

In those days, he and Ruth and Miranda and I had shared countless picnics and parties, laughing and arguing drunkenly together over unfinished meals, never quite resolving our differences. That was back in a time when dreams of life and love and happiness were more important to us than our careers.

CHAPTER ELEVEN

Manipulation of Light

Tuesday's lunch appointment took place at a dumpling and noodle joint in Greek Street. We sat at one of the long refectory tables inches apart from each other, sipping from huge steel bowls of clear broth. At a distance we must have looked like extras from *Oliver* about to break into 'Food, Glorious Food'. I was surprised to find myself eating jellyfish; I thought I had ordered pork.

The two excitable young producers opposite us had managed to secure a co-production deal on their script, had their money in place and were heading into the shoot this month. Now they were looking to FCI for advice on how they could sell their product to overseas territories. Would the film be bought sight unseen, should they get a sales agent, would it be necessary to create a promotional version of the best scenes, or would they have to screen the film in its entirety?

The script concerned a doomed love affair between two elderly female cancer patients who had decided to give their lives some meaning by painting a bridge. Much to Berry's disgust I felt impelled to warn them that their chances of selling the film at all were not high. When I told them that less than

50 per cent of all British features ever got released in their home territory, let alone overseas, Berry spat a piece of chicken back into his bowl.

During the afternoon I sat through the first assemblies of two new British feature films, one about a crippled Irish folk-singing priest who becomes a champion ballroom dancer, and the other about a small-time gangster who has an incestuous affair with his transsexual sister. Hollywood had nothing to be frightened of just yet.

It was too early in the evening to be so tired. There had not been a weekday in eighteen months when I had managed to get home before nine. Miranda had always hated my long working hours. Her father had only come home to his family at weekends. He used to drive his Ford Granada around the British Isles five days a week, selling engineering equipment to local councils. At the age of forty-six he had died of a heart attack on the M4, just outside Bristol. Miranda wasn't prepared to let a child of her own grow up without a father. But she wasn't there now, and nor was Gregory, so the problem would no longer arise.

'Richard, you're not listening to me.'

'I'm sorry, Berry.' I pulled my attention back to the problem in question. We were seated in front of a synchronised row of giant sawn-off shotguns poised in mid-blast, a frozen moment of violence. The bank of eight TV monitors sat against the wall in the orange and blue basement of an offline edit suite in Brewer Street, waiting for Mitch, a twenty-three-year-old skin-head with multiple facial piercings, to manipulate each framed image.

'They need the finished promo tomorrow morning.'

'But we've only just started it.'

Berry tapped the editor on the shoulder. 'How long do you

think it will take to get to a rough cut?'

Mitch flicked through the script, made some mental calculations. 'Eight hours, maybe less if we come in under forty minutes.'

'You'll be home by three at the latest, Richard. Take a company cab.' Berry pulled a cigarette from his pack and flicked it into his mouth.

'No smoking in here,' Mitch reminded him.

'Fucking Christ.' He rose to leave. 'I'll let you get on with it, then.'

Berry wasn't content just to be a producer. He wanted to be involved in every level of film. Consequently, FCI offered a variety of labour-intensive publicity and marketing services, and I was the one who invariably ended up staying late handling this side of the work, supervising the production of promo reels until the last late bars had closed their shutters.

Tonight, the hours passed slowly. The shots fitted poorly together. The editor was not satisfied. Just before midnight we began all over again. By four, we were back to the point we had reached at eleven. At four-thirty and at thirty-minute intervals thereafter, Mitch brazenly consumed a prodigious amount of cocaine from the surface of his mixing desk. Every time he did so he offered some to me, and I politely refused, but I was eventually embarrassed into accepting. The coke smelled as if it had been cut with something else. A bitter mentholated odour filled the room. I had never tried cocaine before my switch into the film industry. Since then I had made up for lost time. An ability to withstand the rigours of narcotic chemistry appeared to be part of the job description, and I enjoyed it a little too much. The trouble with coke was that it dressed you up for a party, then didn't take you there. Quite why the most dissatisfied class of people in London had chosen a house drug that increased their sense of urgency remained a mystery.

I stared at the screens in bored fascination. The shotgun was lowered again and again, firing each time in exactly the same way, the plume of smoke curling first around the muzzle of the weapon, then folding back towards the cartridge chamber. To keep myself awake, I wandered into the optical suite next door and watched another editor at work. On these screens a dying woman fell hard on the steps of a railway station, her white dress spattered carmine. She landed on her left hip, rolling down the stairs, her left hand rising to clutch at bloodied satin. As soon as she reached the bottom of the steps, she began again at the top. The editor altered her skin pigment, draining its warmth. After a while the images were nothing more than a slow motion ballet of pixilated flesh and fabric, the background a miasma of fragmenting electric diatoms. Below the actress was a padded box designed to slow her fall. The editor slid a lightpen across a gridded pad, slowly erasing the box from each frame of the film, replacing the grey area with a section of stone step. He was the sole controller of this electronic world, but seemed to have no sense of his autocracy.

I have some small talent for making connections. The scene tugged a sensation from a different part of my brain, something that had yet to occur. I knew the link would come if I didn't try too hard to think about it. I couldn't see then that I was dreaming of my own death.

When I went back to my own edit suite, Mitch brought his face up from the bench with a jerk and wiped the rims of his nostrils. His eyes were blank blue disks, the eyes of someone who had lost touch with his senses. The men and women who worked in these windowless bunkers were perfectionists, operating within different frames of reference from the normal world. They corrected details, balanced colours, manipulated textures and altered light sources until the tableaux on their monitors were flawless. Behind Mitch, the guns were still frozen on the screens. One of the engineers came in to warn us that the equipment had developed a glitch. It would take a while to sort out. There was nothing to do but wait through the night.

Winged Creatures

Andre Darreau was a French-Algerian zoologist who had worked for many years as a consultant to various world conservation agencies. Now he had retired to breed butterflies and bring a burst of equatorial splendour to the drab north London suburb of Finchley.

'Keep the door closed,' he begged Arthur Bryant, patting the air with his hands. 'We don't want any let out, do we?'

His house was unbearably hot, every ancient radiator steaming and hissing fit to burst. Sitar music rippled exotic glissandos throughout the room as a blizzard of purple butterflies rose from the back of the sofa. Although his lepidoptera were hatched behind glass in a specially constructed conservatory at the rear of the premises, an alarming number of them seemed to be flittering about the overstuffed furniture of the lounge, adding lustre to each surface upon which they landed, like coloured spots of light splintering from prisms.

Bryant stepped forward gingerly and presented what he thought was his ID but turned out to be his library card, because May had bought him a new wallet for his birthday and he hadn't grown accustomed to its pockets. He fished the monarch butterfly from his plastic evidence bag and exhibited it to Mr Darreau.

'Oh, this is one of mine all right.' The lepidopterist lightly turned the frail creature with his fingertips as he examined it with a magnifying glass.

'How can you tell?'

'The adults are laser-marked, a tiny nick.' He gestured at a far wall, where a hundred identical cases were stacked. '*Nymphalidae*, the largest butterfly group. There are thousands of species, of course, but they divide into six basic families. I only sell through long-established connections, you realise. I'm afraid that smuggling has even damaged the world of entomology. One can't be too careful these days.'

'Of course not,' agreed John May. 'I presume you keep records.'

'Certainly.' Darreau crossed the room to a heavy oak desk and pulled open a drawer, releasing a pair of gossamer-winged *Lycaenidae* that drifted out of their dark home and headed unsteadily towards the bright conservatory like souls drawn to paradise.

'There were dozens of butterflies on the body,' May added.

'Body?'

'Yes, sir, a young man found dead in an underground station yesterday. That's where we discovered your specimen box.'

'I don't understand. Forgive me for stating the obvious, but butterflies can't kill you.'

'We realise that, Mr Darreau. They weren't the cause of his death. What we want to know is what they were doing at the scene of the crime.' He explained the circumstances of their visit in more detail.

'Insects can carry germs, of course,' said Darreau, thumbing through his order book and squinting at the crabbed handwriting which filled the pages, 'but they're rarely harmful to humans, although it's true that the insect world is mutating all the time. For instance, there's a problem with the humble honeybee now. British hives are contracting Asian mites. In Europe this isn't a problem because the bees have learned to clean each other, but here they've developed no such grooming skills, and our swarms are being decimated. Nothing similar has been discovered on butterflies, but I daresay it's only a matter of time.'

'Are these at all valuable?' asked May.

'The monarch isn't rare, although there are only a fraction of the number that used to exist in England. When we ripped up all the hedgerows and built supermarkets everywhere we destroyed their natural habitat. No, they're not worth much to anyone other than as a reminder of what we've lost. The monarch is very much a commoner, I'm afraid.'

'What about their symbolic value?' Bryant persisted. 'Do you suppose they could have been left as a gesture, to impart a message to the finders?'

'I think perhaps they play a part in Chinese myth, but I'm not aware of any Western connection. Here we are. The only batch of monarch adults released from here in the last few weeks were sold by one of my assistants to a Mr Malcolm Cotton late on Saturday afternoon. According to this he paid cash.' Darreau looked up at the elderly detective. 'Aren't you hot in that scarf?'

'You mean they really belonged to him?' Bryant threw his partner a look of bewilderment as they left the lepidoptery. 'He was on his way home from here. The purchase receipt matches the date of his tube ticket. What on earth was he doing carrying hatching butterflies around in a box?'

'Well, he wasn't killed for them,' answered May. 'Perhaps they have nothing at all to do with his death. We could be looking for a connection that doesn't exist. It certainly wouldn't be the first time. Anyway,' he added, 'it was murder, not insecticide.'

'Come Friends and Plough the Seas' seemed to be emanating from the car seats. Bryant fidgeted around trying to locate the source, but there wasn't much room to manoeuvre in the rusty little Mini Minor.

'Is this what you're looking for?' May dug into the sprung kapok and pulled a mobile phone up by its aerial. 'I thought you'd left it on a bus.'

'That was another one.'

May did not understand how his partner always managed to reset the ring-tone of the division's mobile phones to Gilbert and Sullivan arias. The man was technologically inept, and besides, *The Pirates of Penzance* was certainly not mentioned as an tone-option in the operation book. Bryant cautiously raised the phone to his ear and listened.

'They've found something interesting in the boy's flat,' he heard Sergeant Janice Longbright explain. 'They thought perhaps you'd know what it was.'

The battered blue Mini pulled away with all the acceleration it could muster. It seemed to take forever to reach their destination. Bryant drove like a man feeling his way through fog, although sudden bouts of stomach-constricting deceleration occurred when the detective realised that the car was about to glide beneath the undercarriage of a lorry or mount the rear of a Routemaster. May kept his head down and concentrated on the file in his hands. Anything was better than seeing where they were going.

'Drug paraphernalia,' May concluded after a lengthy examination of the strange glass apparatus which lay tumbled across the chest of drawers before them. 'Look at the residue on the floor there.'

Cotton had rented the top room of a dilapidated Georgian house in Wardour Street, a place that had fallen victim to Rachmanism; it had been carved into flats with little thought beyond that of squeezing six monthly cheques from the property. Windows had been halved, landings divided into thirds, entire floors subdivided into fractions. In the tiny entrance hall of Cotton's area – 'apartment' would have conferred an unwarranted status upon it – hardboard partitions bowed and split, and the bedroom was disfigured with the tangles of pipes required to supply the building with hot water. The house was living on borrowed time. A new generation of property developers was gentrifying the street; restaurants made more money than flats.

Beyond the single bed, on top of the chest of drawers, a number of tubes had been clipped to retorts and fixed to clear plastic pans with lengths of hose.

'It's a filtration system of some sort. He was distilling something in very small amounts. Look.' May's index finger tipped the balance of a tiny pair of scales that stood beside a magnifying glass. Fine traces of grey liquid hung from the bottom pan like strands of a spiderweb. 'I presume Willis has already taken samples, and I suppose we'll find some kind of cocaine derivative. Either he came to England armed with the knowledge to do this or he hooked up with a friend who showed him how. Started manufacturing, then selling, undercut the locals, trod on the wrong toes, wound up being taught a lesson.'

'And that's it, is it?' Bryant perched himself on the edge of the moth-eaten candlewick bedspread. His tone was stern but his eyes betrayed amusement.

'That's what?'

'Your theory. Pretty severe lesson he was taught, wouldn't you say?'

'A warning to others.'

'It's not exactly a factory, is it?' Bryant gestured at the few pieces of equipment. 'I mean, his output wouldn't have been very impressive. Not enough to worry anyone.'

'Perhaps this was just for his personal use, and there's a much bigger set-up elsewhere.'

'Then he hasn't been very successful. Look at how he lives. Sergeant Longbright tells me they've been over the house from the attic to the cellar and there's nothing more to be found. Where do you see the butterflies fitting in, then?'

May threw his hands up in despair. 'Why does everything have to be a jigsaw with you? In real life, not every piece fits. Nothing is neat. Our existence is a ramshackle affair at the best of times. Cotton was also interested in butterflies, okay? The money he made from selling drugs financed his hobby.'

'So he chose the most common butterflies of all to collect, and was bringing the monarchs back to his breeding grounds – that's this place. I do envy your ability to square everything tidily away. Even when it makes absolutely no sense whatsoever.'

'Well, I'd like to hear your theory,' May complained.

'Happy to enlighten you. He's not producing anything at all. He's experimenting. When you set up apparatus for production you arrange it in stages, so that each part of the process can be monitored and adjusted. There's no such organisation like that here.' Bryant ran his thumb along the edge of the chest of drawers and examined the faintly phosphorescent powder it collected. 'That's not fingerprint dust, it's residue from the wings of butterflies. Look at the scaled-down size of the equipment, like a laboratory in miniature. He's experimenting on the butterflies themselves. Either adding something to them or taking something from them. Cross-breeding. Look at this stuff.' He pointed to half a dozen fine-pointed needles strewn across the counter. 'They were used to inject – or extract – something very small.'

May had to admit it was possible. In the absence of a simple solution, his partner would always find a complex one. A few years after the war they had investigated the murder of a Carmelite nun in a convent room that did not exist. The enclosure in which her body had been discovered appeared to have been built overnight for the express purpose of delaying the discovery of the corpse. 'And I suppose a team of bricklayers crept in and erected it under cover of darkness?' May had sarcastically suggested. 'By my calculation, based on the number of bricks, gallons of concrete, tiles and wood beams, I reckon it would have taken twenty men to finish it before dawn.'

'There you are,' Bryant had solemnly agreed. 'That's your answer.' Oddly enough, he had very nearly been correct. The nuns themselves had covered up the death.

May watched as his partner slowly brought himself eye-level with the surface of the chest. He slid his hand behind a stack of smeary test-tubes and carefully drew out an exercise book.

'I see our lads exhibited their usual thoroughness,' he muttered, raising the cover with handkerchief-wrapped fingers. 'I thought there had to be one here somewhere.'

'Had to be one what?' asked May, exasperated.

'Nobody conducts experiments without tabling the results, John. These are his records. Take a look.'

May examined the pages of miniature scrawl, the taped-in photographs of larvae, the maps, equations and calculations.

'I don't see how this is of any use to the investigation,' he complained.

'Don't you? And I suppose you don't see what it has to do with the Australian Outback, either.' With an annoying smile, Bryant slipped the exercise book into a plastic bag and headed for the door.

CHAPTER THIRTEEN

The Vermilion Hour

The photo album was full. Judy shoved it aside and looked for something else to do. The sun was high in the sky now and scorched through the dusty windows, searing brilliant yellow squares on to the carpet. Soon they would creep to the top of the wall and fade, and she would still be at the window. It was still Tuesday. She had been sealed in here for over forty-eight hours.

She was so thirsty. There was half a can of flat Tizer left, but she was trying to save it, even though she knew that its sticky sweetness would make her thirstier. The fridge had ceased to function for some reason. She had taken the plug apart and could find nothing wrong with it. She should not have drunk the defrosted ice water so quickly. If he decided to reappear right now, she knew she would not have the strength to resist him.

She found a cool part of the window-pane that the sun had not yet reached, and pressed her forehead against it, remembering her second encounter with Midas Blake.

That would have been the July morning after he had frightened off the intruder. Just before nine o'clock, there was a knock at the front door. In the throes of preparing herself for the outside world, Judy leaned out of the bathroom and listened. Another knock. She crossed the hall and paused before the latch. Various portions of her body were covered in face cream, moisturiser, splashes of milk shake, bendi-curlers and old sweatpants, and there was Midas, a big gold god, smelling of something fresh and citrus, standing awkwardly in faded shorts, a grey T-shirt and Nikes, unsure where to place his great hands.

He explained that someone had tried to burgle her apartment last night, and pointed out scratchmarks on the front door. He'd seen the guy off before he could do any real damage. This morning, on the way back from the Wells Street gym he had reported the matter to the police.

'My God, well – good heavens – you have to come in.' She stepped back and allowed him to enter. He was almost as tall as the passageway.

She offered grateful thanks, made coffee, then proceeded to tell him more about herself than she intended. His size was daunting. The palest eyes stared out beneath a heavy brow, so that he appeared permanently angry. She explained about losing the keys, how the police would blame her for keeping her home address in her purse, how she could not afford to change the locks, let alone install a proper security system.

'You have to do something,' he said. 'These front doors are as thin as cardboard. You could put a fist through them.'

When he asked her to come and see the security set-up in his own apartment, she accepted the offer.

And found herself standing in a mirror image of her own rooms – but the decor was radically different. The flat was filled with talismans and mystical paraphenalia, found-art, totems, prayer-wheels, *trompe l'oeil* wall paintings, mandalas and plants, greenery everywhere, thick green stems bursting from all the corners of the lounge, fleshy tropical vines, explosions of red petals, terracotta pots of every size. The kind of place a hippie would have if he was rich and had taste.

Against her better judgement, she was enchanted by Midas Blake, placed under the spell of a charismatic man as simply as a child being told a fairy tale. His speech was slow and earnest, his manner accidentally appealing, as though he had no idea at all that he was attractive. He seemed aggressively prepared to protect his privacy. A simple question would crease his brow in fury, as if he would hit you for daring to pry. He was the first man she had ever met who looked capable of killing. They spent over an hour together. He told her he was good with plants. He owned property in Soho, and worked most nights. He enjoyed 'helping people out'. He was Greek by birth, but had been raised in London. She left knowing little more than these bare details.

She returned to her own apartment, appalled by her taste in men. So it had come to this, the hard-won equality battles, the years of enlightened sexual maturity, set aside so easily in admiration of a big lug with muscles. Shaking her head in wonder, she entered the tiny studio she had built, with its drawing board, its racks of coloured pens, its Apple Mac covered in Post-It notes, and attempted to immerse herself in work. But with no freelance projects coming in she knew she would soon have to consider a full-time office job. Meanwhile, she decided to continue working on her portfolio.

The break came the following week when Daniel Bartek, one of the few friends she had made during her marriage, called her with a commission. He had taken over a key position in the marketing department of Buena Vista International in Kensington Village, and had some ideas for an illustrated movie poster that he wished to explore. He had more confidence in Judy's talent than she did, and was prepared to pay half the fee up front, which would allow her to cover her overdue mortgage repayment. She had a week in which to produce the assignment, a detailed, demanding piece that tested her new computer skills and gave her eyestrain. But it was good to be back in the workforce.

There was much about London that puzzled and bothered Judy Merrigan. Ari, the Greek dry cleaner, had warned her that conmen targeted single women in the nearby flats, and that some of the victims were nurses working at the Middlesex Hospital. He said these men could sense when a woman had been hurt, and gave her a funny look, as though he had decided that she was especially vulnerable.

And maybe she was. She knew that she spent too many evenings indoors tapping the cable remote, nursing a tub of Marks & Spencer's Chocolate Chunk, which was the ice cream for depressed women who needed something more hardcore than Häagen-Dazs. A layer of thick white cloud held the heat in Soho, and despite the traffic noise she kept every window in the apartment wide open. Before the decay of the ozone layer, the British summer had never lasted long enough to require the purchase of air-conditioning units. Now a row of them stood like blanched mailboxes in the window of the electrical store in Old Compton Street.

One scalding Saturday night the weather broke for an hour. As lightning flared and great fat raindrops began to fall, she ran around shutting the windows, wiping up the water beneath the sills. She nearly missed Midas Blake's knock beneath a distant roll of thunder.

'Why close the place up?' he asked, looking around. 'What's a little warm rain on the floor?'

And Judy paused with the mop in her hand and thought, he's right. Why do I always act on the instincts my father bred in me? If I leave the windows open, it gets a little wet. There's no one to tell me off any more . . .

He said, 'I've just opened a bottle of Chablis that's so cold my fingers stuck to the bottle. I shouldn't keep it all to myself.' His eyes stayed on hers as he spoke. She accepted his invitation and followed him across the landing, shifted from her territory over to his. He poured the wine into glasses that released the faint glissando of evaporating frost. They drank, and he talked in a strange soft way that made her listen to the rhythm of his voice but not the words. When he went to the open window and leaned out to look at the sky, spots of rain blossomed on his shirt. He turned and spoke so quietly that his words just appeared in her head. Now she remembered little of what passed between them, but before they parted he said something odd, something about how they shouldn't be scared of going out into the night because there were darker places in their hearts. It sounded familiar, a Robert Frost quote paraphrased. He smiled, and something about his expression chilled her. For a moment he looked utterly helpless, a prisoner of his own image. At the end of the evening – acting once more against her better judgement – she lightly kissed him goodnight. It was an automatic reflex that surprised them both.

The high heavens didn't fall, but Judy was pretty sure the earth moved when her lips brushed his cheek. The trip home across the landing was like stepping between worlds.

Gillian, her agent, warned her against being too cautious with men. 'You wait and they're gone,' she said over lunch the next day, 'and let's face it, you're not getting any younger. What's the worst that could happen?'

'He lives in my building,' said Judy miserably. 'The worst that could happen is that I sleep with him and it goes horribly wrong and everyone finds out and laughs at me and I still have to see him every morning and evening and I end up regretting it until the very day I die.'

'There is that, I suppose,' Gillian admitted.

Mr Midas Blake sent his neighbour flowers. Wild carmine orchids, followed by a tree of fat, petulant roses. He left her glistening, leathery plants with wide pink mouths. He stood a twisted stem of pornographic blossoms on her doormat. And he invited her to lunch. A woman can build dreams around a man who takes her to lunch.

Plants and flowers arrived daily. He called her over to dinner. He was a great chef. He told her he'd learned to cook in the galley of a yacht when he had sailed around Europe. Pointedly mentioned that he'd settled now because he was tired of being alone. There was something about him that was so foreign, exotic and yet familiar, as if he had always existed in a root-memory. Studying his still eyes gave Judy heat-stroke.

The dreams started when she began sleeping with him.

This was around mid-July. She had most definitely not intended to sleep with him, and they were not normal dreams. The sheets stuck to her body as she tossed and turned beneath the carved headboard of his bed, her mind blurred by scenes from a heat-drowsed pagan past. In the ruins of a Grecian temple she saw something scamper between vine-clad columns, watching her with small red eyes. Cherubic children, naked and plump, with the legs of brown rats, sat in shadowed corners heartlessly observing. Panpipes and birdsong filled her head. Fever reveries, she decided, born of hot nights. She would awaken to find him raised on one elbow, watching her in the dark.

And then there was the sex. Good God, the *sex*. His charm became licentiousness, his energy, violence. He knew he could cause her pain, and took pleasure in teasing her at – but not across – the threshold. But before their affair degenerated into some kind of stroke-book fantasy – and Judy was the first to admit that it was less romantic than indecent – mitigating his power was something else, another dimension to the experience. While he was moving inside her, Judy's mind became drenched with fantasies, saturated with images of a forgotten equatorial paradise. When they were combined, the city around them disappeared, the old bursting through the new, flora and fauna reclaiming the streets until all brick and stone had been replaced with dense choking greenery. She felt drugged, transfigured, hauled back to something ancient and harmful.

He told her his semen contained the power to open her mind. She told him she had heard that line before, put slightly differently, and decided it was simply an endorphin rush. She wanted to introduce him to jealous girlfriends who would send him sidelong glances over dinner and whisper behind his back. Her agent Gillian, who was so independent everyone assumed she was a lesbian, would be reduced to coy girliness beneath his intense gaze. He was a *new* new man, unashamedly masculine without being laddish. He loved the night. He spoke of the sunset hour, when the sky above Soho turned vermilion, and how it held more excitement than any expectation of dawn.

But when it came to the ordering of a normal social life, Midas Blake remained infuriatingly elusive. One lunchtime he failed to show up when he knew that Judy had specifically invited Gillian to meet him, then called three hours later with a half-hearted apology. He had no interest in civilised conventions. He was impatient with everything but her. He worked strange hours. Everything about him was strange. And despite the near-domestication of their relationship, he remained a stranger.

But that was then, she thought, and this, this awful hell, is now.

CHAPTER FOURTEEN

Professional Stress

John May stood in the doorway of the darkened restaurant and peered inside. It was now nine-thirty on Tuesday evening, and would be considerably later before he went home. 'Is there someone who can tell me what happened here?' he asked the balding Turkish manager, who still seemed to be in shock.

'She saw everything,' he said nervously, pointing to the sobbing waitress in the corner. The Shawarma was a white-tiled basement restaurant in Kingly Street, and tonight it looked as if it had been hit by a tornado. Tables had been shattered against walls. A bottle had been thrown through a window. Food and broken crockery lay tessellated across the floor. A huge mirror had been demolished with a chair. Shards of glass lay across the tiles like discarded spears. There was so much blood smeared around the room it looked like Damien Hirst had been spin-painting in an abattoir.

The girl sat with her knees and elbows locked together, her head buried in her hands. When Janice Longbright touched her lightly on the shoulder she gave a little yelp.

'It's all right, you're safe now,' she said softly, looking over at the body which lay face down beneath a bloodstained tablecloth, 'let's get you out of here.'

Upstairs, they poured her sweet dark tea and waited until she had finished moistening the best part of a family-sized box of Kleenex. Witnesses always warmed to Longbright's maternal glamour. She reminded them of a sexy fifties starlet slightly past her prime.

The waitress accepted another tissue, her fingers tearing it at the edges. 'He came in just after seven and I seated him at a corner table,' she explained, blowing her nose. Her accent was soft, East European; cheap labour. 'He was by himself. He ordered soup and a steak, and a bottle of champagne, he was very happy, he said he was celebrating.'

'Did you ask what he was celebrating?'

'No, he did not –' she looked bewildered. 'He did not make a lot of sense.'

May knelt down beside her, wincing as his knees cracked in protest. 'What do you mean? He had trouble speaking English?'

'No, it wasn't that. He did not make sense. What he was saying.'

'Can you give me an example?'

'He said something about "prepare to face the enemy" and "have to kill them all". And he kept making these strange movements with his arms.'

'Had he been drinking earlier, do you think?'

'No.' The waitress brightened a little. 'The drunk ones, they don't start coming in till after ten.'

'Please, go on.'

'I brought him the steak and he called me back, said it was too cooked. Our chef, he cooks things very lightly, he will not spoil good meat, and if anything I thought it was underdone, there was blood on the plate, but when I pointed this out to him he began shouting, saying it was ruined and he could not eat it. That was when it happened.'

'What happened?'

'His face changed, like he was really, really angry about something.'

'About the steak.'

'No, something else. Not so angry, maybe, frightened. He kept looking over his shoulder, like he was expecting something to attack him. That's when he jumped up and started –'

Her voice filled with tears. May retreated, and questioned the manager instead. The man had gone berserk, grabbing the steak knife from his plate and slashing at the other diners. Four people had suffered cuts, one seriously. When the waiting staff had attempted to restrain him he had thrown them off, overturning tables, screaming and ranting, hurling plates, cutlery, wine bottles, anything he could lay his hands on. Finally he had turned the knife on himself, dragging the serrated blade across his throat, severing an artery. Most of the blood on the floor was his. He died before an ambulance could find its way through the congested streets.

'Dinner rage, a new crime category.' Bryant harrumphed, pulling his scarf tighter. 'An overcooked steak. Everyone's working too hard, playing too hard, losing their tempers over tiny things. Remember that street trader who banged on the bonnet of my car last week?'

'You ran over his foot, Arthur,' said May, handing Bryant a plastic-wrapped package. 'Are your hands clean?'

Bryant unwrapped the dead man's wallet and riffled through the contents. 'Not typical nervous breakdown material, I must say.' He fanned out an array of credit cards. 'Look at this lot. All solid, sensible accounts. Nothing too clever or high risk. Hang on.' He removed a white identity card. 'My God, how's this for irony? He's a professional stress management therapist. An office at the Middlesex Hospital. Obviously not taking his own advice.' He wedged his fingers into the little leather pocket inside the wallet and carefully withdrew a slim paper packet. 'And what do we have here? Bolivian nostril nonsense? Could he have been having a tooty moodswing?'

'Do you want to let forensics have a go at opening that –' May started to say, but his partner had already unfolded the small square sheet.

'There's a tiny bit of residue here, but it doesn't look like cocaine.'

He turned the paper over in his hand and found himself looking at a picture of a monarch butterfly.

CHAPTER FIFTEEN

Health & Efficiency

That's my excitement over for the night, thought Lucas, finishing his final cider and rising. What a miserable bloody birthday week. Here he was, in the centre of the coolest city on the fucking planet and he had absolutely nothing to do. Suddenly Soho seemed less like a playground and more like a prison.

It was too early and too depressing to head back to his flat in Hackney. He could not shake last night's sighting of Glory from his heat-fevered mind. He considered visiting the bars he imagined she might frequent, Circus, Saint, DNA, but they were too expensive for him. There was a slightly more street-smart joint in D'Arblay Street where some of the wealthier runners drank. Perhaps even that wasn't such a good idea, considering the small amount he had left in his wallet. But for God's sake he was coming of age this week; shouldn't he at least attempt to celebrate?

He found a cashpoint and drew out forty pounds, then cut through one of the dimly lit backstreets that led to the club. It was here, just past a Japanese noodle bar, in front of a shuttered computer showroom, that he encountered the van again.

'Man, I don't believe this.' One Eighty lowered his sunglasses and leaned forward, staring out through the windscreen. 'It's him again.'

'Who?'

'There, on the other side of the road, with the big black case and the fucked-up haircut.' He thumped the glass with his forefinger. 'The scrawny little prick who almost sent me through the fucking windscreen the other day. He was in Meard Street yesterday morning. And I thought I saw him sitting outside a pub in Beak Street last night.'

'You think he's following us? Like, he's working for someone?'

'Seems a bit of a coincidence, doesn't it, three times in a row?'

'He's staring again,' said Waldorf. 'What do you want to do?'

'What do you mean, what do I want to do? Go out and shoot him through the forehead, right in the middle of the fucking street, go on, give us all a laugh.'

'I didn't mean that. I meant we could bring him in.'

One Eighty pulled a horrified face. 'Bring him in? Have you been watching Robert De Niro films again? Waldorf, you've got to understand – you can't just go around kidnapping everyone who annoys you. About thirty people have pissed me off today. Can you imagine what would happen if I grabbed them all off the street? Have you looked in the back of the van tonight? Have you seen what's in there? Do you think it would be a good idea to kidnap someone and place them next to that bag? You have a tendency to overreact, has anyone told you that?' He slammed the van into reverse and guided it back into the shadows. 'Jesus, try to have a little patience.' He shifted the gearstick into 'park' and clambered out. 'Let's hope to God this is the last stop tonight. If he phones in again I'm gonna go mad. I'm gasping for a pint.'

'Where is it?'

'Top floor of number seventeen. Bet there's no lift.'

'At least there's no one around. Where did the little prick go?'

'Down the arcade to score, who knows? There wasn't anything for him to see. Let's do the business.'

Lucas watched from the corner as the van's headlights flicked off and the pair walked away to a doorway beside the computer showroom. One of them stepped back and looked up at the top floor windows. A hand extended from the balcony and dropped down a set of keys. Waldorf stepped forward to catch them, then changed his mind and let them bounce on the kerb. 'Did you ever see *Night of the Living Dead*?'

'Which version?' asked One Eighty, 'the original one George Romero directed or the Tom Savini remake?'

'I don't know, the one where he goes, "They're coming to get you, Barbara." '

'He does that in both of them.'

'Fuck me, *I don't know*, just answer the question.'

'I saw them both.'

'Then what are you going on about? Thing is, right, you know what we're doing at the moment, hasn't the similarity struck you?'

'What, we're the living dead?'

'No, you fuckwit, they are. The bags.'

'Well, no, not really. I mean, they were living and now they're dead. They aren't going to come back to life, are they? People are alive, then they're dead. The process doesn't go back the other way. Once you've gone through the veil, mate, that's it. A one-way ticket. We're doing everyone a favour, getting rid of the rubbish. An efficient public service, this is. The health department should give us medals.'

'We're more likely to get chucked in the pokey, mate. This is technically illegal. The dead are supposed to be processed through a government system, not offloaded down the docks. If they ever decide to dig under the Millennium Dome they'll be in for a surprise.'

As soon as they had entered the building, Lucas slipped into the shadows at the rear of the van and tried the door handles. They turned easily. He pulled open the right-hand door as quietly as he could.

It was dark and hot inside, but he could make out the shape of the nylon bag on the floor. Nothing moved. Perhaps it wasn't a body at all, just an overfilled dress holder. But if that was the case, why creep around in a fake Water Board van? Maybe it belonged to a cool design company and the 'Leak Detection Service' thing was a postmodern joke. These days everything hip pretended to be something else. That would explain why the driver was so smartly attired. That was it. And here he was, trying to make a mystery out of something as mundane as –

His hand was resting on the end of the bag. His fingers could feel a cold nose and an open mouth through the black nylon sleeve. He hadn't meant to yelp. The sound just came out. The thing beneath his hand was definitely an adult male body. He pulled at the metal tab on top and the casing unzipped a few inches, just enough to let him see the crown of a man's head, a mop of dry brown hair, a white ear. Panicked, he quickly pulled the bag shut, catching the earlobe in the steel zip. He could hear voices coming from the front of the van. He pushed himself out, pulling the door behind him, trying to twist the handle upright, but it would not turn. The bag had shifted forward just enough to keep the door from closing. The voices were growing clearer.

'But why the hell would the living dead want to eat brains? It's not going to make them smarter or live longer, 'cause they're dead anyway. What sense does that make?'

'It's just so they can include gory shit,' explained Waldorf, 'sticking their hands in people's skulls, that's all. Like those soldiers getting their brains sucked out in *Starship Troopers*. It's a cinematic device.'

'It's a fucking stupid device. Like the heads and hearts thing. If it's a vampire, you whack a stake through its heart, but if it's a zombie, it takes a bullet through the head. What would happen if you sawed a vampire's head off? If he turned into a bat, would it be headless? It makes no sense at all.'

'Horror movie rules, that's all.'

'Nope. You get the same shit in cop movies. Like the Three Victim Rule.'

'The Three Victim Rule? What's that?'

'No cop ever manages to catch a serial killer until he's murdered at least three victims. Otherwise it's not satisfying.'

There was no time to hide. Lucas could feel the pressure of the body bag against the door. He had no choice but to climb inside and drag the sack further in. As he crept into a pocket of blackness behind the driver's seat, he heard the passenger door slide open. The driver and his companion climbed back inside.

'Where do you get off on this yin-yang thing?' asked Waldorf. 'Why do you always think there has to be retribution anyway?'

'Because there's got to be a balance, that's all.'

'Otherwise what, the universe will fall over? The villains

will win? I've got news for you, pal, they've already won. There is no balance, not now we're getting rid of the old underclass. People's priorities are fucked. They'll believe anything they're told. London's got really clean tap water, right? But how many so-called working-class people do you know who only drink Evian? How many of them own a mobile phone?'

'Yeah, well, that's an essential item for modern-day living, that is.'

'Listen, I was in the video rental shop in Berwick Street Saturday, and this bird next to me is walking along the racks looking at tapes, and she's going, "Brad Pitt, John Travolta, Dustin Hoffman," in this really loud voice, and it turns out she's reading the backs of the boxes into her phone so her bloke can pick what he wants to watch. And that's essential to modern-day living, is it?'

'What do you expect? People work hard, they wanna relax in specific ways. The most important thing is that duty is rewarded.'

'You're always writing screenplays and I don't see anyone rewarding you. You keep telling me there's too much competition. Maybe the scripts are crap, you ever thought of that? I mean, if you're going to create strange situations and get people to believe them, they've got to reflect real life.'

'Real life is boring, man. This is real life, driving a fucking van around all night.' One Eighty turned the ignition and released the hand brake. As they moved off, Lucas slid forward and landed hard on top of the bag. He was wearing cotton Mambo shorts, and could feel the cold skin of the corpse's ribcage through the nylon casing. There was nothing he could do now but wait for the vehicle to stop, and pray that nobody up front turned around until they reached their destination.

He was just starting to calm down when the body in the nylon case began moving beneath him. Waldorf and One Eighty were still arguing about movies. Lucas kept absolutely still, not daring to draw breath. The bag beneath his legs flipped like a dying fish. Shuddering, he clambered away from it.

Lucas crawled to the far corner, but the bag rolled on to him as the van turned into Poland Street. He reached across and fumbled for the zip. Pulling it open a few inches, he gingerly peered inside. The corpse released a great moaning blast of fetid air and suddenly sat bolt upright.

Inside the van, three people screamed.

Above the darkened street, Glory raised her tenebrous wings and smiled into the night.

Wednesday

Because I could not stop for death –
He kindly stopped for me –
The carriage held but just ourselves –
And immortality.

Emily Dickinson

Death is rude.

Damien Hirst

Running On Sand

By 1816 the new trees planted in Soho Square had grown to more than twice the height of a man. Nowadays the little park was disfigured by cars and trucks, but improved by those same great trees, even though three of the oldest and tallest had been lost in the hurricane of 1987. At this time of the morning the sun flickered through them just enough to warm the bench, the path, and a small patch of perfect green in front of my shoes.

I sat with my coffee and my sausage sandwich, pale hands picking nervously at the triangular plastic carton, wondering what the hell I was doing here at eight-forty-five when I was supposed to be rushing to a meeting with Berry. According to my watch it was due to start in exactly ten minutes.

We had finally finished the edit a little after eight. The already-hot streets had come as a shock after the icy air-conditioning of the edit suite. Film executives and production assistants were entering Soho from every portal, like crow-black mourners drawn by the sound of cathedral bells. The secretarial militia, pegged at a different status by their more colourful uniforms, queued for croissants in the coffee shops of Oxford Street. Tousled heads stuck out of doorway sleeping bags, unaware that a new day had started.

I ran a hand across my sweat-sticky face and tried to focus. It felt like someone had tipped grit into my eyes. I dug out my mobile and rang home, cutting the call when I heard my own recorded voice. Force of habit. I knew she wasn't there, but it was hard getting my subconscious to accept the fact. After Gregory left us, Miranda went back to the job she held before her pregnancy, selling advertising time for a Midland TV network while she set up the casting partnership. The new company wasn't doing well. The rent on her office was steep, and there was too much competition to make a decent profit.

Miranda and I had parted amicably enough, but the pressure of our jobs had changed us to the point where we were barely recognisable to each other. We behaved like adults even when we longed to be childish. I had had no idea how to get back to our earlier, more innocent state.

I missed being able to share my problems with Paul. It was Paul who had encouraged me to come to Soho in the first place, Paul who had arranged my introduction to Berry. But for him, work and play had somehow blurred together until there was only one thing he did. Paul performed, delivering a series of pitch-perfect acts – negotiator, host, wit, diner, charmer, procurer, dealer, always one step ahead, always ready to make dull people think they were having fun. He was the optimistic face of the industry, fulfilling everyone's expectations, even if it was all bullshit. When the act ran out, he had nothing more of himself to display. He left behind some disappointed clients and a bewildered, angry wife. Paul's life turned out to be all plot and no character. His death should have become a warning to others. Instead, his colleagues were sneakily impressed. The circumstances of his demise were being turned into a lesson in machismo, an awesome example to those who didn't realise what a tough business this was.

I stood in the shallow end of the pool and tried to rinse away the night's images, the shotgun endlessly firing, the woman falling on the steps. The chemical-tasting water was too warm and clung to my skin. Marshall Street Baths was full of angry young executives thrashing up and down the lanes. The austere Victorian elegance of the place had been blunted, buried in the inevitable modernisation of the building, but squares of sunlight still fractured and reformed in the tiled blue pool. As I dried myself I remembered my abortive attempts to compete in the gym upstairs, watching from the corner of my eye as group heads from Columbia and Warner Bros. overtook me on their Treadmasters.

I tried to tell myself it wasn't like this for other executives, even though I knew that right now, at Heathrow's Terminal Four, thousands of weary business class travellers were preparing for another day staring into laptops and arguing productivity quotas in the capitals of Europe. You saw them congregated in the bar areas, lonely figures in raincoats waiting for their flights to be called, listening to busy tones on their mobiles or staring through the glass at their spectral reflections.

Sweat beaded on my forehead and shoulders as I emerged from the swimming baths. Turning left, I passed an advertising agency housed in an ugly seventies tower block constructed on the site of William Blake's house. Around the corner in Brewer and Lexington Streets were galleries and sellers of artists' supplies. The agency, the artists, the paint-sellers, the patrons; all were still in close proximity to one another, bound by their dependencies. Most commuters failed to pick up on the resonances that sifted down like soot through the centuries. Each section of Soho was defined by the work of its inhabitants, and this in turn reflected much older ways of life. In this manner the city kept its demarcations, even though most were barely visible to the passing eye. In one corner, Marx, Boswell, Hogarth, Thackeray and Dr. Johnson mixed work with pleasure. In another part, Haydn, Mozart and Strauss had laboured, almost on each other's doorsteps. How was it possible that one tiny area could attract so much fame and notoriety, only to forget it all and begin anew each decade or so?

This morning, perhaps because a glaring sun had flattened the cityscape with dead light, perhaps because I had not slept for twenty-six hours, I felt the presence of these ancient residents everywhere I looked. I felt as if I had joined them. I felt dead. It was a strange sensation.

After the meeting I locked my office door and chopped two thick white lines on the lid of a CD case. The off-line editor had given me a couple of grams on the tacit understanding that he would load the bill. It was common practice, like leaving a tip after a meal. Berry passed the extra cost on to the client. If ever I needed to stay alert, I told myself, it was now. Granted, it had been naive of me to borrow money from a company called International Film Investments based above a piercing parlour in Old Compton Street, but I'd been panicked into what Berry would call 'a situation'. Their head office was run by a couple of chimps in sharkskin suits whose inability to fake respectability extended to shouting at each other in front of prospective customers. But what choice did I have? Where else, I asked myself, could I have gone?

As usual, Berry had hit the nail on the head when he said that Miranda had expensive tastes. I had insisted on us owning joint credit cards, forgetting that her idea of a pleasurable day out usually sent the city's retail index haywire for a few hours. It wasn't really her fault. The new casting agency needed furniture. The place had to look good in order to attract quality clients. I asked her to ease up on the spending and she tried her best, but the savings we made were too little, too late. Before I realised what was happening, the building society was threatening foreclosure on our property and the bank was considering the sale of my personal effects.

The new-found enterprise culture of the film industry was no place for a confused liberal. I thought if I borrowed a few grand to ride out this rough patch, I would be able to cover my debts and pay off the interest. I had naively reckoned without the escalation of the loan's repayment terms. More advice from Berry; if you swim with sharks, you can't afford to look like bait. It wasn't enough to feel your way in today's business world, he said, you had to know where you were heading and aim yourself there like a rocket. If you couldn't make the distance there were plenty of others who could.

My one hope was to work harder than ever, and find some way of convincing everyone that I could handle serious pressure. I had to turn the fear to my advantage. I told myself that the more scared I got, the harder I would work, the more my diligence would be rewarded, my talents recognised, my love returned.

It was a nice dream while it lasted.

The acid in your stomach can burn a hole in the carpet, they say. That Wednesday mine could have gone right through the floor, like something out of the *Alien* films.

Lunch took place in an overlit faux-fifties restaurant

decorated in a nineties version of Festival of Britain colours. The design semiotics were headier than the cuisine, in which unreliable Pacific Rim cookery techniques were randomly applied to clumps of fish and chicken and decorated with spots of sauce like spicy bloodstains. It was just as well that a couple of lines of Mitch's coke had robbed me of my appetite.

Today's clients were a pair of producers who had successfully sold a cookery show format and now wanted to make a film. They had written the script and partly financed the production, but could detect no advance exhibition interest in America. They wanted to know how to beat the protectionist policies of the US market. Why, I could not stop myself from asking, was it so important to find distribution over there? Assuming the film was ever made, and given the subject matter – a First World War soldier equates his growing predilection for necrophilia with memories of maternal rejection, but finds peace when he is castrated in battle – that was a brave assumption, why did it have to be accepted by an entirely different country and its culture?

'Firstly, because of the hard cash it could earn. Second, because of our inferiority complex about their cultural imperialism. Third, because we believe they can be led from the path of bad, dumb movies into the pure virgin light of art. Fourth, because we want to wave two fingers at them for always making their villains British. Fifth . . .'

'I get the idea,' I interrupted. I tried to ignore the chunk of garlic-crusted barracuda on my fork – I was sure I had ordered chicken – and concentrated on the woman sitting opposite. I had met Barbara Hanning dozens of times, held easy bantering conversations with her in a host of Soho bars, yet we had never talked about anything important. Our conversation was a litany of complaints about the industry peppered with tasteless topical jokes. She was shepherding our young clients through their rewrites, and had joined us for lunch. I suddenly realised that I did not even know if she was married. She wasn't wearing a ring.

'How did you come to know Paul?' I asked.

'I thought I told you, Richard. I worked in his department at the agency for a while. He was a lovely man. Thought an awful lot of you.' He was the only person who did, I reflected. Barbara sent me a conspiratorial smile before returning to her noodles.

I remembered our conversation at the funeral and looked around the table. Everyone else was wearing black. I was dressed in a crumpled blue shirt, a cream coloured tie and slacks. I looked like a TV weatherman.

I became aware that Barbara was looking at me sympathetically. 'I knew Paul was having problems at the office,' she said, 'I just didn't know how serious they were.'

'Everyone has problems,' said Berry, reaching between us for the salt. He used a lot of salt on his meals because he was an alcoholic. People who drink a lot need extra sodium. We always pretended not to notice. 'The difference is we don't all make such a drama out of them.'

'He killed himself, Berry,' I answered. 'Can't you show a little respect?'

'In Soho terms he's already history. Anyway, he was your pal, sport, not mine. The guy was a lightweight.'

The conversation drifted back to the safer shores of selling celluloid.

'The majority of the world's blockbusters are produced in the most racially divided city in America,' said Barbara, pushing aside her lurid salad. 'The more Europe pressures the studios about exhibition quotas, the more jingoistic their trade papers get. There's not much chance of selling them art.'

Berry flashed a grin at the fresh-faced youths sitting opposite him. 'Perhaps not, Barbara, but that's what we're here to help these young people do.'

'I hate it when Berry talks like that,' said Barbara after the meal. She pushed open the restaurant's etched-glass doors, leaving the air-conditioned foyer for the heat of the street. 'I mean about Paul.'

'No, I suppose he's right. Paul couldn't hack the work, so he threw in the towel.'

'I don't think you believe that for a moment.' She turned to the street, looking for a cab. 'Look, I know you're having a bad year. But you must see that Berry's walking all over you.'

'I'm under a lot of pressure at the moment.' My stomach was starting to churn with the thought of the afternoon ahead. Berry seemed determined to make my last days as strained as possible, and had filled my diary with painstaking chores and meetings.

'Well, we all are, lovey. If you've any sense you'll hide the panic and hang tough. You'll get no respect from anyone if you don't.'

She saw a cab and hailed it. 'Look, there's something I meant to do. I was supposed to let you have it at the funeral, but I completely forgot . . .' She looked at me uncertainly, then opened her bag and withdrew a white envelope. I immediately recognised the italicised handwriting and felt sick. '. . . wanted me to give this to you. I'm sorry I didn't do it earlier.'

I felt foolish and awkward. Berry had walked further along the street and was pointedly waiting for me. I wanted to earn Barbara's respect, but watched hopelessly as she climbed into the cab and directed the driver without a backward glance.

I waited until I was back in my office to read the letter. There was no stamp on the envelope. I tore off the end and pulled out three sheets of paper filled with familiar neat blue biro, then settled back in my chair.

My Dear Richard,

You know, I was cheered up when I discovered how late in life so many people realised their ambitions. My mother was an actress, and in the nineteen-sixties she played a troubled teenager in her first real stage hit. She was thirty-five. Most overnight stars wait for years in the wings. Thinking about her always made me feel that there was still a chance I could be a success.

When I was a kid everyone looked old. Those girls in the St. Trinian's films all looked about thirty, didn't they? They were supposed to be fifteen. I think it was something to do with their hair. All those tight perms and pointy bras. Young authors were photographed for their book jackets smoking briar pipes. I've got a picture of my dad wearing a cravat and a tweed jacket with leather patches on the sleeves. I'm at his age now, and I'm wearing dayglo surfer shorts to work. Something is very wrong.

But he wasn't around to witness the arrival of youth culture. If the past is another country, youth is another planet. Even so, I was never worried. After all, Rousseau didn't start painting until he was in his fifties. I felt sure I had time left to do something grand. I had talents. It was just a matter of discovering my strengths. I believed what my dad told me; you'll see, he said, life begins at forty.

He was probably right. Unfortunately he neglected to

mention that it could end at thirty-one. Just before Christmas I started feeling tired and nauseous. You kept asking me what was wrong, remember? Well, Richard, I was diagnosed with cancer. That's what was wrong. It was slow spreading, deeply buried in my lungs and my stomach, and there was an ominous dark patch on my liver, which explained why my pee was turning brown. The doctor treated me with intelligence and an admirable lack of sentiment. He explained what was happening to my body, only missing out something if it was particularly grim and inevitable. Doctors are scientists. They're cool and accurate. They're not there to make you feel better. Nurses are, though. They plump your pillows and hold your hand and check on you in the night, watching your laboured breathing with their heads cocked on one side, trying to see what more they can do for you. Good nurses should be paid more than water board chiefs.

I remember I went to a cocktail reception for a new television series, and you asked me if I was all right and I waved the question aside. Never mention illness or death in the media world, Richard. It is considered poor taste to talk about the failings of the human body with a woman who has just been on all fours in a cubicle in the Groucho Club snorting cocaine off a lavatory seat.

It took me a while to work out why this was so. Media folk like to think they're unique, and illness is mundane. Anyone can have cancer, it's so dull and suburban. Illness cheats. It's unfair because it allows instant martyrdom, a state which is supposed to be worked for. People in the media industry secretly long to die in harness. We want to be seen to have worked ourselves to death. It's a valid way to go.

Berry once said there's something worse than getting slowly sick, and that's being made redundant after fifty, when it's virtually impossible to find another job and you end up driving a minicab at night to make ends meet.

To my colleagues a long illness meant signing Get Well cards, hospital visits, discreet enquiries, bouquets from Interflora and a series of temporary replacements at the office until the illness became so serious that the idea of a return to work became untenable, at which point they could breathe a guilty sigh of relief and empty the contents of my desk into a bin-liner.

At least I was given notice of my impending departure, even if I didn't confide in you. Most people die unexpectedly, leaving behind small and embarrassing personal secrets. I made sure mine were cleared away. The real problem was that I couldn't get a handle on the process of leaving. I was always the last one out at a party.

My doctor appointed a therapist who was supposed to help me overcome my negative attitude. How could I not have a 'negative attitude' about ceasing to exist, for God's sake? The idea is so simple and final, no more people to love or hate, no more things to like or dislike, nothing at all. Nothing. Black. Like before you were born. Worse, because you can always look back to before you were born.

The people I work for pride themselves on their lack of simplicity. For them there is no God because you can't be complicated and still keep the crutch of religion. Complex adults take responsibility for their actions. So let them think stress made me sick. Let them think I died in the service of celluloid. It's a peculiarly British trait, worrying about what other people think.

My abiding image of childhood is running across the wet sand of a vast deserted beach, the sea to my distant right, cliffs somewhere to my left, a wide blue sky above, the wet sand glittering beneath my pounding feet, the wind at my back, ushering me forward, almost lifting me free of gravity. Then I am an adult, and the tide has flooded in around me, the sand is shifting, the sky has darkened, the wind is vicious, and I am still running, because now I have no choice. I am not running for pleasure. I am trying to keep up. Well, not any more, Richard. I've come to a halt. Think of me with one hand on my knee, catching my breath, waving and retreating in the distance. Life is a long journey home.

I started this letter thinking it might make you feel better. I'm not so sure now that it will.

The night I accepted the decision to put Gregory into care, I cried. Now I found myself crying again. Reading that letter was like hearing a dead person's voice on an answering machine. By the time I finally brought my emotions in check, I found I was late for my next meeting.

CHAPTER SEVENTEEN

Penitence

Barbara was supposed to come by the office to pick me up, but she was late, and I could not wait for her. Crossing Soho was a nightmare. Every street corner was impossibly crowded, drinkers arguing loudly on kerbs and in gutters. From May until September nobody seemed to work. I shoved my way through each laughing group, climbing over stacks of briefcases, my whispered apologies unacknowledged. I had spent the last hour delivering videotapes, work that should have been done by Lucas, our runner. The pavements were slick with spilled beer, wine, gravy and coffee grouts, the leaking juices from restaurant refuse sacks.

Just lately I had noticed that London had begun to smell bad in the summer months. Rome always had, and Paris reeked around the Gare du Nord, but London had remained free from the bitter stink of drainage until now. I wanted to sit in a chair in a cool room, just sit quietly in a chair doing nothing for half an hour, but there was no time left. A schedule of appointments stretched off into the night. Berry's attitude towards me had changed. He was piling on the work, making sure that I earned my final wage slip. It felt as though I was being punished for my inefficiency, but it was hard to find the real enemy in a world where everyone pretended to be your friend.

A solid wall of drinkers spread across Bateman Street, stretching from the Dog and Duck all the way to the Crown and Two Chairmen. The latter pub had been named after the two sedan-chair carriers who used to drink there while they waited for Queen Anne to have her portrait painted across the road, but I doubted that anyone else was interested in this kind of historical footnote.

I recognised at least half of the drinking regiment, familiar guffawing faces behind raised glasses. The adherence to this nightly ritual of hedonism demanded almost monastic dedication from its participants. Perhaps in some strange way these penances reversed the painful transgressions of the day, or at least wiped away the memory of them. After dark, Soho's acolytes performed ceremonies of attrition that cleared the path for the next day's sins.

I arrived at the St Anne's Court post-production facility to find the lift broken. As I began to climb the stairs, sweat trickled down my spine into the waistband of my pants. I wondered if it was possible to hate my life any more than I already did.

I reached the roof and stopped to catch my breath. There had to be an easier way of doing this. If there was, someone younger and smarter would already have thought of it. As the pretence of an amicable parting collapsed, Berry made a point of giving me the really lousy jobs. Pushing open the fire exit door, I stepped out on to the parapet and looked down. A blast of warm stale air hit me in the face. Wardour Street was nine floors below my feet. From where I stood I could see the pulsing neon of Piccadilly Circus. Beyond that, Lower Regent Street sloped away to the Mall. The treetops of St James's

Park were lost in a haze of pollution below the setting sun.

I tried to find a spot to keep the camera steady, but the ledge was too narrow to manoeuvre. Above me rose an angled roof of white concrete. A pair of grey metal derricks jutted out over the street to my left, spoiling the picture. They were fixed on sets of steel rollers, so that window-washing trucks could be attached and lowered. I wondered if there was anyone on duty in the lobby with the ability or authority to move them.

I checked through the lens of the DV3 again and decided not to attempt using the tripod. Focusing carefully, I began shooting footage, panning the camera around in an arc, taking in the buildings Berry had asked me to include. Tomorrow we were shooting a commercial for a new cable infotainment show called *Moira's City*, the idea being to place the presenter somewhere high and have her gesture to London as her backdrop. The fact that I and not one of the juniors had been given the task of reconnoitring the shoot-site showed how little Berry really thought of me. I should have been angry with him, but hadn't the energy to invest in such a violent emotion.

The heat and tension of the day had left me with a throbbing head and a nauseous stomach. A sour mist hung across the buildings, a heated layer of food smells and floating dirt. I longed for the weather to become cold and wet, forcing everyone from the streets back into their offices. A day of rain allowed the city to return to life.

The bricks beneath my feet were hot. I reached the end of the panning shot and pressed 'stop', but the expensive little camera popped out of my sweating hand. Lurching forward, I grabbed at the handle and lost my footing on the stone cornice. The empty sky beneath me reached out with heated fingers, tipping me down towards the air corridor at my feet. The camera cracked against my arm, saved by the strap I had wound around my wrist. Defying gravity, my body swayed nine floors above the narrow streets.

I feverishly imagined the ground rushing up, knowing that these were my last moments alive on earth. My heart inflated in its bone cage as I saw myself tumbling down the side of the building and dropping onto the pavement, skull cracking onto a kerbstone hot enough to fry an egg, to fry my brains . . . but then I thought of Paul hanging there in the doorway and suddenly my equilibrium returned, and I was able to pull myself back to the side of the building. I landed heavily against the coping, juddering my heart, dragging great gasps of air into my lungs.

I felt sure I had glimpsed the moment of my death, but was unable to decipher the meaning of this portent. The feeling stayed with me as I shakily returned into hot streets and churning crowds.

The high priests of the nation's viewing tastes were return-ing home for the night, to be replaced by Soho's partygoing sensualists, the conservative austerity of their day vestments exchanged for sacrilegious red nylon T-shirts, yellow Lycra dresses, khaki baseball caps. I slipped between them, unnoticed.

At Power Post I was occupying two suites on separate jobs. One involved checking a set of edited tapes that my client, Joachim Scheckler of Expando Films, was taking to an important film festival. As I reached the facility, I saw the black van sliding to a stop at the kerbside. There was no chance of entering the building without being seen. The tinted mirror-window slid down as I tried to pass.

'I hope this isn't going to be a clichéd scene,' said the big one with the flat-top, the one I recognised as One Eighty. Apparently they called him that because of the suspicious way he had of giving a room a hundred-and-eighty degree scan as he entered. He was staring straight ahead and gripping the steering wheel with both hands, and I knew he had been waiting for me. 'You know, the one where you tell me you can get the money in forty-eight hours and I tell you that's not good enough for Mr Big.'

I had been preparing myself for this moment. My only hope was to make a clean breast of it. I took a deep breath. 'It's worse than that,' I said, 'I'm going to have trouble raising any money at all. I've been fired from my job.'

'That violates my primary directive,' One Eighty said solemnly. 'Mr Big would be very upset with me if I went back to him and said you were breaking your contract.'

'I just need more time,' I explained.

'He said it! He said it!' shouted the other one, who I knew was nicknamed Waldorf because of his habit of taking afternoon tea there. 'That's a tenner you owe me.'

'Fuck.' One Eighty dug into his trouser pocket and produced a crumpled note. He turned to me. 'Thanks a lot, Mr Cliché. I'll tell you what we'll do. You go to the nearest bank and empty out your account right now –'

'It wouldn't do any good because –'

'Hey! We're not having a conversation, I am talking, okay? You've got no cash in your current account and the bank needs notice to transfer from your deposit account. I know that. We're financial consultants, not chimpanzees. So go to the bank, transfer the full amount – that's this,' he held up a sheet of computer paper and pointed at a laser-printed figure at the bottom, 'and bring it to us before the end of the trading week. Our office closes at 6 p.m. on Friday evening, at which time we will consider our fiscal transactions concluded.' He bared perfectly capped white teeth at me. 'Off the record, let me just point out that failure to comply with our exacting trading standards will result in your legs being torn off at the knees and stuffed up your arse.'

My head started to throb again, just as my mobile phone began to trill.

Barbara's taxi driver refused to nudge the sociable drinkers apart with his front bumper, and braked at the top of the crowded road. 'I'm going no further than this,' he warned her, sounding like a native bearer refusing to lead the way to a forbidden city.

'Fine by me. No effort, no tip,' she snapped, eking the exact change into his outstretched palm. She pushed her way through the throng clustered around the corner of the building like barnacles on a rock and arrived at the offices of Film Creation Incorporated. The doors were locked but there were lights on. She eased her shopping bags on to the hot pavement and dug into her handbag for her mobile.

'Richard, I'm sorry, I had to get some shopping. Where are you?'

'Running more errands for Berry,' I explained, warily eyeing the men in the van. 'I've got Joachim's promo in hand, but I also have to approve some edit-masters before they –'

'I'm not desperately interested in the details, I just need to know how long you're likely to be, hours, days, weeks, that sort of thing. You haven't forgotten who we're meeting tonight, have you?'

Waldorf began cleaning his fingernails with the end of a knife, a parody of Richard Attenborough as Pinky in

Brighton Rock, or so I imagined. One Eighty continued to stare straight ahead.

'No, but my studio time's going to overrun by about an hour and a half, so you'll have to keep him busy for a while.'

'Don't worry, I have ways of keeping a man amused. Not a problem.' She rang off, and I looked up apologetically at my 'financial consultants'.

'She's got you tied up by the bollocks, hasn't she?' offered Waldorf, trying to listen in. 'Is she a trophy wife? An executive accessory? Some attractive skinny bird who runs the house by leaving a list for the au pair, fucking up your credit limit and occasionally gritting her teeth for a shag?'

'Yeah, you see them on their mobiles in all the department store restaurants. Flat little arses, smart little suits, blonde highlights, tons of make-up. Trekking from Selfridges to Harvey Nicks.'

'And the Waldorf,' said Waldorf.

'She's not a trophy wife,' I muttered, 'she's not my wife, just someone I work with.' I surprised myself by adding, 'The woman I loved left me.'

'For another bloke, am I right? And I bet she cleaned you out first. You wouldn't be in this mess right now if you could have had her and her purse barred from the Knightsbridge area. True?' One Eighty removed his hands from the wheel. 'Here's another solution to your dilemma, pal. Get the money from her new fella. Of course, that would mean exposing yourself to further ridicule, but isn't that better than walking around Soho on the ends of your thighs?'

'We're trying to help you regain control of your life,' said Waldorf. 'You can overcome your fear. Take up the reins and get in the driving seat before it's too late. You should thank us. Money can't buy this kind of therapy.'

'No man deserves to die without respect.' One Eighty turned his key in the ignition. 'It's a bloke's basic need, just as romance is to a woman.'

Waldorf grinned. 'Friday evening at six. Don't forget, eh?'

The van pulled away from the kerb, its exhaust enveloping my legs in a cloud of warm blue smoke. I was speechless with frustration. If only they knew what I was going through, the state of mind I was being pushed into. My head throbbed with the stench of carbon monoxide. I wished it would rain.

I had gone no more than a dozen yards when my mobile rang again.

It was the last person I expected to hear from. Miranda.

'Listen, Richard, I'm right outside your office and I have all these bags. Valerie's at the Groucho so I'm having a drink with her, maybe something to eat, but later I thought I'd come by the house. There are some things we really need to discuss.'

I wanted to talk to her, but now was the wrong time. 'I really can't see you tonight, Miranda,' I pleaded. 'I've got so much work on.'

'Why you can't tear yourself away from Soho long enough to see me just this once I don't know.' She gave a petulant sigh. 'Look, I'll probably stay over at Valerie's flat tonight, so perhaps we could meet up at the house tomorrow. You did say you wanted to talk.'

'I do, very much, it's just –'

'It's always the wrong time with you, Richard. I still have a set of your keys, so I can let myself in. I'll see you after work tomorrow. Also, don't forget that it's your mother's birthday on Thursday, and as it's no longer my duty to fake your signature on the card, could you remember to send her some flowers?'

CHAPTER EIGHTEEN

Mortality

She raises her legs and wraps them sweatily around his heavy buttocks, rubbing her pubic mound hard against his testicles until he cries out. The sound drives her down and she buries her head in his groin, impaling her throat on his erection. The coldness of her mouth (she has been crunching the ice in her vodka glass) takes his breath away.

After what seems like an age, she pulls her mouth free from his cock and slowly rises, trailing saliva from the tip of her tongue over the fine black hairs leading to his navel. She drops on to her back with a lipsmacking smirk, fanning her legs wide. The angled light filters gorily through the red curtains, turning the Soho hotel room into a cheap Mexican sunset. Berry lowers himself over her, pressing the livid tip that protrudes from his underpants inside her before teasingly withdrawing it.

'You usually beg me,' he whispers.

'If you don't enter me right now,' says Miranda, 'I think I'm going to faint.'

Berry gives an animal grunt and shoves forward with the full force of his considerable weight.

That was how I always imagined them, anyway. Rutting

like characters in some nasty seventies Jacey-Tatler sex romp, modern-day versions of Fiona Richmond and Robin Askwith, all garter-belts and keeping-your-socks-on and double entendres. This afternoon I wasn't feeling my usual liberal self. This afternoon I hated Berry for sleeping with her. Everyone knew he couldn't keep his dick in his pants. His tales of conquest were the stuff of Soho bar legends. As for Miranda, it had simply dawned on me one day that she was having an affair. It was like solving a murder, working out motive and opportunity. Knowing that she was expending her angry energy beneath the man who paid my wages should have made the infidelity more painful, but by that time I told myself I was reconciled to losing her.

Sometimes, I couldn't believe my own vapidity.

The gradual loss of our loyalty to one another had caused a dull numbness that rendered any further shocks superfluous. I'd been annoyed at being taken for a fool, though. It amused me to think of them furtively creeping in and out of hotel bedrooms. If they had done it to spare my feelings, they needn't have bothered. At least Berry had had the good taste to keep his mouth shut at the office. But knowing that Miranda left me only to spend a good six weeks shagging him before he grew bored with her was humiliating, to say the least.

It took nearly two hours to check the edit masters. The sound level on the second promo tape was too low, dialogue and FX lost beneath a dominant music score, and the engineer was forced to rebalance the audio levels scene by scene. I instructed the transfer bay to provide a single master of all the promos we had edited for my client so that they would be ready for collection in half an hour. It had just gone nine. I planned to come by and pick up the showreel at nine-thirty.

By now Miranda and Valerie would be conspiring together over copious amounts of vodka at the Groucho, destroying the reputations of their friends, gesturing for waiters, cataloguing complaints about their ex-partners. Valerie was bossy and successful, and had just survived an incredibly messy divorce. It was hard not to imagine Miranda using her as a role model. I hated Miranda for leaving, but I was still in love with her. And part of me believed that she would return.

After the day I'd had I should have been feeling knackered, but the quick line I had cut and snorted waiting in the edit bay had left me unnaturally alert and thirsty. There was one more chore to perform tonight before I was through. I was due to meet up with the man from Expando Films, then I could collect the finished tape from Power Post and hand it over to him.

Reds was packed with young professionals filling the aisles from its stainless-steel bar counter to the stairs that led past its spotlit bathrooms. The laughter was so brittle you could etch patterns on it. Everyone was dressed in the latest fashionable-for-approximately-two-to-four-weeks combination casuals. There was a reason why Soho fashion fads were so mercurial; they encouraged the establishment of a hierarchy. The restaurants in which you were seen dining, the clubs you attended, the bars you visited, the clothes you wore, the people with whom you currently associated were all points on a graph that helped to pinpoint your current social status. Your power and visibility were weighed as exactingly as they had been in the court of Louis the Sixteenth.

I thought I'd better inform Berry of my progress and tried calling his direct line, only to be connected to his evening voicemail system. This was unusual, because he rarely left Soho before me. I found my client waiting at the bar with Barbara Hanning. They were standing together with an opened bottle of champagne between them. At any other time I would have welcomed the sight, but as the cocaine wore off I was starting to feel exhausted and unconvivial. Scheckler was charming but tough, a hard negotiator who expected his work delivered on time and under budget. I was running over on both.

'Joachim was telling me all about the new film he's executive-producing,' said Barbara, reaching behind the bar to lift a fresh glass from the counter rack. 'It sounds wonderful. I'm staying under this gorgeous air-conditioning for the rest of the evening. You should try it.' Barbara pulled the fabric of her blouse away from her bountiful breasts and enjoyed the cool breeze in her cleavage. She was a marvel. She could fill any dead space with upbeat chatter. She made dull men look good. I couldn't see why she bothered, but she clearly considered it to be part of her job.

'I'm collecting your showreel in about ten minutes, Mr Scheckler,' I explained, glumly shaking my client's hand. 'Sorry it's running so late.'

'You people are really cutting it fine,' said Scheckler. 'Tonight I am flying to Berlin, and we are screening the reel for the Japanese distributors just after midnight.'

Barbara checked her watch. 'That's a pretty tough working day.'

'Our screening schedule is a great success, but tiring. Everybody in film must work long hours to be successful, I think.'

'But there are rewards.' Barbara had relaxed since lunchtime. She gently tilted a glass and filled it with Taittinger.

'And tonight I'm celebrating. I've just been promoted. They've asked me to be the producer on *The Prisoner of Zenda*.' Miramax were planning to remake the original with a young black woman in the lead.

'Wow. Congratulations.' I accepted the glass and raised it in a toast. I was interested in what she had to say and wanted to talk to her, but I felt so tired that the effort of speaking made me sound forced and awkward.

'So perhaps we will be working together in the future?' asked Joachim.

'You never know.' She waved her hand around the room. 'This is a good time to be in Soho. There are a lot of new movies gearing up.'

Joachim looked vaguely threatened. 'So you don't want to give up work and settle down.'

'And do what? Live in the suburbs, breed delinquent toddlers and drag them screaming around Sainsburys? My divorce settlement came through and my ex-husband has been uncharacteristically generous, so there's no need for me to work at something I don't enjoy. I'm single. I'm career-minded. I'm doing what I love. And I want to make features.'

'Producing a film is an exercise in frustration,' warned Scheckler, rather uncharitably, I thought. 'You can easily become disillusioned.'

'Everyone says that but I know I won't.' I could tell he was starting to annoy her.

'Well, I wish you every success.' Joachim refilled her empty glass. 'Keep an eye on the time, Mr Tyler. I think you should be checking on my reel.' He set down his own glass and headed for the toilet. Obediently, I dug out my mobile and punched in the direct line of the engineer at Power Post.

'Well, I'm getting out,' I told Barbara while I was waiting

for an answer. 'Not through choice, exactly. Berry's firing me. Says I can't handle the job.'

'I know, Richard, he told me.'

'He did?'

Barbara looked as if she was about to be uncomfortably honest. 'Now that the subject has been raised, I have to say that I think you're a little too nice to make your mark in the film industry.'

'I always thought being nice was a good thing.'

'Christ, no. In this business people are only nice if they're scared of being anything else. Of course, it's an ideal quality in other vocations, like social work. I have a conscience but I'm still too selfish to spend my days in King's Cross passing out mismatched shoes to unrepentant drunks. And film *is* a vocation. You need something other than mere ambition to succeed in it; if you don't have a certain amount of righteous anger and a bit of a death-wish you might just as well be selling washing machines. So, what are you going to do?'

'I'll let you know when I've thought of an answer. Maybe I should apply for your old position.' I looked at the glass in my hand and saw that it was empty again.

'You're drinking very quickly tonight, Richard. You don't look terribly well.'

'I didn't get to bed last night.' I shifted the phone to my other ear.

'Have you eaten anything?'

'Not yet. I was – hello?'

'Mr Tyler, I've been trying to get hold of you but your mobile's been switched off,' said Mitch, and I knew it was bad news.

There was nothing on the master tape. Somehow, everything had been erased. I tried to think how such a thing could have happened. Power Post were trying to imply that the reel I had provided for them was already wiped, but it couldn't have been, not unless Lucas had somehow delivered the wrong package. Somebody over there had made a mistake and muddled the tapes. Any minute now they would find the right master and apologise for nearly giving me a heart attack.

'I don't see how there could have been a mix-up. That tape was never out of my sight. Your boy must have idented the wrong one.' A hot flush of sweat prickled my scalp. From the corner of my eye I could see Scheckler coming up the stairs. 'I have someone waiting to take it to Germany, he's here with me right now and I can't – well, look again and keep looking. I'll be over there as fast as I can.'

Scheckler must have seen the look on my face, because he said, 'So, what's the good news?'

'It'll be a few more minutes, I'm afraid,' I lied.

Scheckler gave a grunt of anger. 'You know, if I miss this flight I might as well cut my throat. Don't make me do that.'

Barbara switched on a pacifying smile and gave the German entrepreneur a friendly hug. 'Come on, Joachim, I hardly see anything of you these days, don't begrudge me a few more minutes of your company.'

I tried to think. What if they had really wiped the damned tape? It could happen. It was my fault. I should have stayed there with them while the work was being completed. Scheckler would not be able to make his film sales. He would not pay up, and might even have grounds to sue. A fiery wall of panic descended over me. What the hell was I supposed to do? As I started to move away I could not bring myself to look at either of them.

'I – have to go to the bathroom.'

In the toilet I tipped one more fat white line on to the ceramic top of the cistern and spirited it into my sinuses with the aid of a rolled-up tenner. It was cooler in here, quieter too, like being on the bottom of a stream. Cobalt blues and greys swirled about like water sprites. I wished I could stay here for a while.

I flicked handfuls of cold water on my face, waiting for the red blotches to subside in my cheeks. Loosening my collar helped a little, but something suddenly felt very wrong. My heart thumped like a fist hammering in my chest as the drug was absorbed into my bloodstream. I banged open the bathroom door and pushed my way out to the bottom of the stairs. When I looked down at my shoes, I saw the ground tilt away like a capsizing ship.

I managed three of the stairs, then a fourth, and with greater difficulty a fifth, but then I felt it, a great tearing beneath my ribs, a soaring hot agony beyond anything I could ever have imagined in my most terrible nightmares. Incredibly the spasm intensified, a single knife-twist sprouting a hundred turning blades. The white-hot shafts soared about and plunged deep into my chest, scraping at my ribs, piercing my organs, impaling me on gimlets of pure, clear pain.

My vision speckled with droplets of night, the blackness spreading until I was blinded and freed from gravity, falling slowly back down the staircase as if borne on the arms of angels.

And in that instant, I knew that my heart had stopped.

CHAPTER NINETEEN

Freedom

I could no longer feel it beating in my chest. Where the great muscle-pump had performed in perpetual motion there was now an awful silence, no rhythmic squeezing of blood through my veins, no background beat inside my ribcage, no echoing pulse at my forehead, no answering blips at my wrists. The temperature tumbled about me. Unable to move or draw breath, frozen into silence, I lay on the cold plastic tiles and knew that I was actually going to die, right here, right now.

Surely someone would come down the stairs and find me, I thought, surely in that heaving stew of humanity above someone needed to visit the bathroom. But there were no footsteps on the stairs. The noisy chatter of the crowd receded to a distant soundtrack, like the susurration of a night sea. It was peaceful here, laid out at this most public wake. Strange, too. My life had failed to flash before my eyes, or perhaps it had and hadn't held my attention. How could anything so important be so disappointing?

The sights and sounds of the world retreated, fading from my vision like a rowdy cruise ship drifting off into the darkness. So, after all my unvoiced fears about living, this was the abrupt, unresolved end of everything, the final great terror faced and dealt with. Not so terrifying after all. Just a cessation, a change of state.

Death. A wall that had suddenly appeared before me. One short climb over it and I was free to drop from the other side, my worldly cares dissolving as I fell.

Death. I could say it now, knowing that I finally had the measure of its power.

Death. Each time it formed on my silent lips, it shrank a little.

Death. The word replaced the sound of my heart.

Death. Reduced to a dictionary position.

Death. Its strength vanishing.

Death. Smaller still.

Death. Smaller.

Gone.

CHAPTER TWENTY

Immortality

And life.

For at this moment, when the last glimmering images of my conscious soul should have disappeared from sight, the oddest thing happened. I began to feel warmth again. The dark fuzz inside my head evaporated. The noise of the crowd upstairs returned. The sky cleared like clouds departing after a summer shower and I could see my surroundings, indistinctly at first, then more sharply than I ever had before. I could count the pinholes in the ceiling tiles, the drips of dried paint on the skirting board. Experimentally, I attempted to flex a muscle and found that my right arm moved. Carefully, slowly, I raised myself to a sitting position.

I was alive. Thank God, I was alive! Whatever trauma had occurred in my body, I had survived it. But my heart, what had happened to my heart? I slipped my hand inside my shirt and felt the skin above my left nipple. Nothing was beating. There had to be something, a flow, a pulse, anything, but the silence in my veins persisted. I hauled myself to my feet, swayed for a moment, then lurched back into the bathroom. Standing before the mirror, I ripped open my shirt and heard the buttons skitter across the tiles. Carefully I examined my chest for signs of movement.

This was ridiculous. Clearly I was in a state of shock, and could not find those vital signs of life I saw in everyone else.

But my silent heart knew the truth.

I was dead. In the space of a minute, my body had profoundly changed. The empty stillness inside me was intense, almost a sound of its own. My fingers reached out and touched the rim of the hand basin. They could feel the smooth ceramic curve, but less so than normally. It felt as though I was wearing cotton gloves. My nerve endings had ceased to function. I wondered if I could have suffered a stroke. Then I noticed the changing temperature. The icy air-conditioning no longer felt so cold. Either the system had packed up, or my body temperature was dropping to match that of the room.

I felt other things too. My eyes were raw and dry. Blinking was no longer an automatic response. A strange smell filled my nostrils, a smell of warm wood varnish, like an old mahogany armchair left in the sun. Then I noticed the most alarming thing of all.

I wasn't breathing.

It was as if there was simply no need. My lungs were not filling and deflating. I held my hand in front of my mouth and waited to feel the feathery lightness on my skin, but nothing came even when I tried to force some breath. I exhaled on the bathroom mirror. Nothing. The eerie sensation grew and grew. My blood was no longer pumping around my body. My lungs weren't functioning. I had no pulse, no heartbeat, no breath. I was a medical impossibility.

And in my stopped heart, I *knew*. I knew I was dead. I could feel the physical state of death. I was on the other side. Across the great divide. I had suffered a fatal heart attack and made the ultimate comeback.

Not alive. Just awake.

CHAPTER TWENTY-ONE

Heartless

I knew where the line fell between imagination and reality, and this was definitely real. My first reaction was one of appalled horror, revulsion at my own body, terror at the sudden irreversible and unacceptable change in my health. But it was not a state of mind that I could allow to last long. There was too much to be done.

As I stood in front of the washroom mirror I felt a surge of energy, a hard still power that steadied me and replaced the tingling hyperactivity of my nerves. A man who had come downstairs to pee – *now* he came down – gave me a strange look and moved to a corner urinal.

How could I best come to terms with what had happened? My body had died, and refused to lie down. My brain was unimpaired, although how it would cope with the trauma of what was happening was anyone's guess. I stood before my reflected image and slowly, carefully combed my hair back in place. It would have to be cut in the morning, the top taken much shorter – and I would need some smart new clothes. Change my image according to my new undead status. After all, I could do anything I wanted now. Run up bills. Threaten clients. Assault people. Drive recklessly. Behave like a child.

Nothing could hurt me ever again. There was nothing left to fear. Death was the big one.

Been there, done that. Big deal.

There would be time to think this through later. Now, though, I had to act quickly. Scheckler stared furiously over the banisters as I ascended the stairs. 'Where the bloody hell have you been?' he shouted above the bar noise. Barbara looked as if she had reached the limit of her charm. I threw them a relaxed smile as I approached. Without thinking, I shot out my hand and grabbed Scheckler's arm as I passed.

'For God's sake stop moaning, Joachim, you don't want to be one of these people who has a heart attack before they're forty, do you? Hold the fort, Barbara, we'll be back in exactly five minutes.'

Scheckler pulled free, rubbing his wrist. 'I'd like to know what you think you're doing.'

'Just making sure you stay with me, mein Herr. We'll go and pick up your reel together, shall we?'

At the top of Power Post's stairs I pushed Scheckler ahead of me, grabbing the passing editor with my free hand. 'Mitch, this is your client, Joachim Scheckler, the man who is currently paying your wages. I want you to tell him what you told me. That his tape is lost or wiped, maybe gone forever because you're a cut-rate cock-up merchant who couldn't find his own penis with the aid of a telescope and mint surgical tweezers.'

Mitch was rarely confronted by angry clients. Most tense situations in his job were caused by tight deadlines and panicked producers. One look in his eyes told me that I'd been given the standard runaround line because Mitch hadn't quite finished the work, and needed to buy himself a little time. He'd been planning to call back shortly and calm me with news that the tape had been found intact, and I would have been so pathetically grateful that I would have forgotten my anger at the late delivery.

But I wasn't the same man any more, and Mitch's startled expression told me that others instantly sensed the change, that they would be more careful around me now. There was a new authority in my voice, a new aggression in my behaviour. My body language had changed. I even looked different somehow. And everything I did, everything I said suggested a new inner confidence.

I released the handful of material I had grabbed and allowed the editor to pull his sweater straight. 'Let me guess. You just need a few moments to finish the job and make absolutely sure that my client will be happy with my show-reel, isn't that right?' I gave the editor a look that warned him I might yet lash out, just for the hell of it.

'Uh, that's right, Mr Tyler, I found the tape and just managed to get it finished. I'll bring it to you right now.' Mitch slid along the wall and headed off to the transfer bay as quickly as he could. Exactly two minutes later he returned with the tape and master, already wrapped and packed.

'The truth is, Joachim, this screen-jockey had backlogged too much work. He'll pay for the mistake, because I certainly won't.' I handed over the package. 'Sorry for the delay.'

It felt good to take command. Walking beside the stalled traffic in Wardour Street I realised that I no longer felt frightened of life. How could I be scared of something that had ceased to exist? I had faced the final great mystery and somehow survived. I was free to do anything I wanted. With my death-status came a new strength, a power that I could turn to ruthlessness. I knew I would have to use my gift wisely. Make enough money to take proper care of my son. Settle a few old scores. Build some serious respect.

I was a different man, all right. An older, earlier breed, callous, less controlled, filled with the fervour of right and might, like the rabid Christian soldiers who stormed Delhi in the Indian Mutiny. Not God, but Death, was on my side.

I was crossing the road when an open-top custom-cobalt Ford Mustang nearly ran me over. A pounding drum and bass track blasted out as the owner leaned from his window and bellowed 'Oi, faggot, get out the fucking road!'

I froze in mid-stride, slowly turning in front of the vehicle to size up its owner, a suburban vulgarian Middle Youth in wrap-around blaxploitation shades and last season's D&G. I reached forward and yanked the silvery symbol of a prancing horse from the bonnet of the vehicle. It came free with a tortured twang of metal. As the driver began swearing in earnest, I walked around to the door and pulled him out of his seat by the waistband of his trousers. Thrusting my horse-holding hand down the back of the driver's unpleasantly hot Calvin Klein underpants before he had time to react, I shoved as hard as I could, penetrating my abuser's clenched passage with the horse's chromium head. I carried on pushing until the muscles in my arm ached. Then I walked from the vehicle with the driver's agonised screams bouncing from the buildings.

Pedestrians stared, but no one could quite say what had happened. I slipped away into St Anne's Court. Traffic altercations were an everyday occurrence here. Nobody cared. Nobody saw. The police rarely intervened.

The bellowing driver rolled on to his stomach on the front seat of the car, his legs hanging out of the door, dark blood blossoming beneath his retro-seventies patch pockets as the taxis behind him started honking.

I wondered if my reaction had been subconsciously prompted by the horse's head scene from *The Godfather*. I permitted myself a smile and began to think about getting a drink, finding somewhere to sit and make plans – after I had washed my hands.

CHAPTER TWENTY-TWO

Drinks With the Living Dead

It was time to make my mark in the business world. To substitute my merciless new persona before anyone had time to realise what was happening. Instead of going back to Reds I decided to head for Kingdom, an exclusive private drinking club frequented by the film élite. Up until now the thought of going there had always unnerved me. This was no longer the case.

As I climbed the painted wooden staircase to the club's bar, I remembered something Marcie Beech and Red Banner had talked about over lunch on Monday. Before entering the lounge, I called Banner on his mobile and requested a meeting first thing in the morning. He readily agreed.

'You stood me up, you son of a bitch,' called Barbara Hanning.

'Are you following me?'

'I come here all the time, Richard. I've never seen you here before.'

'I didn't mean to leave you with the tab,' I told her, not

quite apologising. The drinks bill was a claimable business expense, after all. 'I had to make sure Joachim left the country a happy man. Thanks for looking after him. Get you something for your trouble?'

'A single malt whisky, and be quick about it.'

I caught the barman's attention and ordered the same for myself. My clothes felt scratchy and uncomfortable. I stretched and loosened my tie. My muscles had begun to ache. It felt like I'd been lifting weights.

'Are you okay?'

'I guess so.'

'Only you look – different.'

'I do?'

I could tell she was sizing me up, trying to decipher the change. 'Mm. More, I don't know, there's something new about you. Maybe it's the light in here. Have you been using a tanning salon lately?'

When I caught sight of myself in the mirror, I realised what she was talking about. My skin had darkened slightly, giving me a vaguely saturnine appearance. What she had mistaken for a tan was coagulating blood settling in the top layers of my epidermis.

'And you've started working out again.'

'Yeah, I – thought I should make the effort.' Maybe my musculature was settling, too. A terrible thought began to take shape. What if I was still subject to biological laws? What would happen to my physical self?

'I started going again, but a session spent jiggling about next to thirty firm-muscled TWIMs was enough to depress me out of the habit.'

'TWIMs?' I looked at Barbara, wondering if I should tell her what was happening to me, but she had entered her analytical mode, and could not be interrupted.

'Oh, you know, Tough Women In Media. You see them everywhere these days. Girls with *cojones*. You know what it's like. Male executives act like wolves. They mark out their territory when you confront them, tell you where their job boundaries are and just how far you're allowed to approach. Women don't do that. They get on with the work at hand. It used to be because they were grateful to be employed in any decision-making capacity. The new breed behaves just like men, mimicking male arrogance and always trying to go one better. Don't tell me you haven't noticed, Richard. Where men use machismo as a weapon, they use femininity. Not the old, floral kind that was so man-dependent; a stripped-down hardbody version that says, "Fuck me but don't fuck with my career".' She lit a Sobranie filter and jettisoned a spray of smoke towards the ceiling. 'Brigades of slim gymnastic bitches in microskirts are slipping through the ranks of the old guard. Enticement is back on the office agenda. God, we live in interesting times, don't we?'

'You don't see yourself as part of that lifestyle, then?'

'Richard, don't use words like *lifestyle*. No, I'm not part of that lifestyle, dear. I'm living alone and quite settled, thank you. It's about time. My husband and I stayed together for years, heaven knows why. We could see from the start that it wasn't going to work. I finally went for a divorce when he met someone else. And you know what? I pretty much duplicated the circumstances of my parents' separation. From an early age I'd tried to be as unlike them as possible.' She flicked ash at the tray beside her. 'My mother used to say I was my own worst enemy. I resolved to be my own best friend, just like the self-help books. Now everyone I work with thinks I'm a hard bitch. You're better off staying just as you are.'

'It's too late for that.' I could feel the growing need to confide in someone, not caring how they might react. A disorientating sense of panic was spreading inside me. 'There's a new me,' I told her, 'one that has been in existence for less than an hour.'

She looked sceptical. 'Oh? And what does this new you want?'

'To fuck the world up the arse and make a lot of money doing it.'

'Richard! Why would you say a thing like that?'

'Because I'm sick of being *nice*.'

She looked interested. 'I don't understand.'

Scarcely aware of what I was doing, I reached forward and whispered in her ear. 'My old life has ended. I'm not the man I was this morning.'

'Well, that's good to know. You're being very oblique.'

I grabbed her fingers and slipped them inside my jacket, over my still heart. 'Feel anything?'

'Richard!' She nervously tried to pull her hand away, but my grip tightened. Other people started to watch us.

'What the hell do you think you're doing?'

'I'm trying to explain something to you. When I went to the bathroom in Reds, something happened. I had a heart attack. A really bad one.'

'You couldn't have done, you would be –'

'I know what I had, Barbara, I know my own body.'

'If you're so sure of this, shouldn't you be in a hospital?'

'No, I should be at a morgue. It killed me.' I caught a sidelong glimpse of myself in the mirror beside the bar. I looked absurdly angry.

'Richard, you're not making any –'

'I suppose a doctor would say I worked myself to death,

but now I'm going to start living. I've got some hot projects, deals that will change everything. I just have to stay – to keep it – wait a minute – to stay . . .' My head was pounding, shaking. It was hard to see. My body was ticking and cooling like a switched-off boiler. My dry eyes were sticking, staring. My tongue was a piece of cold dead meat in my mouth. I felt as if I was choking.

'What's wrong with you?' she cried, snatching her hand back. My elbow caught her whisky glass, skidding it across the bar and on to the floor.

'Oh God, help me Barbara . . .' Losing my balance, I fell against the bar.

'Drink something.' Not knowing what else to do, she grabbed the whisky tumbler and pushed it across. I drained it, but exerted so much pressure on the glass that it cracked and broke inside my fist. I unclenched my fingers and dropped the fragments, staring stupidly as the opened flesh of my palm filled with sluggish thick blood. There was no pain. I could feel the whisky pass down through my body and drain straight out of my penis, soaking my trousers. I no longer had the muscle control to keep the liquid in my bladder.

I remembered a childhood terror. An electric carriage banging through the doors of a ghost train ride, plunging me into unfathomable darkness. An abyss was opening up beneath me. My face was burning. I clutched at my cheeks, engulfed in an anxiety-attack so intense that my vision spiralled everything away into oblivion. I had to get out while I could still stand. For the second time that night, I left Barbara. Stumbling and crashing into the other drinkers, pushing aside the waiter who tried to steady me, frightened by my minatory behaviour, I fled the crowded bar.

I had no idea where I was going. Revellers blocked my

path in every direction. The brief sense of elation had worn off; all I felt now was dread and a deep, bottomless horror as my warm-blooded living self retreated into a memory. My mind was awash with terrible, grotesque thoughts. My blood was stagnating. My flesh, what would happen to my flesh? It would rot from my bones. I would no longer require sleep, but my brain would stay alert, and couldn't such deprivation send me mad? I dared not lie down in bed for fear that my no longer functioning intestines would settle in coagulated bile. I needed help; but there was no one I could talk to who would understand.

I had to find a medical textbook, but would it cover such a thing as the cessation of physical lifesigns? A vision of Paul's lonely death came to me, and I suddenly envied the peace of such easily obtained oblivion. I thought of Miranda, and her reaction to the news that I was dead and still alive. At best she would run screaming from the house. At worst she would try to have me locked away.

As I stumbled and slipped into the stairwell at Leicester Square tube station, I tried to summon back my initial euphoria, but all that I could see now was a grotesque spiral of physical decay, an endless tumbling fall into the void.

CHAPTER TWENTY-THREE

Barbara

For the second time that night, Barbara picked up the bar tab and paid it. Richard was showing the symptoms of a nervous breakdown. She knew the funeral had upset him badly. He'd been working too hard lately, and she had been shocked by Berry's announcement that he planned to replace his useless partner within a week. She knew Richard's type too well. He was the kind of man who tried to please everyone and ended up getting in everyone's way.

It was good to get out of the West End. She was ravenously hungry. The cab dropped her off at the end of her road. Barnacle Bill the Sailor was the name of a fish and chip shop near her flat. Only now Barnacle Bill was a small smiling Chinaman with an even tinier wife and several impossibly minuscule children. She watched as he slid the foil container filled with chicken pieces in black bean sauce into a plastic carrier bag. By this time of night, the pressures of looking Soho-smart made her long to change into her ratty old dressing-gown and slouch around in front of the TV eating a takeaway with a spoon.

As she walked back along the street, Richard's terrified face appeared in her mind's eye. She hated to see him so distraught, but what could she do to calm his nerves? Offer to sleep with him? The thought had occurred to her before. His helplessness drew something from her, less a maternal instinct than a desire to control, something that always attracted her to flawed men. After her separation she had moved to a two-bedroom apartment on the first floor of an Edwardian house in Crouch End. She was happy enough there, even though she knew she had never truly been happy at any point in her life. The collapse of her mother's stage career had driven the hysterical woman to drink and a breakdown, and her parents' subsequent divorce had been ugly, selfish and protracted. Barbara had been raised by a melancholic aunt in the soul-dead suburban town of Invicta Cross, outside Croydon.

She had married young to escape, only to find herself in an even more disastrous situation. A few months after the wedding she had realised how little her husband interested her in bed. More disturbing was the fact that Martin was so excited by her reluctance to perform that going to bed became synonymous with rape.

The divorce had been unnecessarily protracted by his refusal to accept the truth about their marriage, and took almost two years to become final. Since then she had been careful in her relationships, guarded and reticent, playing the game the Soho way by hiding her feelings beneath glib cynicism, the one problem being that the ruse had worked too well, and the men who knew her treated her like Typhoid Mary. In their eyes, she behaved too much like a man.

Richard was somehow different. He made a poor job of disguising his desire for her, forever locking eyes and guiltily looking away. If only he could get over losing Miranda. That was a tragedy only time could heal. He badly needed someone to help him relax. As she opened her front door, she reached a decision. She would be the one to lead him out of the darkness.

CHAPTER TWENTY-FOUR

The Science of Decay

The station platform was too crowded. As I could not trust myself not to fall – or jump – under an approaching train, I climbed back up to the street and hailed a cab. By the time the taxi reached Highgate I had calmed down a little. I figured that I was suffering from a delayed reaction to my condition. I warned myself that there would be further shockwaves to come.

The house was dark. I changed out of my urine-stained trousers, then tried calling Miranda, but her voicemail system seemed to have developed a fault. I drunkenly remembered that she was spending the night at Valerie's. Just as well, because I was in no fit state to have a serious talk with her.

And there was Barbara. I knew I made a poor job of disguising my interest in her. Whether I liked it or not, my feelings for Miranda stood in the way. If I had developed my new attitude earlier, I might have had an affair with her. But now thoughts of sex were impossible. From her point of view it would be necrophilia.

I dug about in the fridge and found the remains of a chicken casserole, nuked it in the microwave for a couple of minutes and tipped it out on to a plate, but one spoonful forced me to spit the contents of my mouth into the bin. I was no longer manufacturing saliva. The meat stayed as a single spongy lump on my desiccating tongue. The muscles of my gullet could not force food down to my stomach.

Giving the problem further thought, I realised that there was no point in trying to eat at all. The liquids in my gut would probably be drying out by now, and as my system was no longer producing them, any food I managed to swallow would either stick in my throat or lie rotting in the pit of my belly. On the plus side, I no longer needed to move my bowels, but it was small recompense for the loss of epicurean pleasures. I figured I would probably be able to drink, though. It was a matter of consciously remembering not to pee. Presumably I would need to keep my throat lubricated in order to maintain the power of speech.

I removed my clothes and stood before the bedroom mirror, looking for outward signs of my condition. Mauve bruises maculated my buttocks and legs. The skin of my arms at the joints had darkened to the texture of damaged apricots. I was cold to the touch. Pressing my palm flat against the mirror produced no condensation.

I dressed and wandered through the empty, perfect house, past our son's untouchable shrine of a room, wondering how I would pass the night without going mad. Then I remembered the huge old medical dictionary belonging to Miranda's father that was kept in the basement. I brought it up to the study and began to read.

Rigor Mortis

The stiffening of the body following upon death. The more healthy and vigorous the nutrition of the muscles is, the longer it will be before rigor mortis supervenes. Algor mortis, the temperature of death, drops at a rate of about one degree an hour. Livor mortis occurs when the blood's red cells separate and settle in the body's extremities, discolouring the flesh with purplish-crimson patches. After about eight hours, the red cells break down and migrate out of the capillaries into the muscles, and the marks of lividity are fixed wherever they first formed.

Decomposition
Corruption of the body usually sets in about forty-eight hours after death and following the disappearance of rigor mortis, although it will occur much more quickly in warm temperatures and moist atmospheres. In particularly hot weather a body can start to decompose in a single day. Large volumes of sulfide gas inflate the body, hissing from the orifices like leaky boiler pipes. The smell is irresistible to flying insects. Putrefaction begins at about 50°F but accelerates between 70°F and 100°F. It is caused by bacteria migrating out of the intestines, spreading throughout the body via the blood vessels. Corruption of corpses that are carrying diseases is considerably accelerated.

Degenerative Symptoms
The first noticeable sign of decomposition is the green discolouration of the abdomen. This is followed by the veins in the neck, shoulders and thighs turning red. As this occurs, the network of veins beneath the skin becomes prominent. Such an effect is commonly referred to as 'marbling'. After a period of three weeks, gross disfiguration of the corpse is evident. The features become bloated and unrecognisable, and partial liquefaction occurs . . .

I looked away from the page, my fist pressed against my lips, unable to read on for several minutes.

The bodies of elderly people decompose more slowly than those of younger years, and an overweight corpse will break down more quickly than a thin one. Decomposition may be delayed by immersing the body in water, or by binding the body in tight-fitting garments. A body decomposes in air twice as quickly as it does in water, eight times as rapidly as in earth.

Decomposition was a problem I had not considered. I had less than forty-eight hours left, provided I could find a way of keeping cool, and all the signs were bad. I was overweight. Relatively young. And the city was in the middle of a record-breaking heatwave.

It was late. The temperature had finally begun to drop. I had no time to waste. Steeling myself, I read on.

Infestation upon death
The stout-bodied blowfish fly is often the first creature to arrive on a body once life functions have ceased, sometimes within seconds. They deposit thousands of eggs in areas around natural body openings, and these clusters have the appearance of grated cheese. The larvae and adults of flesh flies are the predominant arthropod of the earliest stages of decomposition. Maggots can digest putrifying tissue. The amount of heat they generate can raise the temperature of a corpse by as much as 22° C. An infested body lying on the ground can lose ninety percent of its body weight in a single week. Ants, spiders, silverfish, ticks and carrion beetles (Silphidae) all play their part in the food chain.

At that point, I slammed the book shut.

I sat on the patio steps and looked up into the star-filled night. When I was a child, I had occasionally been able to summon up a delicious sense of terror at the thought of the universe's vastness, and how frighteningly it reduced my role in the grand scheme of things. Unlike the scale drawings in school textbooks that showed stacked double-decker buses equalling the height of a redwood tree, it was impossible to proportion myself against something so eternal and unknown as space. It represented the hidden part of human life.

After a few moments I would halt the feeling before it grew out of control, allowing comforting thoughts of home and family to bring me back to earth. Now once more I felt that dropping sensation of awareness in freefall, and this time I allowed myself to fall with it.

There was another new feeling inside me, a growing understanding of my son's nature. But where Gregory's autism allowed him to glimpse only parts of the whole, I was beginning to sense the reverse. Passing through death allowed me to see the arc of my life. The grand picture was starting to pull into shape.

I was no longer like other men. I had more in common with the freezing space above. As the starfield filled my vision and I soared into the airless void, I opened my arms to embrace the night and knew that somehow I would accept it all, the physical decay, the terror of losing my mind, the loss of identity, the transformation of life into death. I could see to the end of time, and I feared nothing.

CHAPTER TWENTY-FIVE

Mr Bryant has a Premonition

'So why the Outback?' asked John May. He was tired of his partner's guessing games. God knows, he should have been used to them after all these years of working together.

'Oh, *that*.' Arthur Bryant concentrated on cleaning out his pipe with the end of a pastry fork he had removed from last night's crime scene. He had taken to smoking a pipe in order to out-pollute May and his cigars. 'The purchase sticker on the back of Cotton's exercise book, a stationery store in Barrow Creek. I'm pretty sure that's in the Northern Territory. He also makes reference to the Cape York peninsula, which is way up in the direction of New Guinea. Quite a walkabout, eh? What did you get out of the neighbours?'

'Nothing earth-shattering. A couple of them reckoned Cotton was a bit of a religious nut, new-age smells-and-bells stuff. They were kept awake by his evangelistic tones coming through the plasterboard. Thin walls are the curse of modern civilisation. Has Janice heard anything yet?'

It seemed appropriate to have Janice Longbright based at

Mornington Crescent. Sturdy and statuesque, decked out in forgotten brands of make-up and film-star hairstyles of the fifties, she looked like an actress hired to play a glamorous police sergeant in a Sid James caper. But she remained the connecting-point between her bosses, and was the only person in the division capable of explaining their seemingly illogical actions to higher authorities.

Thanks to people like her, Bryant and May's special investigations unit had gained a reputation as the local misfit squad, home to those talents the force were keen to attract and keep, but had failed to find uses for in its regular divisions. Here above the tube station were housed the anti-socials and the academics, men and women who were used to operating as loners, and although team-playing was encouraged, the personality quirks and odd behavioural patterns of the unit's more lateral thinkers were honoured in the same way that universities humoured clever students, or Bletchley employed neurotic scientists during the war.

The office was unbearably hot; air-conditioning units were beyond police budgets. Bryant was still buried inside the heavy overcoat and scarf that Alma, his landlady, always made him wear.

'Aren't you boiling in those clothes?' asked Janice Longbright. She checked the fax machine and gathered up the pages that had come through, tapping the sheets in place with long ruby nails.

'A heart as cold as mine needs a lot of lagging,' grumbled Bryant. 'I've been unfortunate in love. The soul needs romance to stay warm.'

'You could snuggle up with your landlady,' said May heartlessly. 'She's been after you for donkey's years.'

'Alma Sorrowbridge and I have a platonic relationship.

She's quite content doing my cooking and cleaning. Besides, we're not temperamentally suited.'

'Yes, I suppose she's a bit upbeat for you,' May admitted. 'You need someone more like yourself. The sort of woman who makes Sylvia Plath look like Bette Midler.'

'There's no need to be rude.' Bryant's head retreated into his scarf like a tortoise poked with a stick. 'What else do we have on Malcolm Cotton?'

'He spent quite a bit of time in Melbourne's largest juvenile detention centre,' said Longbright, handing John May two of the sheets. 'Auto theft. Eventually got out and went off into the Outback. No record of where he settled, but he stayed there for three years. Then another run-in with the law. This is odd – a drugs issue of some kind but not your usual dope dealing.'

'I can't imagine that drugs are much in demand in the Outback,' said Bryant, stirring his sixteenth cup of tea that day.

'Drugs are big everywhere,' May replied. 'Did you know that 85 per cent of all paper money in the United States has cocaine residue on it?'

'According to this he was caught for selling what the arresting officers clearly thought was cocaine or a coca-derivative . . .' Longbright examined the next sheet, puzzled, 'But it doesn't appear that he was charged.'

'It's an automatic offence,' said May, 'he must have been charged.'

'Nope. The case never came to court, and he was returned to his old parole officer in Melbourne.'

'Can we call them?' asked Bryant. 'What's the time difference?'

'It'll be faster to use the Internet.' Knowing his partner's hatred of technology, May smiled condescendingly. 'Perhaps you'd like to watch me this time?'

The only time Bryant had ever used the police computer network, he had crashed the system, damaged the hard drive, corrupted his disks and got drinking chocolate inside his mouse.

'You go ahead,' he muttered. 'I have my reports to fill out.'

'This fucking heat.' Scott Cronin ran a finger inside his collar and tugged it forward. 'I thought you said we'd meet girls.'

'We will, man. You just have to be a little patient. Let's have another drink.' Glen Dewitt flagged the barman and ordered two more vodka slammers. He peeled off a five-pound note to pay, not realising that the last round, purchased by Scott, had come to eleven pounds. The barman had heard their American accents and listened to enough of their conversation to know that they were new in town and unused to the value of English money.

'This stuff is fuckin' strong,' said Scott, wiping his upper lip. He looked around at the black and silver bar, the microskirted hostesses, the half-empty disco floor. They were in one of the timewarp clubs at the edge of Soho that looked like a white-trash space ship, the kind of damp-smelling eighties hangover that still played T'Pau and the Eurythmics, not because it was hip to be retro but because they had always done so. At this time of night it was populated by third division footballers, women who said they were paid escorts (and women who admitted they weren't), big-arsed middle-Americans and sweaty-looking Euro-businessmen, all of them visitors to the capital on the lookout for an increasingly elusive good time.

Glen and Scott were on the last leg of their European Grand Tour, completing the ritual vacation that heralded the end of their college education. They had not enjoyed themselves. Europe was too weird and foreign, and now the English . . . but they hadn't met any real English, only other tourists. It was as if the real city was in hiding, waiting for them to go home before re-emerging. And expensive – jeezus, they wondered how anyone could afford to live here at all. They had blown what little money they had left on some chemical enhancement for the night – and, with a grim inevitability that made Scott want to punch something – discovered that they'd been gypped.

'Hey, who's this. Check it out, look, look.' Glen tried to point discreetly ahead of him.

'Where, man? Omigod.'

The pale girl sauntered up beside them and tapped her empty shot-glass on the bar. Clad in a black suede bikini and tasselled leather wristbands, she hooked up to a stool and watched as the barman obediently replaced her whisky. Her body was lithe and athletic, rigidly muscular, and she had the blank white face of a painted angel.

'Talk to her, for fuck's sake,' hissed Glen, who was farthest away. But before Scott could work up the nerve, she had turned to face them.

'Hello boys.'

'Hi –'

'Uh, hello –'

'Are you having a good time?' She smiled, and released the rays of the midnight sun.

Glen sniggered. 'Sure we are,' said Scott. 'What's your name?'

'Glory.' It seemed impossible that her smile could grow further but it did.

'I'm Scott. He's Glen. You must work out.' Glen nudged his friend in the back. 'What do you do for a living?'

'I'm an ecdysiast,' replied Glory, and the smile became a laugh. Even the barman was transfixed. 'You should try to catch my act.'

'Sure, where?' They nodded eagerly.

'Here.' She produced a pair of cards and gave them one each.

'Maybe we can take you out after,' Scott ventured.

She looked carefully in their eyes. 'Both of you?'

'Uh, yeah. I guess.'

Her gaze increased its intensity. 'Then what happens?'

'Well, whatever you want.' Glen sniggered again.

'Sex.' She sounded resigned to discussing the subject.

'Well, you call the shots.'

'What are you into?'

'I don't – uh –'

Glory sipped her drink and shifted forward. 'Are we talking one on one? Because that's not me.'

'It's not – well, what do you –'

'Bondage, discipline, role-playing, fetishwear, domination, humiliation, whatever you want, but it has to be the two of you both together. Of course, it helps if you're into each other.'

Glen threw Scott a look of horror. Glory deftly slipped her hand into the waistband of Scott's jeans. 'Do you have a Prince Albert?'

'A what?'

'No? Not even tit-rings? I could pierce you both if you like. Join the two of you with a silver chain, cock to cock.'

'No, hell, I wouldn't like!' cried Glen. Scott shook his head furiously.

'Oh well. You must excuse me, boys, I have to go to work now. While you're here, try the vanilla vodka. I'm sure you'll like it.' She slammed down the whisky shot and ran her fingers across Glen's chest, tweaking his nipple so hard that he yelped. 'Try to have a good night.'

'Reply's in,' Janice Longbright called to the detectives.

'That was quick.' John May joined her at the monitor. 'Somebody over there is working very late.'

Longbright scrolled through the screen information. 'Take a look at this.'

'Wait, let me get Arthur.' May walked quickly back to the staff room. 'Arthur, you roped me into this, the least you can do is – what on earth are you doing?'

'I dropped one of my herbal cigarettes,' Bryant explained, backing out from beneath his desk.

'For God's sake,' May hissed. 'This is a police unit, you're supposed to set an example.' He snatched the joint away and stuffed it into one of the evidence bags lying on the counter.

'I always do,' said Bryant indignantly.

'Yes, but it's not a good one.'

'Your point being?'

'Try to restrain yourself from smoking drugs in the office.'

'I have a doctor's certificate for that. It's alternative medicine.'

'Alternative to reality. Get down that corridor.'

'The parole officer thinks he was crazy,' said Longbright when they entered. 'Messianic tendencies, she's put here. Delusional. Spent a lot of time in therapy.'

The detectives seated themselves either side of the sergeant. 'What else?' asked May.

'Well, according to his father, he could have had a brilliant career.'

'What in?'

'Ecosphere biochemistry, whatever that may be. The boy was extremely bright, but he couldn't handle authority. Suffered continuous disciplinary problems during his first year at college. Finally expelled for conducting unauthorised experiments.'

'Hmm.' Bryant was thoughtfully massaging his chin in a way that usually meant trouble. 'Do we have any profilers knocking around? Who's on the books these days?'

'No, Arthur, please don't go down that route,' complained May. He knew what would happen if Bryant was allowed to bring in his own freelancers. The building would be crawling with psychics, clairvoyants, necromancers, lunatics. He didn't so much mind Bryant's obsessive academic friends, like Dr Harold Masters, who lectured at the British Museum and provided them with useful background information from time to time. It was the other ones you had to watch out for. He did not want Edna Wagstaff and her talking cats to become involved in a case again.

'I have the perfect person for this.'

'Is he in the force?'

'No, she's in Holloway Prison. But she's terribly good. And time, you'll admit, is of the essence.'

May winced. 'She's a professional?'

'Oh yes.'

'What's she in for?'

'Murder.'

'Don't you understand that I cannot let you give out *subjudice* case details to someone serving time for murder?'

'I wish you'd stop worrying so much,' Bryant complained. 'She's completely trustworthy. No one will ever find out that I've visited her.'

'Why can't we try regular procedures first, just once?'

'Because,' replied Bryant, 'I have a really bad feeling about where this is leading.' He released a spiteful smile. 'And if anyone could confirm my worst fears it's her.'

CHAPTER TWENTY-SIX

The Scales of Religion

Wednesday evening, and Soho was as hot as hell. Judy was weaker today. Just crossing the apartment had required superhuman effort. She drank the last of the Tizer, savouring each sickly mouthful. From now on there was only the brackish water from the toilet cistern, and not much of that. She conducted a search for crumbs of food, removing the shelves above the sink on the off-chance that a biscuit might have fallen there. And she thought of Midas Blake.

Was it a coincidence that about the time she began sleeping with him, her artistic ability began to germinate? The Disney designs she had been commissioned to produce became such a delightful riot of colour and chaos that she was promptly hired to develop artwork for an upcoming jungle epic. Her confidence grew with her prowess. The drabness of her past suburban imprisonment was blasted aside by this new fertility of mind. Thanks to the endless gifts of plants, her apartment grew into a tropical jungle. It seemed that even flowers responded to the Midas touch. Their lives together became almost idyllic; the building took on an oddly Mediterranean atmosphere, becalmed and pleasant, an urban oasis drifting above a summer sea of traffic fumes. Only Ari and Maria failed to notice the change. It took a lot to change their perceptions. They lived inside the smell of dry cleaning fluid.

Judy and Midas carefully maintained separate apartments, awaiting invitations from each other before crossing thresholds, a matter of territorial privacy. She painted the overgrown cities of her dreams, filling her bedroom with lush acrylic vistas while Midas –

That was the problem; what did *he* do? He went to his club at midnight almost every night and stayed there until four. He would not allow her to visit the premises, would not even tell her where it was. Could he, she wondered, be seeing other women? Where did he get his money? Why did he have no regular daytime friends? The woman who always rang his mobile – it seemed that Glory did not possess another name – who was she? He'd told her his parents were dead, but surely others were close to him? There were no family photographs in his apartment, no personal mementoes, just things he'd collected on voyages. He drank vast amounts of red wine, as if trying to blot out bad memories, and would behave like a reprimanded schoolboy when she asked questions, dropping his head to his chest, his hair flopping down to shield unforgiving eyes.

He occupied her every thought.

Her prying developed subtlety, and when that failed she tried snooping around his apartment, only to find locked drawers without keys. She complained, feeling their relationship was based on little more than a feral sex-life. Midas was content with the way things were, happy to float on the summer tide. His moods were a series of heatwaves inexorably rippling towards a storm, which broke when he drunkenly barged into her flat one night and accused her of trying to emasculate him.

Emasculate! His fury frightened her. They argued over whether he should have her keys, and the matter added to the mysteries between them. Questions of trust were raised. What did she really know about him? No more than if she had passed him in the street. Judy had held nothing back; why should he keep secrets?

They ended July in deepening bad feeling. The more she complained, the drunker and more unreliable Midas became. On the first Saturday of the month he failed to show up for a dinner party, only to appear at three in the morning smelling as if he'd been dropped in a vat of Chianti.

'Where have you been?' she asked calmly.

'Where I always am at night,' he slurred, sprawling heavily into an armchair.

'And where is that?'

His eyes held hers. 'Where do you think?'

'Midas, I'm tired of playing games with you.'

He turned his attention to his boots, trying to loosen one and failing. 'I work,' he said. 'I'm not the layabout you think I am.'

'What is it you do?'

'You know what I do. I have a club to run.'

'But what do your duties involve?'

'The usual things . . .'

'Apart from the usual things.'

'I wonder. I wonder if I should really tell you. I don't suppose you would approve.'

She called his bluff. 'I'm pretty broad-minded. Try me.'

He stared long and hard at the ceiling, then lowered his eyes to hers. 'We inherited certain – powers – from our parents.'

'Who's we? What kind of powers? Healing powers? Super

powers? Your parents weren't from Krypton, were they?'

'It's not a joking matter, Judy. I have special talents that stem from –' he paused awkwardly, ' – well, from my virility. People need my help.'

'What sort of people?' Judy could not believe what she was hearing. 'Where do you meet them, Midas?'

'Sometimes at the club. Sometimes at parties.'

'You go to *parties* without me?'

'These are specially arranged parties. I am in great demand, especially with older women. And some men. They pay me well. My sex gives them strength. It opens their senses. As it has done to you.'

'Are you trying to tell me you're paid to attend *orgies*?'

'They're not orgies. They are ceremonies. Ceremonies of pagan veneration. Glory organises them and tells me what to do. It's very important to maintain the balance of urban life. Glory knows – '

'Are you having an affair with this woman?'

'Who, Glory? Of course not!' He seemed horrified by the idea. 'She not supposed to have sex with anyone. The consequences can be fatal. I don't think there's any way I can make you understand if you don't already trust me. I don't see why I should have to explain this. It has no bearing on our relationship.'

'Think again,' she said, attempting to drag him from the chair.

'But we're good together,' he said, 'you know that. Don't spoil it now, Judy.'

'I'm a pretty liberal person,' she explained, 'but I draw the line at allowing other people to worship at the shrine of your dick.'

He shook his head in disgust. 'You can't forsake me now. I

cast spells. I can help you. Your life would be much less pleasant without me.'

Judy didn't want to believe what she'd heard, but instinctively knew it was true because the role fitted him so perfectly. Now she just wanted him out of her flat. She would never have managed it if he hadn't been so drunk. By the time she had slammed the front door and double-locked it she was shaking with anger and fright. This, she told myself, was her reward for trusting too fast. This was the danger of cities.

She avoided him. There was no question of moving out, or of coming to terms with what he had told her. She refused to be bullied, and could not afford to leave. He slipped a note under her door begging for the chance to explain. She tore it up and posted it back through his letterbox. The next time she passed him on the stairs, she warned him to leave her alone if he didn't want her to report him to the police as a pest.

Two nights later, the real trouble began.

CHAPTER TWENTY-SEVEN

The Angel of Loneliness

In Macclesfield Street Lucas Fox sat on the kerb outside the former Dutch resistance pub, De Hems, and watched the firemen playing Russian roulette. The fire station was in Shaftesbury Avenue, behind the pub, and the firemen drank here when they were off duty. They had a fondness for noisy drinking games, and in summer when the wooden front doors of the saloon were folded back, their laughter could be heard above the cries of the Chinese street traders far down the street. The polyglot pub, verging on Chinatown, was visited by Dutch residents, jovial Rastafarians, giggly English shop assistants and bemused American tourists, who consulted their maps and clung to each other like lost children until they sighted the nearby McDonald's, and felt safe again.

Every Soho public house enjoyed patronage peculiar to its site. Even bars that stood within a few hundred feet of each other had customer characteristics that remained unchanged through decades of ownership. The Golden Lion had traditionally performed its civic duty as a rent-boy boozer, but that wonderfully unwholesome image had been tainted by the mass murderer Denis Nilsen, who allegedly picked up his victims there. This was too disturbing even for Soho, and the pub had subsided into nondescript repute, out of fashion, out of time.

Other troubled sites lived on under new names and new disguises. Prostitutes' apartments regularly changed tenancy and ownership throughout Soho, but the same buildings continued to provide established bases for their working girls. The rowdy Helvetia pub had become the even rowdier but gay Comptons; the boy bars were capable of more serious hellraising than straight joints, and managed to do so non-violently, which was probably why Soho had so many of them. Wardour Street's the Intrepid Fox was named after Westminster's gambling-mad Radical candidate Charles James Fox. In 1784, the beautiful Duchess of Devonshire had won Fox the coalmen's vote with a pint of stout and a kiss. A plaque had long commemorated the spot. But now the Fox was a goth-rock pub, its history buried beneath photographs of soon-to-be-forgotten bands. Many of Soho's pubs were well on their way to three-hundred-year anniversaries. In Bateman Street, the Dog and Duck had been named for the hunters who once shot snipe in nearby Leicester Fields. These days, Lucas was more likely to see a genuine Hollywood movie star seated inside, relaxing after a hard day's ADR – Additional Dialogue Recording, formerly known as 'looping' – in the De Lane Lea dubbing studios opposite.

The runner sat with his drink and pondered his fortunate escape. They had thrown him out of the van! One Eighty had angrily grabbed him by the throat and shaken him as if emptying a vacuum-cleaner bag. Then he had looked at Waldorf and burst out laughing. Lucas could not see what there was to laugh about. The writhing body beside him was fighting to break free of its plastic shroud, and all his abductors could do was roar with glee. Then Waldorf had climbed over the seats, grabbed him by the collar and shoved him out of the rear doors, like an angler tossing back a sprat. Lucas lay on his back in the road as their choking mirth was lost in the exhaust roar of the van.

Why had they let him go? With a flush of embarrassment, Lucas realised that they had looked at him and seen that he posed no threat to them. He had no proof, no power. He was just a kid, a know-nothing nuisance who had caught a glimpse of the world beneath the city. It had appeared for a second like a flash of forbidden flesh, and had vanished so quickly that he could only wonder if he had imagined it.

And as if to confirm that he had not, Glory walked past.

She was dressed in her outfit of sparkling black satin, with black seamed stockings and her impossibly tiny feet encased in high heels, like a showgirl in search of a venue. Lustrous black eyes above an upturned nose, pearlised crimson lipstick edged in black, make-up that would register from the back of the one-and-nines. The bonnet of black chiffon that was pinned to her honey-curl hair lifted and floated in the warm evening air. Radiant in the stage-filters of an orange sun, Glory never acknowledged her audience. She skipped across the road without checking for traffic – those familiar with the Soho streets knew that this was an awkward cul-de-sac for vehicles and never bothered to look – and left traces of a long-gone scent behind, Arpege or Misty Roses.

Lucas was aroused by her, enticed and intrigued, even though her age seemed oddly to fluctuate, her appearance altering from one day to the next. He knew she would not look twice at someone like him, but the mere sighting of her gave him comfort and pushed thoughts of loneliness from his mind.

He stayed for another beer but the special moment had

passed and the sun had dropped behind the buildings, mono-chroming the street in preparation for the night ahead.

He walked through the summer mist along Shaftesbury Avenue in the direction of Piccadilly Circus, in no hurry to be home, at a loose end with the world, watching and listening, catching snatches of conversation, cutting corners across lives, waiting for his time. And then, at the end of Rupert Street he saw the van again, and knew that fate had drawn him in this direction. One Eighty was leaning from the window talking to an elegantly dressed young black man whose haircut looked like a tarantula. As a handshake concluded their conversation, Lucas broke into a run. It was now or never. He had come so close to touching something beneath the surface . . .

The van pulled away, and for the first hundred yards he paced it, shouting at the driver, but One Eighty had not even seen him, or if he had, did not acknowledge him. It tipsily crested the corner of Brewer Street and picked up speed, leaving him in the middle of the road with his hands on his thighs, gasping for breath in the dusty evening air.

Thursday

I am a part of all that I have met;
Yet all experience is an arch wherethro'
Gleams that untravell'd world, whose margin fades
For ever and for ever when I move.
How dull it is to pause, and make an end,
To rust unburnished, not to shine in use!
As tho' to breathe were life.

Alfred, Lord Tennyson

'Cogito Ergo Zoom'

David E. Davis Jr

CHAPTER TWENTY-EIGHT

After Life

'Cut it very short at the back and sides, flatten the top, scissor the front. And put a little grease on it. Got that?'

Angelo studied his customer in the mirror and ran a hand through his own neat grey hair. The usual visitors to the narrow Dean Street barbershop were Soho club types wanting radical clipper-cuts. This guy was harder to place. Sensing no forthcoming interest in the discussion of the day's sporting news, he set to work in silence.

'And give me a shave when you've done.'

Once Angelo had finished the haircut, carefully checking the sides for perfect evenness, he wrapped the upturned face in a hot towel and stropped an open razor on a belt attached to the counter. It was an old-fashioned approach, but gave the closest, smartest shave that money could buy. Then, with infinite precision, he worked the blade around his customer's throat. He had nearly finished when the man in the chair gave an involuntary shudder, causing him to nick the flesh below his right ear. Angelo quickly reached out for a towel, but when he turned back he saw that no blood had yet appeared in the cut.

'I'm sorry,' he apologised quickly, 'I've nicked you.'

'You have?'

I stared at my neck in the mirror, then slowly raised my fingers to the wound, touching it. No pain, no blood, just a thin pale line of parted flesh.

'You want me to put something on that?' The barber looked worried.

'No – no, it doesn't matter.'

I knew that I would have to be careful about physical maintenance. The important thing was to keep my body in one piece for as long as possible. I tilted my head from side to side, studying the haircut. It definitely made me look younger. This morning I had followed the advice in the medical book and donned a tight black T-shirt that would keep my body fat pressed tightly in place and delay the process of putrefaction. I slipped a black shirt over the top and buttoned it, tugging the cuffs over my bruised purple veins. I decided to treat myself to an expensive black suit. If I was going to do the business, I needed to look it.

Angelo held up a hand mirror. 'Very smart, sir. A new you.' He removed the gown with a flourish.

'You've done well.' I handed the flabbergasted barber a twenty-pound tip. It was time I got used to throwing my cash around. After all, I could owe all the money in the world and nobody would be able to do a damned thing about it. How could you collect from a dead man?

The cab took me straight to the designer menswear collections in Bond Street. I commanded the shop assistants with confidence and paid for everything on my credit cards in the full knowledge that there would be no incoming finances to clear the debts. One hour later, dressed in a crisp new Donna Karan suit and Patrick Cox shoes, I walked through Soho and knew that, sartorially at least, I was someone to notice.

It was clear to me now that my old self had entirely mis-understood Soho life. Everyone had great ideas, but no one had finance. In my attempts to appreciate how money was generated, I'd failed to see how the system worked. I had tried to impose a sense of order in my daily job, but the business defied logic, existing in a climate of confusion, its inexplicable successes creating endless non sequiturs. Film hits were always justified with hindsight. The box-office future was virtually impossible to predict. Creativity was born in disobedience and thrived in chaos. Any attempt to impose a structure ended in disastrous compromise. There-fore, I decided, it would be necessary for me to become a force of chaos. I needed the freedom to act in an irresponsible manner. Being dead was a pretty good way to free myself from accountability.

'The street-gang thing,' I reminded her, 'you mentioned it when we last met.'

Marcie threw a look at her partner. *Did we tell him about that?* 'Right,' she agreed guardedly, 'what did we talk about exactly?'

'You implied that most of the financing had been in place before – I don't know – something had happened to the project.'

This time it was Red who threw her the look. They worked with each other's approval. Seated side by side in the offices of Shattered Glass Productions they stared at me as if they had never seen me before. Admittedly, I had changed a little since we had last met.

'The working title was *Cityville*. We had a director on board and a green light. The whole thing was cast, packaged and approved, then Rupert Everett changed his mind and pulled out. I have a prospectus here somewhere.' He reached down beside the arm of the red cord couch on which they sat and pulled out a glossy folder. 'The money was supposed to come from three main sources. Each company had script approval, but everyone was happy with the final draft. PolyGram put up most of the cash. A Canadian corporation and an independent UK source split the remaining costs between them. We replaced Rupert and were about to go into pre-production –'

'And start spending PolyGram's money –'

'When the independent UK source pulled out.'

'What was their problem?'

'They didn't believe the film could be successfully shot on location in the centre of London.'

'Why not?'

'You know what the film commission used to be like. It's better than it was, but it's still a logistical nightmare shooting in a city of eight million people. And the script called for the kind of huge crowd scenes you never see in London-based features.'

'Surely there must have been ways around the problem. Set it somewhere else, change some of the scenes, scale it down.'

'Absolutely not. The London backdrop is essential. Much of it was high angle stuff, shooting from the rooftops looking down. The roof scenes were so central to the action that we considered recreating them in a studio and matching the exteriors, but then the cost became prohibitive. We looked at the production from every angle, but time ran out on us.'

'So even if you could solve the problem now, you couldn't recover the package?'

'Sure we could. The money's still in place. It was just that we had Cannes coming up, so we shifted our attention to financing *Quincy's Rogue*.'

'Mr Tyler, forgive me but where is this conversation leading?' asked Marcie.

I waited for the traffic to stop hooting in the street outside, then, like a stand-up comic planning a punchline, made them wait a little longer. 'Suppose I told you that there was a way of saving your film.'

'Even if we could go back, we're involved with *Quincy's Rogue* now, it would be hard to –'

'Let me level with you. You'll never complete your elephant movie so long as you insist on shooting it in India.'

'But your partner told us –'

'Forget what he told you. He's after his commission. Go with the *Cityville* project. Tell your UK backers you've found a way to handle the wide shots.'

'How?'

'CGI. You wanted to use computer graphics on the elephant, but that's already been done in movies like *Jumanji*, *George of the Jungle* and *The Lost World*. Do something new. Use a graphic imaging system to populate London instead of using it to create creatures. Think of Jim Cameron's money shots in *Titanic*.'

'That was the most expensive film of all time, Mr Tyler!'

'We had considered the possibility,' Red cut in, 'but nobody could convince us that the technology was fully in place. Now, of course –'

'It would be a different matter. But the process would be way too expensive and time consuming.' Marcie waved the thought aside. 'A nice thought but forget it, we'd never get that kind of budget.'

'I have a way to do that. It's not an issue here. Trust me, it's

just a phone-call.' I could tell that my casual air of indif-
ference was getting to them. 'Let's cut to the chase. Which
project would you rather see realised?'

'*Cityville*.' They spoke in unison.

'Then let's do it.'

'There's another problem, a serious time constraint.'

'How serious?'

Marcie looked sheepish. 'The deal would have to be put
together before next Monday. That's when our option
officially runs out. We don't have the finance to renew.'

'Then we'll need to have it signed and packaged by close of
business tomorrow. My team can handle the paperwork.'

They looked at each other. 'You can do that as well?'

'Believe me, it's the easy part.'

Marcie held out her hand. 'I'll believe it when I see it, but
until then I guess we have a deal.'

'Good.' I smiled from one to the other. 'Let's make a bang
and blow the bloody doors off.'

'I'm sorry?'

'A line from Michael Caine in *The Italian Job*,' I explained
to Marcie, whose filmgoing experience probably extended
back no further than *Jurassic Park*. 'Don't worry. Soon,
audiences will be reciting lines from your film.'

CHAPTER TWENTY-NINE

Shafting The System

I knew that my ability to pull off the *Cityville* deal would be a good test of my new-found confidence. Time to see what happens when you accelerate from nought to sixty, I thought as I snorted the second fat line from the washroom counter. I wasn't sure that cocaine could have any effect on me now, seeing that it could no longer be carried in my bloodstream to my brain, but I was prepared to give it a try. Hey, it couldn't harm me; I was dead.

I checked myself in the washroom mirror, half-expecting to find some tell-tale sign that would tip colleagues off to my posthumous state, but so far nothing showed beyond a certain glassiness in the eyes. My voice had dropped half an octave, though. I wondered if it was something to do with the fact that my trachea was no longer receiving any lubrication. The whole process of my necrobiosis was a mystery to me. Would my brain-pan dry out, leaving the brain itself to atrophy? Would my muscles become inelastic leather straps, like pieces of Boerwurst? Once again I found myself trying to inject logic into an impossible situation. I knew I had to accept my circumstances without question, otherwise I would not achieve anything in the short time I had left. I had passed through the vale of tears, answered the final question, handed back my soul, become an ex-parrot, popped my clogs.

It was payback time.

The clever part of my plan was the deal with the edit suite. I knew for a fact that the studio had a cash-flow crisis and was close to bankruptcy. It wasn't generating enough business to pay for the leases on their equipment, and the staff they hired was second-rate because they couldn't afford to cover the salaries of decent producers. If I could bring in a sizeable chunk of work to feed their cash-haemorrhaging new graphics system, they would cut a bare-bones cost arrangement with the production company and I would profit on both sides. The best part was, the deal actually had a kind of warped integrity. It allowed the moviemakers to take a crack at their dream project and save money on the production, it kept Power Post afloat, it allowed me to prove my business credibility, and it solved my immediate financial problem – I was sure that one of the edit suite's joint-owners would front some credit until our business was concluded. And I would do all this without compromising anyone's artistic ideals. I knew Berry couldn't say the same about the kind of deals he put together.

Okay, I thought, straightening my immaculate jacket in the washroom mirror, priorities, one, lock the deal in place with Red and Marcie, two, visit Power Post and leave with a credit guarantee, three, check in with the bozos at International Film Investments. Then I thought, why bother to pay them off? Earlier in the week I was frightened they were going to tap-dance on my face. Now they could come at me with machetes for all I cared. They were the ones who needed to be scared. They *all* had reason to start feeling scared.

Time to concentrate on the serious art of making money. I could not afford to waste a second. I had now been dead for around fourteen hours. The day's temperature was already growing unbearable. *In particularly hot weather a body can start to decompose in a single day*. I couldn't help wondering what was happening inside my body right now, even though I knew it was best not to think about it. I didn't need to be aware of the mechanics. It was possible to use a toilet without having to envisage the drains.

My main problem was the elephantine slowness of the industry's negotiations. The backers of *Cityville* needed to be convinced that the script's essential wide-shots could be handled with computer effects, and it had to be done today. It was usual to tape up wide-angle photographs of locations during pre-production and match them with the story-boarded action. In this case, if such material was in existence, the effects house could calculate a ball-park figure for the digital work involved. But Red was now in a meeting and so was Marcie, and the secretary didn't know where the boards were because she'd only been there a fortnight, and the man who usually kept the pre-production stills was a freelancer, and she thought he was away on a shoot and didn't have his mobile number in the office even though he was her brother-in-law.

This was typical of the manner in which the industry operated; it was littered with inefficient relatives, talentless sons and arrogant daughters pressured into ill-suited positions. In every single office in the whole of Soho, some-one was waiting for someone else to call back.

There had to be a faster way of getting things done. It was necessary to radically accelerate the entire business process. I needed staff, people who would do exactly as they were told and carry out my bidding without asking stupid questions. And most of all, I needed my body to hold out for at least forty-eight hours. According to the book, this was the outside limit of the time I had left.

First I cleared some working space and mapped out an elaborate agenda for the day's events. As soon as this was achieved, I commandeered Carol, Berry's secretary, Beth, his personal assistant and Julie Saito, the super-efficient production manager, assigning each of them duties and responsibilities. My only remaining social engagement of the week was a farewell lunch with Berry tomorrow. Given that it was neither possible to swallow food nor desirable to have it sitting in my dry stomach manufacturing bacteria, I decided to cancel the date. There seemed little point in maintaining social niceties now, and it was important to keep focused on the matter at hand.

Most of all, I was determined not to panic. Nothing could be gained by doing so. I had been given something no one was ever granted – a little extra time in which to realise my ambitions. It was important to take full advantage of what I had left. I turned to the great stack of unsolicited scripts behind my desk. Most of them were unreadable, derivative and impenetrable, filled with semi-literate copycat Tarantino dialogue or pretentious high art symbolism. Some read like faded photocopies of bad Hollywood action vehicles. Some were just deeply eccentric. Quite a few were vanity projects, bland scripts penned by rock stars and TV performers who had earned their royalties in another medium and now fancied themselves as artists. A handful proved promising. Unfortunately I had always been too busy to nurture the small percentage of decent ideas nestled in the great swathes of A4 paper that decorated my office. Now I pulled down the first half-dozen scripts that my wrinkling fingertips touched and began to make two piles.

It took me an hour and a half to speed-read sections from thirty-seven scripts and reject them. I finally set aside five that met my initial criteria. I sacrilegiously avoided dialogue that displayed the peculiarities of English writing. These scripts would have to be capable of attracting foreign money. I rang the five production companies involved and told them the good news; that I was interested in actioning their scripts. It was funny how I managed to find someone to accept all five calls. How easy it was to get people to the telephone when you had advantageous news to impart! Producers, writers and directors offered to rush over that very minute and explain the visions they nurtured for their projects. I transferred these meetings to Berry's assistant. Then it was simply a matter of dealing with agents and offering scale financing. Nobody asked me where the money was coming from. Nobody questioned my credentials. For all its suspicion and cynicism, the industry proved very gullible when it came to accepting offers of help.

I called banks, investment houses and international film funding consortia to arrange meetings, and wasted several minutes having one phonecall fruitlessly transferred around the various extensions of the Arts Council. I sent the five scripts out for copying and arranged for a secretary to have them hand-delivered by Lucas, our runner. I rushed out press releases for *Screen International*, *Screen Finance*, *Moving Pictures* and the *Hollywood Reporter*, and gave them to Carol, Berry's secretary, to email. The industry press published weekly, but there was still time to get production news into the latest copies, especially as I was prepared to blackmail them with threats of withdrawing essential advertising revenue. It paid to have contacts, and for the first time I was able to start putting mine to some use.

By the time another hour had passed I was the proud executive producer of five go-projects in pre-production. It didn't seem to matter that I had no cash or security with which to finance them, that I had no personal commitment to any of them, that I had no distribution guarantees, no collateral of any kind, that I had nothing at all legally signed on paper and could not even remember the titles of the scripts. In theory, I was already a success. Once the press reports I had bullied into tomorrow's papers appeared, my personal stock would skyrocket.

The five scripts I had picked shared one common element. Each provided an opportunity for a spectacular central performance. That would make it easier attracting big American names to these projects, especially when you could offer them any amount of money because you had nothing to begin with and were prepared to say anything the agent wanted to hear.

Julie Saito called to say that the *Daily Mail*'s entertainment journalist was on the phone. I was impressed by the speed with which the news had leaked from the trade to the national press. With any luck, I would be able to encourage them to write yet another 'British Film Renaissance' piece.

As I took the call, I opened Berry's humidor and clipped the end from an obscene Havana cigar. It was so easy getting projects off the ground, I had no idea why I hadn't done it before.

CHAPTER THIRTY

Choose Death

'What the hell is going on here?'

Returning from lunch, Berry stormed past his secretary's desk and entered his office. His desk was half-hidden by stacks of scripts, contract files, research material and documentation. Phones were ringing, people were running, sheaves of paper were spewing from the photocopier, the fax machine was buzzing. Beth was adding names to the production chart on the wall. Carol passed cradling scripts in her arms. Julie was conducting an argument with her mobile.

'Richard told us we were to give his work precedence today,' she explained, cradling the phone beneath her chin. 'He said you sanctioned it.'

'I did nothing of the kind. What on earth are you doing?'

'I think you'd better talk to him,' she replied warily.

'I'll soon bloody sort this out. Where is he?'

'In the conference room. He said he needed more space.'

Berry peered into the small shuttered area he had designated for client meetings, and could not believe his eyes. There were six Japanese men inside the glass booth. Richard was in his shirt-sleeves, pointing to a diagram pinned on the computer clipboard, and not only was he allowing everyone to smoke, he had one of Berry's own special cigars clenched between his teeth. Something else struck him: this timid, awkward man was now aggressively haranguing his audience, stabbing his finger at each of them in turn, virtually daring them not to pay the fullest attention. He slapped the figures behind him and made what sounded like a concluding statement: 'The days when fortunes were made and lost on a film's performance during its initial release are gone, gentlemen. A modern film is like a train. The engine is the theatrical run, the first carriage is the video release, the second is the cable sale, the third is the network showing, and each one gives you a chance to recoup. The bottom line is, there's virtually no risk to you.' Richard was not exactly telling the truth, of course. Even though he was angry with his former employee, Berry couldn't help but be impressed.

I took another drag on the cigar and waved aside a hazy blue cloud. Although I had never indulged the habit before, I now found smoking a pleasantly soothing experience. The aromatic fumes circulated easily in my dry nasal passages. I watched as Berry sidled into the room and smiled wanly at my guests, who dipped their heads and smiled back.

'Richard,' he hissed, trying to sound pleasant, 'can I see you outside for a minute?'

I smiled pleasantly. I had reached a natural break-point in the presentation anyway. 'If you will excuse me, gentlemen.'

The moment the door had shut behind us, he turned on me. 'Perhaps I could trouble you for an explanation? You hijack my staff without authorisation, you take on projects for which you have absolutely no authority, you conduct meetings without my knowledge or consent –'

'I can see how it may look to you, Berry,' I replied

reasonably, 'but after all this is my last week and I feel I still have something to prove, if not to you, then to myself.'

'This is a joke, right? You're doing some kind of crap number on me.'

'No, a crap number is Sally Ann Howe singing "Lovely Lonely Man" in *Chitty Chitty Bang Bang*. Those gentlemen in there are considering a major investment in British co-production even as we speak.'

'Oh really? And what are you planning to use for capital?'

'Don't be such a slave to textbook production methods, Berry. You don't need cash to make deals.'

'Of course you do!' he ranted. 'It's at the heart of the industry. Without co-production money pumping the system, you'll never bring a single project to life.'

'There's nothing pumping my system, and yet I live.'

'What are you talking about?'

I placed my arm around his shoulder and guided him away from the conference area. 'Your problem is a slavish adherence to the laws of physics. It's all cause and effect with you. Here, let me show you what I mean.'

We had walked a short way along the corridor, and were now standing by the entrance to the stairwell at the rear of the building. I pushed open the door and invited my colleague to step forward into the gloom. When he hesitated in confusion I urged him forward.

'What happened to the lights?' Berry asked innocently, looking up. The second you removed him from the protective cocoon of his brightly lit world there was something childlike about him. I could almost see what had appealed to Miranda.

'I have a high concept for you,' I said softly, 'about a movie executive everyone treats as a doormat, and the man who shagged his woman.'

'Wait a minute, you don't think I'm – we're –'

'Turn around, Berry, and walk down the stairs.'

'You don't think you can push me around in my own office –'

'You're not in your office. You're in the dark.'

'I'm not going to be told what to do by you –'

'There's a lot less to being ruthless than I'd thought.' I gave him a gentle shove in the chest. 'Start walking.'

'I suppose you think this is funny, well, have your little –'

'Walk, Berry.' Another shove in the chest, harder this time.

'This is absurd, I don't know what you think you hope to –'

'Isn't it obvious? I'm going to kill you, take over your company and get my woman back.' The next shove carried an audible smack. Berry threw out his fist, but I blocked the punch. Berry's fingers closed around my bare arm. He could still not believe that this particular worm had finally turned. It had to be a practical joke, and it was going too far.

I slammed the palm of my hand into Berry's chest so hard that the startled executive nearly toppled backwards. His fingers gripped the dead flesh of my bare arm and with an awful sucking sound the skin tore free, slipping away from the bone like the shedding of an evening glove. Even in the gloom I could see fear and revulsion register on Berry's face.

'You're a decision-maker, Berry. Choose death. Start walking.'

With a yelp of horror, Berry shook away the sheet of flesh that was stuck to his fingers. Frightened now, he turned and took a tentative step down into the dark.

I had used picture wire because it was fine and very strong. Ideally I would have used fishing line, but I couldn't think where to buy any in the West End. Berry's right shoe caught the wire stretched across the steps. There was nothing in the world he could do to keep his balance after that. I pushed at the small of his back as he fell, just to make sure.

Berry flipped over into the stairwell so quickly that I was nearly kicked in the head by his feet. Somehow he managed to stop his fall by grabbing at the balustrade, but it only took a moment for the heel of my shoe to kick away his fingers. Berry's skull cracked against the edges of the concrete staircase twice before he reached the basement. If he wasn't dead when he landed he would doubtless bleed to death, alone in the dark and unable to move. My one worry was that he might manage to call out, so to be on the safe side I popped down to the bottom of the stairwell and carried out a hasty examination.

Berry was on his back, moaning faintly. Fluid was leaking from a cut so deep and wide that it looked like a crack, just above his right ear. Suddenly he let out a startling yell that frightened both of us. I booted his jaw about a bit until I heard something give and, after a weird rattle in Berry's throat sounded, like a football turnstile revolving, he became still once more, and silence descended on the basement. I returned to the third floor and unwound the wire from the base of the banisters.

I tried to remember the correct procedure for taking revenge upon the living, as laid down in countless 'back from the dead' horror films. The bullying boss, the faithless wife ... it was predictable, I knew, but these conventions had to be honoured. I returned to my meeting, concluded it successfully, then decided to telephone Miranda in order to carry out the next phase of my plan.

Abducting her in the traditional manner would be impossible, of course. I would have to wait until she donned a heavy négligé before appearing on the balcony outside her bedroom window, wait for her to sight me, scream and pass out, then carry her up/down to my rooftop/underground lair. This approach would not work for a number of reasons. Miranda slept in a baggy T-shirt, her bedroom windows had no balcony and she was not much of a screamer. She was far more likely to berate me with withering sarcasm before returning to her make-up mirror. Besides, she was staying at Valerie's, and Valerie was the kind of woman who kept a rape alarm in every room.

I loved Miranda too much to cause her harm. But perhaps it would be possible to reason with her. I would have to reveal the hideous truth about myself, but perhaps then she would repent, if not for my sake then the sake of our son –

– and then what? –

Return to a normal life with me? I had less than thirty-six hours left before I became a putrid, collapsing heap of rotting flesh. There were no prospects left for me. This was it. My final stand. I had passed the point of no return last night in the downstairs toilet of a bar, just as poor Paul had . . .

I knew that if I started thinking too hard I would go mad. It was best to bury speculative thought in positive action. I punched out the number of Miranda's mobile and waited for her to answer.

CHAPTER THIRTY-ONE

Mutual Mutilation

'**You realise** nobody has made a positive identification of the body,' said Danbury cheerfully. 'Cotton's father can't get here until tomorrow. Until I carry out the post-mortem my hands are tied, if you'll pardon the pun.' As Malcolm Cotton was discovered with his wrists and ankles bound together, John May found himself in an unforgiving mood.

'Just give me a rough outline of what you've found so far,' he snapped. Eddie Danbury was a bright, instinctive pathologist whose promising future had been damaged by a devastating nervous breakdown. Facing expulsion from the force and an uncertain future on the lecture circuit, his career had been saved when May requested his services at a new pathology unit recently set up in Camden Town by the North London Serious Crimes Division. The mortuary there was small, but uniquely geared to dealing with the kind of problematic case-histories that arrived on Bryant and May's desks. It required a special kind of intelligence, someone not too hidebound by traditional methodology, and Eddie fitted the role perfectly.

Aware that he had been bailed out by a man who recognised his talents, Danbury maintained a grateful loyalty to

May. His biggest handicap was an almost total lack of social skills. He had the knack of embarrassing everyone he met. Arthur Bryant found the young man unbearable. There was, he felt, no room for levity in a house of the dead. Bryant shared the opinion of the former medical examiner, Oswald Finch, who kept a sign above the entrance to the morgue reading '*Taceant colloquia. Effuiat risus. Hic locus est ubi mors gaudet succurrere vitae*' – 'Let conversation cease. Let Laughter flee. This is the place where death delights to help the living.'

'We've got our hands full here, Eddie. Tell me anything, just don't make me wait for the post-mortem.'

'Well, it's as old Miseryguts Bryant thought. The bullet wounds were the eventual cause of death, but Cotton took a while to die. The alignment of the holes with his jacket and sweatshirt suggest that he was shot standing the right way up. He's a well-developed, well-nourished white male measuring six feet one inch and weighing – '

'Can we skip this bit?' asked May impatiently.

'I thought you'd be interested in identifying marks.'

'Were there any?'

'One. A tattoo on the back of the left calf. A red butterfly.'

'Can you take a shot of it for me?'

'Sure thing. And I'll have a preliminary internal for you soon. Sorry it's taking so long, but there's a bit of a backlog. I think we're going to find narcotic traces in his system. Cocaine abuse stays in the hair follicles for as long as a year. I'm sure I'm going to find that.'

'Why do you think so?'

'It's difficult to say. Nothing certain. The eyes are odd, the lymph ducts look a little swollen. Some candida in his mouth, he's quite spotty; his immune system's down. There's something that might be a recent needle-mark on his right thigh. I don't know, he just has *the look*. Give me a few hours.'

Bryant pulled his coat tighter and stepped into the cellar bar, a long narrow room that smelled of stale beer and disinfectant. 'Can you put the lights up?' he asked.

'They are up,' said the barman. 'There are only a couple of bulbs left and that's as bright as they'll go.'

'Janice, make sure the photographer brings a couple of extra spotlights. Does anyone have a torch?'

The New Brunswick Revuebar looked like Aladdin's Cave, if one assumed that the tales of the Arabian Nights had been first told in a mildewy Soho basement. Its red satin walls and grimy chandeliers had survived since the fifties, although the room no longer played host to the neighbourhood's more classically-trained strippers. In its heyday the Krays, Christine Keeler, Mandy Rice-Davies and various minor British movie stars had hit the bar for a late drink, from where they could watch the exotic fan-dances and nude tableaux that only just kept within the Lord Chamberlain's laws.

Dozens of damp-warped photographs in chrome frames still lined the rear wall. There was even a picture of Miranda's mother, the leading player in three films each worse than the last, her career as a film star over by the age of thirty-eight, her career as a Soho alcoholic just beginning.

In the nineties, the bar had fallen on hard times. With the change in licensing laws the Brunswick became a relic of the past. It was no longer necessary to tolerate smelly underground bars with complicated and expensive membership laws just to get a drink after eleven. The only people who still frequented the place were the old regulars too set in their ways to shift their loyalties, and a few tourists who blundered in mistakenly thinking that it was still a strip joint.

It was here that Scott Cronin and Glen Dewitt had taken their last drink. Their bodies lay huddled together in the corner of the room under a single plastic sheet.

'Tell me something I don't understand,' Bryant asked the barman. 'How on earth could you have let them do this to each other? Didn't you try to stop them?'

The barman puffed and shifted, threw a look at the bouncer and puffed again. 'Billy and I tried to get near them but they were –' he faltered, desperate for help.

'Crazy,' Billy the bouncer cut in, 'fucking crazy. The tall one, 'e had a knife. The other one fucking bit me.' He pulled back his sleeve and revealed a suppurating bandage. 'Took out a chunk of flesh the size of an 'alf-crown. There was no other punters left in the bar, so I run out to grab one of you lot.'

'And you found PC Crowhurst. What happened then?'

'By the time we got back down the stairs they was both lying on the floor.'

'And where were you while this was going on?' Bryant asked the barman.

'I came out and pulled the door shut behind me. No point in me stayin' in there with 'em.'

'Quite. And I assume there's no other exit to the room. You must be tipping Westminster Council's safety officers a bob or two. How did they fall out, these lads? What were they arguing about?' He looked from one blank face to the next. 'Which one started on the other?'

The barman stared back blankly. 'They weren't arguing,' he explained.

'I don't understand,' said Bryant, trying to remain patient. 'One of them must have upset his pal. You were here at the bar, you must have seen or heard it start.'

'I did, it's just that they wasn't arguing. The tall one picked up a knife and stuck it in his stomach. Then the other one did the same.'

'You're trying to tell me they attacked *themselves*?'

'Well, I ain't makin' it up.' He looked so desperately miserable that Bryant was inclined to believe him. The elderly detective walked back to the bodies and picked up the clear plastic envelope the forensics team had set beside the sheet. He could see the contents clearly: two wallets, loose change, some keys, club flyers, and a plain white packet with a red butterfly stencilled on it.

'Bad shit.'

'I beg your pardon?'

'That's what we're looking for, isn't it?' asked Bryant. 'Bad shit.'

'Arthur, where on earth did you hear that?'

'Oh, seventies' films. Black American people used to say it. "Man, that's some baaaad shit." *Shaft's Big Score*, if memory serves. Richard Roundtree. Jolly good it was, too.'

'Sometimes I despair of you. I thought you said that the last film you paid to see was *A Town Like Alice*, in 1956.'

Bryant smiled secretively. 'I did occasionally go out in the sixties, you know. It wasn't all work. I remember the first Summer of Love as clearly as I remember anything.'

That wasn't saying much. Bryant's memory was appalling and suspiciously selective.

'What I mean to say is, suppose Malcolm Cotton was making some kind of weird new drug and selling it. Suppose there was something wrong with what he was selling.'

'And suppose this business with the butterflies is purely a coincidence, and we're getting our signals crossed.'

'Oh come on, the designs are identical, the one in Cotton's exercise book, the one on the dead therapist, and now the one on Cronin and Dewitt.'

May shrugged. 'You know as well as I do that it could simply be a cultural thing, a symbol used on the club circuit, a record label, a designer clothes tag.'

'It's a home-made stencil, John. Cotton liked it enough to have one tattooed on his body. You're going to find drug residue in that little packet.'

'And what if we do? It still doesn't mean that the drug stemmed from Cotton.'

'It does if the residue in his apparatus matches anything on three dead men.'

'When will we know that?'

'Tomorrow morning. Until then, I suggest we proceed on the assumption that Cotton was the source and got in the way of an established Soho supplier, who decided to remove him. What I don't understand is how a drug that had presumably been tested for toxicity on the apparatus in Cotton's flat could cause such a violent effect. How psychotic do you have to become to stab yourself to death? And how much more is there out on the street, waiting to be ingested?'

'I don't see how we can act if we don't know what it is, or where to find it.'

'Maybe not, but I know where we should start looking,' said Bryant. 'In Malcolm Cotton's exercise book.'

CHAPTER THIRTY-TWO

Forcibly Bewitched

She knew it was Thursday evening, because she could hear the discordant New Orleans jazz band at the corner and remembered their schedule. At this time every week they launched into their horrible music and spread good cheer around Soho like the plague. For some unearthly reason, Judy was feeling quite happy. She had lost weight, and could now comfortably fit into her jeans. If she ever got out of this alive she would be able to boast to friends about her miracle diet. Friends. She wondered what had happened to them. Presumably someone somewhere had tried to call her, but of course both of the telephones were dead. Perhaps Midas had told them she had decided to take a sudden vacation. Perhaps no one had bothered to call. Everyone was so busy with their careers these days . . . she knew the lack of nutrition was the cause of her light-headedness. A tense euphoria crackled and buzzed behind her eyelids like a demented insectocutor. To calm herself she tried to recall the exact circumstances of her imprisonment.

Late in July, just a short while ago. She was trying to paint, staring at a great blank sheet of Daler Board. Nothing was coming out right. Judy told herself that the idea of Midas affecting her artistic ability was simply some form of psychosomatic suggestion. Just then, the walls of her flat started shaking with the sound of Greek music. That night, Midas had held a party that carried on until dawn. People were still arriving at four in the morning. She donned earplugs and went to bed, but could not sleep a wink.

'You missed a great night,' Ari said the next day when she passed him on the stairs, 'a great night! How we danced and laughed! Midas is such a wonderful host.'

'I thought you said he was very quiet.'

'Yes, but a party, that's different! Such singing! It's a pity you couldn't come.'

I wasn't asked, she thought, eyeing the seven binbags filled with winebottles that stood by his front door.

Slightly jealous of his ability to enjoy himself, slightly annoyed that she hadn't been invited, she decided to live and let live. Maybe this was his way of coping with rejection.

But it was just the first of the parties. From being the quietest guy in town, Midas suddenly became the neighbour from hell. Crashing and banging, deafening her at all hours with music, howls of laughter and even what sounded like screams of pain. People came and left at three, four, five in the morning. Sometimes she went on to the landing and saw them climbing the stairs, dangerous types, criminal lowlifes, drug dealers, crazies, whores. Each night it got worse. Several times she got up the courage to hammer on his door, but he would never answer. She angrily complained to Ari and Maria, who were dumbfounded.

'But you must be able to hear the noise, even two floors away,' Judy insisted.

'No,' they said, shaking their heads, 'we haven't heard a

thing. As far as we know, Midas only ever had one party.'

'But the rubbish he throws out on to the landing, the people, the mess . . .'

'You see any mess around here?' asked Ari defensively. 'I think maybe you're overreacting. We never have any trouble from Midas.'

She knew she was *not* imagining it. The woman in the apartment below was spending summer at her daughter's house in Cornwall. That just left the top floor occupied.

The noise and the mess continued. Judy asked the residents in the buildings on either side if they had suffered disturbances, without luck. She visited a harassed young man at the Westminster Council Advice Centre and was unhelpfully informed that nearly 50 per cent of all flat owners move because of problems with neighbours. He outlined the alternatives, patience or the police, and counselled the former. She was reluctant to involve the law, as she had done during the stormy end of her marriage, and finally persuaded the community officer to call on Midas. The report he sent her after his visit made her wonder if they knew the same man; it was virtually a love letter. Her neighbour, her ex-lover, had certainly turned on some full-strength charm. As the community officer was almost certainly gay, she found myself wondering if he had done more than that.

Judy felt like selling her story to the *Enquirer*: I DATED A PAGAN GIGOLO. Surely he was just an ordinary man with a smart line in seduction. Could Midas have found a way of preventing others from hearing his noise? If he really could cast spells, perhaps he wasn't just directing them at her. Legally her hands were tied. No previous problems had ever been recorded at this address. If anything, she was the nuisance, not him. Perhaps she was going crazy. She could imagine the community officer's official report: *Ms Merrigan complains that her neighbour is forcibly bewitching her.*

Her patience was pushed to the limit. Her relationship with Midas became a war of nerves. Thunderous music that no one else ever seemed to hear played all night. Bags of stinking rubbish split and spilled against her front door. Creepy characters sat at the top of her stairs drinking, picking their teeth and flirting; a smacked-out kid who played with a knife, a laughing fat whore with gold teeth, a boy who stood on the landing outside her flat shouting at the top of his voice, a sickly bald man who constantly hawked and spat – Midas's acolytes. Ari and Maria swore they saw nobody pass them, but how else did these sleazeballs get on to the staircase, by flying in through the skylight? The first few times she saw someone sitting there she raced down to the ground-floor apartment and dragged Ari upstairs, only to discover the landing deserted. It was like living in a carnival funhouse. Judy could feel her ordered life cracking apart as quickly as the plants in her flat were drying and dying.

One hot evening she heard a noise outside her door and opened it to find Midas drunk and nearly naked, smeared with paint and slumped on the landing smiling at her.

'I'll call the police if you come any closer,' she warned, trying not to panic.

'And I'll send them away with love in their hearts,' he replied, smoothing his stomach, allowing his hand to brush his genitals. 'Don't you know the story of the wind and the sun, and their wager to remove a traveller's coat? The wind tries to blow the coat off but the traveller pulls it more tightly around himself. The sun just smiles and warms his victim until he sheds his clothes . . .'

He was tumescent now. Judy yelped and darted back into

the apartment, slamming the door with a bang. There was no point in ringing anyone for help. She knew Midas would be sober, clothed and full of charm by the time they arrived.

That night her dreams betrayed her, conjuring Midas into her bedroom, pacing before the bed, whispering happy obscenities. Wherever his bare feet touched the carpet, grape-vines sprang up in verdant knots. Wherever his hands touched her, silvery green tendrils traced lines of moisture on her skin. She reached between his broad brown thighs and buried her face there, at the source of his musky heat, to fill her head with searing comets. In the morning she awoke feeling spent and sluttish. Later she passed Midas on the stairs, smartly attired, going out.

'Sleep well?' he asked with a knowing smile.

Judy thought she was going mad. She sought Gillian's advice over lunch, and after trying to persuade her to go to the police she produced a more workable idea. 'Find out about him,' she said. 'Make him your quarry. The more you discover of a man like that, the less strength he has over you.'

It seemed like a good idea. She knew Midas often received mail from a woman. Her unwanted letters, handwritten in purple ballpoint, accumulated in the hall. When she returned home, Judy made a note of the return address.

Her name was Danielle Passmore. She lived in Notting Hill, on the top floor of one of those grey Victorian houses large enough to garrison a regiment. The front garden was filled with dead rhododendrons, the ground floor boarded with corrugated iron, so that at first sight it looked as if nobody lived there.

Judy rang the bell and stepped back, squinting up at the filthy windows, wondering what she would say. Danielle took so long to come to the door, she was about to leave. The woman in front of her was small and shy, thirtyish, fair and very pale, probably once attractive. It was hard to tell now, because her face was disfigured. A livid crimson scar traced a series of crescent-shaped indentations from forehead to chin, as if someone had tried to cleave her skull in two. She had something wrong with her right eye. Skin had dried dark and tight across the socket. Judy tried not to look too hard.

'I hope you don't mind me just turning up like this,' she said, but before she could continue Danielle interrupted: 'It's about him, isn't it? You've come about him. I knew someone would eventually.'

Judy asked her what she meant, and was invited into the silent heart of the shadowed house, cold even in the summer heat. They sat facing each other in faded armchairs, in a shuttered room that showed too many signs of a woman living alone for a long time.

'He is still beautiful, isn't he?' she asked. 'Did he touch you? He did, I can tell. You smell of him. Have you felt his potency? He places people beneath the spell of his fertility, the spell of the satyr. You knew he was a satyr, did you? The distilled essence of everything male. A priapic satanist, a pagan. A god. Of course, it was her idea. Glory bestowed the power upon him. She can do that to her favourites. People have no idea of the extent of her abilities. Soho belongs to Glory.'

While Judy was trying to form a response to this, Danielle followed a different train of thought. 'I tried to leave him, you know. We were lovers for months but he frightened me. He showed me things inside myself that I couldn't bear to think about. He lived in South London then, in the great old house he used for ceremonies. I told him I'd have no more to do with him. He was very gracious. Said he was sorry I felt that way. Kissed me on the forehead as I left.' She touched the first of her scars, retracing his lips. 'When I reached home it was late and the hall lights were out. The timer wasn't working. I made my way upstairs, let myself in and boiled a kettle. Then I heard a noise in the lounge, a clanking sound. Metal on wood. Couldn't think what it was. Went in to see, but there was nothing to see.

'There was a chest of drawers against the far wall, and that's where the noise was coming from, a steady rhythmic knocking, the only sound in a silent house. It was where I kept a few tools for home repairs. Curious, I opened the drawer and a wooden-handled claw hammer flew out at me, smashing into my face. Each time I shoved it away it flew back, hammering at my eyes, my nose, my teeth. I saw it returning through a curtain of blood, over and over. Eventually I passed out. In the morning I awoke and managed to call someone. I was in hospital for nearly a month. They wired my jaw but couldn't save my eye.'

'My god, what did the police say?'

'It was just a hammer. There were no prints on it except mine. There was nobody else here, Miss Merrigan. What could the police say?'

'Who else knows about this?'

'No one. I knew he wouldn't want me to speak of it.'

'But we have to tell someone. If he has some kind of – power – over people, he must be stopped.'

'You don't understand,' whispered Danielle, wiping her good eye with the heel of her hand. 'He refuses to see me. He ignores all my letters.'

'It sounds like you're safer if he does –'

'I still adore him. I pray for us to be together again. Why else do you think I call and write? I have no control over this awful – desire. He has left me with a thirst that can't be quenched. I worship him. That's what he wants.'

Judy left the poor thing shortly after that. In the desiccated garden she looked back up at the window and studied the broken, crooked face that stared forlornly down. She believed in darkness then. Perhaps Danielle's wounds were self-inflicted and she was simply deranged. It made no difference. Her suffering was real. Judy understood now. The price of the gifts Midas bestowed was slavery. Every god needs to be worshipped. Those who lapse are cast into damnation. The old rules were the hardest to break.

She couldn't just walk out of the apartment. Aside from the financial problems it would involve, those rooms represented every shred of independence she had mustered for herself. She wearily returned home to find the landing at the top of the stairs sombre and silent, but when she listened at Midas's door she could hear a faint chanting of madrigals. It filled her with dread to think what he might be up to in there.

Two days later, Judy's ex-husband came to London to discuss the maintenance payments he had failed to keep up. When she returned from the station with him, Midas was lying in wait, standing casually outside his front door as if keeping a pre-arranged appointment.

'Judy's told me so much about you,' he said, extending his hand, which was shaken in puzzlement. 'She and I are neighbours but I like to think we share much more than just a landing.'

Judy attempted to shepherd William into her apartment, but Midas caught his arm. 'Before you two go off and talk business, I'd love to offer you a drink.' William looked at her unsurely, but she could tell that he was prepared to be swayed.

'Judy says you collect science fiction. I have quite a decent collection myself.'

His door was open. His arm was extended. His smile was wide. William was lured inside, and Judy followed like a fool. Over the next half-hour, Midas exuded so much sincerity that she nearly passed out with the strain of smiling back. The two men sat cross-legged on the floor pulling books out of racks and laughing together. William was completely taken in and proved reluctant to leave, even when she insisted on keeping their restaurant booking. The neighbours of serial killers never noticed anything unusual. What did they see? Smiling strangers who quietly closed their doors. Good citizens. Likeable men. It was like people who discovered they were living next door to drug dealers. They always thought they were builders or decorators.

Judy's personality withered beneath the force of Midas's onslaught of charisma. How could she be expected to compete? He was more believable than her, more fun to be with. All she did was moan through dinner. It didn't take a genius to see that William would rather have spent the remainder of the evening bonding with her neighbour. It was a guy thing. She had no allies. Midas could direct his fury at her and shield others from any awareness of it. She realised with some alarm that she had a less forceful personality than the enemy plaguing her. When William left, he told her that she was lucky to have someone so interesting living next door, and that she should see a doctor about her depression. Perhaps, he suggested, she should try Prozac. Judy told him to mail her a cheque or she'd see him in court. Somebody had to play the bad man.

She wished they hadn't parted on bad terms. He shouldn't have been driving; he was way over the alcohol limit. His car ploughed into the outer lane barrier on the M2 at the Medway Bridge, a hundred feet above the winding black estuary. He was lucky not to have been killed.

Midas stopped her on the landing to tell her that her ex-husband had not been wearing a seat belt at the time of the accident. Shocked into silence, she tried not to imagine how he knew.

The first week of August was unbearable, the hottest for years. The ice-maker in Ari's store broke down and all his vegetables spoiled. The days were stuck together, melting into nights. In the height of summer a London night has less than five hours of darkness. Many of the clubs and bars in the area close up with the rising sun. Midas's guests stayed long after that. Judy Merrigan lay sleepless above Wardour Street, lost and alone in an empty hot bed, listening to the obscene laughter of the revellers on the landing and in the street. She could feel her nerves fraying further each day. The most she could ask was for Midas to leave her the hell alone. And he did until six days ago, when his familiar knock had heralded the start of this nightmare.

CHAPTER THIRTY-THREE

Far From Creation

It was a little after 2:00 a.m. I was sitting on the patio steps with my knees drawn up beneath my chin, staring at the stars. It was the way Gregory sat when he watched the sky.

Barbara had just rung up, annoyed with me. She had spent the evening sitting alone in L'Etoile enduring the stares of diners while she waited for a man who had not even bothered to ring her mobile and explain why he was unable to make dinner. Elena, the restaurant's formidable doyenne, had seen too many women abandoned at her tables back in the days when she managed Bianci's and L'Escargot, and sent over a glass of champagne as a sign of commiseration, but even that had not helped. She had left the West End tired, angry and drunk. I had been so wrapped up in getting this film deal off the ground that I had completely forgotten our arrangement. I apologised and promised to make it up to her tomorrow.

I replaced the phone, and Miranda appeared, as I knew she would. She didn't see me at first. I had not heard her come in, and didn't turn around when she switched on the lounge lights. She jumped, surprised to find me sitting in the dark. She looked tired and rather beautiful, a little windswept, a little less perfect. She kicked off her shoes from force of habit.

'I've had an awful evening,' she explained. 'I couldn't get a cab from Valerie's. I tried to call you but you've been in meetings all afternoon. I'll stay in the spare room and be gone before you're up in the morning.' She rattled ice into a chunky glass, poured herself an alcohol-heavy gin and tonic. Even with the windows wide open, the house was unbearably hot. 'Christ, I'm tired of working for a living.'

'You try to see all of it, and can only make out the tiniest part. It's so – unsatisfying.' I returned my gaze to the sky. 'We used to believe we were at the centre of creation. Instead it turns out we're trapped on a minuscule planet turning around a rather small star, which revolves with thousands of millions of other stars in one of the less interesting galaxies, among billions of others. We're not even at the centre of our own galaxy, we're on the very outer edge. In galactic terms we're a distant, forgotten, meaningless speck. If there is a centre to the universe, we're about as far from it as you can possibly get. And by the time we've finally figured all this out, we sicken and die. In the life arc of the universe we have a billionth of the lifespans of butterflies.'

Miranda peered over the rim of her glass at me. 'Your point being, exactly?'

'We think we're so terrific. That's like someone in Aberystwyth thinking they're on the cutting edge.'

She was not in the mood for the kind of argument you had with other sixth-formers after smoking a few joints. 'Well, we earthlings don't have much to compare ourselves to. You want a drink?'

'Whisky.'

Not my usual tipple, but I had found that it soothed my aching throat. The scotch had been a Christmas gift, barely touched until now. She shrugged and unsteadily poured a generous measure of Glenfiddich into a tumbler. 'I hear you're out of a job.'

She handed me the drink and seated herself in the wicker chair at my back. I knew that I had started to smell bad, stale and decaying. During the day I could cover it up, but one look at Miranda told me she was making a mental note to change the kitchen bin-liner, then checking the thought when she remembered that she no longer had to worry about keeping the house fresh.

'I suppose Berry told you.'

'Well, I called up to speak to you this evening and he answered –' The excuse trailed away. She knew neither of us believed it, although she didn't know that Berry was lying in the basement with his jaw a foot from his face. 'What are you going to do?'

'I'm working on something.'

'You know, I don't think I've ever seen you sitting out here before. You always used to hate it.' She sipped her drink, clicking ice against her teeth. 'Are you all right?' After Berry had torn the skin, my arm was in a bad way. My jacket sleeve was stained and I was nursing it, hiding the damage from her like a child with a secret.

'I'm fine.' I continued to watch the indigo sky, the city aglow in the distance. Some nights it looked like it was on fire. The effect was usually a man-made one. Spotlights from movie premières criss-crossed the clouds as if searching for bombers. 'Tell me something, Miranda. If you had just a few hours in which to tidy up all the loose ends of your life, how would you go about it?'

'A few hours?' She gave a hazy frown. 'Why?'

'Indulge me for a minute.'

I swirled my glass and watched as she thought. The ice was

delicious against my palms. The evening's refusal to cool down made me feel tired and disconnected. I could tell Miranda was pleased to find me at home, even in my reflective mood. She looked as if she felt sorry for me, in the way that one feels sorry for a half-drowned dog. She had no need to any more.

'I guess there are two ways you could go. Make amends for all the things you did wrong in your life. Or take revenge for the wrongs that were done to you.'

'Which would you choose?' My eyes never left the sky.

She smiled. 'What is this, Richard?'

'Come on, which would you choose?'

'Well, I'm not exactly waiting to enter the kingdom of heaven, so I guess there's no point in trying to repair the past. I'd take revenge. At least it would get rid of some anger, and clear the air before I died.'

'That's what I thought.' I turned to look at her now. 'You're the revenge type.'

'Well,' she said defensively, 'it's better than doing nothing.'

I wondered. Here I was, trying to make this extra time count for something when perhaps I should simply have accepted my fate. If I hadn't fought so hard against dying perhaps my soul would have departed, leaving my body inert on the floor of the toilet.

Miranda rubbed at her temples. It was something she did when she was tired of playing games. She wanted to be loved unconditionally, to be the sole centre of someone's attention. She had always complained that the men in her life were so busy untangling their own problems, they hadn't any time left to concentrate on her. 'I don't understand what we're talking about, Richard. You want to tell me what's on your mind?'

I didn't suppose she'd given my feelings much thought lately. Since reaching the decision to leave me she had not come near the house. I knew she didn't miss the place. It reminded her too much of us fighting, and Gregory.

'You didn't speak to Berry this afternoon.' I dropped my voice to little more than a whisper. I didn't mean to torture her, but it was so damned satisfying to do so. 'He didn't return your call. And he won't return it tomorrow, either. Or the next day.'

Miranda shrugged, not bothering to cover the lie. 'Berry has a habit of disappearing without telling anyone where he's going.'

'What I don't understand is how you two managed to stay friends. He dumped you. Wasn't that humiliating?'

'No more humiliating than you having to work for him.' Miranda usually managed to have the last word in an argument. 'Where is he? You haven't fought with him, have you?'

'About you? No.'

'Then how do you know he didn't ring me back? What's happened between you two?'

I finally turned to look at her, and smiled. As I did so, I caught sight of myself in the mirror. There seemed to be something wrong with my face. I had twisted my features at an odd, lopsided angle, and my eyes seemed to be staring too hard. A thin strand of spittle hung from one side of my mouth, as if I had suffered some kind of paralysing stroke. Quasimodo on a bad-hair day. No wonder she was looking startled.

'I'm worried about Gregory,' I told her, changing the subject.

'What do you mean?' she asked, annoyed by my refusal to answer her questions. 'He'll stay where he is. They're looking after him well. He'll be fine there.'

'I don't want him in that place, Miranda. He won't make any improvement unless he's around the people who love him.'

It had been a mistake for Miranda to come back here. I knew she couldn't bear to have the same argument for the hundredth time. 'When will you face the truth, Richard? He's never going to improve. It's not a psychological condition, it's a physical handicap that no amount of love is ever going to change.'

'You know I don't believe that.'

'What more proof do you need?' she cried impatiently. 'Christ, you've been told by experts often enough. Sometimes it looks like he understands, but he's just reading your facial expressions and interpreting them.'

'The doctor said his social referencing tests –'

'They'll gauge his ability but they won't change anything. His mind is like a broken mirror – remember being told that? – and he'll never possess the mentality to bind the pieces into a whole. Others can but he can't.' She pressed the cool glass to her forehead and closed her eyes. 'He can't.'

'Listen to me, Miranda. What I want to do is provide you with a quarterly income –'

'There's no need, Richard, I'm earning good money now and – '

'Whatever the settlement you and the lawyers decide upon, providing you personally look after Greg.'

'You're asking me to give up the agency. You know I can't do that.' She wasn't even prepared to give the idea a moment's thought. She rose from the chair behind me and returned to the lounge. I had been sure that she would return here when Berry failed to call her. I wondered what she would do if she knew that her ex-lover was lying dead in the bottom of his own building.

I heard the clink of ice cubes again and wondered how much time I had left. I thought the temazepam tablets I had taken from the bathroom shelf were in 20 milligram caplets, but could not be sure. I certainly did not want to kill her. I just wanted her to understand and learn, but she could not do that yet, not until I had completed my task. That meant taking care of her until she had come to the right decision about her life. I had emptied the contents of ten caplets into the bottle of Bombay Blue Gin. The bottle was less than half full, and she poured large measures. Would that be too strong?

'Tell me how your affair with Berry began,' I asked pleasantly, waiting until she was comfortably back in her chair.

'It wasn't an affair, Richard, it was an escape valve,' she sighed, tipping the glass. 'Therapy, exercise, getting rid of tension, call it whatever you want.'

'So you didn't love him?' I felt heartened by the news. Perhaps there was hope for her yet.

'Good God, no. People like Berry want everyone and end up with no one.'

'Then why pick him?'

She set down her drink and lit a cigarette. 'He knew the rules. He was looking for a woman who wanted the same thing. No strings, no memories, no sentiment, none of that shit.'

'You make it sound like a business transaction.'

'That's what it felt like. That's what I needed after being with you, endlessly analysing everything. Can we talk about something else?'

Certainly, I thought. We can talk all night long. While we talk, I'll wait for you to sleep. And once you are asleep, you will be mine again.

FRIDAY

There is no greater joy in life than first proving that something is impossible and then showing how it can be done.

Barnes Wallis

Natural Additive

By 9:07 a.m. on Friday morning, the sun was high and hard as a diamond above the roofs of Soho. Norman Balon, the rudest pub landlord in the civilised world, was striding along Greek Street towards the Coach and Horses, looking more than ever like Walter Matthau's disgruntled twin brother. He remained one of the area's few surviving 'characters', uncompromising and merciless when it came to insulting the few tourists who foolishly ventured inside his smoky saloon bar. Most of the other eccentric residents who enhanced the locality's pungent reputation in the last two decades were gone. Jeffrey Barnard, AA's worst nightmare – an intelligent, contented alcoholic – was finally dead. The comedian Peter Cook, the artist Francis Bacon, bar legends Muriel Belcher and Ian Board had all passed away, as had most of the original members of the notorious Colony Club. Many of the Italians, the Polish and the Maltese had shut up shop. The area's legendary restaurateurs had moved on. The days – and long nights – of the Doll's House, Mandy's, the Establishment, Jimmy's, the Gargoyle, the Mandrake, the Two I's, the Bag O'Nails and other premises of borderline respectability had come to a sorry end. The red-bulb doorways of the old strip-bars and drag joints had vanished in a new era of sexual freedom, replaced by brasseries and mega-restaurants, T-shirt shops and designer bars. Only the prostitutes remained where they had always been, sharing their first-floor backstreet walk-ups with elderly 'madams' who still cleaned for them and arranged their appointment books.

The new Soho was not disrespectful enough for Arthur Bryant. He felt that every city needed an environment where artistic and moral freedom could exist side by side. An area's reputation was consolidated on the vision of its artists, not the gimmickry of its restaurants. Still, there was good news; 'The Vice', Soho's long-running problem with the criminal underworld, had been cleared away. And new generations of artists, film-makers, writers and designers had made the area their home. The wheel had turned once more.

Switching his attention away from the baking tarmac of Wardour Street, where a truck was spraying water, he patted his forehead with the corner of a neatly laundered handkerchief, then passed the swipe card through the slot again. Nothing happened.

'The stupid thing is broken,' he complained.

'You've probably got it upside down,' said May patiently. 'Give it to me.' He examined the plastic oblong in Bryant's hand and sighed. 'That's your Safeway discount card. What did you do with the one Janice gave you?'

'Um. Ah.'

'Oh, for God's sake.' May dug about in his partner's voluminous overcoat and located the entry-pass. Unconcerned, Bryant unwrapped the paper bag he was clutching and peered into it.

'Who wants lemon and who wants apple?'

'I don't consume man-made chemicals,' said Sunshine Day, the heavyset Antigua-born woman who was standing between them. Sunshine had been christened in London during the hippy, dippy days of the late sixties, and lived up to her name.

'Don't give them to me,' said May. 'They get sugar all over you and make you hyperactive. No wonder American policemen get trigger-happy after hanging around doughnut shops.' He inserted the card and ran it through. This time there was a click and the door swung inwards. 'After you, Sunshine. I'm sure Mr Bryant would like your first impressions.'

Sunshine had been released into the detectives' care for the morning. They had promised to return her to Holloway Prison by noon. There was little danger that she would try to escape from their custody. She was wearing an electronic homing tag on her left wrist. Besides, she had no desire to stay in the outside world. She had come to prefer life inside the jail. All her friends were there, and she understood how things worked. She had barely known any other society.

They had returned to Malcolm Cotton's flat because Bryant was convinced they had missed something. The boy's exercise book had yielded several names, but no addresses or telephone numbers. Either they had been stored in his head, or they were written down somewhere. It wasn't much to go on, but the detectives had uncovered precious little else. Willis and his forensic team were thorough, but not particularly imaginative. They smothered the flat in graphite powder, and lifted faint fingerprints with sheets of adhesive plastic and aerosol glue, but so far the only whole prints they could identify belonged to Cotton himself.

The secondary searches Bryant liked to conduct were narrower, and concentrated on evidence that had become germane to the case following the initial findings. It was here that the unit's more lateral thought processes came into play. Willis had struck a deal with the detectives that allowed them back into crime scenes once he had concluded his own tests and his reports had been accepted and signed off, but it annoyed him to think of Bryant tramping about, ignoring hard scientific evidence in favour of his own fancifully concocted theories. Technically they were operating beyond their jurisdiction, but with so many staff away on summer leave, their help was grudgingly accepted.

A draft of Willis's lab report indicated traces of cocaine and amphetamine in the residue scraped from the glass pipes in Cotton's filtration apparatus, but a number of rarer compounds could not be identified. Upon hearing this, Bryant had insisted that they search the flat more thoroughly, and brought along his wild-card consultant. He knew that murder cases quickly grew cold with the passing hours, as evidence and motives became muddied by conflicting testimony, theoretical analysis and the unwanted attentions of the press. So far the deaths had barely been reported – they had, after all, been filed as drug-overdoses – but who knew what could happen with the weekend about to begin?

Sunshine Day was a self-styled 'organic chemist'. She had an abnormally high I.Q., and knew a lot about drugs. Her interest had developed at an early age, when she had watched her parents shooting up heroin, and had witnessed her musician father's fatal overdose in an illegal Soho drinking club. He had died on the night of her sixteenth birthday. As a consequence she had put her formidable knowledge to good use, but her evidence was inadmissible in court by virtue of the fact that she had spent a considerable part of her life operating on the wrong side of the law. When she finally used her expertise to murder a violent lover and had been placed behind bars, paradoxically she was granted permission to make discreet use of her skills in the service of the police. Sunshine was a good woman who'd had bad luck. But she had killed a man, and was quite capable of doing so again. Today, though, she was happy and smiling.

She had not stopped smiling since the detectives collected her from the prison. She was thoroughly enjoying herself.

As they climbed the steep stairs, May recalled something that had been bothering him. 'If we're looking for links to a drug,' he asked, 'what form of ingestion do you think it would take? A needle?'

'Danbury was mistaken about the needle-mark on Cotton. Of course, there's no reason to assume that he was a user.'

'If he was, he knew how to handle it.' Sunshine stopped on the stairs to regain her breath. 'I think what you're looking for is more likely to exist in the form of an easily absorbed powder. When it comes to sales, there's a big psychological barrier between powder and liquid. Folks think it's okay to shovel dust into their nasal passages but balk at the idea of opening a vein. Needles are serious shit. You're talking heroin, morphine, methadone, DMT.'

Sunshine had studied photographs of Cotton's apparatus, and one thing bothered her. The boy appeared to have been doctoring his drugs, liquefying, mixing and drying them, but why? She explained that any chemistry student could turn morphine sulphate into heroin, multiplying his supply on a 1/11 basis. He could cut the resulting crystals with synthetics, laxative, speed, baby powder. Diluting the merchandise helped to keep profits up, but you couldn't go too far. In an area like Soho there was a constant demand for high-quality narcotics, not the £65 packet but the £90 one. Dealers were more likely to be friends doing someone a favour, and repeat customers knew when they were being gypped. Cotton's filtration equipment was not necessary for drug-cutting. It suggested some other form of experimentation, something a little more complex, but the chemical analysis report was annoyingly open-ended.

Cotton had half a dozen books on butterflies above his

bed. These, along with other volumes cataloguing spiders, ants and centipedes had been removed and carefully examined. There were several scratch-pads filled with notes and doodles in his desk, along with another large exercise book labelled 'Flora and Fauna of New Guinea'. These had been placed in bags for later examination. The sparsely furnished apartment offered few opportunities for surprise.

'I want to dismiss this business with butterflies,' said Bryant, checking between the cooking pots in the kitchen, 'but I can't. It's Cotton's only obsession, one of his few distinguishing characteristics. He spent years in the Outback. He could have returned here to specialise in the field, to capitalise on his knowledge. Instead he started dealing drugs. Why?'

'Perhaps he needed to finance his work,' offered Sunshine. She had opened the fridge and was checking the shelves. 'A lot of people fool themselves by figuring they'll just deal within their circle to make a little ready cash.'

'His father is pretty well off,' said May. 'I'm sure he could have asked for the money. No, it's something else. Specialists are usually rather messianic about their findings. They're desperate to discuss their favoured topic with anyone who's interested. What do you think interested Cotton?'

Sunshine held up a set of six small plastic flasks. Five were empty. The last contained a tiny amount of pinkish-grey fluid. 'I think you may have part of the answer right here.'

'Where did you find those?'

'Back of the fridge.'

'Looks like prepared baby formula.'

'They're old organic yoghurt bottles, and that's what your men would have thought was in them. They've been rinsed out and reused. I've seen this kind of thing before,' said Sunshine, 'but not very often. This is definitely the result of chemical experimentation. The set is labelled with a batch number.' She held the bottle close and examined it against the light. 'You said there were numbers in his exercise book?'

May laid the book on the desk in the bedroom and leafed through the pages until he reached a lengthy series of matching numerals. 'The number on your bottle is right here,' he pointed out. 'Whatever Cotton prepared, this is the last of it.'

'How many earlier batches?'

'Seven. Looks like there are six of these little buggers in each batch.'

'And those aren't in the flat.'

Sunshine clicked her tongue in annoyance. 'Which could mean that there are over forty bottles out on the street.' She shook the plastic container, waited for it to settle and clear, then reluctantly passed it to John May. 'Now we need to find out what's really in it.'

'What do you think he was doing?' asked May.

Sunshine's smile broadened. 'You're not going to hold me to a wild guess?'

'Absolutely not. Just give me an opinion.'

She rested her hand on an ample hip. 'I think he was cutting cocaine with whatever's in this little pot, diluting rock crystals into the liquid, boiling it, then drying the resulting compound and grinding it into a powder.'

'Why would he go to so much trouble?' asked May.

'I'm wondering if this stuff is some form of synthetic intoxicant that would allow him to use less coke without the purchaser noticing. It's the dealer's holy grail, the invention of a cheaply produced substance that'll maintain or enhance the effect of whichever drug it's cut into. Imagine the profits to be made!'

'And you think the boy discovered a way to do it.'

'Maybe he thought he had,' replied Sunshine. 'Looks like he

turned out quite a few early experimental batches, probably trying to get the balance right. The problem is, we have no idea of knowing how far he managed to stretch each sample. Clever boy. He brings enough new dope into the public arena to get itself noticed, but hides it inside a known drug.'

'How much exactly?'

Sunshine puffed out her cheeks and thought hard. 'Let's see, by the time it's dried, cut and poured into spindles, say a minimum of three hundred and fifty grammes and a maximum of several thousand. It all depends on the strength of the compound. I know it doesn't seem like a large amount if you compare it to the kind of hauls that get picked up coming into the country, but if its chemical structure is being deliberately altered, there's no telling what you'll have to deal with on the street. Unless punters are being supplied with instructions for its correct usage, which I doubt.'

Bryant set down another half-dozen books on species of lepidoptera. 'Does it have to be synthetic, this additive?'

'No, I guess not, but it would be highly unlikely for someone to discover a natural substance that hasn't already been tabulated for its narcotic properties.'

'Hmm.' Bryant sat down at the table and opened one of the books. 'I don't suppose it would actually come from butterflies, would it?'

'Some kind of chemical secretion? I've never heard of such a thing. Maybe we could look into the problem over a beer.'

John May checked his watch. 'I have to take you back now, Sunshine. I'm sorry. You know the rules.'

'Hey, that's okay.' She placed a plump hand on the warm bedroom window and looked down into the street. 'Boy it's nice, the sun and all, but there's too much bad air out here.' She gave a glorious smile. 'Take me back to prison, where I can breathe.'

CHAPTER THIRTY-FIVE

The Enchantment

At the same time that Arthur Bryant was trying to open the door to Malcolm Cotton's apartment building, three doors further along Wardour Street and two floors up, Judy Merrigan lay on her lounge rug and felt the sweat trickling down the insides of her legs. How could it be so hot, so early? With nothing else to do today, she lay watching the burning light fold back and forth beneath the curtains.

Her thoughts turned back five days to the previous Sunday morning, the last time she had been able to contact another human being. Once more she had heard his persistent knock at the front door, and wished that she had not answered it.

'I must talk to you,' Midas said quietly. 'May I come in?'

After a moment of hesitation, she held open the door. He had lost a little weight, looked great. She felt a wreck, not up to confrontation.

'You've changed things around.'

'I had to,' she said. 'All the plants you gave me died.'

'I can't afford to lose you,' he said suddenly. 'I've never lost anyone.'

'Oh? What about Danielle Passmore? Do I look as much of

a victim as her? Did you think I'd be easier to convert?'

He showed no surprise. 'I can do so much for you, Judy, if you believe in me.'

'Oh, I believe. You're no crank, Midas, I'm sure of that. But I prefer to rely on myself.'

'Then I have to make you realise your mistake.' He disclosed a clear plastic tube in his hand and snapped open the cap, allowing the milky contents to leak on to the doorframe. 'My seed brings fertility to the barren lives of others, but it can be used in more persuasive ways.'

As soon as she realised what he had in the tube, she shoved him out of the doorway. He knew his strength, and allowed her to do so.

'I'm calling the police this time, damn you,' she shouted through the closing gap.

'Let me know when you're ready to reconsider,' he called back as she slammed the door shut behind him. 'I'll be waiting for you.'

She had no idea what he meant until Monday morning arrived. She had taken two sleeping tablets, and groggily awoke to another cauldron-hot day. The bedroom was stifling; the window had slid shut in the night and wouldn't budge when she tried to open it.

None of the lounge windows would open, either.

She thought perhaps the paintwork on the sills had become sticky – until she tried the front door. The latch refused to move even a tenth of an inch. The wood had become sealed in its frame. There was no other way in or out of the apartment. As ludicrous and impossible as it seemed, she could not gain access to the outside world.

Determined not to panic, she picked up the telephone receiver to call Ari, but found the line dead. The junction box in the skirting board looked as if it had been damaged. Okay, she thought calmly, I'll just have to break a window. At first she considered using a hammer, but remembering what had happened to Danielle she decided to stay out of the storage cupboard where she kept the toolbox.

Instead she entered the lounge clutching a hiking boot, wrapped a teatowel around her arm, shielded her eyes and whacked the window with all her might. Nothing happened. No sound, no shatter, nothing. The glass did not even reverberate. It was as though the pane had been recast in transparent steel.

That was when she started to lose her temper. She screamed her lungs out for a while, hoping that someone would hear her through the walls, but no one came running up the stairs. In the boiling streets below, pedestrians passed without stopping to look up and listen.

By midday the temperature in the flat was 104 degrees Fahrenheit, and she forced herself to stop panicking long enough to take stock of her position. She carried out an inventory of supplies; there was half a day-old loaf, a little butter, some yoghurt, a tin of beans, a packet of sliced ham, an almost empty jar of peanut butter, some breakfast cereal but no milk. That was it. She usually stocked up at the beginning of the week. At least there was an unlimited supply of tapwater. She tried the windows again, this time hammering on them with a steel-framed kitchen chair, but they seemed to absorb the sound and impact of every blow.

The computer. She ran to it and switched on the modem. Her attempt to e-mail Gillian through the internet resulted in the message rerouting itself back to sender, endlessly scrolling down the screen until she was forced to shut the monitor off. The next time she tried to boot up the system, it didn't work at all. The screen kept printing the same message: AN ERROR OF TYPE 078 HAS OCCURRED. A little picture of a bomb appeared beside it.

Her clothes were stained with sweat, so she took a shower. She did her best thinking beneath the scalding jets of water. There had to be another way out. Presumably it would be a waste of time taking up the floorboards or trying to burrow through the walls with the puny hand-drill William had left her. There was an attic above the apartment that might be able to get her to the roof – except that the entrance to it was set in the landing ceiling, just beyond the front door.

If Judy was truly under some kind of enchantment, she knew she would not be able to escape so easily. She thought about the few friends she had made in London. They never came around without calling first. How long would it take them to report her dead telephone line? How long would it take an inquisitive friend to climb her stairs?

Monday seemed to last for ever. Through the front door she could hear Midas's damned madrigals and the imbecile laughter of his acolytes. What frightened her was the feeling that he wasn't even at home. She had heard him early that morning, whistling on the stairs, slamming the entrance door. Secured up here in her airless, baking cocoon, Judy began to consider the possibility that he had decided to let her die.

CHAPTER THIRTY-SIX

Theatre of Cruelty

I **was** having terrible trouble with the wheelchair.

It behaved like an airport trolley, refusing to turn corners. I pulled at the left wheel, yanking it around, then pushed straight ahead across the floor of the basement. It seemed appropriate to place Miranda beside the body of her former lover. I decided to leave the tape across her mouth. She appeared to be breathing normally, and I didn't want her screaming the place down when she awoke and saw where she was.

I carefully bound her wrists and ankles to Gregory's little wheelchair with strong brown parcel tape, then locked it into position against the wall beneath the stairs. I had managed to squash her into the tiny seat, but she looked very uncomfortable. Here at least she would be safe from my rampaging mood-swings.

My earlier fury with her had given way to pity. I wanted to depart my life leaving behind a full, tidy set of achievements; enemies dispatched, kindness rewarded, debts settled, faith renewed. I realised that drugging my ex-girlfriend and carting her off to a Soho basement was probably not the best way to go about it, but in the crucial hours that lay ahead I had to be certain of her whereabouts. I would need to talk to her, to arrange her future. I felt sure she would not hate me for killing Berry. She might even forgive me before it was too late.

A single surfacing thought disturbed me. The stairwell was accessible from any floor. There was no reason for anyone to use it, except in the event of fire, but even so, could I risk leaving her here when so much depended on the next few hours? I looked around at the darkened concrete well. The sealed door set in the far left-hand corner opened into a narrow brick corridor that, in turn, led to a fire escape exit.

Beyond this, though, was not an alleyway but a disused viewing theatre. In the twenties the building above it had housed a restaurant with a small ballroom. As the properties were carved into smaller packages, balconies, landings, corridors and annexes were grafted on to the original structures, and the downstairs section of the ballroom became stranded without any access. Soho was filled with redundant rooms like this. Developers would purchase an old house and discover that it came with an unwanted addendum, a room to which the only available access was through someone else's property. Other developers purchased offices at bargain prices and prepared to rip out the interiors so that computer wiring could be laid, only to find that the rooms' original features were listed and untouchable. The buildings of Soho tunnelled down beneath the streets, and many of them had become connected over the years, at least until the boom in the eighties, when many properties were sub-divided according to their new leases.

The little ballroom had been converted into a preview theatre in the sixties, but the film company that had built it had since been bankrupted. Now Westminster Council refused to renew their licence because the room's only safety exit crossed the property next door, and had been bricked up. It was into this room that I decided I would push Miranda's wheelchair.

Berry had the key for the basement lock on the office set he kept in his trouser pocket. I turned over his body and dug them out, one corpse molesting another. Once the padlock was removed, the door opened easily. This time I had remembered to bring a torch, and shone it across the grimy gilt walls. The theatre's red plush curtains hung in tattered swathes like bloody bandages. Four rows of old cinema seats were spotted with clumps of furry grey mildew. I rolled the wheelchair to the end of the first row and turned it to face the screen, so that it looked like Miranda had come here to see the film.

The little theatre would have seated about thirty people, but now its chairs were broken, its screen torn in two. The huge carbon-arc projectors in its booth were the old, dangerous kind that could blister and ignite celluloid if left unattended. The carpet was spongy with moisture and reeked, but at least in here there would be no danger of Miranda being discovered. Perhaps it was appropriate that I should make this theatre, the scene of so many projected celluloid tragedies and fantasies, the scene of my own final drama.

I dragged Berry across the basement floor by an arm and a leg, along the corridor and into the cinema, leaving him beside Miranda. A black patch of blood had pooled around his skull. I was careful not to slip over in it.

I had to return to what I knew would probably be my last working day on earth. I left Miranda sleeping soundly in the child's wheelchair, beside her ex-lover's corpse. Just before I resealed the door, I stood and watched her for a moment. I longed to bury my face at the nape of her neck, to smell her hair, to kiss her ear. Too late now. I knew I could not afford to indulge myself like this. All would be gone soon enough. It was time for me to prove my mettle, and act.

The hot night had affected my body condition. My skin was starting to slough. I could feel it drying and shifting on my bones, like meat separating from a boiled chicken, the epidermis stiffening like chamois leather. My mind was a scalding hell of half-ideas and unfinished plans. As I returned to my office and set about arranging the day's appointments, I smiled grimly at the paradox in which my death had placed me. Just when I had reached the perfect state in which to conduct my life, I found that I no longer had one to live. Was it this way for everyone? Was dying always so inopportune? I forced such thoughts from my deteriorating mind. There would be time for madness soon enough.

In the heat of the year's hottest day, Soho awoke and went to work. An aura of pleasure settled on the area at the end of the week. On a Friday it was virtually impossible to dine without booking. The bars were busy as soon as they opened. People loitered on the streets as if preparing to witness lights in the heavens. Elderly men began queuing outside the Sunset Strip club on Dean Street long before it opened, as patiently as they would wait to see a dentist.

The hard indigo sky let light into this little brick world, and encouraged by the sense of impending release, office workers greeted one another with the cheerfulness of passengers who had just confirmed their places in the lifeboats of a sinking ship.

They were certainly cheerful in the offices of Film Creation Incorporated. The trade dailies were in, the word was out, and I was suddenly hot, and by a process of osmosis so was the company. The breaking news was splashed across the pages of every important entertainment periodical. The *Daily Mail* was running a full page on 'Movieland's New Movers and Shakers', and had managed to dig out an old picture of Berry and I attending last year's BAFTA awards. Yesterday my negotiations were conjured from nothing more than the sooty Soho air, deals more fragile and invisible than spun glass, but already this morning they were on their way to becoming concrete.

An eavesdropper listening in on the phonecalls I had initiated would have heard talk of cross-collateral promises, qualifying contract-breakers, brokered talent packages, and all of them to be instantly actioned. Yes, it was all talk, but at its heart there was something oddly real – a promise of product, in the form of scripts, finance, casting and production ability. All it took to make the dream tangible was confidence.

Here was the paradox at the heart of the film trade. A man could be a fool one day and a superpower the next. He could have nothing to his name, no experience, no talent, no sense of honour or decency, but if he could survive on sheer energy until the signing of his first production, he would have a chance to become all the things he most assuredly was not when he set out. The industry was divided into those who acknowledged this fact by honouring idiots, and those who would only deal with their professional peers. But as yesterday's idiot was often tomorrow's professional, it paid to keep an open mind. It was a question of how much rubbish you were prepared to listen to without becoming cynical. In the last few years I'd done a lot of listening. Now it was time for me to be heard.

By midday two of the five scripts I had selected for

promotion had taken their next step towards the blinding light of the projector. Money had been raised in the heat of the moment, on the back of good press, on shows of bravado, on nothing at all except the collective will for it to happen. I acted more speedily than I had ever moved on anything. I zigzagged across Soho, clasping hands, initiating agreements, preparing deals, meeting, acknowledging, acquiescing, impressing. I talked the talk. I looked the business. I had the confidence and nerve that my partner – and where was Berry this morning? everyone asked – usually displayed. I worked fast and without fear. I felt no terror of failure, and my sure-footed confidence spread to others like the warmth of the sun. Most importantly, I broke the rules. When someone said, 'Let me get back to you on that,' I said, 'No, let's do it right now or not at all.' Anyone could make friends. It was important to make the right enemies. That morning, I was really cooking. But inside, the cracks were starting to show.

There was a dark place deep inside my head, a black nothingness that said forget all this, there is nothing you can do, your own life is over and that means so is theirs, because your world only exists while you are aware of it. Soon, I knew, I would start to fail physically. Already my right foot felt odd, and when I removed my shoe I found that the nail of my big toe had come away inside the sock. The bones of my hands were moving strangely, and kept clicking out of position. In the last few hours my right eye had started to lock like the ball jamming in a roll-on deodorant, and I found that I had to moisten it with a dab of water on my finger to get it moving again.

I needed more time. I had until the close of trading today to make my mark. I was sure that even if I managed to survive the weekend, I would not be presentable enough for personal appearances come Monday. Making the deals was one thing, making them cast-iron enough to survive my physical destruction was another matter entirely, and one that I now attempted to address. I worked on Berry's mobile, calling non-stop as I ran in and out of the traffic. Everything I had silently absorbed in the past was suddenly being called into play. I knew I could do it. I only wished I had more time. Everywhere I looked there was a clock urging me on.

As I passed the entrance to the Soho Villa, one of the industry's most respected senior producers smiled and raised his hand in greeting. 'I've been hearing good things about you,' he said, genuinely pleased for me. 'I hope you have as much success with your projects as I had with *The Last Emperor*.' I thanked him warmly and ran on. Already the people in power were starting to ask about me. I was on my way to becoming another overnight Soho celebrity. But behind the smile was a screaming voice, a terrified warning shriek that I had to ignore until my task was through.

The method of my attack was in place; like an army's battle-plan it capitalised on the enemy's weakness and closed a tight pincer-movement around the foe. At lunch I would set the seal on the deal for the third screenplay. I would not be greedy; three films were enough for my purpose. I would draft out my terms and leave the power of attorney for all future negotiations with Miranda. Whether the films were produced or not, the money would accrue and pay for my son's care at home, in his mother's loving arms, to provide for the future security of my reunited family.

In time Miranda would forgive me and forget the cruelty I had been forced to inflict on her to make her see sense. In time Gregory would improve. The family would heal. All would be well. And I would be forgiven. I would not be forgotten.

CHAPTER THIRTY-SEVEN

Where Dreams Come True

Barbara sat in a restaurant called The Last Supper and peered through a rippled perspex sculpture of a vagina at the other diners. Richard was seated three tables away. He certainly seemed to have recovered from his strange attack last night, although he didn't appear to be eating. He was also having lunch with four of the most powerful men in the industry, and there was no sign of Berry. What was going on? Even from this distance she could see where the balance of power lay. For Richard, the wind had most definitely shifted. People were starting to take notice of him. He was all over the trades, getting things done, moving projects on. She didn't understand it. It was not in his nature to be a player. He cared too much about other people's feelings. You couldn't get very far with an attitude like that.

And where was the money coming from? Even the financial film press seemed vague on that point. Could he have found a secret source in the city? A number of corporations had let it be known that they were looking to invest in British movies, but their boards were notoriously slow to absorb the long-term complexities of feature finance. Most of the big guns were waiting to see if the country could sort out its distribution network before committing their millions. And once the money was agreed, the risks grew and grew. A film required confidence. If it started going wrong in mid-production you had only two options; shut it down and lose everything, or continue to pour more money into it.

Why wasn't Richard eating? He looked more aggressive than ever today. His posture was more rigid, his smile broader, his confidence unbounded, and yet there was something unhealthy and unnatural about him. His strange behaviour in the bar, all that talk about being 'dead', it made no sense. Overnight he had taken control of his life, and also lost it. What was happening?

They were all supposed to be attending the première of Benny Carver's debut feature tonight. Benny was a twenty-six-year-old rich kid who had directed some flashy MTV videos, and *Chemical Man* was a desperate last-ditch attempt to keep the big-budget no-brain action film alive. The producers had originally planned to have Joel Schumacher direct Schwarzenegger, Stallone and Seagal in a movie based on a failed TV pilot about a government agent who can change the chemical composition of his body, but after endless salary wrangles they had opted for a first-time director and cheaper stars, and had put the rest of their expenditure into special effects. Everyone would be going, if not to the film, then to the extravagant bash afterwards. Barbara decided to take Richard on one side at the party and find out what was really going on. Powerful men were supposed to be sexy, but she preferred his woolly-minded former self. In her presence he had always been indulgent and attentive. Now she sensed an unpleasant change when he glanced across at her, as if he was sizing up her value.

Barbara set down her fork, annoyed. Ten minutes ago her lunch companion had wandered across the restaurant to talk to someone, leaving her to eat alone. She looked back at

Richard's table. His lunch meeting was breaking up. He had pushed back his chair and risen amid much hand-shaking. When he looked over again she found herself staring into his eyes. He did not break contact once as he came over and stopped beside her table.

'Don't bother eating that, it's full of tiny bones.'

She looked down at the unenticing slab of grey fish that sat on its bed of wilted nettles, a culinary investment of approximately twenty-two pounds fifty, and sighed. 'I don't know why I ordered this. I wanted a steak.' She looked up at him.

'Are you okay?'

'As fine as I'll ever be. Who's your lunch date?'

'Some arsehole from a TV network who's seeking to asset-strip a film company for its back-library. They're too mean to film their own productions and they're looking for a cheap way to fill the schedules. He's asking me for recommendations. I recommended that he doesn't do it. So he's gone table-hopping over to someone more important. In the middle of the meal. He's over there talking to some guy about the video rights of *Space Babel Seven*. That's what the world needs, isn't it? More TV time devoted to platitudinising Californian spacegirls in Lycra suits?'

'Then leave him, Barbara. Stop suffering fools gladly and come with me. Why wait around just so he can stick you with the bill? Sometimes you just have to walk away.' Richard held out his hand, and she found herself taking it.

'Oh, Richard, if only it was that easy.'

'But it is. You've proved yourself. You don't need this prick. You have nothing to be scared of. You can do anything you want if you have no fear of failure. Let's get some fresh air.'

'You're right,' she said suddenly, looking down at the congealing meal and shaking her head. 'You're absolutely right. What the hell am I doing here?' She eased herself from the seat and threw her napkin down on the table. 'Let someone else pick up the tab for a change.'

'When movie directors get older the movies they make change, have you ever noticed that? I'm talking about European directors, not employees of the Hollywood system. They start their careers making the kind of small hyper-realistic films that usually win the Palme d'Or at Cannes. But once they hit fifty or thereabouts the subject matter becomes more magical and whimsical. Locations are replaced with stylised sets. A certain devil-may-care playfulness steps in. Look at Fellini filming Rome and Woody Allen shooting New York. Why hasn't anyone done that with London? Look down there, it's like the set of an old musical.'

I folded my arms on the yellow brick parapet and leaned forward. The moment I did so, I could hear the noise of the hot streets below. We had brought our drinks up to the deserted roof of the Soho Villa and were looking down at the lunchtime crowds in Old Compton Street.

Barbara rested her arms alongside mine on the warm stone. 'Funny how New York has its Broadway songs,' she said, 'but London has no single voice, just a great cacophonous fuzz of sound. You can't set this chaos to music. If you try to think of a song about London you always end up humming something twee and awful aimed at tourists, full of Cheery Victorian cockneys and strutting Ascot toffs.'

'If I could direct a movie, I'd set it in the streets of Soho and tell a real story.'

'I thought you could do anything you liked now, Richard. Isn't that what you've been telling me? Cast aside fear and achieve the impossible?'

EXTERIOR SHOT – SOHO STREET – DAY
The road is deserted as our black-clad STAR walks alone down its centre. As he looks up into the camera, he throws out his arms and starts to sing.

                    STAR
          My alarm goes off and I head into town . . .
          Now I'm out on the street where
          they can't keep me down . . .

Cut to BUSINESSMEN and WOMEN marching out of their offices with briefcases, swinging their arms, everyone suited-up in black. They fall in behind STAR, joining him in the chorus. Other cheery Soho characters move into shot and start to dance and sing.

                    STAR
          I'm back in Soho . . .
          With the pimps and the whores . . .
          In Soho . . .
          Where they break the laws . . .
          In Soho . . .
          Where you never feel blue . . .
          In Soho . . .
          Where your dreams come true . . .

The black-suited EXECUTIVES throw their briefcases to one another. Jolly COSTERMONGERS dance with crates of lettuces. BUILDERS jump acrobatically over piles of bricks. BARMEN and WAITRESSES strut past with silver trays held high. SEX WORKERS in bust-hugging fetishwear lean waving from windows while TAXI-DRIVERS pirouette between high-kicking RENT BOYS, and MOBSTERS shoot each other dead in a mime-ballet gang war. Through them shoves a determined woman in a spangled fishtail frock, SHIRLEY BASSEY, for it is she.

> BASSEY
>> We always know what's going down . . .
>> (Blimey, guv'nor, it's a laugh!)
>> We're the guys and gals of London Town . . .
>> (We never do fings by half!)
>> 'Cause it's SOHO – that – we – love!

Cut to the word SOHO strung across street in red, white and blue neon. Fireworks, confetti etc. Everyone throws their arms in the air.

'Well, maybe someone younger than Shirley Bassey,' I said, 'that fifteen-year-old girl who's in the charts, I don't know. Get a first-time director with experience in music videos, or maybe even I could direct. You could mix modern dance music with retro to catch both audiences, like the Propellerheads did.'

'Hmm. I'm not so sure . . .'

She was still considering the idea when I pressed my cool face against hers. She closed her eyes, allowing the afternoon sun to warm her cheeks, and I knew that she wanted me to kiss her. I felt her arm slip around my waist, her lips slowly parting over mine. I knew that my tongue would be dry in her mouth, and drew saliva from her to moisten it. My hands cupped her heavy breasts as my tongue probed deeper. I shifted my hard-muscled thighs against her legs as my right hand slipped to the back of her skirt.

She would have let me make love to her, right there, standing on the silent rooftop in brilliant sunlight, but suddenly the terror returned and I knew that I was contemplating madness. I pulled away and twisted aside, frightened to let her see my face, knowing that my muscles were contorting uncontrollably.

'Richard? What's the matter?' She came closer, raising her hand to mine, but I knocked it away.

'No, don't look at me.'

'If there's something wrong, at least let me try to help. Are you ill? Talk to me.' She took another step forward. 'I don't know what you imagine is the matter with you, but I'm sure it's something we can work out.'

'It's too late for that. There's nothing you or anyone else can do.' I stumbled away along the terrace, following the guard-rail like a blind man, keeping my face turned from hers.

'Don't do this to me again, Richard,' she cried, 'I can't take it. Please, don't run off again.' For a brief moment I had forgotten my undead status, but kissing her brought me back to the few senses I had left. What could I have been thinking of?

I forced myself to consider my physical condition. Although I still felt sexual desire, the need for love and tenderness, I could not allow myself to touch a living human being. Aside from the grotesque implications of such a union, there was a physical problem – my atrophying muscles could not produce an erection. I would never again be inside a woman.

A wave of revulsion prickled over me. I had been despoiling her, dirtying her, pressing my corpse-flesh upon her living skin in the most degrading way imaginable. If she only knew of her narrow escape! Releasing a moan of anguish, I fell back to the stairs and the darkness of the world below.

As I ran through the streets, a vision consumed my sight. Miranda, my Miranda, was waking from a strange dream. She had been watching sharp stars shift across a sable sky, gently gliding away from her house, borne aloft like a mummy in a sarcophagus. A rhythmic bumping had followed, a flight down a stairway, and then a stifling sense of being trapped.

I imagined what would happen when she opened her eyes. At first she would see nothing. Gradually a lighter plane would reveal itself; a million iridescent flecks of mica rising above her, the soft grey wall of a movie screen. She would perceive that she was in an abandoned cinema, seated at the front of the auditorium but facing the wrong way, looking back at the seats. She would glance up at the chunks of pink plaster hanging down from the ceiling. In the gloom they looked like stalactites in a cave.

Then she would realise that her movement was restricted. Her wrists were bound tight, her hands cold and numb. Worse, she would not be able to open her mouth. And then what happened the night before would start to piece itself together, and she would know that I had drugged her and hidden her away from prying eyes. But why, she would be wondering, what did I hope to achieve?

I began walking faster. Poor Miranda. She'd remember how I came to terms with the break-up of our relationship, how we sat down and discussed the matter in a sensible, adult fashion. And before she could think of Berry, before she had time to conjure his face she would find him right there in front of her, tipped on to his head like a broken puppet freed from its strings. His bulky form was instantly recognisable, even though it was half hidden in the gloom. His face was turned to her at an impossible angle. His eyes were abnormally bulbous, and she would see that there was something wrong with his collar and tie. They were almost torn off. Then she would discern that his shirt collar was in fact his shattered jaw, and the tie was his bloodied tongue.

That was when she would begin screaming into her gag.

No more fear for me. Plenty for her!

CHAPTER THIRTY-EIGHT

Tea With Waldorf and One Eighty

One Eighty slapped his hands rhythmically on the counter, waiting impatiently for his cappuccino. He would rather have been ordering an ice-cold beer, but the management had forbidden drinking on the job ever since he had uprooted a bollard and taken the rear bumper off an ice-cream van in Argyll Street. The coffee bar had scuffed-steel counters and tall, sharp-edged stools on jagged faux-rust stems that could give you a nasty slash if you walked past them with your elbows out. The place had been open for two months, which at the current Old Compton Street turnover rate meant that it would fold before the leaves started dropping in Soho Square, or as soon as customers grew tired of drinking coffee that tasted like yesterday's grouts tainted with chlorine gas fumes, which ever came first.

'You know the trouble with you?' said Waldorf, who was always prepared to tell his colleague what the trouble with him was. 'You're like the guy who thought he was a pair of wigwams. You know, too nervous.'

'Tense.'

'Oh yeah. You gotta learn to relax. You crunch those damn mints all the time –'

'It's easy for you,' replied One Eighty. 'You smoke. You're – cool.'

'What do you mean, I'm cool?'

'You know.' He gestured at Waldorf's face. 'Cool.'

'You mean I'm black.'

'No, that isn't the only –'

'That's what you're tryin' to say, though. I'm cool 'cause I'm black. Fuck you, One Eighty, I'm cool because I take time to enjoy life and I stop for tea in the afternoons and I don't own a jacket that costs less than £700 and the babes damn near hump me in the street, that's why I'm cool. Don't tell me it's 'cause I'm black. It's because I'm a civilised man in a world of fucking chimps.'

'Okay.' One Eighty admitted defeat. 'Maybe I should be more like you.'

'That's more like it,' Waldorf agreed, 'now you're talking sense.' He pushed the coffees aside and threw a five pound note on the counter. 'Come on, don't drink this shit, I'm gonna show you a more relaxing way to spend your break.'

The harpist on the balcony of the tea room at the Waldorf Astoria was plucking her way through the opening chords of Massenet's *Meditation from Thais* when two young men smartly attired in black suits and shirts arrived at the maître d's desk.

The ethereal music, watery lighting and aqua-blue decor imbued One Eighty with a sense of tranquillity as he scanned the room in his customary fashion. 'Fuck me,' he said as they were seated behind a pair of tall fronded palms, 'Oscar Wilde goes to Seaworld.'

'An oasis of serenity.'

'And senility. It's some kind of chill-out room for the over-sixties.'

'You say that now, but wait 'til you try the sandwiches,' said Waldorf. 'They know me here, so I don't want you nicking stuff. You can take that cake-slice out of your jacket for a start.'

One Eighty dropped the silver utensil back on the table-cloth, and they ordered pots of Darjeeling just as a quorum of county ladies shrugged off their shopping bags and seated themselves around the neighbouring table.

'There's some pretty good-looking women in here. Mature but fit, you know?' One Eighty ducked his head as he spoke, as if he was expecting to be overheard. 'Do you ever, like, pull any of them?'

'Piss off, this is a refined establishment. It's not the done thing to buy a couple of Eccles cakes and nip upstairs for a quick shag. Anyway, they all have to catch trains by five.'

'So, like, you come here by yourself, do you?' One Eighty was amused by the idea.

'Yeah, when I want to sit and think.'

'About what?'

'My career, man. I'm twenty-eight. I look around at all these twenty-two-year-olds coming into Soho thinking every-thing's going to happen for them and the world's a fantastic place, and I know someone's going to come along and slap them down really heavily, and they're going to end up just like me. Doing the jobs other people won't touch with a stick.'

'The risks are big but the money's good. The hours are okay. I get time to rework my screenplay.'

'Yeah, but it's never going to get made, is it? I mean,

realistically. Who's gonna want to see a film about a demonic rogue elephant that attacks people, for fuck's sake.'

'I've got a lot of interest from a production company,' said One Eighty, talking through a mouthful of prawn sandwich with the crust removed. 'This bloke reckons he's close to raising the finance and getting a director on board.'

'What's his name?'

'Red Banner.'

'And that's a real name, is it? It sounds made up. You trust these people?'

'They told me they loved the script.'

'Yeah, well, everyone says you're a great fuck until they can't get you into bed.'

'Since when did you know more about the film industry than the experts?'

'Since I sat through the last Demi Moore picture. Now listen, we need to have a serious talk about something.'

'What's the problem?'

'Your shoes.' He waited for a reaction, but none came.

One Eighty looked down at his feet. 'What?'

'Your shoes. The ones you – you know.'

'No, I don't know.' One Eighty sucked his fingers and selected a slim wedge of cucumber and relish. He pushed the whole thing into his mouth with the tip of his right forefinger.

'You took them off before you sorted out the Cotton boy.'

'Oh, right. They were brand new. Italian. Expensive. I didn't want to fuck 'em up. So?'

'And your socks. You took your socks off as well.'

'Yeah, I didn't want to fuck those up, neither.'

'The boss thinks you left your prints in the tube station. He's heard something about the police getting a lead. Gave me a right bollocking on the phone.'

'He doesn't know what he's talking about. Your toes don't have fingerprints.'

'You're right, they have toe prints.'

'Exactly.'

'They're traceable, you mook. Just as traceable as your fingers.'

'You're fucking joking.' He pulled his shoe and sock off and started to examine the sole of his foot, which forced the waitress to stifle a laugh. 'Christ, I never thought of that.'

'He wants to see you tonight, after we sort out what's-his-face, Mr Tyler – and I don't think he's going to be very happy.'

'Great,' grumbled One Eighty as he tugged his sock back on. 'I take care of someone else's problem, and all I get is complaints. Make an example of the boy, he said, put some fear about. Doesn't he realise that taking someone's life can leave you feeling quite depressed? Psychologically damaging, this job is. I should receive counselling. I could become traumatised.'

'Unlikely,' muttered Waldorf.

Having fought the temptation for the last hour, the harpist finally succumbed to Debussy's *La Mer*. One Eighty eyed the sandwiches once more. 'Yeah, well, you fuck about with the law, you expect to get hurt.' He lowered his hand over the cake stand and raised a watercress sandwich by its corner like a crane seizing a trinket in a seaside arcade.

'I don't think the police know what they're doing,' said Waldorf, hypnotised by his partner's bizarre attempts at table manners.

'I didn't say the police, I said the law,' One Eighty explained through a mouthful of watercress. 'The law according to Midas Blake.'

CHAPTER THIRTY-NINE

The Etiquette of Whoring

It was 4:09 p.m., and the body was gone.

Berry had landed in the far corner of the stairwell, and I had dragged him through the corridor into the little theatre. A black patch of blood still marked the outline of his shattered jaw on the concrete floor of the passageway, but now there was no corpse. I sat on the edge of the filthy stage and peered out at the back of the parked wheelchair, trying to think. Surely he couldn't have survived the fall? And if he had, where was he now? Suppose the same strange biological anomaly that had occurred in my own body had happened in Berry's? Was he wandering about drooling and jawless somewhere, planning revenge?

I switched my attention to Miranda. She couldn't see me from where I was sitting. I felt sure that she would be awake by now, frightened, hungry, soiled, angry. I could not face her yet, not while there was still work to be done. Besides, part of me wanted to punish her. Let her take stock of her position. I decided that I would confront her later, after dark. By that time, tearful contrition might make her more amenable to my plans.

What if I had killed her? What if she had choked behind the tape? No, her head remained motionless but was upright. It was nice and cool in here. She was dozing lightly. I had seen her like this so many times before. Stressful situations made her sleep.

I crept to the bottom of the stairs and moved carefully forward. Pulling the plastic water-bottle from my pocket, I removed the lid and inserted a bendy-straw, fixing it in place with a piece of tape. I did not want her to see me yet, but it would be necessary to free her mouth in order to allow her to drink. When I tapped her shoulder she started violently and tried to look behind her, but the chair's high back prevented her from doing so. I tore the tape back from her lips so that the corner of her mouth was exposed, lowered the Evian bottle in front of her face so that she could see it was ordinary water, then attempted to slip in the tip of the straw, but she twisted her head aside and tried to scream.

The slap was meant not to hurt but to act as a warning, but was harder than I had intended. She immediately became still and accepted the straw, tentatively drawing on the liquid until she could be sure of its purity. I allowed her to drain the bottle before putting the tape back in place, only now her lips were wet and it would not stick down, so I was forced to add another piece. I was determined to remain behind her. I knew that one look in her eyes would make me relent, and I could not afford to weaken now.

I closed the door behind her and returned to the office. The hot afternoon was adversely affecting my body condition. My skin was drying in yellowish opaque patches, giving my arms the texture of old pastry. The skin at the top of my thighs had rubbed raw to the muscle. I wondered how much longer the cartilage between my bones would continue to flex. Lunch had been a long hard sell, the financiers unwilling to be rushed, suspicious of my insistence upon not eating.

The episode with Barbara remained inexplicable even to me. Part of me was so angry that I was finally achieving success after it was too late to enjoy, and part wanted to return quietly to a normal life. All I could do to stop myself from going mad was concentrate on the deals, and make sure that they would continue to work their way through the system when I was no longer around to guide them.

My stiffening fingers made typing difficult, but phone calls could only achieve so much. Agreements had to be legitimised on paper. Documentation had to be provided with post-dated signatures. Nothing could be left to chance. Lawyers would search for loopholes later, and I had to be sure that they would find nothing. By five o'clock I decided I could squeeze in two more short meetings before the première, see the first ten minutes of the picture, then slip out and return to Miranda. I would have to miss the party. In the film world, premières have a hierarchy and parties assume a rare significance. You may have a ticket to the première, but do you have one for the bash afterwards? You may have a ticket for the party, but do you have a pass for the VIP lounge? You may have a pass for the VIP lounge, but do you have any decent drugs? You have no idea of the depths one can sink to in the pursuit of pleasure.

But hey, I thought as I dropped someone's script – the summation of five years' hard work – into the waste bin, life is composed of such trivialities.

I couldn't stop myself from searching for a hit. Just one decent script could provide work for hundreds of people, generate a fortune, build an empire. It may seem obvious but even art films are made to turn a profit, and a film has a better chance of being made if it features a big star doing what the big star is best known for doing. But big stars bring their own problems; basically, most are a pain in the arse. The alternative answer is finding a script so beautifully written that the worst performer in the world would have trouble fucking it up. So far I'd found five good scripts, but not one perfect one.

I checked my watch again and thought about the party for *Chemical Man*. Movie parties are attended by two types of people; non-industry rubberneckers who've managed to blag a ticket and spend the whole evening looking over their partner's shoulder going 'Don't look now, but Cindy from EastEnders is standing in the corner', and industry folk who welcome the chance to attend so that they can complain about the poor celebrity turn-out this film has, compared to the one they most recently worked on. Factions sit together plotting the downfall of friends and enemies in equal proportion, agents target potential clients, producers hustle, actors flirt, writers are ignored, directors expound film theory, distributors and advertisers claim total responsibility for the film's success, financiers allow themselves to be wooed while carefully avoiding promises or commitments, waiters shamelessly hand out their phone numbers, and everyone gets a little bit of what they want. To understand how to work the room at a film party is to comprehend the etiquette of whoring.

I had one working hour left to close my deals. Trying hard not to think about what might have happened to Berry's corpse, and what might be happening to Miranda, I set to work with a fervour that would have alarmed Moses.

Imago

The engraved Tibetan human skull was a constant source of disagreement between them. It was, May supposed, beautiful in a grotesque way. The problem was that it stank to high heaven and Arthur Bryant was the only person who had failed to notice. He kept it on the shelf above his desk to remind him of the Chinese injustices committed in Tibet, next to a Victorian papier mâché hand-puppet of Mr Punch's hangman, several obscure volumes of criminal law, books of Sufi philosophy, a history of the Crimean War, an original floor plan of Newgate Prison, several valuable sixties' Superman comics, a photograph of a drunken human pyramid the detectives formed at his Bow Street leaving party, an unread copy of *Captain Corelli's Mandolin* and a balsawood model of the *Titanic* which Bryant had started in 1947 and set aside unfinished with the advent of television.

'I was thinking about the Indian Mutiny this morning,' said Bryant, tipping back his chair and staring up at the ceiling. 'How the sepoys refused to bite the ends from their gun cartridges because they were coated in animal grease.'

'Not sure I'm entirely with you.' May's head appeared above his computer terminal. 'Don't quite see the relevance.'

'Ingestion,' said Bryant. 'How concerned we are about what we put in our bodies. We buy free-range eggs, yet talk to a chicken farmer and he'll tell you battery eggs are safer because the chickens haven't been feeding in their own excrement. We switch to butter substitutes to reduce cholesterol but won't give up our cars, even though the choked atmosphere causes lung damage and early death. Then there's America, making more trash than anyone else on the planet and refusing to reduce their emissions, thus harming the rest of the world. Which brings us to China.'

Bryant's train of thought had clearly become unhitched again. May was fed up with waiting for the internet to download the information he required, and pushed himself back from the monitor. 'Does this have something to do with the Cotton murder?'

'Most certainly. Drugs, you see. All this concern over diet, and yet when it comes to chemical intoxicants, people have no qualms about taking whatever they're given because they've paid a lot of money for it. They could be snorting powdered rat droppings up their noses for all they know.'

'This is your butterfly theory again. I thought you'd put someone on that.'

'I have. In fact, I expect to have results from him later tonight.'

'It would make more sense to wait for the lab report on those bottles.'

'I don't hold with sense, John, it reminds me too much of Jane Austen. Besides, that will take until Tuesday at least.'

Janice Longbright peered in. 'I think one of you should come to the interview room. They picked up a young lad in the West End about an hour ago. He was carrying one of the bottles.'

May studied his partner thoughtfully. 'I'll tell you what, Arthur, why don't you conduct this interview? It'll do you good to talk to young people again.'

'Are you suggesting I'm losing my faculties?'

'Not at all. It's just that you're a bit of an old fart sometimes.'

'That's a bit rich, coming from someone who still asks where the little lion is on his eggs.' Bryant rose to his feet, indignant. 'Fine. I'll do this one by myself.' He opened the door and shouted. 'Sergeant Longbright!'

Janice had been applying a fresh layer of vermilion lipliner when Bryant called, and the sound of his voice made her skip the edge. She sighed and walked out into the corridor. 'Yes, Mr Bryant?' she said, making a stab at civility.

'How come you always call him John and me Mr Bryant?'

'Because, well, you've always been Mr Bryant.'

Bryant looked miffed. 'From now on please call me Arthur. After all, we have been working together for a long time.'

'Twelve years, sir.' Longbright suppressed a smile.

'Do you have the boy's admission form?'

'Here.' She hastily grabbed the sheet from her desk and thrust it into his hand. Bryant ran his eye down the page. *Name: Damien Gossage, age 19, no current employment, two previous convictions, both drug-related.*

'How did the arresting officer know to bring him here?'

'Mr – John – circulated a fax containing a photograph of the bottles you found in Cotton's fridge. The officer watched the boy hanging around outside an arcade in Windmill Street. When they went through his pockets they found a tiny piece of what appeared to be hash, and one of the plastic bottles. The officer recognised it from the fax.'

'Anything left in it?'

'Empty, I'm afraid.'

'Lead me to him.'

Bryant peered through the wire-mesh window of the interview room. He saw a tall, stick-thin boy with bad skin, nose rings and lousy posture sulkily hunched over in his chair. One look gave him all the background he needed. A housing estate somewhere in the suburbs, parents who didn't give a damn, years of junk food, an attitude born from a lifetime of being ignored. As he entered the little room, the boy looked up in astonishment.

'Did somebody ring for the butler?'

'Believe it or not, I'm a detective,' said Bryant sarcastically. 'Any hilarity you might be experiencing at that thought can be dispensed with now. I've had a rotten week, my piles are playing up, I'm freezing cold even in this ridiculous heat and last night my landlady backed over one of my cats in her Landrover. I know it probably seems nothing compared to the life you're currently leading, but it still depresses me.' He seated himself opposite. 'Have they given you a cup of tea?'

'Uh, yeah.'

'Good. Let me explain a bit about the position you're in. I'm sure you're growing familiar with the routine. The officer who arrested you thinks you're dealing drugs, and looking at your sheet, guess what? So do I.'

'No, I –'

'Try not to embark upon a sentence until I've finished. I'm not talking about your previous troubles or that disgusting speck of hashish they found in your pocket. I'm referring to the little plastic bottle you had on you. Those bottles are believed to contain a drug, the kind of drug that carries a mandatory sentence if you're caught trying to sell it. Now, I don't want your life story, I'm not interested in your present state of hardship, but I would like to know how you came by the bottle, what was in it and where it went. Think you can tell me all that?'

The boy cleared his throat and shifted forward, attempting to make a decent impression. 'I've never been in trouble with the law before,' he began, 'in fact I never –'

'This is the part I told you we could skip?' Bryant reminded him. 'Let's move on to the bottle.'

'The bloke told me how to use it but there was nothing in it when I –'

The kid was falling over himself in an attempt to explain. This was a boy who did not want to go to prison. 'The beginning,' said Bryant softly. 'Just take a deep breath and tell me from the beginning.'

'I was in a pub in Soho.'

'Which pub?'

'The Nelly Dean.'

'The one at the top of Dean Street. Go on.'

'This bloke started talking to me. He asked me if I wanted to get high, said it would cost me a monkey, and I told him I didn't have it.'

'What did he look like?'

'Just a bloke. I don't know, I wasn't really looking.'

Bryant sighed, but knew what the boy meant. The young tended to avoid eye contact as a way of controlling unknown situations.

'He said he had this stuff, and what you do is you put two drops of it into a cigarette –'

'A *cigarette* cigarette?'

'Nah, you put hash into the tobacco then drip this stuff on before you roll it up.'

'And it gives you a better high than if you just use the hash by itself.'

'Yeah. He said you could use it in all sorts of ways. I only had a tenner so he sold me a bottle he'd nearly finished, but the lid couldn't have been on properly 'cause when I went to use it it was empty.'

'I wonder how many other twerps he'd switched bottles on before he saw you,' mused Bryant, sipping his tea. 'Did he say where this magical potion came from?'

'Dunno.'

'What's its street name? He must have told you that.'

'Yeah.' He thought for a moment. The effort was painful to watch. 'Imago? Would that be right? He said it was Imago.'

Bryant recognised the word from his study of Malcolm Cotton's books. It was the term generally used to describe the adult stage in the life-cycle of a butterfly. 'Imago? Are you sure?'

'Yeah.'

'Have you ever heard of that before?'

'No.'

'Would you recognise this man if you saw him again?'

'No chance. He pissed off pretty quick.'

'With your money.'

'Then there was these other blokes.'

Bryant sighed. Why did the young always insist on tangling their stories so? 'What other blokes?' he asked.

'I dunno, two geezers. Black guy and a white guy. They wanted to know where I got the bottle.'

'They witnessed the transaction?'

'I s'pose so. They told me to let them know if I saw any more of it being sold on the street.'

'Then they must have given you a way of getting in touch with them.' But not a telephone number, thought Bryant. If they were professionals, they wouldn't risk discussing drugs with streetkids on their mobiles.

'Yeah. There's a nightclub in Greek Street called the Hot House. Strippers an' that. They said I could find them in there any night after ten.'

Bryant looked down at the admission sheet. 'Mr Gossage. I bet they used to call you Sausage at junior school. Damien. I want you to have a good hard think about the man who sold you this.' He produced the plastic-sealed bottle from his jacket and held it up. 'I want you to be sure that you've told me the truth, that someone didn't actually sell you the whole bottle, and that you haven't been selling it to other people. Because this is a brand-new drug, and we think there's something wrong with it. We know that a number of people have had very bad experiences after taking it, so if it turns out that you sold it to any of them, it would make you a dealer – and a murderer.'

The boy appeared to shrink as he released an anxious moan and sank down in his seat. His body language was enough to suggest to Bryant that he was telling the truth.

'Okay,' said the elderly detective, slipping the plastic bottle back into his coat, 'let's start with some descriptions. Someone is spreading these poisonous little things around Soho, and I need to find out who.'

CHAPTER FORTY-ONE

Urban Jungle

Judy Merrigan watched from her window as the street grew busier. She had dragged the sofa over to her viewing point, and lay there in her bra and pants, breathing the hot, stale air as slowly as she could, hardly daring to move.

The wall clock read 6:50 p.m. She had been trapped in the apartment for five days now. Back on that first day, the Monday, she had tried a few ruses to attract attention; turned the TV, the radio and the CD player way up until the collective volume was ear-splitting. No effect at all. Midas was keeping the sound in, just as he kept others from hearing his celebrations. It was like being sealed away from the world in an impenetrable bubble.

The day before yesterday her food supply, with the exception of a few items like gravy mix and maple syrup, ran out. She had carefully bagged her garbage but the flat had still begun to smell funky, and she was out of ideas, trying not to panic. What could she do but sit and wait for someone to find her?

She watched TV, read books, played music, then listened at the sealed front door as Midas prowled back and forth, laughed, partied, came in, stormed out. In here it was as if she had already died. Life restarted inches beyond her front door.

Judy could not believe that she was being held prisoner in the middle of a city of eight million people. It was as if nobody thought she was still alive. Perhaps they didn't; the idea flipped her stomach. Perhaps Midas had changed their perception of her. Perhaps, like an unloved octogenarian, her bloated body would be found weeks after her death.

On Wednesday afternoon she had torn up a patch of carpet in the bathroom and removed a short section of plank that had been cut for easy access to the central heating duct. She had hammered on the copper water-pipes, praying that Ari might hear her on the floor below, but there had been no response. She found a gluey chocolate bar in her coat pocket and voraciously consumed it, smearing the sticky dark confectionery around her mouth. She lay staring at the wall and tried to think of a way out, but the heat distracted her.

'And what did you do today?' she asked herself aloud.

Yesterday, her fourth day sealed in the apartment, was the hottest yet. As the temperature crept up, sweat dripped from the nape of her neck, collected in the crooks of her elbows, the backs of her calves. Even the traffic in the street below seemed listless. The people who usually looked so busy and important were diminished by the smoggy haze that settled between the buildings. She was tired of being punished, being victimised without a way of fighting back. All those movies she had seen where feisty heroines stripped to singlets and squared off against their enemies were bullshit. Few of the women she knew had any way of matching a man for sheer vindictiveness.

And at night, all night, every night, the satyr sang his song. It pounded against the walls, rattled the crockery cabinets and shook the windows, a high, atonal wind instrument rising beside his voice – and nobody heard it but her. She lay on soaked sheets and held the pillows over her ears, but the sound seemed to come from somewhere deep inside her head.

On Friday morning she rose unrefreshed and switched on the TV. The weatherman promised that the summer's endless heatwave would result in a storm, then a talk show host encouraged a pregnant girl to fight with the father of her child before a cheering audience. Judy nervously followed her usual track around the apartment, trying to think of ideas and clutching at even the most foolish, running to the radio to catch a phone-in number before remembering that the phone would not work.

She carried out her daily inventory; she was out of soap, shampoo, washing powder and suddenly she was out of water. Turning on the tap produced a thin trickle, then nothing. Midas must have turned it off at the mains supply in the attic. She had drained the last of the half-can of flat Tizer she had been saving in the warm fridge. How long, she wondered, could a person survive without water? Three days, four, more, less?

She lay on the floor of the lounge, drained of energy, watching a simpering couple win a video recorder on a game show. The thought of giving in to Midas no longer occurred to her. She knew now that the apartment was to be her oubliette. She would die here in front of the white-trash talk shows, an unremembered martyr.

She should not have drunk the brackish water that had dropped from the icebox into a row of saucepans; it had made her throw up. But she had known there was worse to come. That afternoon she carefully scooped the last of the water from the toilet cistern into a saucepan, boiled it, then sealed it in a jug. Going to the bathroom wouldn't be a problem; there was nothing to eat. Her stomach growled constantly, but there was no pain. She reminded herself it was like going on a diet. But she knew it wasn't. It was dying by degrees. She felt herself slipping into a state of fugue, aided by the incessant drone of the television and the stifling heat of her cell. The door and windows remained unbudgeable. She lay on the sofa with her burning forehead pressed against the window as the tide of passers-by ebbed and flowed. She missed the outside world.

Soon day would fade to night and back to day. She could feel herself wasting away, stomach shrinking, tongue swelling, muscles atrophying, and she no longer cared.

The heated, hallucinatory hours crawled by. In a brief moment of lucidity she noticed the appalling state of the apartment. Empty food wrappers littered the lounge. One of the wastebags had split, a dark stinking residue leaking on to the kitchen floor. She no longer dozed, existing instead in a perpetual mental twilight as his delicate, persistent jungle sprouted around her; in her overheated mind, phosphorescent sprays of greenery sprang up to shield her body from the sun, the fragile tracery of ferns brushed her bare flesh. Bright insects buzzed around the engorged shoots that pulsed with rhythmic growth, rooting her into dank hot earth. More than anything, it was the suffocating heat that made her tear off her clothes with the little remaining strength she possessed, a humidity perfect for succumbing to an orgiastic pagan past.

And like a true pagan, she decided that she needed a phallic totem, a spear, something primitive to carry beside her.

In her weakened condition it took most of the afternoon to loosen and remove the wrought-iron embellishments from the coat-stand that stood beside the front door. By the time she had removed a four-foot, bevelled metal rod, it was nearly nightfall.

This was the time he came home, to rest before leaving for his club a few hours later. It was then that she called out to him. She had no need to summon loudly. A whisper would have done as well, providing it was done in good faith. She dragged herself back to the door and called softly once more, then held her breath and listened, knowing he would come.

She heard his boots scuffing together, just outside the sealed entrance to the apartment.

'Judy,' she heard him murmur, 'oh, Judy.' Behind her, one of the lounge windows gently slid down a few inches from its jammed position, and an eddy of cooler air twisted through the lounge.

With a gasp of relief she turned and presented her sweat-slick throat to the petrol-tainted breeze. 'Release me, Midas.'

The front door lock loosened and unclicked. The spell was waning with his arrival, and her acceptance.

And with her last ounce of strength she ran at the door, ramming the point of the stand through the thin plywood panel until it met with resistance. There was a shout on the other side as the rod passed into some kind of obstruction. She prayed it had struck a damaging blow to his stomach. But the iron shaft she retracted was not smeared with blood. The window slammed shut, and a moment later the door rebolted itself with a loud bang.

She was beset with a feeling of infinite loss as her freedom was snatched away. Once more she was a terrified animal trapped in the death-heat of the rainforest. The sudden exertion had been too much for her. The room shifted, the floor tilting above her. Then there was only the solace of oblivion.

CHAPTER FORTY-TWO

Disintegration

7:20 p.m. I adjusted my bow-tie, preparing to walk through the police cordon and up the red carpeted staircase to the cinema where the première of *Chemical Man* was being held. The crowds had gathered to see the stars of the film and other sundry celebrities attending the première. They had waited behind the grey metal barriers for hours in the dusty heat of Leicester Square, just to catch a glimpse of an eternally-youthful screen legend, the bare shoulders of an exotic child-woman alighting from a limousine, the wave of a golden LA teen idol, the sexy twinkle of a caring, muscular action hero, the scented smile of a glamorous Hollywood superstar.

What they saw alighting from the first car was a dwarfish man with an orange face and fat, grey sideburns poking from beneath his wig. This turned out to be the youthful screen legend. His heavy make-up gave him the skin-tone of a faulty Belisha beacon and ended just above his shirt collar, so that he looked like he had borrowed someone else's head for the evening. He appeared so much older and smaller than his screen image that for a moment I thought I was looking at his father, or even an uncle.

The exotic child-woman almost fell out of her limousine.

When the crowd cheered her she looked up at the sky in confusion, as if this auditory signal heralded the arrival of a rainstorm. The touchingly gamine appearance she affected on screen was translated in real life to a gawky anorexic colt-ishness so exaggerated by her knock-knees and bony elbows that she looked like a stack of chopsticks tied in satin.

The golden LA teen idol looked ill. His lustrous skin had been dulled by his prodigious drug intake. His eyes had dropped in their sockets, the skin beneath them yellowing to the colour and texture of a very old library book, the cheeks caving in, the lips drawn tight. He was wearing an eighteen-thousand dollar suit that helped to distract public attention from his ravaged appearance, but still headed in the wrong direction when he alighted from his car, and had to be turned around by his manager, like a battery-operated toy.

The caring, muscular action hero fulfilled everyone's expectations as he unfurled himself from his limo to pump and preen for the cameras, then spoiled the moment by attempting to make an impromptu speech about supporting French nuclear protests. This, in retrospect, was a short-sighted move on behalf of the action star, who failed to recall the fact that the French Ministry of Defence had graciously lent the film their state-of-the-art military hardware. When he was reminded of this fact at the party afterwards, he fired his PR team.

The glamorous Hollywood superstar failed to turn up. This was her fourth no-show to the British première of one of her films, and she still received hopeful invites.

The cast of *EastEnders* put in an appearance, but then they always did. Most of them were prepared to attend the opening of a biscuit tin.

The film world had been hard-hit by the loss of Princess

Diana. Of all the royals, she had succeeded in attracting attention, in the form of heavy donations, to a large number of trusts and charities connected with British film premières. Without her there was no one modern enough or glamorous enough to draw crowds and open wallets. Tonight Princess Anne was gamely having a stab at it, and the foyer of the Odeon was filled with hangers-on.

I joined up with a dozen familiar faces as I reached the red carpet. People I barely knew touched me on the shoulder as I passed. The change in their behaviour towards me, brought about by some exciting rumours and a handful of paragraphs in the industry trades, was phenomenal.

The audience fidgeted in hushed expectation while it waited for Princess Anne to stop asking the manager of the Odeon if he had far to come to work, then she arrived inside the auditorium and they all stood up and craned around for a glimpse of her, then she sat, then they sat, then the Dagenham Girl Pipers filed off, then the stars of the film came on to tell everyone how thrilled they were about all sorts of things, then they tried to leave by the wrong side of the stage, then the film began. As soon as the credits were over I headed for the toilet, sneaking out through a side exit before anyone saw me. I had no desire to stay and see the film, the script of which consisted of six fights, one sex scene, two plane crashes, a runaway train and a speedboat chase joined together with smutty puns.

Back at the office I resisted the temptation to head straight for the basement and tend to my poor Miranda. To tell the truth, I was starting to feel very strange indeed. I caught sight of myself in the mirror, and the vision caused me to draw a sharp breath. The baking night had begun to affect my corporeal condition even more seriously than I had expected.

My epidermis felt as though it was separating from my body. I smelled bad. Something deep inside me was turning rotten. In the bathroom I carefully washed, soaked my skin in moisturiser, then doused myself with expensive cologne. I pulled a comb through my hair and found that much of it was loose. Untangling a knot, I very nearly pulled my entire scalp from my skull. I could feel it lifting from the bone like old lino. I felt as though I was being held together with bits of string, that any minute I might fly apart and dissolve in a putrefying mass of bones, guts, bad meat and marrow jelly.

My mouth was so dry that I drank a litre bottle of Evian in front of the toilet, allowing the liquid to sluice straight through my body and out into the bowl. Actually, I doubted I would have been able to keep it in any more. My muscles had weakened considerably in the last few hours.

There was something wrong with the skin below my ears. It had dried out in tight skeins, and indents had developed along my neck. My blood had coagulated, and my arteries were collapsing. The insides of my wrists were undergoing the same change. There was nothing I could do to disguise this effect. I was able to control the bloating of my green-tinged stomach simply by pushing down hard and forcing the bacteria-laden air out of my body, although the noxious smell and the bizarre noise it created were spectacularly revolting. I felt myself growing lighter as my remaining body fluids evaporated.

More worrying was the fact that something was moving about inside my chest. It felt like termites, tickling and prickling as they scurried back and forth beneath my skin. I dreaded to think about the microscopic creatures that might be breeding in there.

I found some make-up in one of the secretaries' desks, and

carefully applied it to the blotchy patches that had appeared on my cheeks. Then I lacquered my fragile hair into place with an entire aerosol can of Sunsilk Superhold and, emboldened, even applied some colour to my corpse-pale lips.

By the time I had finished I felt sure that I looked pretty good in the soft evening light, and could probably pass for normal even under bright electric light.

Of course, I was too close to see how I really looked to others. Like a cross between Ronald McDonald and Barbara Cartland, probably. Throwing myself one last bravado-inducing smile in the mirror, I checked my watch and went back to work. There was still an hour before the film turned out, and I had one final task to perform.

As I seated myself at my desk, I felt something tear. I pushed back my seat and rose, examining my trousers. It felt as if something had given way beneath the fabric. I loosened my belt and lowered the legs to the knee. The skin on my right thigh had developed a horrible transverse split. The dry crimson musculature of my leg was showing through the rupture.

Gingerly, I felt around the side of my thigh and gently pushed the taut skin. It tore again, developing a further split at the back of my knee. If the lesion completed its route around my thigh, I imagined that the derma would drape down like a baggy stocking. I grabbed a roll of Sellotape from my desk and attached the loose end to my leg. Carefully pulling the edges of the split together as much as I dared, I wound the tape around my leg until I had finished the entire roll.

With the problem temporarily alleviated, I rebuckled my trousers and began to draw up my last will and testament.

CHAPTER FORTY-THREE

Doomsday Scenario

It had gone six o'clock on a hot Friday night. In the ratty little office of International Film Investments, that was usually a cue for Waldorf to go over to the Coach and Horses and bring back two pints of lager. Glory never drank before a show. Afterwards she hammered the scotch, as though the performance drained something out of her that only strong liquor could replace. Tonight was different. One Eighty was in a filthy mood because Tyler had clearly welshed on his debt, and was slamming around as he closed up for the night, swearing under his breath. Also, he had started smoking again, and hated himself for it. He abhorred weakness, especially in himself.

Glory couldn't settle. She shifted from one worn armchair to another, pulling at the neck of her T-shirt, unable to catch her breath. She barely spoke, and looked malevolent. That was a bad sign for everyone. When she was in a mood like this the only way she could calm down was by going over the road to the tattoo parlour and having something pierced.

It was up to Waldorf to do something. He decided to ring Midas for advice, but the boss was short-tempered too, and seemed so preoccupied that it was impossible to get any sense from him. The endless heat was annoying them all.

'There's no point in getting so angry,' said Waldorf. 'We know where Tyler works. We'll go and see him first thing Monday. Take him up to the roof, beat the shit out of him, then push him off it. Will that make you happy?'

One Eighty lit a fresh Marlboro from the stub of the last one. 'No, it bloody won't.'

Waldorf knew what was really wrong, and it had nothing to do with Tyler's non-appearance. The fallout from Malcolm Cotton's death had hung over them like a pall of crematorium smoke all week. Beneath his bravado, One Eighty was disturbed. The police presence in the neighbourhood – usually low to non-existent – had suddenly jumped, so they were obviously on to something. There were three more sacks in the van awaiting disposal, which would mean another trip out to their favourite spot by the river at two in the morning, and Midas would continue being shitty to everyone until the rest of the bottles turned up. What a fucking mess.

One Eighty had hoped that Glory would be able to sort it out for them, as she had so often done in the past, but even she seemed unable or unwilling to act.

'Glory, I've been meaning to ask you,' he said with forced cheeriness, 'that thing Midas does, the clouding thing, you can do it too, can't you?' Waldorf shot him a warning look. She turned to study him as slyly as an alligator measuring up a meal.

'It's a mind trick. You wouldn't understand.' She smiled bleakly. 'I could do it to you if you want.'

'Well, I think we'd better be off.' Waldorf rose and turned off the company's only computer, which was largely there for show, anyway. 'At least let's go and have a beer. Glory, you coming?'

She shot him a look like a knife-thrower taking aim at an unfaithful lover.

Waldorf threw up his hands. 'Fine, I guess it's down to me to do something. I know we all have a bad feeling about this but we can't just sit around waiting for the situation to solve itself.'

One Eighty had a coughing fit and thumped himself on the chest. 'What are you planning to do?'

'I don't know yet,' Waldorf admitted, 'but it'll involve random acts of violence, some running and screaming, and a fair amount of bloodshed. Then, if we can get everything back under control before the night's out, maybe *she* can get a good night's sleep again and we can all stop worrying.' He threw Glory's furious stare back at her and slammed out of the office.

By 7:15 p.m. Lucas was well and truly pissed off.

It was his twenty-first birthday today and no one – *no one* – had remembered. His mother had called him this morning, but for fuck's sake you expected that. At work, everyone had been running around in such a panic he thought the company was going bankrupt or something, but it turned out the reverse was happening. They were going into production, no longer just discussing it but actually doing it, gearing up to shoot a feature film. Everyone was talking about Berry Elliot's partner, Tyler, and the great deal he had put together. Nobody had seen Berry for a couple of days and there were conflicting stories about where he was, somebody said the Maldives, which was weird because he never went anywhere. Nobody had time to talk to Lucas because he didn't matter, he was just a runner to be ordered about and shouted at, but if they took the time and trouble to talk to him for just five minutes they would discover that he had talents that could help them.

And now, even Malcolm Cotton had not turned up. Lucas had arranged to meet him for a drink in the Admiral Duncan, a mental-looking gay pub with purple and gold walls that made a change from the aggressively straight bars around Soho where blokes would happily start trouble with you for glancing at the wall behind their girlfriend. At least gay blokes smiled and nodded as if you were a mate, there were no punch-ups and the barmen were too ditzy to short-change you.

He had not known Cotton long, and probably would not have bothered to maintain the friendship if Malcolm didn't throw his money about so wildly. The boy was always flush, chucking cash at waitresses and buying all the rounds. Lucas found it easy to listen to his wilder theories about the flora and fauna of Australia while he was being plied with expensive drinks. He had told Cotton at the outset: listen, he'd explained, I'm straight, but if you don't have a problem with that we can be friends, can't we? And Cotton had laughed and said of course, you're not at all my type anyway, and Lucas had actually felt a bit rejected, which was deeply weird.

And now they were supposed to have their usual Friday night piss-up together but the bastard had failed to show, even though he had promised to turn up. Lucas dug into his rucksack and his fingers closed around the small plastic bottles Cotton had given him. He wondered what he should do with them. There was something unreliable about Malcolm. He spent too much of his time locked in his apartment experimenting with drugs; not taking them himself, he insisted, but trying to invent something that would sell and make his name around Soho.

What he really wanted to do next was make a movie, and everyone knew that these days the drugs scene and the film industry were in each other's pockets. Get to know the right people in one, and you automatically had a connection with the other. It all sounded very dodgy. Maybe the police had got him. Either way, it made no difference. It just meant that Lucas was stuck here by himself once more, alone in the most crowded part of one of the most crowded cities on earth. Man, it was embarrassing to be this unpopular.

Perhaps it's me who's vanished, he thought, finishing his pint. Perhaps I've become so insignificant among all these people rushing about their lives that I've actually become invisible, and can walk through things and shout without anybody hearing a word I say. So I can do whatever I like, because no one will take any notice of me anyway. Maybe Soho has broken away from the rational world and is spinning out into space, maybe if I go to the corner of Regent Street all I'll be able to see is the whistling black void of eternity. There's a screenplay in that somewhere.

Allowing the thought to console him, he ordered another beer.

At 8:57 p.m. Arthur Bryant tried the intercom again, but it released a howl of static until he removed his finger from the button. His partner stepped back and looked up at the building. 'Do you know which floor he's on?'

'The top. End flat. There's no lift.'

'Come on. The walk will do you good.' They followed a small Asian woman laden with plastic shopping bags into the block, and swallowed back the pervasive reek of disinfectant. The flats presented a daunting exterior, but were pleasanter inside. Recently sold off by Tower Hamlets council, they overlooked the East End's Columbia Road, whose crowded Sunday flower market ensured that every resident of the area could afford to display all manner of lurid blooms in their front windows.

The block's top-floor balcony was a broad, windswept platform of tile and concrete – or rather, it would have been had each resident not created a front garden by constructing fences from their section of front wall to the balcony. As this was a public thoroughfare, every extension had to be fitted with a latched door, so that the detectives had to pass through half a dozen strange private garden-worlds before they reached Andrew Brockenhurst's flat.

'What an extraordinary place,' said May. 'I've never seen so many fake wishing wells and garden gnomes. What's Brockenhurst like?'

'I've only met him once but he seemed a good chap,' replied Bryant, pulling his scarf tighter. 'One of the country's top graded biochemists, had a marvellous career ahead of him but couldn't take the stress. Complete mental breakdown at the age of thirty-three, never fully recovered, lost his MoD security status, took up a consultancy position, now writes for technical publications. I don't understand why we push our best men so hard.' He knocked on the door and stepped back. 'Oh, one other thing,' he whispered, 'don't be surprised if his behaviour is a little – unusual.'

May was used to his partner's colleagues acting strangely. Oh, they appeared normal enough at first but quickly betrayed themselves by becoming too enthusiastic for their specialist subjects, and before you knew it they were conversing with the dead, producing stigmata, arguing with Elvis and summoning Egyptian spirit guides. He'd had trouble sleeping after meeting that creepy woman who brought cats back to life.

So it was a pleasant surprise when the door was opened by a very ordinary-looking middle-aged lady in a blue blouse covered in cornflowers, an apron and fluffy pink slippers. She smiled and stepped back. 'Right on time. Please go through to the lounge, Mr Bryant. He's expecting you.'

May followed his partner into the flat, past china poodles and photographs of grandchildren. A delicious smell of baking scones wafted through from the kitchen. The lady of the house ushered them to a sofa.

'So, how are things?' asked Bryant cheerfully. 'Oh, I'm sorry. Daphne, this is my partner, John May.'

'Pleased to meet you, Mr May. Any friend of Arthur's, as they say. Andy will be down in a minute. Can I get you a cup of tea?'

'That would be nice. Thank you.' May smiled, and Daphne slip-slapped off to the kitchen. He turned to Bryant, and caught the edge of a mischievous grin on his partner's face. 'I don't get it,' he whispered. 'She said her husband would be down in a minute.'

'Yes. He will be.'

'This is the top floor, Arthur. They haven't got an upstairs.'

'Oh, you'll see.' Bryant was barely concealing his amusement, proof that there was something definitely odd going on.

They sat and waited. No sound came from the kitchen. 'I can't hear Mrs Brockenhurst making tea,' whispered May.

'I don't suppose she is,' Bryant replied mysteriously.

They waited some more. Finally they heard someone in the hall.

'Oh, there you are!' boomed a deep voice. 'Good to see you again!' A man strode into the room and shook their hands violently. 'Andrew Brockenhurst. Please call me Andy.'

May stared. He was looking at the same person who had gone out minutes earlier. 'Mrs Brockenhurst' had removed his wig, combed his hair and changed into men's overalls and workboots, but was still wearing make-up and lipstick. Bryant caught his partner's astonishment and his grin broadened.

'Did Daphne offer you tea?'

'Yes, she was the perfect hostess.'

'Oh, good. I've had a chance to look at your evidence, Arthur, and I think I have something for you. Let me just chase up your refreshments.' He rose abruptly and left the room.

'Oh, for God's sake,' complained May, 'he's not quick-changing again, is he? It feels like I've wandered into a touring production of *Charley's Aunt.*'

'No, he'll bring the tea in himself,' said Bryant. 'His "wife" won't put in an appearance until we leave.'

'And we have to go along with this, do we?'

'When Andrew's real wife died after a long illness, he just adopted her role. It seemed the most natural thing for him to do. He's not harming anyone.'

'They must have fun going to the shops together.'

'Here we are.' Andrew laid out cups and biscuits with unnecessary precision.

'I asked Sunshine Day to call you,' said Bryant, pouring milk into his cup.

'I talked to her earlier today. She's very bright, isn't she? No pun intended. It's a pity she's under detention. I'm sure you could use someone with her talents in the division. What do you know about the properties of narcotics?'

'It depends on which of them you're talking about,' answered May.

'The most powerful ones of all are distilled from the world's natural flora. They can be augmented with synthetic combinations, of course, but the core illegal manufacturers aim for purity because they know the product will be radically diluted between the factory and the street.' In command of his subject Brockenhurst was all business, but the lip-gloss was hard to overlook. 'Purity means a good refinement system, although anyone can lay their hands on filtration equipment. More importantly, it requires a plentiful source, and access to it.

'You specifically asked me if it would be possible to distil a drug component from an unusual source – namely, butter-flies. The request intrigued me because I immediately thought about the narcotic properties of nectars and pollens. I tried all the major pharmacological listings for the areas you specified, namely the Antipodes and surrounding northerly islands, but I didn't come up with much, certainly nothing that would crop up in the feeding cycle of lepidoptera. The butterfly part misled me because I imagined them feeding from biologically mutated flora and manufacturing some obscure narcotic. Then I thought about earlier life stages, pupa to caterpillar, and remembered this.' He opened the heavy book that lay on the coffee-table between them, and turned to a page he had marked with a Post-It note.

'The Trough Caterpillar. It's a rare Australian caterpillar that operates in an extraordinary fashion. It's found in remote, inhospitable areas of the Northern provinces, and feeds on a very particular species of plant. Problem is, the area where the plant grows is the home ground of a voracious breed of soldier ant. Their bite is poisonous, and they kill and devour the caterpillars whenever they get the chance. So, as it tends to do in these situations, nature has evolved a unique system of symbiosis deal to with the problem. The caterpillar has developed a trough on its back, into which its glands secrete a kind of nectar. It's a very powerful narcotic, and the first couple of ants that try to attack the caterpillar are drawn to it. Once they drink from the trough they're hooked for life. They enter a fugue state and stay with the caterpillar, living on its back. They fight off any others of their own species that attempt to board. Usually two are enough. And the caterpillar is able to continue up to its plant, where it can find the succulent leaves required by its diet. The ants stay on the caterpillar's back right up until they die. The aborigines know of the drug and use it to induce trance-states. It's a very pure high, with no known ill-effects, but there's one obvious drawback. Its high level of addiction.'

'And you think this is the stuff that Cotton put on the street?'

'Obviously you'll have to run some tests, but I can show you what to look for.'

'I don't understand,' said May. 'If it's a pure high, why are buyers suffering psychotic episodes?'

'Could be for any number of reasons,' said Brockenhurst. 'The most likely explanation is that the small supply Cotton has managed to bring into London has become contaminated by man-made chemicals. The French have been conducting toxic gas tests in the region for some years. Pollutants are mutating within the cell-structures of the area's indigenous life-forms for the first time. The only reason I know about this creature is because it's on the endangered species list. It's certainly not the only drug-producer of its kind, but there's only one similar natural euphoric I can think of, and that comes from a beetle native to Western Africa. It lives in the roots of the Akee, *Blighia sapida,* a plant that is filled with a poison called ligustrin. Its food-chain became contaminated with man-made chemicals used by local farmers as a defoliant, and it started to spread viral infections from ingestion. It transmitted a kind of motor-neuron disease via any liquid that came into contact with the victim's body apertures. In that case the symptoms were extraordinary.'

'What were the symptoms?'

'At first – extreme euphoria, then dizziness, increased heart rate, erratic pulse, hypertension, blood-tinged diarrhoea, dilated pupils, respiratory difficulty, hallucinations, increasingly aberrant behaviour, murderous anger, tachycardia, oliguria, kidney failure, anuria, insanity, paralysis, cytotoxicity, eventual death from ventricular fibrillation.'

'Let's hope we haven't got something like that on our hands,' said Bryant. 'On a hot summer's night in Soho, who can spot the difference between extreme euphoria and ordinary high spirits? How do you tell the revellers from the victims? And if it could be borne in solution like bilharzia, how would you stop it from eventually entering the water supply?'

'Good question, that. A classic doomsday scenario,' Brockenhurst said, nodding agreeably and helping himself to a chocolate biscuit. 'Though in your case it's clear that not all of the users are suffering psychotic episodes.'

'Which brings us back to the question; why are only some users affected?'

'From the reports your department have made available to me, they appear to exhibit the classic symptoms of overdose. If more than a small amount is used, it undoubtedly becomes lethal. It's possible your distributor underestimated its properties in solution. It's not diluting down as quickly as his calculations predicted. Perhaps he was a better chemist than he was a mathematician. Also, it may have different effects depending on its use in combination with various street drugs. If it did carry through to water-borne infection, it would eventually dilute itself out of the system.' He gave a grim smile. 'But by God, you'd see some fireworks before it did.'

CHAPTER FORTY-FOUR

Stressed

With my will dated and signed but not yet notarised, I finally went downstairs and re-entered the viewing theatre. It was now a little after ten. I shone the torch across the seats at Miranda and saw her flinch. Still no sign of Berry.

I knelt in front of her and slowly removed the tape from her mouth. She could scream all she liked here and no one would hear her. Everyone had left the building and besides, theatres like this were fully soundproofed. But she did not scream. She stared at me in an angry haze, blinking away the bright torchlight that illuminated the musty air between us.

'We have to talk, Miranda,' I said, watching her carefully. 'First of all you must understand that I'm not going to hurt you. God, I'd never do anything to hurt you, but we have to talk.'

'So you keep saying,' she replied hoarsely. 'Give me some water, damn you.'

I found the bottle and refixed the straw for her. After she had drunk, I set it aside and placed my hands on her knees. I felt her try to move them away, recoiling disgustedly from my touch. Not a good start to our negotiations.

'Miranda, this is about our future together, about us and

Gregory. You know I still love you and I'd do anything for you.'

'You've a fucking funny way of showing it,' she croaked. 'How could you do this? You can't run around abducting people. Christ, cut my arms free at least. My hands went numb hours ago.'

'I can't just yet. I have to explain.' I pressed my knuckles against the side of my head. It was so hard to think clearly. How could I tell her that I was dead? There was nothing for it but to give her the facts, keeping everything clear and simple. I spoke softly for a while, modifying my tone in a rational and friendly cadence, then paused to see how she would react. For a minute only our breathing sounded in the damp theatre. While I waited for her response, I picked apart the tape that held her left wrist.

'Look, Richard,' she said finally. 'We can get you professional help. This can all be explained. You're not dead, you're having a spectacular nervous breakdown of some kind.' Her speech was too measured and wary to evince genuine concern. 'You hear about it all the time, people in stressful jobs. You've been working too hard, you've had too much to worry about, and I don't suppose I've helped matters much. I know how upset you were by Paul's death. But it can all be fixed, I promise you.'

She was lying. I knew her too well. She didn't believe a word I had told her. Nothing she said rang true, no matter how reassuring she tried to sound.

'Tell me, can you fix this?' I asked, and tore open the front of my shirt, revealing the pustular grey skin that writhed beneath my torchlight. 'Can you stop the maggots from breeding in my guts?'

I pinched my arm just below the scaly elbow and picked

off a flake of dried flesh the size of a fifty-pence piece, as hard and dry as a toenail. 'Can you stop my skin from cracking off? Can you stop my teeth from dropping out of my head?' I pushed my hand into my mouth and gripped one of my eye-teeth, easily twisting it out of the rotting gum. The entire root came with it, and the rancid stench it released was so repulsive that I hammered the tooth back in place with my fist.

'Or how about this cute trick?' I shouted.

I tilted my head close over hers and stuck my fingertips hard into the socket of my right eye, allowing the dry ball to drop forward into my hand like a marble. 'Do you think that's caused by stress, you deceitful two-timing self-absorbed media-slut?' I bellowed, losing control. 'By God, I'll show you how the dead take revenge.' The handful of hair she grabbed for as I confronted her came out of my scalp by its dead roots, ripping away a patch of skin that revealed the ivory dome of my skull, but I could not be stopped now.

Her screams were absorbed by walls that had heard ten thousand dramatic scenes from thirty years of lousy motion pictures.

CHAPTER FORTY-FIVE

Corporate Entertainment

In order to escape ancient prohibitive building laws, many houses in Soho – and indeed the whole of London – had built upwards over the centuries and dug down into the earth, creating polyfenestral attic rooms and dank, labyrinthine basements. There was hardly a single old building in the area that resembled its original plans, if indeed there had been any to begin with.

The Hot House was part of a sprawling underground complex beneath Greek Street. Its entrance was through the lower-ground floor of a popular French restaurant that had illegally expanded its dining-room across a mutually shared passageway. No signs promoted the club, and no board announced its bill of fare, but excellent word of mouth ensured that a stream of wealthy punters arrived throughout the night.

John May flicked his identification at the doorman and made his way through to the bar lounge. In recent years, Soho's few remaining strip-clubs had gained the cachet of respectability, legitimised by their place in the district's bawdy history. The decor reflected this new popularity, and the bar had been fitted with retro-fifties stage lights and red leather seating. An angular chromium bar and restaurant filled the rear half of the auditorium. May was surprised to see a number of attractive women in the audience.

Just before eleven-thirty, an announcer introduced the main attraction of the night. 'And now, ladies and gentlemen, for your delectation and delight, the Hot House presents the living embodiment of London, the Spirit of Soho herself.' The applause began before he had finished. 'The one and only – Glory.'

A peal of Big Ben's chimes rang out on the tape, fading through to a hard Britpop beat as on to the stage stepped an extraordinary woman, masked to the chin, chained at the wrist and dressed from throat to ankle in sparkling black nylon. She reminded May of Hollar's 1643 etching of *Winter*, in which that season appeared as a lady in exotic black garb, walking in smoky Cornhill. Glory's representation was sexed up and modernised, of course, but the resemblance was clearly quite deliberate. From the moment she strolled on to the stage, Glory owned the audience. She led with her pelvis and dragged her dainty feet, satirising the movement of a twenties' vamp, throwing the audience a lascivious kiss. She was the kind of woman who could turn a man back into a little boy. She snapped apart her steel cuffs and removed her mask to reveal glittering silver nose and lip rings, then strutted to the front of the stage, analysing the audience to see how far she would take her show tonight. She looked very dangerous, but it was a danger that most men here would consider worth risking.

May attracted the barman's attention. One Eighty had seen May enter the lounge and had taken him for another elderly punter, but when the police credentials came out he quickly adopted a more deferential manner. He led the detective to a quiet horseshoe seat at the rear of the room and offered him a drink. Unusually, his offer was accepted. May was tired, parched and overheated. The club was air-conditioned but the management never turned it very high; more refreshments were sold that way, and the hefty mark-up on soft drinks made them more profitable than champagne. One Eighty introduced himself, reluctantly using his real name, which was Marcus Sherbourne. Nicknames were too revealing to the police.

'It's an interesting show.' May indicated the stage.

'There's no one else to touch her,' said One Eighty proudly. 'Glory is our resident *femme fatale*. She makes the punters fall in love with her, then scares them half to death by taking their offers seriously.'

'And that's all part of the act?'

'I wouldn't call it an act. She is what you see. Let's just say, like the rest of us she has a personal agenda. A woman like her can get a man into some heavy trouble. But that's some-thing the management has a responsibility to deal with. What can we do for you?'

'I'd like to have a friendly chat with your manager. Is he available?'

One Eighty was respectful of the Soho police. They worked long and hard through the Bacchanalian summer nights, resolving arguments, calming tempers, separating pugilists. On the other hand, Midas Blake had been uncom-fortably awaiting the arrival of the law all week. The barman could not decide whether to lie, then, realising that he had tipped his hand, agreed to go and look.

'Tell him it's about Malcolm Cotton,' May called in his friendliest manner. His instincts told him that there was no point in mentioning Gossage, the boy from the Nelly Dean. If the owner recognised the name of the source, they had something to talk about.

The tall, tanned man who approached the table a few minutes later wore a black silk shirt and a smart black Armani suit. His eyes were lined with kohl, and his blond hair reached an unshaven square jaw that accentuated a jagged scar on his chin. His appearance was both innocent and threatening, like a damaged god. It was a studied look designed to attract women and perturb men. He towered above the table and offered a broad hand.

'I'm Midas Blake,' he said amiably. 'How can I help you?' He seated himself opposite May.

May explained the situation. 'I understand that the chemical enhancer currently entering circulation is known as Imago,' he concluded. 'Perhaps you'd like to tell me your side of the story.'

'I'll be happy to do so, Mr May,' said Midas, sitting back to allow the waitress to settle their drinks, lager for the policeman, a grappa for himself, 'but before you paint me as a villain, let me tell you a little about how my club runs.' He raised his hand and waved it expansively around the room. 'This place – or rather, the establishment that had made this building its home since the war – used to have a terrible reputation. The Golden Girl Club was a hangout for thieves and whores. The men and women who drank here were among those responsible for Soho's bad reputation. But times change; the days when you could sell diluted alcohol at inflated prices and tickets from street doorways to clubs that didn't exist are gone. Soho has become legitimate. It only trades on its past for nostalgia value. When the imported water you stock makes more profit than the watered beer you used to sell, why bother breaking the law?' He raised his grappa glass in a toast before sipping and replacing it on a coaster. 'This isn't your usual jurisdiction, is it?'

'Not any more,' explained May. 'Many years ago I used to spend my nights on the beat around these streets, a mere footsoldier. It was very rough in those days. We had a lot of slashings, faces with razors. You don't get that any more.'

'I wonder why not.'

'The gang rivalries disappeared when the old families moved out. People are less protective of their turf these days. And plastic surgery is affordable enough to make scarring pointless. But I imagine this was all long before your time.'

'Don't count on it. I'm a lot older than I look.' His lips parted to reveal a white wall, too perfect to be natural. The smile fanned fine lines around his eyes. 'I thought I'd seen your face before. Remember how the local coppers used to behave around here, acting like little gods, pulling a few hundred a week from every club and bar because they all knew we were bending the by-laws?'

'Ah, the bad old days.'

'It took us a long time to realise that if we behaved and followed the letter of the law, we wouldn't have to pay protection. We could afford to mount decent shows, pull in the big money. In the seventies nobody would dream of coming to a club like this and charging it on a credit card.'

'Well, there weren't that many credit cards around.'

'It wasn't that. You couldn't put in an expenses claim for something that was considered disreputable. This was a cash industry. Now we operate on nothing but plastic. We're not notorious any more. We're fashionable. And if the girls take their clothes off, why, that's ironic, a postmodern take on fifties frolics. I preside on the business board that provides Soho with adult entertainment. We own smart, bright strip-clubs like this, some expensive blonde-wood-and-pastel-wall gay bars, and controlling interests in several chic restaurants, all of them clean and modern and making a fortune. My colleagues and I can provide you with the perfect New Labour-voting, art-loving, easy-listening, Conran-dining, mood-enhancing corporate night out.'

'But how do you keep it like that, Mr Blake? Do you constantly test the water, discuss with your board how best to ride the zeitgeist into the next trend? Or are you simply lucky? That's what interests me.'

Midas smiled and sat back, reassessing his guest. Something told him he could afford to take a gamble with the detective and speak with relative honesty. 'Well, Mr May,' he explained, 'my places stay fashionable because I keep out the trash, and that means removing undesirable elements, and *that* means controlling the drug scene. Which is not as easy as it sounds. Keeping drugs out means becoming actively involved. We're club-owners, not a crime force. Besides, if you become too vocal with the dealers you attract the attention of the wrong people, and you end up getting hurt. You say the old gangs have gone, but I'm sure you're aware that there are Russians here now, and they don't fuck about. The owner of the Seventy Two club in Kingly Street had his head cut off and left on the back of a milk float. I don't need to tell you how many people have died in fires around here over the last few years. As a businessman, you have to make your position clear from the outset and try to contain the situation. Like every other major international city, London is awash with drugs. Most of its paper currency – '

'Has cocaine residue on it, I know. So what do you do when things go wrong? I assume they occasionally do go wrong?'

'What can you do, Mr May?' He turned his palms face up. 'You clear up the mess and sweep it out of sight. Issue a clear warning. Try to stop it from happening again.' Midas was glib, but what he was saying made sense. May sipped his whisky and sat back. 'Tell me about your staff,' he said. 'Not the regular employees. The ones you trust with your life.' May knew that around here no one could afford to operate alone.

'Listen, I've got no secrets. I employ two special gentlemen. One of them is the big guy behind the bar. The other is out on business at the moment. When they're not working at one of our clubs, they undertake various housekeeping duties.'

'What do those duties entail exactly? How far would you ask them to go?'

'That's hard for me to say.'

May and Blake understood each other perfectly. There was a line here that was inadvisable for either of them to cross. As the detective did not reply, Blake finally broke the stalemate. 'Until recently, policing our own property was a pretty straightforward job. The drug territories were kept separate. You know what it's like around here, Mr May. The film mob got their gear from the runners in Dean Street, the indie TV companies got theirs from Brewer Street, the music people have clubs off Tottenham Court Road, the big orders get biked to hotels and corporate-lunch restaurants and the loose stuff on the ground goes to spendy punters looking for parties. The dealers aren't going around playgrounds trying to hook schoolkids, they're producers buying and selling a little for their friends. Why else do you think anyone talks to them? The users aren't *Trainspotting* clones, they're high-salaried execs using drugs to reach that little extra energy they need when they're working late.'

May sighed. 'The world is getting faster.'

'You'd better believe it, Mr May. Cheap computers, mobile phones, instant communications. Industry around here used to stop at night. If you were a designer, your typesetter went home at six. If you were a producer, your film footage had to make the night-bath to be developed. Computers invented the twenty-four-hour day. So editors work all night and restaurants stay open to accommodate them, and suddenly there's no such thing as nine to five. With this software you can do the work in half the time, says the computer salesman. That means we can take on twice as much work, says the boss. Overnight, the media world doubles its speed. What do you think gives everyone the fuel to stay awake through one more deadline? When does a drug stop being a menace and start becoming a productive part of the system?'

'But Imago wasn't included in the package.'

'Not until now. Everything was fine until about a couple of weeks ago, when my boys found someone throwing up in the toilet after smoking a joint. They asked him what he'd taken and he produced some weird shit in a little plastic yoghurt bottle. None of us had seen it before. Over the next few days it started turning up more frequently. Word was it was something new, and everyone seemed to know who the supplier was. In fact, this kid was going around telling everyone where to get it, trying to build himself a reputation.'

'Well, he succeeded, although not in the way he imagined. Malcolm Cotton was found dead in a tube station five days ago.'

'Now, that is a shame.' Midas's cool stare never wavered for an instant or betrayed a flicker of surprise. 'Perhaps you'd like another drink, Mr May?'

'Why not, Mr Blake? It's getting late. I can afford to relax a little. Tell me about the boy in the Nelly Dean. The one you saw being sold one of the bottles.'

As they talked, Glory strode bare-breasted across the stage and glared furiously at the men in the audience, most of whom shifted in their seats with uncomfortable excitement. The atmosphere of anticipation was electric.

Spectral, scratchy music began, a twenties dance-band filtered through an electronic mix. A dazzling spotlight shone as Glory raised her iridescent wings, and the club's occupants fell victim to their nightly nyctalopia.

CHAPTER FORTY-SIX

Martyrdom

I. Simply. Wasn't. Getting. Through. To. Her.

'You must understand what I'm trying to create,' I tried to explain one more time, 'I have left everything to you and Gregory. I've worked it all out. The moment I die, you will start to become rich.'

I calmed down a little now. I needed to obtain her full appreciation of the situation. I gripped her thin wrists, trying to get her to look up, but she kept her face lowered and turned aside from mine, frightened to look at me.

'I thought you just told me you were already dead.'

'Yes, I am – technically – but it won't look like I'm dead until all my bodily functions cease. I don't know how long this conscious state will remain, but I don't want to wait around and watch the disintegration occur before my eyes. I'm already coming apart at the seams, Miranda. I must choose when to die in the eyes of the world, so what I propose to do is this.' My fingers pinched her chin and tried to raise it, but she pulled away once more. 'I am going to "kill" myself. Tomorrow morning I will go down to the underground and, oh, pretend to slip from the platform or something, and fall under an arriving train. I no longer have any sense of pain, so you needn't worry about me feeling anything, I'll just make sure that my skull goes right under the wheels, and I'll cease to be. My death will be ruled accidental, and you'll get everything. All the insurance money, the territory sales, the box office profits, the merchandising tie-ins, the video rental and sell-through deals, the terrestrial TV and cable percentages, the sequel rights. The films will continue on into production without me, but none of them will be able to proceed without following the ground rules laid down in my documentation, I've made sure of that. And you'll be able to take care of Gregory properly, get him out of that dreadful clinic and care for him at home, really be a mother to him –'

'Christ, will you stop this?' Miranda screamed suddenly. 'You realise you've gone completely mad, you've nothing left for yourself, so you've thrown all your hopes into something completely impossible. All this trying to make things work for the best, it's ridiculous. Don't you see? There is no hope, and even now you can't face that fact!'

'Of course there's hope,' I said, wounded. 'I know in my heart you love me, just as much as you love Greg –'

'I don't love Greg!' she yelled at me, still avoiding my eyes, 'I never loved him! How could I? I wanted a normal child but I was cheated. I was given that sad little thing that wailed and thrashed and couldn't tell if he even had a mother.'

'Of course he can tell, you've seen him –'

'I've seen him react to a basic stimulus in the same way that a dog reacts to the mention of dinner. He can't tell when there's someone in the room. He doesn't know if it's night or day. He doesn't even understand that you love him. All he can feel is whether he's wet or hungry. I wished I could have cared more but I couldn't. I used to lay there next to the pair of you, fighting to find something inside me, some spark I could nurture, but there was *nothing*. I wish he'd been born to some other woman, someone brave enough to give up her own happiness for him. Why should an accident of fate turn me into a martyr? I know it sounds awful but I don't want to waste my life looking after a child that can't show the simplest signs of being alive.'

'You're wrong. He knows I love him.' I sat back, aghast. If my tear ducts had still been functioning, I would have cried. 'Let me ask you this,' I shouted at her. 'What was it all for? What was the point of me working so hard, trying to become someone?'

'I thought you were doing it for yourself,' she replied blankly.

'I was doing it for you and him.'

'Then you shouldn't have bothered.'

'Without me you'll have nothing,' I threatened. 'I'll put it all in Gregory's name, not yours. Then the film deals will have to be managed by whoever I appoint as his guardian. You've a good business head, Miranda. This could give you a successful career as well as motherhood. I need someone to nurture my films to fruition and bring about a renaissance in the British movie industry. I've planted the seeds from which highly profitable motion pictures will grow. Films, not products, stories with human scale instead of technical wizardry. I thought it was the perfect plan.'

'Too bad you didn't check with me.' She leaned forward, pulling at the straps of parcel tape I had reattached around her wrists. 'You can't just make plans without involving others, Richard. I know this is a shock, but sometimes people don't want what you want for them.'

'And how do you feel about me?' I asked slowly.

'Oh, Richard.' Her voice softened a little. 'I loved you.'

'And now?'

'And now I can't.' She made a little shrugging gesture with her mouth. 'Just can't.' Her eyes were glassy with tears.

'You're sure.'

'What we had is dead.' She gave a sad little nod, her wet sapphire eyes finally locking with mine and widening with horror.

Dead. As dead as my own flesh. How blind could I have been? 'You're right,' I agreed, 'we have nothing more to say to each other.'

I thought fast. Miranda would never change her mind. I would have to rethink the plan. My hands closed around her throat before either of us understood the decision I had reached. I squeezed until I heard the bones break in her neck, and then squeezed some more. I stayed like that for five minutes or so, until the ruptured blood vessels in her skin had discoloured her flesh, turning it to the colour of winter roses. I removed my hands and the imprinted hollows of my thumbs stayed in her neck, like impressions in clay. Her head slowly tilted back, as though she was falling into a drunken stupor.

Miranda was as lifeless as I would be in a few short hours. I cut loose her straps and walked back from the scene to the rear of the theatre. I was still contemplating her body when a hand grabbed my ankle.

I admit I screamed. It was a classic *Evil Dead* moment. The hand's fingernails dug in hard, shredding the dried flesh above my ankle right through my sock. I looked down and was surprised to see the bloody, jawless Berry grimly clutching at my leg as though strap-hanging in a railway carriage. I had underestimated his stamina. Somehow he had managed to drag himself to this part of the auditorium. Obeying a faulty internal compass he had unfortunately headed away from the only exit.

With my left leg pinioned, I shifted the right one over his neck and stamped down with all my strength until I heard a crack as sharp as celluloid snapping in the gate and prayed that it was the top of his spine, and not my ankle, that had just broken. Then I unpicked his fingers from my sock. He had torn the flesh beneath the cotton into shards, like a Chinese waiter separating crispy duck with a fork. It felt like my shoe was full of cornflakes. I shook out as much as I could, and left the screening room, redoubling my efforts to find a solution for my dilemma before the night was through.

As I left the building, the answer came to me in a blinding flash. Barbara was the only one who still had faith in me. Barbara had the fortitude, the independence, the kind heart. She could nurture my films and become the co-architect of a national revival of British cinema! And she would make a pretty good mother. I decided to go after her.

CHAPTER FORTY-SEVEN

The Politics of Pleasure

11:35 p.m. Midas lit a Cuban cigar and took pleasure in drawing the musky warm aroma through it. The penumbral room seemed to close about him as he conducted his discourse with the detective.

'As Mr Cotton was so keen to become famous in the Soho area, I thought it might be a good idea if we had a little talk,' he explained. 'He certainly had a lot of nerve, I'll give him that. You don't come strolling in here and announce your intention of weaning customers over to your supply without upsetting the Chinese, the Indians, the Cypriots, the Russians and any number of splinter groups. He came in here and sat down where you're sitting, bold as brass. I couldn't figure him out. He seemed to be operating entirely alone, so where did he get the confidence? Kids like him can't keep their mouths shut. He was bragging, and he couldn't resist telling me his secret. The stuff was addictive, highly addictive. And I knew it wasn't properly tested. Not at the speed he'd claimed to have perfected it. When I asked him if it was safe, he lied to me.'

'How do you know he lied?'

'Come on, Mr May, the kid had pound signs in his eyes.

Didn't take the stuff himself, he said, and only made it in small batches because the central ingredient – whatever that is – couldn't be easily imported. Then I realised, he was trying to cut a deal with me. With me! He'd somehow got the idea that I knew all the local suppliers. Well maybe I do, but I wouldn't tell him. He thought he could strike a deal to bulk-buy cocaine from them, enhance it with or without their help, and sell it through the clubs.'

'I wonder where he got that idea. You certainly wouldn't deal drugs in any form, would you?' There was only a faint hint of irony in May's tone. Midas leaned forward and almost blotted out the light.

'Let's get one thing clear, Mr May. Our clubs are more than just drug-free zones. We're entrepreneurs who are prepared to get our hands dirty so that you don't have to. These days the world comes to Soho. We won't allow ourselves to be made fools of in the eyes of our international partners.'

'So what did you do to stop this boy from operating? Maybe you should have tried picking up a telephone and having him arrested.' May was sure that Blake's men had made an example of Cotton, but wondered if he could prove it on a single toe-print, which was all he had at the moment, and probably all he was ever likely to have.

'Tell me something I don't understand,' May pushed. 'If Cotton sparked an epidemic with his new chemical compound, what could you do about it?'

'We have a multi-million-pound business community operating here in a handful of narrow streets, Mr May. You only have to look at us to see who has the power. Haven't you ever wondered why there's so little real trouble in Soho these days? It's a potential powder keg of lunacy. The lid stays on because of us. When somebody starts behaving like an arsehole we take him out of the equation, give him a talking to, send him away for a while.'

'And if that somebody winds up dead?'

'They don't, Mr May, not on our turf. Perhaps they're found somewhere else, but they're never, ever found here. They might break an ankle tripping down the steps, but that's all. I send my boys out each evening to clear up other people's messes. I send them out in the van and don't let them come back until their work is done to everyone's satisfaction. It's just part of the service.'

'Interesting.' May watched while the crowd applauded Glory. She stood before them in a minuscule black g-string, her wings discarded about her in shards like those of a tortured butterfly. The chains had left a crosshatch of fine red cuts over her small, pale breasts. Barely bothering to acknowledge the audience, she took a bow and swept off behind the curtains.

'How did you conclude your talk with Mr Cotton?' asked May, draining his beer.

'When he'd finished boasting about Imago, I gave him my advice. I told him I couldn't help him, that it was a bad idea to tread on so many toes.'

'Did you ask your boys to get rid of him, Mr Blake? Did you save someone else the trouble of doing it? No offence, you understand.'

Midas looked as if the idea had never crossed his mind. 'None taken, Mr May. I told you, I couldn't do such a thing. That would constitute direct involvement.'

'You know I can put an investigation team on you.'

'Why would you want to do that? We're on the same side, you and I. That's why I'm taking you into my confidence. I know you need our help. Imago is contaminated. It's bad mojo, and it's out there. The guy who flipped out in the restaurant, the pair who killed themselves in the New Brunswick? We heard about them minutes after it happened.'

May knew better than to ask from whom; the Metropolitan Police made the *Titanic* look watertight.

'And you're sure the contaminated supply is on the street?'

'You must know how much the boy manufactured, Mr May. There are probably several thousand doctored grammes being traded around town this evening. If only a handful of punters suffer bad effects, that's still a lot of trouble for a hot Friday night.'

May leaned forward. 'I'll tell you what I think, Mr Blake. Cotton died in the early hours of Monday morning. The dates in his journal suggest that he only perfected the filtration process of Imago two Fridays earlier. He had no money in his bank account. Unless he was able to lay his hands on an awful lot of cocaine, he couldn't doctor much of it. He needed to turn some fast cash before he could build his little empire. He wasn't able to raise enough capital to buy the cocaine he needed. That's why he came to see you. Of course it would be more profitable to control the entire process, but why would he want to do that? He was a stranger here, he didn't have the connections. But he could sell the bottles on. The dealers could cut their coke further and would profit from the newly-addicted return custom, and Cotton would provide the sole supply because he was careful to be the only person who knew where it came from. He developed the drug in batches, but we can only account for eight bottles: six in Cotton's fridge, two on the victims and the one your lads found. I need to know who he sold the undiluted bottles of Imago to, and what I'd like from you, Mr Blake, is a list of possible contacts.'

'You know I can't do that. I have a certain standing in this community. There would be serious repercussions.'

'There will be anyway, when we settle the blame for Malcolm Cotton's murder. Right now I'm more interested in preventing an epidemic. We have to treat this like a communicable disease.'

Midas pointed back at his customers. 'They're not patients, Mr May, and I'm no doctor. I have to protect my people, and my stake in the land. As long as the punters don't die on my property, I have no ethical compunction to help them. In Soho the concept of morality shifts like sand. Thousands of people are out there tonight seeking self-gratification, and their actions will affect each other in varying degrees. Some will find happiness at the expense of others. Every hot night brings pleasure and pain. It's a system of supply and demand, and anything that damages the system must be stopped or rerouted, but if the rest of those bottles have been repackaged, remixed and sold we won't hear about it until the bodies start turning up.'

'That's a situation I am naturally anxious to prevent,' replied May. A perturbing stillness in the Greek commanded authority. He was completely ruthless in the protection of his interests. And there was something else at work within him, something older and darker that May could only glimpse and guess at.

'As you said, Mr May, your job is to assign blame.'

'And yours is to provide entertainment. I think we're both prepared to go quite a long way beyond our remit.'

May's mobile phone rang.

'Another outbreak,' said Janice Longbright, 'a big one this time. Arthur is already on his way there.'

'I thought he was going home?'

'The call came in just as he had put his coat on. I tried to stop him –'

'Give me the address.' He glanced up at Midas Blake, who was clearly curious about the call. 'Well,' said May, 'it looks like we both have our work cut out for us tonight. I don't want you to leave the club until I get back. If you do, you might find some trouble on your doorstep that your boys can't sweep up.'

CHAPTER FORTY-EIGHT

Madness in the Air

Alex and Natalie were just warming up.

Natalie worked in an Italian sandwich bar, and Alex was a waiter at the gay cafe next door. He'd been offering to take her out for ages, but she had misread his signals, assuming that his interests lay elsewhere. Finally he explained that it was just a job, and they had made a date for Friday night.

They met up in the Pitcher & Piano just after ten, smoked a couple of joints, bought some rubbishy coke from an illegal minicab company that operated out of Old Compton Street, then spiced it up with something a boy in the Bongo Lounge had recommended and sold to them for a few quid. At that low price they figured it couldn't be anything special.

The boy knew Natalie, and explained that you were supposed to mix the stuff with something else because it was too strong to take on its own. It was in liquid form, and was supposed to turn low-quality drugs into something that kicked like high-grade Columbian, but it made the coke damp and impossible to snort, so Alex said fuck it and drank some neat, and instantly felt great, and gave some to Natalie, and they both wanted to do some more.

They went to another bar but it was too noisy and

crowded, so they returned to the Bongo Lounge, but now Alex had a headache, and suddenly felt very impatient with the slow drinks service, so he reached across the counter and grabbed the barman by his jacket lapel and shouted in his face, and the next thing he knew all hell had broken loose and there were people screaming at him, and he looked down to see the broken bottle in his hand and blood smeared across his shirt-sleeve, and the barman was lying across the counter with blood boiling out of his mouth as if it was spouting from a jammed tap, and he looked around to try and find Natalie, but she had used her Bic lighter to set fire to a pile of paper napkins, and the burning paper was drifting through the air like a snowfall in hell, and it had set fire to her hair and she was making such a terrible fuss that he just wanted to stab her, so he did.

And then the police arrived.

The neon clock in the window of the Italian barbershop read 11:50 p.m. 'You know what I hate?' asked May, falling into step beside his partner as they pushed their way through the crowded streets. 'The sheer lack of innocence. Everyone's got a smart answer. I'd like to give some of these kids a clip round the ear. Midas Blake acts like London's landlord. He isn't telling the truth about Cotton. For all I know he might have talked the boy into giving him the bottles for safekeeping.'

'Unlikely. We know that Cotton was a lone operator.'

'Suppose he hid them somewhere?'

'The mix was in his fridge because it probably has a limited shelf-life. I should think he needed to unload it as quickly as possible.'

'If he managed to sell the bottles, how come there's no money in his bank account or in his apartment?'

'Maybe he was carrying it on his person, and the killer took it from him.'

'No, that would mean he – oh, no.' May raised his hands to his forehead. 'I know what he did . . .'

'What?'

'Of course. It fits . . .'

'What? *What?*' Bryant hated information being withheld.

'He gave Imago away. All thirty bottles. That's how one of them ended up in the hands of the Gossage boy in the Nelly Dean. Midas Blake told me that Cotton had wanted people to know where it came from. First he thought Blake could personally supply him with coke. When that didn't pan out he asked for help with the drug's distribution, but Blake wouldn't provide the necessary contacts. Cotton knew that Imago was highly addictive. He didn't need a middle-man when he could hand it out for free and create an instant market. He figured he'd have both suppliers and punters coming to him.'

'You realise that makes the drug virtually untraceable,' Bryant complained as he stifled a weary yawn. 'If Cotton hit his consumers directly there's no point in tackling the usual suppliers, not if he went waltzing through Soho tossing poisoned candy at anyone who wanted it. All we can do is co-ordinate some kind of warning system and get the relevant emergency information out on the street.'

'Do you have any idea how many bars, pubs, clubs and restaurants there are in this neighbourhood?' asked May. 'If Cotton gave the bottles away, you can bet some enterprising dealer is decanting it into saleable ampoules as we speak.'

'I was on my way home,' complained Bryant. 'I'm knackered. My feet hurt. It's past my bedtime. I get nasty if I'm not tucked up by midnight.'

'Arthur, you're nasty all the time. Your moods differentiate themselves by degrees of bad temper.'

'That's not true.' The old man bridled. 'My landlady considers me charming.'

'Alma Sorrowbridge is in love with you, it's not the same thing.'

'Don't talk rubbish, John. It has nothing to do with love. Alma has been washing my underwear for nearly twenty years. She drives me insane. We might as well be married.'

'Exactly. Why do I think this must be the place?'

Smoke was billowing from the doors of the Bongo Lounge. Firemen had cordoned off the road and pavement in order to allow a tender to reach the front of the building. Police and safety officers stood noisily arguing at the club's blackened entrance.

'You wouldn't believe what's been going on in there,' one of the constables told them. 'We've got arson, assault and what appears to be mass hysteria. Everyone's out now, but there's a girl up on the roof.' He pointed up to a stick-thin figure spotlit against the steeply raked slates.

Arthur Bryant had no head for heights, and was happy to let his partner accompany their officers up the rusted fire escape. When May reached the top, he saw that the girl was standing in a foot-wide concrete gully running around the edge of the roof. She was shaking and crying, facing out above the street, oblivious of her surroundings. The back of her head was blackened and looked scorched. Her dress was torn, charred and spattered with blood. For a minute or so May stood and watched her. He was joined by a pale young man who showed his credentials in a plastic slipcase; drugs counsellor.

'Your name is Natalie, isn't it?' he called softly. 'Right now

I'm sure it's easier for you not to move a muscle, because you don't know what you might do if you try to move, so listen carefully to the sound of my voice . . .'

She appeared not to have heard him. Her hair was stuck to her cheeks in sooty tendrils. She looked down and released a hopeless sob. May slowly realised that the counsellor was hypnotising her.

In the crowd that had gathered below, Lucas Fox stared skyward and thought he recognised the girl on the roof. She looked like the one who worked in the Italian sandwich bar in Wardour Street. He had been talking to Natalie just a couple of hours ago. She was going out on a date, and asked him if he had any drugs, and he'd been about to say no when he had remembered the little plastic bottles he still carried in the bottom of his portfolio case. She'd insisted on giving him ten pounds for one of them, even without knowing what was in it, and he'd thought fuck it, why not take the money. Malcolm hadn't bothered to reclaim them. He'd probably pissed off back to Australia. Anyway, he'd given him the bottles, telling him to pass them out to anyone who wanted to try a new high.

Lucas had forgotten the usage instructions, but figured that anyone who was prepared to try the stuff would know how to use it. He never touched narcotics. He had no need. Alcohol made him just as wrecked and depressed. What the sandwich bar girl was doing half-burned and covered in blood four floors above the street was a complete mystery to him.

Lucas's evening was growing more surreal with each passing hour. People's behaviour around here was a little out of whack at the best of times, but tonight there was madness in the air. His fantasy recurred – that he was trapped in Soho like some latter-day Midwich Cuckoo, doomed to wander the increasingly hellish streets for all eternity. He recalled the tenner Natalie had given him and decided that he might as well make some money out of a thoroughly fucked-up night. Where was the harm?

And with that thought he set off along Old Compton Street to sell the rest of the bottles.

CHAPTER FORTY-NINE

Party!

It was midnight when my taxi pulled up next to Battersea Power Station.

The driver had asked too many questions, so I didn't leave him a tip. I did, however, leave a fair amount of dried skin on the back seat, and something that looked like a piece of worn-out calf muscle. I popped it in his ashtray as a surprise for later, and noted how quickly I had grown accustomed to this autumnal shedding of flesh. Although my corporeal form wasn't waiting until autumn. It wasn't even waiting until tomorrow. I had the feeling that if I started jumping around on a dance floor I'd explode in a miasma of putrid body-parts.

I was already looking forward to my eternal rest. Just a short way to go now. My mother once said about my Aunt Mary, 'Her death came as a welcome release.' I knew how Aunt Mary felt just before she died. This bitter little woman had grabbed at the Angel of Peace and clung on for dear life, praying to be taken away. When I reached that point of oblivion, I would walk proudly beside my soul-taker. Chat to him about his work, probably. Offer him an option on his story.

I alighted just as members of a former girlpower pop group were attempting to excite the interest of the tabloid press by pulling their skirts over their heads. Photographers were stacked on bleachers beside the gates, oinking like seals waiting to be fed. Half the cast of *EastEnders* walked past, surprising no one.

There were differences between this party and an ordinary night at a club. No mile-long queue, for a start. No drug dealers patrolling said queue asking everyone if they were sorted, and no botulism-riddled burger vans waiting for dehydrated stoners with the munchies. Instead, meet-and-greet PR teams lined the entrance while the baying paparazzi attempted to incite photo-op punch-ups between washed-up soap stars.

Inside the overheated tent where the party was taking place, gigantic inflatable dolls waved serenely back and forth, an acoustic disaster that was ruining the set of the one-hit-wonder band playing on a far stage. The dolls were meant to represent the leading characters from *Chemical Man*, but had been underinflated, so that they appeared as diseased, squiffy-eyed, hunched, wrinkling gnome-versions of the stars. Personally, I would have sued.

I surveyed the territory. Elegant drunk women tried to maintain their poise as they tripped over guy-ropes. Creepy old producers prowled the premises like praying mantises looking for mates. Troops of slender young models patrolled in outfits designed to showcase their genitals. Desperate TV stars who had been drop-kicked from prime-time to cruise-ship cabaret the moment public opinion turned against them looked for someone currently famous to stand with. I saw far too many people I recognised.

Waiters provided the marquee with its 'gymnasium-on-a-hot-night' aroma by stalking about with trays of deep-fried squid and insufficient underarm deodorant. DJ bass-and-drum stuff thudded dully from a sparsely-populated dance area. Everyone was dressed in the very latest fashions, which meant, of course, that they looked like escaped mental patients. Tiffany, the networking tart from Tuesday's funeral, had stuffed her voluptuous body into a shiny pink rubber sheath dress. She looked like a balloon animal.

Accepting a glass of champagne from a bored waitress, I began my search for Barbara. I set off in the direction of the VIP lounge, which, if memory served, was usually sited at the rear left-hand side of the room. Most post-première parties were either under- or over-invited. This one was under-, with six hundred guests swallowed up in a temporary plastic structure imbued with the intimacy of an aircraft hangar and the melancholy ambience of an abandoned church.

Julie Saito grabbed my arm as I passed near the bar. She was effusive, and cheerfully drunk. 'Look,' she bellowed in my semi-detached ear, 'that's Bethany Zen, the German supermodel.' She made a grimacing face. 'Her thighs are thinner than my arms! I've been watching her eat. It's incredible. Two entire trays of fried canapés so far. The waiters can't keep up. She must have the intestinal tract of an armadillo.' Julie swivelled around, slopping gin from her glass. 'My God, don't look now but there's Melanie Benn, the girl who presents the sex shows on the Porno Channel. She's dating that psychotic Essex drug lord who's financing the Millennium Dance on Film season.' Melanie was wearing a shiny purple nylon wig the colour of a constricted penis. Her skin-tight gold catsuit left her pubic mound looking like a camel's foot. She gave a girly laugh as she palmed out packets of coke to thick-set young men in shiny suits. Drugs were everywhere. The party guests were saturated in them, subsiding with the weight of them, slinking and sinking and slowing beneath their onslaught.

'Richard, I've got something for you.' Julie was mood-swinging between hyper and spaced. 'Quick, quick, quick. Where's your glass?' I looked down. It was still in my hand.

'Okay, now empty out half of the champagne.' Barely listening, I made to tip the contents on the floor, but she stopped me. 'No, silly, drink it!'

Why not? I thought. Nobody in here would see the result. I half-drained the glass and held it out. Julie produced a small plastic bottle from her purse and popped the lid. 'Try some of this.'

'What is it?'

'Don't worry, it'll make you feel wonderful. You deserve it after the week you've had. Go on, it tastes of peaches.'

I drank it to shut her up. It tasted like the smell of formaldehyde. Mentholated, clinical. She studied me with wide, unnaturally bright eyes. 'You have to wait a few minutes for the full effect. It lasts for about half an hour. Forget Es, forget coke, this is the real thing. I'm on my third. It's *the* drug of the moment. Everyone's trying to get hold of it and of course it's very, very expensive, but I have a friend who knows someone.' Her smile broadened. 'You can start to feel it now, can't you?'

It was true. I could feel something happening inside my head, but it was not something good. A tingling sensation rippled across my brain, a thousand pinpricks fragmenting my vision like a bad migraine. I shoved her aside and walked off.

'What's the matter? Richard!'

I stood at the edge of the dance floor as colours rolled across my vitrifying skin, and fought to keep my balance.

Someone was walking towards me with a slow, steady gait, as though keeping balance on the deck of a ship. As the figure grew closer, I saw that it was Paul, poor dead Paul, and then I knew I was hallucinating. He looked moth-eaten and pale, as if he'd been kept in a drawer like an unloved jumper. He wore the suit in which he had been buried, a smart black off-the-peg number he had never worn in life.

'Dear Richie, here you are at last,' said Paul, holding out his hand. 'I was hoping you'd be able to make it.'

'I think you'll find that you're dead, Paul. You're not s'posed to be up and about.' I tried to distinguish his features but could not see clearly. 'You don't go to parties after you're dead.'

'Why not? You're here,' Paul pointed out. 'That's probably why you can see me. Anyway, this lot's already half-dead. Hey, thanks for coming to my funeral. I couldn't see you, of course, closed lid and all that, but I heard your nice comments. I thought you might learn something from the letter, but it doesn't look as if you have.'

'What do you mean?'

His eyes widened so far they nearly fell out. I know how eyes look when they're about to fall out, believe me. 'Well, bloody hell,' he cried, 'you're dead and you're working harder than ever. The point was to make you recognise the falseness of your life and get you to relax before it was too late. Start living like a normal person. Obviously you weren't paying attention.'

'Working is like getting married,' I replied, 'you either do it properly or not at all. You can't set a speed limit. There are things that have to be done.'

'Only if you're competent enough to pull them off. Look at the mess you're in. Okay, you've turned your career around in less than a week, but I think you need to work on your people skills. You've murdered Berry and Miranda.'

'Are they here, by any chance? Be unlike them to miss a party.'

'No, Richie, murdered people don't get to come back. Besides, if they were here they'd probably be attacking you with steak knives.'

'I thought I could solve all my problems.'

'Yeah, right. Like you think abducting Barbara can solve your problems.'

'I have no other way out, Paulie. She'll understand in time.'

'She'll think you're mad.'

'She already knows I'm dead. How much worse can it get?'

Paul cast his hands about airily. For a moment it looked like his scraggy little arms might fly off. 'Accept what has happened and be content with the outcome. The living view their lives as a road seen a few yards at a time. They never take the overview.'

'What overview?' I shouted back. 'I didn't start living until I died.'

'Everyone has a tragedy, and that's yours. You didn't wake up in time. Don't feel bad. Most people don't. There's nothing you can do about it now.'

'I can try to end things properly.'

'All right, but don't say I didn't warn you. You're dead. You don't *have* to go into work any more. That's the whole point.' Paul turned to leave, but looked sadly back. 'Life's a joke, and most poor sods don't get the punchline before they die. But you can. You can go out laughing, Richie. Work it out.' Then he slowly walked away into the pulsing lights of the dance floor. I tried to watch him leave, but the sapphire and crimson flashes stuck needles in my brain, and I was forced to look away. 'Paul. Don't leave me, Paul. I'm alone.'

I would never be able to cry again. I rubbed my sore, dry eyes and attempted to locate him, but he had gone. I set off in search of Barbara once more.

The DJ was playing the Propellerheads' 'History Repeating', and its retro lounge-rhythm was getting to me. My skin seemed to be crawling in time to the saxophone. It felt as though at any moment my right hand might detach itself and scuttle about on the floor like the one that menaced Peter Lorre in *The Beast With Five Fingers*.

The VIP lounge had been constructed from what appeared to be a portakabin covered in regency wallpaper. The entrance was guarded by two bouncers who kept out the riff-raff. Inside, gold plastic candlesticks and Victorian sconces protruded from wobbly partitions, like the set of a travelling production of *Lady Windemere's Fan*. White plastic vases containing arrangements of dry-cleaned flowers greeted the chosen few who had been afforded this array of special decor privileges. In one corner a row of superior portaloos had sporting prints hung above miniature bars of hotel soap marinating in leaky washbasins. So many guests had cut coke lines on the plastic-glass of the sporting prints that their frames were now glued to the walls.

Barbara was standing alone, staring into the middle distance in that studied manner people adopt to hide the fact that they feel awkward standing by themselves. She greeted me with an enthusiasm born from loneliness. Stepping forward, she prepared to land a couple of air-kisses on me, but drew back with a gasp when she saw the condition I was in.

'Good God, Richard, what's happening to you?' she asked,

horrified. 'What's wrong with your skin?'

'Whatever do you mean?' I slurred. I was feeling weirder by the second. The tingling in my brain was intensifying in spiny waves.

'It looks like it's – well –'

'Yeah, it's sort of coming off,' I explained. I shifted to a mirror – actually a sheet of stretched plastic in a gold-sprayed frame – and studied my twisted visage in the dim light. What I saw was pure horror movie material. Boris Karloff shying from fire. Lon Chaney under the mask. Dorian Gray's painting revealed. My condition had deteriorated alarmingly. My jaw was showing. The pale bone appeared through yellowish skin that had split like a dried-up shoe. My discoloured left eye had tipped up and inward. A section of scalp above my right ear hung down like a poorly glued poster. The backs of my hands had cracked open to reveal their skeletal structure. When I tried to speak, my thick dry tongue prevented articulation.

The image presented to me was the living antithesis of everything beautiful, youthful, natural, wholesome. I was debauched, obscene, unholy. I had finally grown as grotesque as the times in which I lived.

I lurched towards Barbara with a grunt and she gave a little scream. Then she gave a big scream. I was half-expecting her to faint into my arms, so when she did it came as no surprise, although she was heavier than I thought she'd be. If anyone saw her fall, they made no attempt to come forward and help. Nor did anyone try to stop me when I slipped my hands beneath her back and thighs, and carried her off into the shadows.

Holding my new bride thus, in outstretched arms, I stumbled towards the building's fire exit.

Path of Contagion

'**Oh, man.** This isn't fair. This really isn't fair.'

'I'm sorry, One Eighty, but you heard what Midas said.' Waldorf walked around his colleague's head and pulled the top from a hip-flask of armagnac. 'I gotta do it.' He had a sudden thought. 'Unless you want to do it yourself.'

'Fuck off! No way! Look at my hands, man.' He was right. They were shaking.

'Here, drink some of this. Drink a lot.' He handed down the flask. One Eighty took several large swigs, wiped his mouth and passed it back. It was 12:15 a.m, and they were on the top floor of the multi-storey car park in Brewer Street. They usually parked in the NCP in Wardour Street where they had a cash-deal going with the Africans, but it was too well patrolled for their purposes tonight. One Eighty lay on an oil-free patch of ground behind the van, with his head propped on a cushion. Waldorf checked that the pistol's silencer was properly attached.

'I wish it wasn't me having to do this, but at least I'm your friend, I'm a good shot, I'm someone you can trust.' He peered down the barrel and took aim.

'Wait! Listen! Couldn't I go to a hospital and have it done surgically?'

'And what are you gonna tell them? There's nothing wrong with it, you just don't like it anymore and you want someone to cut it off?'

'Midas must know a doctor, someone who'd do it,' he moaned, raising his head and looking along his prostrate body.

'There's no time left,' Waldorf explained. 'We fucked up. Imago is out on the streets and any of us could be taken in for questioning. Okay, so they won't be able to pin anything on Midas, but the moment they take your shoe off, you're fucked.'

'A toe print. A fucking toe print. I can't believe that's all they have to go on.'

'That's all they need, buddy-boy. Now hold still, and get ready to bite down hard.'

One Eighty reinserted the rag in his mouth and scrunched up his face. Waldorf squatted before his colleague's naked right foot and took careful aim at the big toe.

'Lay it flat, man. Keep still, you're wiggling it.' Slowly he squeezed the trigger. Even with the silencer on, the gunshot made a hell of a noise because the bullet ricocheted off the concrete floor and went through the windscreen of a Honda Civic. One Eighty spat the rag from his mouth and screamed the place down.

'JEEEESus CHRiiiiST!!!'

He looked down at his ruined foot, aghast. Blood was pumping from the shattered end of his big toe, forming a puddle around his ankle.

Waldorf was pleased with his work. 'Keep the noise down, man, it's gonna be okay. I trained with St John's Ambulance.' He tipped the rest of the armagnac over the splintered toebone, picked off several fragments of bone and skin, and applied a tourniquet. Then he cleaned and trimmed the stump, wrapping it in medicated gauze as One Eighty screamed and groaned into his jacket sleeve. 'Think of it this way; what use is a big toe?'

One Eighty shouted something into his sleeve.

'Okay, balance, but apart from that. You'll have to lay off football practice for a while. Think of the extra time it'll give you to work on your screenplay.' He snickered as he pulled a white plastic sleeve over the end of One Eighty's foot. 'And you'd better cancel your step classes.'

Seventeen minutes into Saturday morning, and the streets below were growing more chaotic by the minute. She sat shivering inside her blanket in the steaming night, her bony legs dangling from the fourth-floor parapet. She had lost a shoe. Mascara blurred her eyes as she stared out through the demons that filled her world. The counsellor knelt beside her, speaking softly, maintaining a stream of soothing hypnotic phrases that would keep her distracted until the officers above him could pull her back inside. May watched the scene in sadness. The girl was no more than nineteen, the age of his own daughter when she had died, slimmer than Alice and paler, although her anaemic appearance was probably the result of toxic shock.

'Look at them all, so many of them,' she called suddenly, her high thin voice cutting through the rumble of traffic, 'they keep coming in waves. Why don't they ever stop?'

For a moment May wondered if the drug's bizarre origin could have somehow percolated through to a human system, bringing with it some kind of primitive trace memory.

'Can't fight them,' she declared, rising sharply, 'better to die.' As she stepped forward, the counsellor signalled and two men dropped down to grab her waist, pulling her back from the edge of the parapet. Natalie began screaming, kicking and punching the men until all three of them fell over in a heap. Two other officers rushed in with the medical team, and they managed to hold her down long enough to sedate her.

One saved, thought May, rising from the roof. He wondered how many others would be tempted to try a little chemical experimentation tonight and get more than they bargained for.

'I'm sure drug-induced epiphanies can take many forms,' said Bryant, when his partner had returned to ground level. He squinted up at the grey night sky, looking more than ever like a tortoise emerging from hibernation. 'You don't think she saw herself in the body of an insect, do you?'

'What, galloping about on the back of a caterpillar fighting off ants?' asked May. 'I suppose it might be bio-chemically possible that some deeply ingrained sense of social regimentation could surface, but surely the species jump is too wide to give it any serious consideration.' He looked up at the pedestrians aimlessly threading their way back and forth past each other in Old Compton Street. 'I mean, what do human beings have in common with six-legged creatures with jointed thoraxes – and – highly developed social patterns – of –'

'I think you'd better stop there,' remarked Bryant. 'You know, none of this would be happening if people weren't so determined to have a good time. Janice was just telling me about this club in Windmill Street called the Chill Zone. It opens at five in the morning, and you go there to calm down after a night of drugs and dancing – and do you know what they get up to in this den of iniquity?'

'No. Enlighten me.'

'Jigsaws. They play Cluedo and do jigsaws and drink cocoa and listen to Burt Bacharach.'

'How extraordinary.'

'It strikes me that they're living their lives back to front, behaving like adults while they're still children, and relaxing with the pursuits of childhoods they never completed.'

'So what's the answer? You can't bring back the Victorian family, rosy-faced children silently sitting at a parent's knee. Not when the world is so near and available. Malcolm Cotton's father is a diplomat, probably gave his son the best of everything, but Malcolm still got away from him. He didn't want to be given money, he wanted to make it for himself. This is the school playground for kids like him.'

One of the fire officers stuck his head above the fire escape and began warning the gathered crowd to stand away from the front of the building. May peered through the neon-filtered smoke that still pulsed from the club's entrance as bloated hoses emptied water into the smouldering basement. 'We'd better get on,' urged May, 'we're not finished yet.'

Sergeant Janice Longbright was arguing with her headset. 'Several more incidents incoming, sir,' she called. 'Three – no, four – one in Frith Street, the others in Old Compton Street.'

'What do you mean by "incidents"?' asked Bryant.

'Acts of violence, by the sound of it. Two badly injured in Frith Street, a place called Garlic and Shots, that's a restaurant, serious affray in –' she paused, cupping her hand over her receiver, 'wait, one dead in the Turkish House, I think that's a bar –'

'Get the exact addresses, will you?' May turned to his partner. 'We'll start at the most recent scene. It's like following the progression path of a virus.'

Bryant looked glumly at strips of purple neon tinting the faces of the passing crowds. 'If it's a virus,' he said, 'it's one we have no cure for.'

Longbright brought over the crime scene addresses and began checking them off on one of the tourist pocket-maps given away by the area's clubs. The detectives dragged together several tables outside the Bar Italia and huddled around them, while bad-tempered waiters glared and complained darkly to one another about lost custom.

'Look at the pattern,' said Bryant, banging the end of a teaspoon on the folded paper. 'It looks like the work of one person. He's criss-crossing the roads, see, down Greek Street, up Frith Street, down Dean Street, and each time he has to pass through a short section of Old Compton Street. Join them together and we get the path of all the outbreaks reported so far. So, if the pattern holds, the next one should be at the corner of Old Compton Street and Wardour Street.'

'Why would he keep to a routine that could be followed?' asked May.

'He can't have any idea he's leaving a trail,' replied Bryant. 'He's not aware that this stuff he's handing out is harmful. There's no reason why he should be. Taken in the correct dilution, it's not.' He studied the map again. 'He's like some latter-day Typhoid Mary. What's on the corner of Wardour Street?'

'The "O" Bar. It'll be packed at this time of night.'

'We need a couple of drug lads in there right now. Nobody conspicuously narky, none of the blue shirt-and-haircut brigade. And no uniforms on the street. If he sees a heavy police presence it'll drive him inside, but it won't stop him. We need to make this person cocky and careless. There's no description to home in on. They just need to keep their eyes peeled for signs of deals being cut. Post as many as you can in Wardour Street.'

'What if he turns off somewhere? There are literally hundreds of places he could vanish into before we spot him.'

'He's in plain sight,' said Bryant, rubbing at his rheumy eyes and wearily folding away the map. 'He's not even acting suspiciously, because he doesn't know anyone's looking for him. That won't make him any easier to find.'

'Then what do you suggest we do?' asked May.

'What can we do?' The elderly detective shrugged. 'Head for the next co-ordinate. Like Daedalus imprisoned within the labyrinth he designed, we must ensure that he cannot escape.'

CHAPTER FIFTY-ONE

Mind in Chains

00:22 a.m. She lay in her customary position, with her knees curled beneath her and her forehead pressed against the window, feeling the vibrations of the street beyond. The trembling pane acted as a seismograph. For the last five days and nights it had provided her only human contact. She tried to hate Midas, but could not find the energy within herself to do so. He acted with the elemental instincts of an animal. She wanted to understand how his magic worked, but abstruse reflection eluded her. Her needs now were more basic, water and food, unparched air. They overrode her every thought.

Judy knew she would die in this position, beside the window, imprisoned in the amber of her sweltering apartment, pinned into position like a butterfly in a specimen jar. She heard his footsteps on the landing and rose with difficulty, thinking that she should call out, even though he knew she would not capitulate. She had long passed that point, and could only continue to her death.

She felt sure that the man she had known as Midas was someone quite different in the outside world, that he had only presented one face to her. She suspected he had many other names. He was the stranger who came to lead the world into temptation, the one who could give people everything they needed in return for blind allegiance. He might appear at a certain co-ordinate on the map, to a certain type of person, when the skies were high and the time was right, and to many people, stronger people, he might never appear at all. An arid marriage, four years of loneliness, how ripe she had been for his attentions! Even if it were possible, there would be no point in returning to Danielle Passmore and asking to see a photograph; she knew his likeness would not be the same. He would never adopt the same guise twice. Perhaps he didn't exist at all . . .

He had cut the electric supply to the apartment, as if he had already decided that her life was at an end. The lights had gone out. She had found some candles in a kitchen drawer, and had recklessly decided to ignite them all. What point was there in hoarding the light? The rings of the gas stove still burst into noisy flame, but made the kitchen unbearably hot. Anyway, the street lights and the neon illuminations of Wardour Street's restaurants and clubs flooded the lounge with arrogant nocturnal rainbows. She could trace the contours of the flat without need of sight. What she needed was water, cold water to drip upon her dry tongue and ulcerated lips.

She heard his boots scuffing the landing mat outside her door. There was a scrape of metal on metal – a key in a lock. He was letting himself into the flat! The thought filled her with terror, and excited her with the possibility of escape. But now she listened to the door opening and realised that he was entering his own apartment, not hers. She held her breath. The door clicked gently shut, and there was silence.

But he was here, just a few metres away, and that meant there was still a chance that she had not been abandoned.

How could he be so close and not think of her? Finding some small supply of energy, she hobbled to the door and tried to see through the splintered hole she had made with the makeshift spear, but it was too dark to see anything.

Suddenly, a thin bar of light. His door, opening. Darkness, as his body filled the gap. The click of a lock, tumblers turning over. The sound of the key relocking. Silence as he turned and stared at her door, thinking. She remained frozen against the door, not daring to breathe.

She knew it then; he was going to leave. After a moment's hesitation his footsteps retreated back down the stairs. She heard the building's entrance door slam shut and saw him walking briskly up the road towards the club, unconcerned about her fate. Not for the first time, she wondered if her imprisonment was simply a state of mind, a suggestion he had planted in her head. In the normal world windows could be broken, and doors unlocked. Perhaps her mind had sealed her in here at his command. She spread the fingers of her right hand across the humming glass. It felt stronger than steel.

If there was a way out, it would have to come from outside. Bleached by the gaudy indigos and scarlets of the street, she resumed her position beside the window, returning to her lonely vigil.

CHAPTER FIFTY-TWO

Angel in Respite

For a small woman she was bloody heavy, a dead weight in my arms as I manhandled her from the back door of the venue to one of the taxis queuing outside. I checked my watch: 00:41 a.m. The party had barely begun. Nobody was leaving yet, so my exit route was unimpeded. I dug a miniature of scotch from my overcoat pocket and poured a generous measure into Barbara's open mouth. She coughed and spluttered but eventually swallowed most of the contents. With her auburn hair flowing over my arm she looked like a sleeping pre-Raphaelite angel.

I felt guilty about what I was doing, but knew that it was for the best. Barbara's life was an empty mess, going nowhere. She needed love, she needed respect, she needed to be a success, and these were the things I was going to give her just as soon as she regained consciousness.

Whispering soothing words in her ear, I pulled open the door of the nearest cab and lifted my beautiful burden inside. I laid her gently back against the headrest, followed her in and gave the driver his instructions. He glanced in his rear-view mirror a couple of times, but did not speak.

By the time we reached the West End Barbara had begun to

stir, but the alcohol in her system was clearly hampering her co-ordination.

As our taxi drifted, becalmed, through the sluggish traffic around Piccadilly Circus, I tried to plan my next move. Barbara lay with her head against the passenger window, rolling it back and forth against the glass as if experiencing a traumatic dream. The skin on my hands kept sticking to the warm leather seat; I could feel new rips and stresses developing on my palms. The constant bacterial churning in my gut had swelled my groaning stomach, ripping the material of my shirt around the buttons. I needed to find a quiet spot, but instinct drew me back to Soho, where there would be no peace for hours to come. Above us, a distant scrape of thunder warned of the approaching storm that would break this suffocating heatwave.

My office was empty. The keys to the alarm system were in my jacket. I directed the cab into Rupert Street and told the driver to pull over. All I needed this night was an assurance from Barbara that she would take care of my films and my child, and in return I would take care of her for ever.

Perhaps I had been deluding myself. Perhaps the movie projects would not weather my disappearance and the financial structures I had set in place would collapse, but at least I had to try. What else was there left for me? I was disappointed not to have located a perfect screenplay, but perhaps one of the other projects would make up in direction what I had been forced to overlook in script execution.

We double-parked in the crowded street and I tipped the driver generously. I backed out of the rear door, pulling Barbara into my arms and planting her shoes on the pavement. It was just a short walk to the office from here, no more than twenty-five yards. I had pushed her against a wall and was looking for my keys when I heard a voice hailing me, right at my back.

CHAPTER FIFTY-THREE

Revolution

It was just before one. Lucas had discovered that earning money, even illegally, was hard work. So far tonight he had made almost three hundred pounds. Stopping to collect his thoughts in the rowdy pink quarter of Old Compton Street, he checked his bag and saw that there were still over a dozen ampoules left. It would be easy to call it a night, but the street was still packed with punters looking for a good time and willing to pay for it. As the hour grew later they became more reckless with their money. He could jack up the price of the bottles and make the same amount again, maybe even more.

If he had thought consciously about what he was doing he might have had second thoughts; he was not without a conscience. But he was angry with Malcolm, angry with everyone, angry for not being important, for not being listened to, and being given money was easing the pain. It wasn't fair. He knew he was surrounded by producers who had never produced anything in their lives, directors who had not been on a sound stage since film school, chancers who got by on energy and bullshit, artists who never produced any art, people who merely arranged meetings, but arranged so many of them that eventually, by some miraculous osmotic process, money was generated. And now here he was, generating money just like them, because everybody knew the old days were gone, the gentlemen of the industry had retired to second childhoods in their Surrey gardens, and for the new boys drugs were just a handshake, a calling card, an introduction that waived the queues at a million parties. Besides, he'd been to film school. Directing wasn't that difficult if you had a decent Director of Photography and an experienced editor. He knew the difference between an Elemack Cricket and a Fraser Dolly, a Split Diopter and a Grad, but what was the point if everybody else knew as well? Media Studies was the most popular college course in the country. But if it turned out that familiarity with the 35mm lab process was less important than getting a reputation as Mr Goodtime with the people who counted for something in the film world, then he'd be stupid not to use the foothold, wouldn't he?

He reached the corner of Wardour Street and dodged between the taxis that sped up from Shaftesbury Avenue. He was going to turn right, but decided to head into the racier quarter behind the office, where Soho's neon-lit sex clubs still thrived. What he needed was someone who carried a wad, someone with more money than sense. He slipped past the singing drunks who filled the piss-reeking alleyway of strip-joints leading into Rupert Street. Searching the pavement on the far side, he suddenly felt like a gambler on a lucky streak. There was the last person he expected to see. Richard Tyler, pushing some drunken girlfriend up against a wall.

'Hey, Mr Tyler, you need a hand?'

Richard twisted around, trying to keep his face in shadow, but his eyes stared glassily at a boy he did not recognise. 'Who's that?'

'Lucas? Your runner? I usually work for your partner, Mr

Elliot.' The woman was virtually unconscious. She looked familiar. What the hell had he done, knocked her out? 'You seem to be having some trouble there.'

'Oh, I – uh – she just, she drank too much. I thought I should get her to the office.'

His voice was strange, weirdly guttural.

'Okay.' Lucas took Barbara's left arm and lifted. Together they turned her in the direction of the office door.

'The alarm will be on,' said Lucas. 'Do you have the code?'

Richard suddenly appeared to change his mind about going up to the office. 'Look, why don't I just set her down over there?' He pointed to the little cafe on the corner. 'A black coffee will probably bring her around. We'll be fine.'

But Lucas wasn't about to be dismissed so easily. They sat her between them on an unstable plastic chair and the runner ordered three espressos. Richard pushed his chair back against the wall, out of the light, so that Lucas could barely see him. Barbara was in a stupor. Lucas could smell whisky on her clothes. She must have taken a bath in the stuff. 'So,' he asked, 'I guess you had a good evening?'

'It's not over yet,' Richard muttered darkly.

'That's true.' Never drink with your boss after midnight, thought Lucas, this is like pulling fucking teeth. 'Will your friend be all right?'

'She'll be fine.'

'Do you want a brandy or something?' Richard sounded like he had a sore throat.

'No, I'm – fine. I just need to get my breath back.'

'Wait, I've got something that might help.' He pulled the portfolio case from his shoulder and dug out one of the ampoules. 'This'll keep you going all night.'

'More drugs.'

'Nah, more – medicinal. The price of this stuff on the street is going to skyrocket, trust me.'

'Trust you.' Richard tried to concentrate on what the boy was holding. His vision kept fuzzing out of focus. He saw a small white bottle turned over in pale hands.

'I must stay awake. I still have much to do.'

'Then this is what you need. It normally sells for about –' he took a breath, 'eighty pounds –'

Richard gave no reaction. He stayed with his chair tipped back, his face lost in darkness, unmoving. Okay, so he had pitched a little too high. No harm in trying.

'– but I can let you have it for, say, fifty-five.'

Richard dragged his hand through a jacket pocket and threw a stack of crumpled, sweat-stained twenty-pound notes on the table, not bothering to count them or even look at them.

'All right,' said Lucas, grinning as he gathered the money. A hundred and forty quid! He wanted two and had already figured the discount! Who'd have thought that square old Mr Tyler would turn out to be such a cool customer? He pulled another bottle from the bag and handed it over. Richard left them on the table, sitting there in the open air, like they weren't part of a drug deal at all but bottles of fucking milk. Lucas looked up and saw a policeman walking on the other side of the road.

'Better put those away, I mean they're not exactly legal,' the boy prompted, but Richard made no move to pick them up. There was something wrong with his hand; it looked damaged, burned or something. The chemical bottles stayed where they had been set. Lucas could see a huge neon arrow above them blinking DRUG DEAL. He swept them from the table and emptied the contents into their espressos, one bottle in each.

'Believe me, if you're feeling tired this'll put you back on top,' he promised, sliding the cup across the table. There was another policeman opposite now. The two of them were talking, and pointing down the street. There was something going on. He shifted uncomfortably on the chair.

Barbara was reaching a state of consciousness. She fidgeted and rubbed at her eye. Alarmed, Richard reached from the shadows and grabbed the tiny cup. He downed the scalding liquid, then threw the cup aside. It tasted familiar, bitter and mentholated. A rumble of thunder made them both look up.

'Barbara, don't worry, you're safe.'

She opened her eyes and tried to make sense of the fact that she was sitting on a chair outside a coffee bar. 'Christ, what – what happened?' She tried to pull herself upright and take a look around, but nearly toppled the chair.

'You drank too much, Barbara. We've been looking after you.'

'Oh, Richard! Richard –' She was remembering. He saw a look of horror contort her features and pushed himself back into the darkness. 'Show me what you've done to yourself . . .'

'No, I–' He felt ashamed of causing such revulsion in others.

'Please, I need to see how much harm –'

She leaned forward to see, but he gently pushed her away.

'Your hands,' she gasped, 'what have you done to your hands?'

He could see shreds of dried skin hanging from his fingers like loose-fitting gloves, and hastily retracted them. Outside the cafe, the black Water Board van cruised to a stop, then reversed into a parking space right in front of them.

'Listen, you two obviously have a lot to talk about,' said Lucas, rattled. 'I've got to go.'

But the door of the van was already sliding back, and Waldorf – his eyes still encased in neon-reflecting Ray-Bans – was clambering out. Lucas looked across the road to where the two policemen stood.

'A pleasure doing business with you, boss.' Lucas rose from his chair as Waldorf spotted him. 'Enjoy the rest of your evening.' He darted around the front of the table but Waldorf threw out his arms and grabbed the strap of his portfolio case, pulling him back. There was no point in calling to the police, not with drugs in the bag. He was trapped.

'I remember you, smart-arse,' grinned Waldorf. 'Get in the van.' Lucas yanked at the nylon case as it slid from his arm and Waldorf began to haul in his catch. The strap strained and snapped open at its clasp, slithering through Waldorf's hands. They had been pulling so hard that Lucas fell back, firing the case over his head into the air. It turned once and was lost in the searing electric night. A moment later it could not be seen. It never hit the pavement.

As Lucas shoved himself away, puzzled by the bag's disappearance, Waldorf grabbed him by the shoulder and yanked him back behind the van, out of public sight. Lifting him inside, he hurled the boy over the back of the passenger seat on to the pile of black plastic shrouds and slammed the door shut.

'Let's get out of here,' One Eighty snapped from the passenger seat, where he lay with his right leg awkwardly outstretched. The van veered out into the traffic, cutting up the cars behind.

'What are we going to do with him?'

'Let me out,' shouted Lucas, fighting for balance as the van rounded a corner, 'I know what you put in these bags!'

'Give yourself a medal, boy.' Waldorf turned to his crippled partner. 'Slow on the uptake, isn't he? I blame the comprehensive system.'

'You're a pair of fucking body snatchers!'

'Yes and no,' replied the driver, trying to be fair. 'They're dead, but they're not buried.'

'That one I sat on wasn't dead.'

Waldorf spun the steering wheel, rolling One Eighty across the seat. 'No. He surprised us all. I think his nervous system decided to have one last fling. He'd taken enough chemicals to poison a rhino.'

One Eighty clawed himself upright, twisting so that he could keep the boy in his sights. 'The people in the bags, the moment they finish work they jack into anything they can lay their hands on. Sometimes they're braindead and their hearts have stalled, but their nerves and livers are still doing the Lambada. Those bottles you're flogging around town – they're not yours, are they?'

'Fuck off.'

'Ooooh. Big man.' The van hit the brakes and One Eighty winced. 'What's in 'em?'

'He doesn't know,' said Waldorf, crunching gears, 'he's got no idea what trouble he's been causing.'

'That stuff you're cheerfully bunging around Soho is called Imago, right?'

'So?'

'So, it's lethal if you don't mix it in exactly the right proportions, do you understand? Have you been telling punters how to use it?'

Lucas felt sick. Worse. His mouth was so dry he couldn't speak. What had he done? What the hell had he done?

'Weren't you given any instructions?'

'Yeah, but I forgot what they were. I didn't think they were important.'

'Great.' He poked One Eighty in the shoulder. 'Call Midas, see what he wants done with this mook.'

One Eighty punched out the speed-dial code, spoke to the barman at The Hot House, then listened. 'He's not there,' he explained, folding away the cellphone. 'He's going to some party. Eddie reckons he's gone back to his apartment to change.'

'Can't we leave the boy at the club?'

'What, we just tie him up and walk him through the bar? That'll give the punters something to talk about. Bollocks, let's take him to the flat.'

'I can do a deal with you,' Lucas pleaded.

'Oh, right. Like those deals you've been doing all night.'

'Listen, I don't know who you are, I'd never recognise you again, let me out and nobody will ever know—'

Waldorf brought the van to a stop. 'You don't seem to understand, sonny. You've been killing people. You're a murderer. A public health hazard. A walking toxic waste dump. You're bad for Soho and you're bad for us. We have to leave you with somebody official and let him decide what's to be done with you.' He turned to One Eighty. 'You'd better wait here.'

'What, you don't think I should have a go at four flights of stairs?' cried One Eighty in surprise. 'Don't you want me to get better?'

'What's he like, your boss?' asked Lucas as he was bundled out of the vehicle and in through the entrance to Midas Blake's apartment building.

'Very decisive,' answered Waldorf. 'One look at you and

he'll know exactly where your body should be dumped. He'll probably pick a quiet spot below Waterloo Bridge, very popular that is. If the tide's going out, you won't get a boat-hook in your collar until you're well past Woolwich.'

Glory raised the portfolio case by its strap, allowing it to revolve slowly in front of her. Placing a hand beneath the side-pocket, she felt the bottles inside and smiled. She was tired of seeing Soho awash with drugs. She wanted change. Not physically engineered change, but a revolution brought about from within the collective psyche of the residents. Revolutions hurt, but people were resilient. They survived. Drugs were everywhere.

It was an odd situation for her; she usually felt she knew exactly what was best for Soho, but tonight was different. Instead of destroying the bottles, suppose she distributed them? Some users would live, some would not. Perhaps the wrong people would survive. She could imagine the chaos. The area would be affected for years to come. Bars and restaurants would be closed. Tourists would shun the neighbourhood. Property prices would fall. Vice would move back in. Their business interests would be damaged beyond repair. But perhaps the place would grow into something entirely new. Soho was not a Christian place; it remained the responsibility of older, crueller gods.

Glory's grip on the case tightened as she reached a decision and turned her glittering heels in the direction of the nearest nightclub.

Arthur Bryant tried to make himself heard above the noise, then gave up. All around them people were running, shoving, trying to get away. The man who had burst from the doorway of the Japanese restaurant could not be stopped by either of the officers in this part of the street. Their steel-weave vests were too heavy and uncomfortable to wear for long on a hot night like this, and they had removed them. This lunatic was waving a meat cleaver and screaming as he swung the blade around himself in great sweeping arcs. Nobody wanted to get near him. They had all seen commercials for Japanese knives.

'We can bring him down, sir,' said one of the men.

'In an area this crowded? Absolutely not,' warned May. 'Besides, he doesn't know what he's doing. It's the effect of a drug, you can't shoot a man for taking an overdose, for God's sake. Put someone in suitable clothing and disarm him.'

'There's some riot gear in the back of the van,' said Janice Longbright. 'Two of the boys are suiting up.'

'I've never seen anything like this – this mafficking.' Bryant turned about in horror as he witnessed the unfolding chaos. Two panicking pedestrians had slammed into the bonnet of a car, causing it to veer into a shop window. There was a second fall of glass, and more people began to scream. 'This is beyond a civil disturbance,' said Bryant, 'it's madness. What are we supposed to do?'

'Contain and control – Christ, I don't know.'

They watched helplessly as Soho ran riot around them. When May turned back he found Bryant walking purpose-fully away down the middle of the road. 'Wait,' he called, 'where are you going?' But the old man had made up his mind to act, and was conveniently deaf to any protest.

Behind the turquoise neon ziggurats of the Bar None, Glory had taken over at the counter and was mixing the world's most dangerous cocktails. The bottles spun in her hands as she bounced along to the Japanese techno-mix, grinning madly as she distributed the bright, lethal shot-glasses to her eager customers.

'What are they called, Miss?' asked a Texan tourist.

'Suicide Cult,' Glory answered with a sour smile. She sat back and unfolded her black wings, waiting for the next wave of cleansing lunacy to begin.

CHAPTER FIFTY-FOUR

Anabiosis

I heard the clock in the tower of St Anne's Church distantly striking one.

'Let go, Richard, you're hurting me!' Barbara twisted away from me, but I tightened my grip on her wrist, causing her to cry out in sobering pain.

'I have to talk to you somewhere quietly, I can't do it here,' I called back. Around us, mortals ran and stumbled as deranged satyrs threw bricks, litter bins, chairs, anything they could lay their hands on. Thank God there are no children in Soho at night, I thought. Across the street the plate-glass frontage of a nightclub, the Bar None, suddenly fell out onto the pavement, neon tubes splintering and exploding around a screaming man.

'Tell me what you want, Richard.' Barbara was crying now. 'I don't understand.'

It seemed as if she was deliberately refusing to keep up with me, lagging behind, pulling back. With one strong kick I brought her legs out from under her and caught her as she fell. Hoisting her into my arms, I began shoving angrily through the crowded confusion, but she screamed bloody murder, long and hard and loud, and within seconds people were shouting things back like 'Leave her alone!' My God, I thought, they think I'm one of them, one of the crazy people, and before anyone could pull us down I broke through the malcontented mob into the street beyond. Thunder reverberated through the sky in an oceanic roar, making everyone stop and look up.

Racing along the cobbled street with Barbara's warm body in my arms and Soho's villagers closing in behind me, I understood how Baron Frankenstein had felt. But there was no castle where I would be safe, for I knew – just as the monster and his bride had known – that I belonged dead.

'By the morning I'll be gone, and this night will just be a bad dream.' I talked to calm her, and pushed ahead into Shaftesbury Avenue. The streets were still crowded, but there was less madness here. The pavement was more open, the area more exposed. Our pursuers wheeled around the corner behind us, calling out to others to stop me. Flustered by so many conflicting signals, people parted to let us through and watched as we passed, wondering whether to interfere. Barbara was growing heavy in my arms, so I stopped beneath the narrow glass canopy of the Palace Theatre. The stage door was closed, but the fire escape exit gave when I tried it. Pulling down on the handle, I lowered Barbara and shoved her inside.

There was no one at the doorman's box. If there was anyone left in the theatre, I knew that they would be in their dressing rooms, far from us. I forced her ahead of me, and she stumbled up the shadowy stairs.

I felt close to death now, real death, a blessed release from my suffering. By the time I reached the second floor I could hear the rabble shouting below, but now there were police sirens, and it sounded as if they had stopped outside in confusion.

'Richard, where are we going?' Barbara cried, blundering ahead in the dark. At the next landing, the stone staircase became a steel fire escape ladder. I pushed past her and led the way, gripping her arm, almost pulling her off her feet. Our escape route led to the angled gables of the roof. Slamming the firedoor shut and picking my way along the gulleys like Oliver Reed in *Curse of the Werewolf*, or Christopher Lee in *Taste the Blood of Dracula*, I brought Barbara to the brink of the building. Below us, traffic barged boisterously across Cambridge Circus.

'I have to be sure that you'll help me,' I explained, allowing her to lean and catch her breath against the warm terracotta tiles.

She was trying to be rational, trying to say the right thing. She was frightened. There was a smear of dirt across her forehead. It endeared her to me even further. 'Richard, if you're in trouble, you know I'll help.'

'I want you to take care of my legacy, my films and my son. Is that too much to ask for? Gregory will be cared for financially, but he needs the devotion of a decent woman –'

'What on earth are you talking about?'

'I've explained this to you, Barbara, and I only have a short time left. The bacteria in my stomach is growing by the second. I can feel it becoming ever more lethal. It's eating into my brain. I will die before dawn, and when it happens I must be alone. Someone will have to look after Gregory. You're kind, you're good –'

Her eyes widened. She looked angry about something. Already I could see what her reply would be, but I hoped she would change her attitude; I did not want to have to hurt her.

'You know I'd be happy to help Gregory, but you must stop this nonsense about being dead, Richard.'

'Miranda wouldn't do it. I killed her, Barbara, I strangled her even though I loved her. She wouldn't listen to me, wouldn't help me. She never wanted to be a mother. She didn't love her own son. And now she's gone.'

'I know Miranda's dead, Richard. How could I forget? I went to her funeral with you on Tuesday.'

'What are you talking about?'

'I sat in the front car right next to you and held your hand, remember?'

'Don't be stupid,' I cried, 'she's not buried yet, I left her body in the old theatre – I killed Berry, too. You mustn't be angry with me. I had to.'

Barbara was searching my face, looking for something. She was making me feel very uncomfortable. A dull pain began to grow behind my dry, ruined eyes.

'Richard, listen to me, you didn't kill Miranda. She was very ill, she had a tumour and she died. Don't you remember? We went to her funeral together. I gave you a letter from her.'

Sapped of energy, I slumped against the wall at my back. I was becoming confused. 'No, the letter was from Paul.'

'Paul who?'

'My old friend, Paul, my best friend Paul.'

'Listen to me, Richard, you've been under a lot of pressure and you've got everything tangled up. Berry's away on vacation. He was too upset about Miranda to stay in town. He left this morning. He's gone scuba diving in the Maldives.'

'That's impossible.' I sat up, ever more puzzled. 'I killed him yesterday.'

'You didn't, Richard. I spoke to him, for God's sake. He came into our office first thing. He was wearing a Hawaiian shirt, and was carrying goggles and flippers. He didn't exactly appear to be in mourning.'

'Barbara, I don't remember –'

'Miranda died ten days ago and you went to her funeral on Tuesday with me. The letter was from her, not your friend Paul. Paul died nearly a year ago. He had a breakdown and killed himself. Miranda was very ill. You accused her of having an affair. You said you'd never forgive her, but when you finally found out that she was ill, you wanted to so badly. And she died before you could talk to her. Have you been taking anything? You've been hiding your eyes all night. Let me look.'

'No, you're lying, I don't want you to see me like this –'

She seized the collar of my jacket and pulled me towards the light. The sodium glare from the floodlights on the front of the theatre shone harshly upon my features.

'Oh Christ,' she cried, 'what have you done to yourself?'

'I warned you,' I said miserably. 'I told you not to look.'

'We have to get it seen to at once, Richard.' Puzzled by the tone in her voice, I pressed my fingertips to my face, trying to understand.

'How ever did you get those awful cuts? Your hands and dear God, your arms too, the tissue will scar – those blue bruises –'

Couldn't she see my flaking raw features, the craquelure of my tortured skin, like some perished shop dummy in its final stages of decay?

'I'm dying,' I stated simply.

'You're a total mess but that's about all,' she said firmly. 'You've fallen over a lot and it looks like you've been cutting yourself with something. Some of these wounds look infected. You're going to need some stitches. What have you been doing to yourself?'

'I – don't know.'

I dropped to the ground and started to cry. 'I don't understand.' She knelt beside me and examined my eyes, yanking at the lids. 'Jesus, your pupils are like black basketballs. Is that coke?'

'No,' I mumbled, feeling ashamed. I thought of the coffee cup Lucas had passed to me. That awful menthol taste. So familiar. Where had I tasted it before?

'What have you taken, Richard?'

The answer slowly surfaced. The bitter mentholated smell, it always filled the edit suite, it was always on Mitch, always on Berry, in the little white packets they passed me, little doses of slow poison.

'What – have – you – taken?'

I thought back through the week. I'd taken some on Monday, then on Tuesday before the funeral. I'd been up all that night snorting the stuff. And the next day – more than I had ever taken before, just to keep myself on the edge . . .

'We should get you to a doctor.'

Then why hadn't Mitch been affected? He'd been taking all kinds of drugs from all over the place, why hadn't he succumbed to these paranoid delusions? I fought the pandemonium in my brain and tried to understand what had happened.

The weird familiar smell, it was on Berry's clothes, it was on Lucas, it all came from the same source. Suddenly everything began to make sense. Berry got it from Lucas and gave it to Mitch. The editor's stash came from different sources. Everything I had taken stemmed from Lucas.

'I'm not dying,' I gasped, 'I'm not dying.' Disbelief flooded over me. I tried to stand up, but my limbs had grown suddenly heavy and I staggered against the parapet. Not death at all but a series of guilt-ridden delusions.

'Thank you, thank you.' I seized her shoulders and embraced her, bringing my face against the pulse of her neck, her ear, her warm hair. 'God, Barbara, you don't know what a week I've been going through. Nightmares. Worse. Much worse.'

I stayed like this for ages, gently rocking her back and forth in my arms as tears streamed down my cheeks. As I broke away, I was surprised to find her asleep, her body once more heavy in my arms. As I watched, a helpless grin spread across my face, growing wider and wider until it seemed in danger of splitting open my skin. It was so hard to tell what was real and what was imagined. I supposed I would continue to suffer hallucinations until the stuff I had swallowed in the coffee cup wore off.

But I had not taken one sip.

I had drunk the whole thing.

And this had to be my hallucination, Barbara telling me that everything was all right, this, *this* was just a phantasm. Isn't a dream something you want to believe? I looked back at Barbara and saw that she was unconscious. Her eyes had rolled up in their sockets. I had almost succeeded in crushing the life from her. How long had she been out? How much had I imagined? I began shaking her hard but she looked dead, as dead as everyone else in my life.

'Help me, Barbara,' I shouted, 'I can no longer trust my senses.' Behind me there were footsteps on the stairs. Someone was coming. I had promised myself one thing; that I would settle my life before leaving it. At least I had managed to help Gregory, and that counted for something, didn't it?

Fists were hammering angrily on the fire escape door. People shouted my name as they threw themselves against the lock. Their booming blows echoed over the roof like a giant's footsteps. Then the sounds faded away, the cacophony of the traffic became muffled and flattened, and the world was silent but for the wind in my ears.

I tried to rise, but the bones of my legs had been damaged in the climb to the roof. My right femur splintered and split as I tried to put my weight on it. Behind me, Barbara burst into spluttering life, coughing and gagging as she rolled over on the slates.

'Help me!' I screamed, 'I don't know what is real!'

Lightning buckled the sky, flash-framing the rooftop. I twisted back to her, unable to walk. The sharded pale bones of my leg poked through soft, rotten flesh as the musculature around it stretched and tore. I reached out to her with a clawed right hand, knobbles of raw bone thrusting through the ends of my fingers. The clouds above us flashed an angry vermillion. Thunder punched the air, echoing through stone canyons.

'God, won't you help me! *I don't know what is true!*'

Barbara stared at me in horror, pushing herself back against the parapet as I lurched towards her. With a sharp, dry crack my other leg shattered at the knee. I looked down in horror as my right thigh-bone wrenched out of my tortured pelvis, and felt a lurch deep inside as the bacteria breached my stomach wall. The torn epidermis, as dry as tissue paper, opened to expose intestines that shifted from coiled order into ungainly loops, obscenely bare, reeking and stinging in the polluted night atmosphere.

My body was disintegrating quickly now, decaying beneath me, my internal organs splitting and popping and dissolving. It felt as though cracks were opening in my head, as though for the first time my trepanned brain was reaching out into the air, like a fire exposed to oxygen.

Using my left hand to grip the parapet, I pulled myself towards her. 'I don't know if I am a man or a monster!'

'Richard, whatever you may have done, you must know you are a man.' Barbara reached out her arm. Anyone else would have been immobilised by the sight of my corporeal form rendering itself down into offal.

The door behind us exploded back against the wall and men began pouring through. They were brandishing staves, knives, shotguns, their faces contorted with self-righteous fury. Barbara screamed as one of them tried to pull her from me. I swung my scarecrow arms at him, sending him sprawling on to the tiles. I turned back to Barbara, longing to hold her one last time. They were almost upon me when I pushed myself back to the concrete lip of the building and looked down to the distant street.

It was time for me to leave, to launch myself into the sky and conclude the matter of my corruption. I knew I would fall with my dilemma unresolved. I would fall knowing it could be no other way, because what I had been asking for was an absurd paradox. It is impossible to satisfactorily conclude one's life before dying. No life can be closed without the act of death, and as that moment remains unfixed, no life can ever be completely resolved.

I looked down at the street far below. The moment of my end was here. I would fall not understanding if I was a murderer or a victim, a chemically-corrupted psychopath or the product of some physical refusal of death. I would fall having spent my entire life doing the wrong thing. I pulled myself over the cusp of warm, wet concrete and heard Barbara scream as I felt the stone beneath me drop away.

But then, as my body tumbled through the raging night sky, I felt the truth in my heart. And what I saw within brought me comfort, because it concluded the events of my life, decided my fate, and closed my little world. It would be hard for anyone to understand that the shattered form hurtling towards the pavement had ever once been a man.

CHAPTER FIFTY-FIVE

Karl Malden and the Meaning of Life

Barbara's hand was knotted over my forearm.

It was raining hard. I looked down at the pavement, then back at her desperate face. I was sprawled on my stomach, halfway over the parapet. We were alone on the roof. 'You've come back,' she cried, relieved, 'my God, you've come back.'

'What's happening?' The thundershower was falling heavily around us, bouncing up from the orange stone brickwork of the theatre.

'You're getting some colour back in your cheeks,' she laughed, 'that's what's happening.' She turned her face to the rushing clouds and allowed the downpour to flood over her. I felt the chemical effect leaving my system in a single hard rush, like dropping through the first freefall on a roller-coaster.

'Whoah!' I clutched at my head, feeling my body temperature start to fall with the surrounding atmosphere. And with it, the rush of events that had marked the last year of my life. Paul killing himself. Miranda's illness. The terrible, wrenching letter she had given to Barbara to pass on to me after her death. Her affair with Berry had been real. Miranda had been no saint. The institutionalisation of our son had placed us both under a lot of pressure. I had been angry and frustrated, pathologically unable to take control of the situation, still working for the man who had once made love to her. Then to be the last to know that she was dying, to be unable to forgive her. There was never any time. I had reached her hospital room minutes too late.

I was beginning to see how the accumulation of poison in my system had distorted my vision. Virtually everything I had imagined over the last five days had been drawn from the vast repository of stock film situations that sat inside my head. My love of motion pictures had burst the banks of my rational mind, overflowing into my life, fleshing it out with celluloid dreams.

I warned you at the start. I told you when I took you flying. My imagination has always run away with me. And I played fair with you. Look back at these notes and you will see. It's all there, just as it happened to me.

But as the skies opened up on us and I knelt in the warm dirty water cradling Barbara in my arms, I remembered how I always wanted a happy ending.

'You saved me,' I told her.

'No.' She shook her head. 'I'm not here to save you. You can do that for yourself. I'm not a substitute for Miranda. But I'll help you.'

'I'm scared of dying again,' I whispered, looking into her eyes. 'I know there's a life beyond Soho. I need to get away from all these people in black. They're ready to die. I'm not. I want to live a normal life among normal people.'

For a moment I thought she was going to kiss me. Instead

she gave me such a resounding slap around the face that she nearly knocked my teeth out.

'Oh, get a grip, Richard,' she snapped. 'Have you seen what life is like out there? It's awful! You want to be among *normal people*? Most normal people have the charisma of gherkins. They creep around Tesco hypnotised by non-stick pans and oven chips. They pick their noses at bus-stops and read car magazines and lay farting in front of the television watching dramatic reconstructions of accidents. You want to become a vegetable in the suburbs? Normal life *sucks*. Its homes stink of baby sick and spring-dew toilet cleaner and *clichès*. And the older you get the more clichèd it gets, until you exist in an atmosphere of total jet-black hatred, masturbating over underage models in Argos catalogues and arguing about the boundary lines of hedges. By the time you die or get bunged in a home you've lost interest in everyone and everything. Normal people are lifetime moaners who only perk up at the misfortunes of others. You don't belong in that world. You have a shot at something different, not the kind of different they show on TV, not skydiving grannies and excitable arseholes in off-road 4×4s, but something uniquely, unhealthily you. Do you understand?' She shook me violently. 'You're here in Soho because there's something very wrong with you, something that prevents you from fitting in. You're special as in missing-a-limb-special, because you have an obsession. An awful, crippling, debilitating, depthless obsession with films. You can describe a plot and send normal people fleeing from you like vampires in daylight. You can't name the senior members of the cabinet but you can name every film in Alfred Hitchcock's career. And it goes much deeper than that. If you thought about it, you'd realise you could name every film *Karl Malden* ever appeared in, including the Italian ones he did when he needed the money. If someone asked you for the connection between Bryan Forbes' *Deadfall* and Guy Hamilton's *Goldfinger*, or between Ridley Scott's *Legend* and Stanley Kubrick's *2001*, you'd give them answers like a shot. *It's what you do*. You needn't be in denial about your power anymore. Other people get obsessed too, but yours is a usable sickness. Just keep away from normal people. Brick up the wall. Stay in the ghetto where you belong. Ghettos are the last bastions of individuality.' Finally she paused for breath. 'And this is all I know. Maybe one more thing. The real and lasting pleasures of life consist of a million small, memorable moments. Just pinpricks of light in the dark.'

'Movies always tell you that life amounts to something much more meaningful,' I protested.

'Fuck 'em,' she laughed as she kissed me in the tumbling, sparkling rain, 'they're only movies.'

CHAPTER FIFTY-SIX

Recruitment

Lucas tried to tip himself on to his side, but the bindings were too tight. Midas Blake had not arrived at his flat yet, so Waldorf had knotted his hands together with electrical flex and looped the end through the landing banister before gagging him with a filthy handkerchief and leaving him there as a present.

His watch read 01:47 a.m. The hall light was on a timer, and had clicked off seconds after the front door had shut behind them. The landing was in darkness, although a little light filtered in from the street. He kicked out at the banister, but it was difficult to see where he was aiming. After a few minutes, one of the wooden bars began to crack but would not give.

Judy heard the noise on the landing and woke with a start. She listened carefully. It sounded as if someone was trying to break into the flat next door. Perhaps Midas had lost his keys.

With great difficulty she pulled herself into the little hall and laid down so that her mouth was below the door. 'Hey,' she called, her voice little more than a croak. 'Hey.'

'Who are you?' replied a man. Not Midas, someone younger.

'I'm locked in here.'

'You are? Jesus, that's fucking inconvenient. I'm tied up. They left me here for Midas.'

'You must get free before he comes back.'

'I can't. I'm tied to the banisters. I need like, a knife or something.'

'Wait a minute.'

She headed for the kitchen and began searching through the drawers for something sharp. It took her a while to return to the hall, and she could hear him starting to panic. 'Someone's at the front door,' he hissed, 'hurry.'

She slid a breadknife beneath the door but it caught on the handle. She hit it with the heel of her shoe, and it scraped under. She watched as the blade vanished, taken from the other side. On the landing, the timer-lights went on.

'Shit, he's coming,' she croaked. 'Don't let him catch you.'

'Don't worry, I've no intention of doing so.' Lucas sawed through most of the flex and was able to bend the last piece back and forth until it weakened and broke. Below, he heard heavy footsteps on the stairs. He looked over the banisters and saw the top of Midas's head.

'Stand away from the door,' he called, charging it. The centre panel fractured beneath his shoulder, but the frame held. He charged again, and this time the panel fell inward even though the frame remained firmly in place. As he hauled himself through, the smell of rotting garbage stung his nostrils.

'What happened to the lights?' he asked. The footsteps were on the final flight of stairs. Lucas stared at the woman he was rescuing. She looked terrible. 'Christ, lady, what happened to you? What's been going on here?'

Judy pushed anxiously past him. 'We've got to get out of

here before –' She stopped. Lucas followed her frightened gaze. Midas was framed in the remains of the doorway.

Before the boy could move he was seized by the arm, lifted and thrown across the kitchen. He crashed into a chair and fell hard against the far wall. As he tried to pick himself up he saw Midas grab Judy by her hair and drag her across the room. She screamed and flailed at him but he ignored her, hurling her into a corner so hard that Lucas felt sure he must have broken her neck. She fell beneath the window and lay there unmoving. He studied her for a few moments, brushed a lank strand of blonde hair back in place, then headed across the floor with an exasperated grunt.

Lucas was hauled back on his feet. Midas dragged him from the kitchen, holding him so high that his trainers did not touch the ground. Out and across the landing, shoved under one enormous arm as Midas unlocked his front door, then into a bizarre tropical retreat filled with lush ripe plants and sickly perfumed flowers.

'You and I need to have a little talk, my friend,' he said, punching him backwards so that he stumbled and fell on to a low couch. 'You've broken the local rules. Have you seen what you've caused out there?' He crossed the lounge and pulled open the window. Shouts, sirens, the anger of running men. The shriek of braking tyres on wet streets. It had finally begun to rain. 'Malcolm Cotton is dead, and the damage has been halted at its source. You're the last remaining symptom.'

'Why was she locked up in there?' Lucas was scared, but not enough to overcome his curiosity. 'What have you been doing to her?'

'Judy broke the rules as well. It was a matter of loyalties, sonny, I don't suppose you'd understand. Stuff like that creates a structural weakness in the system. We can't afford to be distracted, not for a moment, not by anyone. She'll be fine. She could have left at any time.'

'How?'

'It's a mind thing. Of no concern to you. You should be worrying about yourself.'

Lucas was about to press his case, but the murderous look in Midas's eyes stopped him. There was no point in lying or trying to excuse himself. This was one time when honesty might be the only way out.

'I got greedy,' he said simply. 'Malcolm had left the bottles with me. He wanted me to give them away, just hand them out to people. It was a chance to make some money. They would have found their way on to the street one way or another.'

Midas considered this for a minute. 'I know, but what you did was wrong. You see that, don't you?' He paced across to the open window and turned his face to the sky, allowing the rain to soak him. 'Soho will always need protectors. It's hard to find people with real dedication to the job. They don't stay long.'

'I could do it,' he answered eagerly. 'Let me work for you.'

Midas considered the offer. He had misgivings about the boy, but Glory had behaved just as irresponsibly, and there was nothing he could do about her. 'Order needs to be restored,' he decided. 'It's fitting that you should make amends for your mistake.' The trademark smile started to appear. 'Perhaps we can work something out.'

'The mind thing –'

'Forget about it. It's something you're born with, and it's a curse. Let's take one day at a time.'

It seemed impossible, but she felt raindrops on her face.

Fat wet baubles bursting on her parched skin. A cool zephyr traversing her arms and exposed breasts. More rain.

And thunder, blessed deafening thunder as the promised storm finally broke above her . . .

'Miss Merrigan.'

An elderly man with bright false teeth, upside down. And Ari's wife, Maria. She was holding out a mug of tea, her panacea for all ills. Judy tried to raise her head. She could hear the rain falling steadily, thrumming on the roof, dripping from gutters, churning through drainpipes. The air was cool. Her mouth and throat were dry, too parched to speak. She gulped greedily at the tea, scalding her tongue.

'How did – how did you get in?'

'You have no front door to speak of,' said Arthur Bryant. 'Are you all right?'

'I – think so.' She promptly threw up on the floor.

'Ah – the gas,' said the elderly man. 'All the taps were turned on. I wouldn't try to stand up just yet.'

Maria was at the other end of the flat with her hand over her mouth, opening the windows. Clouds of flies were settled on the rotting binbags beside the sink as fast as she shooed them away. One thought passed through Judy's disordered mind. She had to confront Midas in the company of Maria and Ari and this elderly stranger, to prove to someone that she was not mad, that she had not done this to herself. She pulled her shirt down over her breasts, staggered painfully to her feet and rubbed the lump on the side of her head.

'Who is this?' She pointed at Bryant.

Maria waved the old man forward. 'He comes to look for Mr Blake and sees your door, smells the gas . . .'

Judy all but dragged them across the landing to Midas's door.

'Are you *sure* you're all right?' Maria was asking, and the old man was saying something about getting her to a doctor when the door opened and there stood the skinny young man with the bad haircut who had managed to break into her flat.

'Where's Midas?' she shouted. 'He didn't hurt you? Is he in there?'

Puzzled, Lucas stared at Maria, then back at Judy. 'What is she talking about – ?'

Judy was hysterical now. 'Where is Midas Blake?'

'I don't understand,' Maria was telling Bryant, 'Miss Merrigan, she's not been well and she –'

'*Where the hell is he?*'

' I live in this apartment,' said Lucas. 'I don't believe we've met before.'

'You're lying, can't you see he's lying!' She pushed past the boy. 'He must be in here!' But there was nobody else in the flat. There had been a framed photograph of Midas on the coffee table. She grabbed at it, only to find herself looking at a Polaroid of the boy with his arm around some girl on holiday. 'You know where he is,' she screamed, 'why are you protecting him?'

They're all in it, she thought, *he's got to all of them*.

Her last remaining strength left her. The game had ended in a stalemate. She stumbled back to her apartment and fell on to the sofa, then slept all the way to the hospital.

Later, many things continued to puzzle her. How could the boy have been won over so quickly? Had Midas used his ability to cloud minds? Where was he now? The thought plagued her that he might be planning to come back and finish the job. Perhaps he thought she was dead, or worse – alive and weak enough to accept him.

But finally, she knew that he had lost interest in her and moved on, in the way that some males thought nothing of exchanging their women. In the weeks and months that followed, she took to walking around the Soho streets searching for him. Sometimes she thought she saw Midas through the windows of a restaurant, but when she drew closer the features changed and she always found herself staring at the face of a stranger.

She sensed he was there just beyond her reach, slowing his step at a street corner so that their paths would not cross, or suddenly turning his back as she approached. She felt sure she had been part of a greater drama, that he had taken something from her, anger, lust, some vital force that he had used to augment his own strange power, but the worst thing was – she could not be sure. She only knew that there were things she would never understand, and that even if she reached the end of her life with her goals achieved, her relationships resolved and everything neatly squared away, there would be a part that remained forever hidden in darkness and chaos. But perhaps, she decided, this was how life was meant to be. Good was rooted in evil, just as light was born in shadow, and the rational world was no more than a beam flickering brightly in the darkened auditorium of her mind.

CHAPTER FIFTY-SEVEN

Defenders

Sergeant Janice Longbright pulled up the collar of her rain jacket and stopped in front of the basement steps. Just a few hours ago this whole area had been in an uproar. Now it was Saturday, and the streets had been washed clean of their sins. Soho possessed the early-morning composure of a small town waking up, except that a pair of green-haired transvestites in see-through plastic raincoats were sitting on the back of a milk float eating kebabs.

Longbright gripped the iron railings as she descended the slippery steps, then halted in front of the door. The sign above it had been torn out from the brickwork. A bare flex hung from the wall. The plaque and the entry bell had also been removed. Three wide planks had been hammered into position across the entrance, heavy mortar nails pounded into the brick. A note had been attached to one of the planks with a piece of Elastoplast. It read: NO DELIVERIES UNTIL FURTHER NOTICE.

'The Hot House is a funny place,' said May, fishing the teabag from his cup with the pointy end of a dart and flicking it expertly into the wastebin.

'Funny, why?'

'It's gone. Boarded up. Closed down. Just like that. Janice went there this morning and couldn't find anyone who had the faintest idea where Midas Blake and his entourage had disappeared to. It looks like the carnival left town.'

'You half expect it in that locality,' said Bryant. 'Those short-lease places come and go so quickly.'

They watched the rain stream across the windows of their office above Mornington Crescent tube station. Vans sloshed over blocked drains and flooding roads. The city had plunged prematurely into autumn.

'Oh, he'll resurface somewhere. The only thing we can be sure is that he won't go far. He and his troupe have taken it upon themselves to protect the area. Soho is Blake's domain. He wouldn't be able to leave it even if he wanted to.'

'I have a feeling you're right,' Bryant agreed. 'I'm not sure whether to be worried or relieved.'

'What made you try to find Midas?'

Bryant threw his partner a look of exasperation. 'I was standing in the middle of a riot, John! At my age, broken bones don't heal fast. I thought I'd go and see the only person who might be in a position to tell us what was happening. I'm convinced the boy was our "Typhoid Mary". Pity he wasn't carrying any proof.'

'No, but the epidemic stopped.'

By 3:00 a.m, everything had returned to normal. The panic had peaked, giving way to an eerie calm. Bar owners swept up broken glass. Ambulances removed innocent victims. With the exception of a few boarded-up windows, the streets of Soho looked no different from the way they had appeared before, the inhabitants only a little more dazed than usual.

'An outbreak of violence on that scale was a direct threat

to Midas Blake's livelihood,' said Bryant. 'It was in his interest to take action. The way you described him stuck in my mind. You said he was like London's landlord . . .' He shook the thought from his head. 'I'm going mad. Forget it. The main thing is that we nailed Malcolm Cotton's murderer.'

May laughed. 'What a buffoon! You'd think if he was going to get rid of the incriminating evidence, he'd blow off the right toe.'

'And by that you mean the left one. Eurgh. This tea is stewed.'

'I'm not surprised. You made it an hour ago.'

'Sod it, I'm going over the pub.' Bryant rose and made a grab for his serpentine scarf. 'Are you coming?'

'I suppose so. Are you going to wear that hat in public?'

'Alma knitted this bobblehat. It's very fetching.'

'It's what it might fetch that worries me.'

Bryant and May crossed the wet road arm in arm, like children in the dark, never stopping to consider that they too were spirits of the city, the defenders of its dreams, the guardians of its future.

CHAPTER FIFTY-EIGHT

Family

'**What did** you expect of me?' Glory stretched herself across the sofa like a cat lazing in a shop window. Rain-squalls hit the penthouse roof with metronomic regularity. The Soho loft was cool, almost cold, the space sparely decorated with two gigantic white canvases, a bright red sofa, emerald cushions on the polished wooden floor. A cat prowled somewhere.

'I just thought you could have acted with a little more – restraint,' said Midas, carefully choosing his words. 'Seven people died.'

'A small price.' She yawned, settling further into her position for sleep. 'Sometimes I don't know why I do things, but it usually turns out to have been the right course. At least I didn't sleep with any of them.'

'Thank God. That usually kills them, anyway.'

'I don't see what you're complaining about. The poison was flushed through the system. Soho abides. Sometimes I think we should let it die, for all the thanks we get. Besides, how dare you accuse me of cruelty. Look at the way you treated your little girlfriend.'

Midas sat beside her. 'I let Judy go.'

'So you should. She was too mousy for you, anyway.'

'She could have left the flat at any time.'

'Ah yes, the power, the wonderful power. Such a gift. Such a burden.'

'It's only in the mind.'

'And sometimes not even there. God, I'm so tired.'

He gently stroked her hair. 'I love you, Glory.'

Her eyes were closed now. 'I love you, little brother, but you've a lot to learn.'

'I've been thinking. I have an idea for a new venture. I'll need your help.'

She softly blew a kiss. 'Tell me later. Let me sleep now.'

As always she's right, he thought. Hard times require cruel gods. He stayed beside his slumbering sister, watching her until the amber light grew once more in the sky.

The rain had finally stopped. The five of them walked briskly along the wet tarmac of Berwick Street, masters of all they surveyed. As always, they wore black suits and tight black T-shirts beneath long achromatic raincoats. Dark glasses hid their eyes. Waldorf was describing a film he had just seen. Lucas was trying to memorise the complex, bizarre instructions for his initiation. Midas watched his apprentice with grudging approval. Glory strode ahead of them, alone and aloof, her glorious golden body wrapped in a black riding cape lined with stars. They traversed their territory, surveying their kingdom, marking their inventories, planning their changes. And as they walked, they took the life of Soho with them.

CHAPTER FIFTY-NINE

The Whole Picture

Things moved quickly for me after that extraordinary week. Berry was still in the Maldives – no one had thought to tell him what was going on – and everyone was still running around at the office. I couldn't desert them now so, as stitched and patched as any street drunk, every bone in my body aching, I went back to work.

The first person who came to see me was Lucas. He silently handed me a letter of resignation and waited until I had read it, hovering by the door.

'Was there something else?' I asked.

'Last Monday I saw you and Mr Elliot going into a restaurant.'

'Yes?'

'The people you were with. Was one of them a producer called Red Banner?'

'Yes, that's right.'

Lucas seemed satisfied, and went away. Wheels turned. An hour later he came back.

'There's someone I think you should meet,' he said.

Rain pattered from the canopy of leaves as I stood beneath the plane tree and watched her crossing Soho

Square. She was wearing a shiny black plastic raincoat with the collar turned up, and a matching rain-hat. I knew she was probably naked underneath it. Even wrapped in plastic she was glorious. Her face was thickly painted. I wondered if anyone had ever seen her without make-up, if her natural face was a blank that allowed her to be whoever she wanted.

'We could have met in my office,' I said, holding out my hand.

'I don't like offices,' said Glory, sweeping past me and seating herself on a wet bench. 'I've seen you before in the square.'

I never imagined she had noticed me. 'I've seen you too.'

'One of our men wrote a screenplay about an elephant.'

'*Quincy's Rogue*,' I replied.

'I understand you helped to get him a deal. He can't continue with that project.' She paused to light a cigarette. I was surprised to see her smoke. I don't know why I should have been. I knew nothing about her. She gave off feelings, not facts.

'My brother and I have considerable resources. We are interested in making a film set in Soho. Something that would make our home look – appealing to outsiders.'

'Do you have an idea of what it should be about?'

She sprayed blue smoke into the cold morning air. 'We rather thought you might have.'

'I've spoken to a lot of agents, but so far I haven't been able to find anything –'

'No,' she said, reaching forward and tapping my chest with a painted fingernail. 'We thought you might have something in there, Mr Tyler. Tell me, have you ever thought of directing?'

I had never considered the idea. 'What makes you think I could?'

'Oh, a sixth sense.' She gave a conspiratorial smile.

It was only afterwards, when I was scripting our project, that I began to appreciate the whole picture. I had been gently led forward, through Lucas and One Eighty and Glory to Midas, the man with the gold, and Midas had made his fortune from the characters upon whom I now modelled my screenplay – the people of Soho. A full circle. I always said life was a movie, so I made my life into a movie.

And this time I was able to correct the structure, glamorise the characters, polish the dialogue and most importantly, add a neat conclusion.

After all, isn't that what everyone wants – a happy ending?

Soho Black

(20th Century Fox, Dir: Richard Tyler, 1999, US.)
Brad Pitt, Cameron Diaz, Drew Barrymore, Ethan Hawke.
107 min.

Lovers of bizarre cinema may cherish this oddball trip into the life of a failing film producer whose unexpected death puts his career back on track. All others, beware! Garish lighting, strange camera angles, offbeat production design from newcomer Lucas Fox, a deafening percussive score and a script that sometimes loses its way will deter the casual viewer, but those who stick with it will find many perverse pleasures. Nominally set in London's creative square mile, the film bows to American tastes by adding sickly love interest and a ludicrous finale filled with computer-generated effects. Barrymore's turn as a stripper named Glory will raise a few eyebrows. First-time director/writer Tyler steals from virtually every bad horror movie ever made and even throws in a staggeringly inappropriate musical number from Shirley Bassey. Inside this overblown melodrama is a small human tragedy trying to get out. Still, Tyler's film has already started to achieve cult status, and it'll be interesting to see what he does next.

Time Out Film Guide

Quincy's Rogue

(Paramount, Dir: Red Banner, 1999, UK.)
Oliver Reed, Paula Yates, Jane Horrocks, Hugh Grant.
94 mins.
Ludicrous monster-on-the-loose farrago set in Africa but
shot at Pinewood by producer-turned-director Banner, whose
crippling inability to frame a single decent shot makes him
the new Michael Winner. An embarrassing career low for
all involved, especially Reed as the Great White Hunter
searching for a legendary elephant that guards sacred gold
and contains the spirit of an ancient demon. Yates displays
the charisma of a car park puddle, waggling her hands and
screaming her lines as she runs through the (patently phony)
undergrowth. Grant provides comic – and audience – relief
when he is eaten by a crocodile. Horrocks employs an acting
style that has not been seen since the advent of sound. The
ropy special effects are heavily utilised in a finale that sees the
demon tusker swimming a raging river to exact vengeance on
the terrified Reed. 'My God,' cries Quincy, 'it can swim!' And
indeed it can, unlike the film, which sank without a trace.

Time Out Film Guide

The Answers To Barbara's Questions

Deadfall and *Goldfinger* both had their title tracks written by John Barry and sung by Shirley Bassey.

Legend and *2001* both had their original scores replaced at the last minute. Jerry Goldsmith's music for Ridley Scott's fantasy was dumped in favour of a more contemporary Tangerine Dream soundtrack, while Stanley Kubrick replaced Alex North's music with a mixture of classical and experimental sounds from his temp track. All six scores have eventually surfaced on CD.

Richard Tyler's film *Soho Black* is now available on PolyGram Video, priced £14.99 from all good stockists.

THE END